Native of Ohrid, The Republic of North Macedonia.

A Bachelor of Arts in English literature and culture at the Johannes Gutenberg University in Mainz, Germany.

He has written a previous work albeit unpublished. This is his first attempt at going public.

Is a fan of mythology and folklore, which serve as part of the inspiration.

Is a beginner author in the genre of fiction and fantasy.

I would like to dedicate my work to my grandmother, Irinka, and my mother, Mirjana, to whom I read the book as I was writing it, and whose eagerness to hear more gave me the drive to finish it until the end.

Ivan Lekoski

INVICTVS

AUSTIN MACAULEY PUBLISHERS™
LONDON * CAMBRIDGE * NEW YORK * SHARJAH

A CIP catalogue record for this title is available from the British Library.

ISBN 9781398425767 (Paperback)
ISBN 9781398425781 (ePub e-book)

www.austinmacauley.com

First Published 2023
Austin Macauley Publishers Ltd®
1 Canada Square
Canary Wharf
London
E14 5AA

Table of Contents

PROLOGVS

The continent of Avalon, its west side home to the eight kingdoms of: Men, Dwarves, Elves, Vampires, Werewolves, Angels, Demons and Faeries. There are a great many other races thriving at this piece of land but these eight are the most advanced and prominent ones. At present, they live in peace, untied and prosperous but this was not always the case.

Since the foundations of these kingdoms, they have been at war, constantly at their throats, fighting for centuries. The most insignificant of them all were the Demon race. Comprised of three different clans of Demons: Fire, Storm and Dark. Amidst the First Great War, they were locked in a Civil one, a war that threatened their very existence. The other warring races decided to leave them on their own and simply defeat the last standing tribe, and this might have been so had it not been for a single miracle.

The Demon Magdabolg was born in the Fire Clan, and he was blessed with immense power that once he came of age, he used it to become the First Demon King. With an iron fist, he brought an end to the internal strife and united the tribes under one banner, which still carries his visage in his honour to the present day. The united Demons quickly switched the tide of the war and proved a formidable foe, one that threatened to overrun the other armies. That was until Magdabolg was defeated and slain by the combined efforts of Angel and Elf under their kings Lumiel and Singorin who had called for a temporary truce in order to counter this threat. Magdabbolg's death threw the Demon army in disarray and soon they were yet again fighting against each other; this time for the position of a king, inviting ruin upon themselves.

During the time of the Second King Demiurgos, who was of the Dark clan did the Demons saw their revival. Having decided to stay neutral from the ongoing Second Great War, he dedicated himself to the restoration of his race and for hundreds of years his kingdom thrived and prospered in peace. He also made many reforms including the system of inheritance which dictated that the eldest child of the king, regardless of gender, will inherit the throne, a system which was also used by the Men and the Angels.

As much as 'rainbow and roses' this may sound, it is not in this period that the Demons saw the peak of their kingdom; it was during the reign of Demiurgos' only son, the Third Demon King Abaddon. A child prodigy much like the late Magdabolg, he was feared and respected from a young age. His talents grew so immensely that in his early years he had already surpassed his father, and at the age of 400 he had already taken the throne. The power Abaddon wielded was so immense that it felt like a pit of a bottomless abyss; seemingly infinite. Being discontent with the state of his kingdom he set his sights on grander things, conquest. Thusly, he amassed a huge army partly of his brethren and partly born from his own magic.

Having subjugated the Dark Dragon King Argyros and his kin he used them and his armies to quickly overrun and crush the neighbouring kingdoms of Viloth and Sanclunea. Soon, Volkodakia and Elviun followed. Thus, he transformed Dhalsarria from kingdom to an empire, ushering in a rule of darkness and despair. None dared challenge his might until one day an unlikely alliance of the remaining races stood up to face him. Rebellions broke out in the conquered kingdoms; the imprisoned rulers were liberated, and Abaddon was challenged to a final bout. But so great was his power that the other rulers only managed to destroy his physical body which was no easy task despite their combined might. His spirit fled to the depths of the Earth never to be seen again.

The surviving Dragons, Argyros being one of them, retreated to their homeland where they stayed in hiding ever since. The defeat of the mighty king rejuvenated the morale of the alliance so much that even the ordinary people as well stood up to fight their oppressors. The Demons put up a valiant fight under the leadership of Abaddon's peerless generals but alas they could not hope to defeat the combined might of all seven armies and they themselves were slain.

The empire was lost, and the Imperial Capital Dishum was reduced to rubble from the forthcoming siege. The rest of the races saw that they function better in unity and after a passionate victory speech from the then Prince Arthur Pendragon, son of Uther Pendragon a formal pan-species peace was made.

For one hundred years the kingdoms of Camelot, Viloth, Volkodakia, Elviun, Nidvelir, Sancluneaa and Faeran saw tranquillity, and prosperity. Although all of this may seem like 'rainbows and roses', something will happen that is going to shake this state of equilibrium…

CAPITVLVM I

FORTVNE ROTA VOLVITVRi

Camelot, Kingdom of Men

Arthur: Morgana!

Says while walking through the corridor in fury.

Arthur: Has anyone seen my daughter?

Soldier: As per my knowledge, she has not left her chambers, sire.

Arthur: Well, she is not there!

Soldier: That is odd, no one passed through here, there is no way I would have missed her.

Arthur: Merlin!

Growls his name.

Arthur: Fetch me the Court Magician at once!

Soldier: Yes sire!

***

Arthur: Let me guess, he was not in his chambers either.

The soldier lowers his look.

Arthur: What am I to do with those fools…

He frowns and sets out on his own.

***

Morgana: (giggling) Are you sure this is safe?

Morgana, Arthur's daughter is a very comely girl, with a well-defined face and a pale, smooth complexion. Her hair is long, reaching her waist and it is slightly wavy, she also has two strands tied behind her head, going down in a braid that reaches the base of her neck. The colour of her eyes is hazel. She is wearing a long, blue, velvet dress.

Merlin: Oh yes, it's perfectly safe; no one knows about this secret place.

Arthur: There you are!

Morgana: I thought you said nobody knew about this place!

Merlin: I guess I was wrong.

Arthur: Have you forgotten that the old dungeons were my favourite spot when we played hide and seek, old friend?

Merlin: Oh right…must've slipped my mind (smiles).

Arthur: You, out! And get yourself cleaned; you reek of damp.

Morgana: Yes father (she gets up and leaves the premise).

Merlin waves at her. He has the appearance of a young adult in his late twenties but is much older than that. His hair is short and black, his eyes are dark brown going towards black. His face is well defined and comely.

Morgana was about to wave back but goes on her way after her father's scornful gaze.

Arthur: Damn you, Merlin! Damn it all!

Merlin: What? We were having fun!

Arthur: I warned you not to sway her with your mischief!

Merlin: 'Sway her'? She loves me, and I love her.

Arthur: She is but a child!

Merlin: She is almost sixteen! Not a child anymore!

Arthur: Not a grown woman either! It is not love she has for you, it is blind infatuation, nothing more, what does she know about love?

Merlin: You give your daughter less credit that she deserves.

Arthur: I will give her credit when it is due.

Merlin: And when will that be?

Arthur: When it is due.

Merlin: There you go with your stubbornness again! Always the same.

Arthur: Hold your tongue! We may be sworn friends, but I am still the king here.

Merlin: What will you do? Have me flayed?

Arthur: Do not test my patience, Merlin.

Merlin: Pah!

Arthur: And stay away from Morgana, this is your final warning, should I see you with her again I will have you exiled.

Merlin: You wouldn't.

Arthur: Like I said, do not test me.

Merlin: This wouldn't happen to have any relation to her betrothal to that pig Gryffydd, would it?

Arthur: Lord Gryffydd is a very powerful man and a marriage to him shall secure me the loyalty of 2,000 men.

Merlin: There you are thinking about politics again instead of your daughter's feelings.

Arthur: Feelings do not rule a kingdom, politics does.

Merlin: What need of an army anyway, we are at peace for 100 years now.

Arthur: Peace? There can never be peace, not while he is still alive.

Merlin: Abaddon has been dead ever since then, you should know; we were both there.

Arthur: Dead yes, destroyed no. His soul still lingers in this world and while it remains, we can never have true peace, a sorcerer of your calibre should be well aware of that.

Merlin: You are just afraid of spectres of the past.

Arthur: And so should you. Every wise man should be…

Merlin: Ah! This is not getting us anywhere!

Arthur: No matter what you say you will not persuade me otherwise, my decision stands.

Merlin: Well, I hope you're aware that your decision will earn the contempt of your daughter forever.

Arthur: Morgana is well aware of what is at stake here.

Merlin: Whatever makes you feel better, old chap.

Arthur: Pah! I have wasted enough time dealing with you, the conversation on this topic is over. Now go and make yourself presentable, I need you by my side at the meeting.

Merlin: (sigh) Whatever you say, your highness…

He gets up and leaves the dungeon with Arthur following right behind.

***

Arthur: Sorry I am late; I had some errands to attend to (throws a scornful look towards Merlin).

Sindri: Not at all, your majesty, we all have our personal matters beside state affairs.

Arthur: I am grateful for your understanding.

Sindri: (nods politely, looks towards Merlin) Master Merlin, looking young as always, I see.

Merlin: You don't look a day older as well, your lordship.

Sindri: Well… (strokes his beard) I do like to consider myself young, for Dwarven standards at least (lightly chuckles).

Merlin: Nonsense, you look young as a fiddle by all standards.

Sindri: Ho-ho-ho, you do have your way with words.

Merlin: I'd like to think so as well.

Arthur: Now that the small talk is out of the way, let us get down to business.

Sindri grumbles.

Arthur: Surely you must know why I called this meeting, Lord Sindri.

Sindri: Unfortunately…

Arthur: The monthly ore supply has dropped by 20% this year, that is unacceptable.

Sindri: I'm afraid that my hands are tied in that matter, we have our own people to look after you see.

Arthur: As do I, which is why in response, I shall have to revoke some of my magic tutors.

Sindri's aide: What! But my lord! Their number is already scarce as it is, if you were to revoke them –

Sindri: (raises his hand in protest, silencing his aide) I do apologise for my aide's misbehaviour, he is young and eager; do not hold it against him.

Arthur: I understand, I was young and eager once as well, so I will overlook this lapse this once.

Sindri's aide bows in apology.

Sindri: Your Highness, about the ore, our own reserves are already beginning to thin out and we are having trouble finding new sources, as you know, manalith[1] is very hard to obtain.

Arthur: Hmmm…

Merlin: We'll double your grain supplies.

---

[1] A crystallised cluster of mana used in the magical production of armour and weapons.

Sindri looks at him puzzlingly. Arthur turns towards Merlin as well.

Merlin: **If** you keep the ore supply per the agreed amount, we will let you keep the tutors **and** we'll double the grain supply, not a bad deal, isn't it?

Arthur: Can we even afford such a thing?

Merlin: Of course, we've reached a surplus last month.

Arthur: I still have not received the reports from last month.

Merlin: I'll talk to Fion.

Arthur: Make sure that you do.

Arthur: (turns to Sindri) What say you, sir?

Sindri: Aye, I'll bring it up to the King. You should expect an answer soon enough.

Arthur: That is pleasing to hear.

Sindri: One more thing, sire, if you don't mind me asking, whatever do you need so much ore for? We've been at peace for a hundred years, a peace that you brought on, is there really any need for more armaments than you already have?

Arthur: (his face turns grim) Peace, peace, peace, everyone is on about peace when it is nothing but a superficial farce! And all those who think otherwise are fools beyond reckoning!

Sindri: You speak of the Dark One's soul…

Arthur: Of course, I do! I certainly do not mean my grandmother's undergarment! … Everyone has been dulled by this false sense of peace, unafraid of the danger that haunts us.

Sindri: Even if he were to return by some dumb luck, we'll just destroy him all over again, there is nothing to fear.

Arthur: If he were to return it would be the end of us all…we are not the same as we were hundred years ago.

Sindri: If you ask me, I think your fears are baseless.

Arthur: But I do not ask you, do I?

Merlin: I think, it would be best if we called it a day, hm?

Sindri: Couldn't agree more.

Sindri's aide: Thank you for your patronage your highness (bows).

Sindri: Sire (bows).

Arthur: Do give Baldur my regards.

Sindri: Will do.

Sindri's aide: Senir aldur perduz[2] (murmurs under his beard).

---

[2] Senile old fart.

Sindri: Quiet fool! (Hits him on the head) They can understand us!

Sindri's aide grumbles while stroking his head. Merlin snickers in secret.

Arthur: Something on your mind?

Merlin: No not at all.

Arthur: You are free to go.

Merlin bows and leaves.

***

Later that day, at the Gryffydd mansion

Gryffydd: Merlin! How rare to have you come and visit me, sit, have a drink.

Merlin: With all due respect, Earl, I didn't come here to sit with you nor for a drink.

Gryffydd: What did you come here for then?

Merlin: I came to talk.

Gryffydd: Well, we can't have a proper conversation without a cup of scotch now, can we? Please, I insist that you sit.

Merlin sits down while Gryffydd pours him a drink then, using telekinesis, Merlin pulls the cup towards himself.

Gryffydd: Ah, magic, how convenient.

Merlin downs it in one go and slams the cup on the table furiously.

Gryffydd: Judging by your demeanour, I reckon you're upset about something.

Merlin: It's about princess Morgana.

Gryffydd: Ah yes, it has come to my attention that you are against our future marriage.

Merlin: Against? I abhor the idea!

Gryffydd: I wonder why?

Merlin: I love the princess and she loves me! And I will not have her married to the likes of you!

Gryffydd: Love, such a wonderful thing, too bad that neither of you have any say in the matter.

Merlin: You only care for the position it brings and nothing else!

Gryffydd: My, my, how cruel, I care more about the princess, the throne is something that comes along with it.

Merlin: You care for her as much as you care for your own shit!

Gryffydd: You want to hear me say it? Fine, I care for the position.

Merlin: You fuckin' bastard! Listen to me now and listen well, you will call off the wedding or by the Gods, I will make you do it!

Gryffydd: Be careful who you're threatening sorcerer, how would the king feel if he found out that you're intimidating his future son-in-law, I could have you hanged for treason.

Merlin: You underestimate my abilities.

Gryffydd: Go on then, work your magic, the king will know immediately that it was you.

Merlin: ... This is far from over!

Gryffydd: (finishes his scotch) I believe that you have exhausted the extent of my hospitality; now, I will ask you to remove yourself from my premise.

Merlin: You can take your hospitality and shove it up your arse!

He storms out of the door, crossing paths with a maid who was eavesdropping on the conversation.

Merlin: (stops and looks at the startled maid) Well? Don't you have anything better to do?

Frightened, she goes in the opposite direction.

Merlin: Bloody maids... (after walking away for some distance, he vanishes).

***

The same night, Gryffydd's mansion

Merlin: (materialises inside, drunk) Gryffydd! I've decided that I don't give a flying fuck about your threats! I'm putting a stop to your betrothal to Morgana! Gryffydd!

He waddles inside his office and spots a grizzly sight; Gryffydd, lying on the floor in a pool of his own blood with a dagger thrust in his back.

Merlin: Oh no! (Rushes towards the body).

He checks the pulse, but it is too late, no use in attempting healing magic.

He reaches to pull out the dagger and just as he grips the handle, the same maid walks in and lets out a deafening scream.

Merlin: No, no! This is not what it looks like!

Maid: Help! Help! Murderer! He killed him! He killed the master! Murderer!

Merlin: Shut your mouth woman!

Maid: Guards!

Merlin: I said shut up! (Makes her pass out).

Eirene (Gryffydd's younger sister): Hilda, what is all this ruckus? (Gasps from the sight) Brother!

Merlin: Eirene, I can explain (goes towards her unaware that he is holding the dagger).

Eirene: Stay away from me, murderer!

Merlin: It's not – (sees the dagger and throws it aside). *In that moment the guards come in and apprehend him.* By Bethor's beard… (he gets taken away).

***

Arthur: What in Lugos' name is going on in here? (Still in his nightgown) Eirene?

Eirene: Your majesty…he killed my brother… (sobbing heavily).

Arthur becomes outraged.

Merlin: Arthur, it wasn't me I swear it on my life…

Arthur: Take him to the dungeons!

Morgana: Merlin? Merlin!

Merlin: Princess!

Arthur: Go back to your room, Morgana!

Morgana: Where are you taking him? Let him go!

Guinevere: Morgana! (Going after her daughter).

Arthur: Take her away this instant!

Guinevere: I'm sorry, my love, I tried to stop her…come sweetie.

Morgana: No! Let me go! Let me go!

Merlin: It's going to be alright, princess, I promise!

Arthur: What are you still waiting for! Take him!

Guard: Sir!

Morgana: No! Mother! Mother, please make them stop! They can't do that to him!

Merlin: It'll be alright, I'm innocent! (Yells as he is being dragged away).

Morgana: What is going on!

Eirene: He killed my brother!

Morgana: Lies! You lie! He couldn't have done it!

Eirene: I saw him hold the dagger!

Morgana: You wench, I will see you burn for your lies!

Arthur: Why are you still here! Move woman!

Guinevere: Morgana, stop making a scene; it is unbecoming of you as a princess!

Morgana: I don't care!

Guinevere: Enough! (Slaps her).

Morgana: (holds her cheek) I hate you! I hate both of you! (Runs to her room).

Guinevere: I'll talk to her…

Arthur: Talk some sense into her while you are at it.

Guinevere goes after her.

Arthur: Come child, tell me everything.

***

Merlin: Arthur…

Arthur: Silence!

Merlin: …

Arthur: Do you have any idea! Any! Idea! In the shit you have gotten yourself into!

Merlin: I didn't do it.

Arthur: That is not what Eirene says.

Merlin: Eirene doesn't know anything!

Arthur: She knows enough! …You were seen all bloodied, holding the murder weapon, the testimony of the maid puts you on the scene, leaned over Johan's body with said weapon in your hands as well, with no signs of a break in.

Merlin: I was going to pull out the bloody dagger!

Arthur: That is not what it looks like.

Merlin: And what of the bloody dagger itself!

Arthur: Investigation shows it is one of your agla.

Merlin: Impossible!

Arthur: Perhaps you would have noticed if you weren't drunk as a pole!

Merlin: …I was set up.

Arthur: It matters not, all the evidence points against you.

Merlin: Emrys…it was Emrys, he's the only one besides me who has keys to my study, he must have taken the dagger! And materialised himself –

Arthur: Enough! You are grasping at straws; you have no clear proof that it was the boy.

Merlin: But you believe me, don't you, Arthur?

Arthur: I do not know in what to believe anymore…

Merlin: Arthur…

Arthur: A trial will be held this afternoon; you will be found guilty and hanged for murder.

Merlin: At least exile me! Banish me! Anything is better than death!

Arthur: You know I cannot do that; the people will settle for no less.

Merlin: You would condemn your friend to die just to satiate Gryffydd's army?

Arthur: It is not only that, how will it look if I pardon the murderer of the most powerful noble in Camelot? The people will think I am being impartial and that will set a precedent, which must be avoided at all costs.

Merlin: Even at the cost of my life?

Arthur: I am deeply sorry, but the law is the law and even though I am your friend, first and foremost I am the King of Camelot.

Merlin: The Great Arthur, forever the people's champion, protector of Camelot even when the very laws he protects are wrong!

Arthur's eyes widen in ire.

Merlin: Tell me, 'friend', what kind of a king gives away his daughter in return of the servitude of the people who supposedly oh so love him?

Arthur: (slaps him with his backhand) You will not talk to me that way! Am I not the King!

Merlin: You are not my king!

Arthur slaps him again.

Merlin responds by spitting in his face.

Arthur wipes away the spit then hits him in the gut.

Merlin: (lashes out at him but the chains hold him at bay) These chains won't hold me.

Arthur: They are made of anti-magic steel, the best quality; not even you can escape them, and should you attempt to flee, I have given orders to the archers to shoot you dead on sight.

Merlin: I curse you!

He turns around and walks away.

Merlin: I curse you, Arthur Pendragon! And all of Camelot! Aghhh!

***

Morgana: Merlin!

Merlin: Princess!

Morgana: Oh Merlin! I can't believe that they would treat you like a common criminal.

Merlin: In your father's eyes that is what I am, a murderer.

Morgana: My father knows that you're innocent, it's just that his position as a king would have him do otherwise…

Merlin: Yes, he would have me executed.

Morgana: What! But the trial…!

Merlin: Oh, my sweet love, the trial is just a formality, a sham, nothing else…

Morgana: They can't do that! My father can't do that, you're his friend…surely, he would settle for exile wouldn't he?

Merlin: (shakes his head) No…

Morgana: But…I – I'll talk to my mother! She will talk some sense into him!

Merlin: It's of no use, I am doomed.

Morgana: There must be something I can do!

Merlin: Kiss me…one last time…

She leans forward and kisses him, and he returns it.

Morgana: (places her hand on his cheek, tears come out) I don't want you gone…

Merlin: Sometimes Fortuna plays cruel tricks on us…it can't be avoided.

Morgana: I curse Fortuna! I spit in her face!

Merlin: (half smiles) You have to be strong and move on and one day become a great queen.

Morgana: Unless I get a baby brother (chuckles).

He smiles.

Morgana: I promise (kisses him again).

Emrys: Princess, the Queen requires your presence.

Merlin: Go…

Morgana: I love you (whispers).

Merlin: I love you too princess (whispers).

She leaves the dungeon.

Merlin: Emrys…you traitorous cur!

Emrys: Come now Merlin, is that any way to talk to your friend and protégée?

Merlin: I curse the day I took you in!

Emrys: Ah a bit too late for that.

Merlin: Why Emrys? Why!

Emrys: Because I'll always be in your shadow, as long as I am your protégée I can never move up, I mean who can become greater than Merlin! The greatest sorcerer this kingdom has ever seen.

Merlin: Ah of course, blind ambition.

Emrys: Is it? Blind? With you out of the way, the King will have no choice but to promote me as the Court Magician and I shall receive all the glory and acclaim that comes with it while you remain deep in the ground, fodder for worms (evil smile).

They speak in Thyrodian so that the guards may not understand them.

Merlin: Oh, you poor sad creature, you may take my place, but you can never **BE ME**!

Emrys: No, I shall become better than you ever were or ever will be.

Merlin: I will watch you from the Heavens and laugh at your failures!

Emrys: That remains to be yet seen, 'master'.

He walks away.

***

Unknown voice: Merlin…Merlin!

Merlin: Huh? (Wakes up from a nap) Who's there?

Merlin: Blimey! I must be going crazy…

Unknown voice: Oh no, you are far from that, Court Magician.

Merlin: Who's there? Show yourself!

Guard: Be quiet in there!

Merlin: Kiss my arse!

Guard#2: Poor sod, started talking to himself.

The voice takes a form of a shadowy silhouette and stands before Merlin.

Merlin: By Bethor's beard! Who…What…are you?

Unknown voice: You already know the answer to that, Merlin.

Merlin: Abaddon…

Abaddon: Correct, or what's left of me at least.

Merlin: Why don't the guards see you?

Abaddon: Fools without magic are imperceptive to my form.

Merlin: Makes sense.

Abaddon: Talk in my tongue so that they may not understand, I know you speak it.

Merlin: What do you want from me?

Abaddon: I want to help you.

Merlin: Help me? Why would you want to help me?

Abaddon: I need a body, Merlin, and yours is perfect, give it to me and I will release you from this fate.

Merlin: Of course, there's a catch; no thanks, I'd rather die than be your vessel.

Abaddon: Did you not put a curse upon Arthur Pendragon and the whole of Camelot?

Merlin: I was angry and beside myself.

Abaddon: Don't be a fool, Merlin! Think about it, what do you have to lose? Your most gifted student betrays you; your friend betrays you and the girl you love will probably be married to another pompous noble. Tell me, what do you have to live for or rather, die? You were right to curse them.

Merlin: … Morgana, she loves me, I can't stand her seeing me become a monster…

Abaddon: Even though you can never be together in life or in death?

Merlin: …

Merlin: Do not take me for a fool, Demon, I know what happens if you possess me, you will eat away my soul until the being known as Merlin ceases to exist and only you remain.

Abaddon: Well, aren't you a clever one, there is no fooling you, is there.

Merlin: I told you, I'd rather die, go find yourself another body.

Abaddon: Perhaps the Princess will heed my words, and her body is suitable, she is of the Pendragon house after all, a daughter of Dragons.

Merlin: No! NO!

Abaddon: Broken and distraught as she is, surely, she will say yes to the opportunity to save her beloved Merlin.

Merlin: Alright I'll do it! I'll do it! Take me, take my body.

Abaddon: Oh Merlin, I knew you would come around.

Merlin: …It is as you said, I got nothing to live for, but Morgana has so much she can achieve…and I will be damned if I let her become you.

Abaddon: And they say chivalry is dead.

Merlin: Get on with it.

Abaddon: With pleasure.

He lunges forward and enters his body, causing Merlin great pain which makes him scream.

Guard: Oi! What's wrong!

Guard#2: Open the gate!

The two guards rush to the screaming Merlin who soon passes out from the pain.

Knight: It's time, bring the prisoner.

Guard: Yes sir!

Guard#2: Come on, on your feet.

Both lift him up.

Guard: Should we tell him?

Guard#2: Nah I'm sure it's nothing.

Guard: Ye, probably stomach pains from anxiety.

Knight: Come on soldier, move it!

Guard: Yes sir! Sorry sir!

Knight: Bloody guards…

***

Square of the Royal City Londwyn, place of the trial

The square is filled with people who are shouting 'traitor', and 'murderer' towards Merlin, who is hearing all of this muffled up as he is still dazed by the possession that took place.

The royal spokesman reads the accusations placed against him and unanimously, he is proclaimed guilty.

Spokesman: The people have spoken! The esteemed judges have spoken! His Majesty has spoken! Merlin, Court Magician and Advisor to the King, you have been found guilty of the charges placed against you and therefore are sentenced to death by hanging!

Morgana: Noo! He is innocent! Merlin!

Merlin: Princess…

Morgana: You can't do this!

Arthur: Guards!

The guards restrain her as she tries to make her way to him.

Morgana: You are condemning an innocent man! Is this what Camelot stands for!

Arthur: Woman, do something!

Guinevere: It's always 'woman do something!' Why don't **you** do something for a change? (Walks away)

Arthur: Guinevere! By the Gods!

Lancelot: (restraining Morgana) Princess, calm yourself.

Morgana: You know he's innocent, Lancelot, you all do!

Lancelot: It has already been decided! It is the word of the King!

Merlin meets Arthur's gaze.

Arthur: (meets his as well) … (extends his hand and after a few intense moments shows thumbs down).

The spokesman nods to the executioner who then places Merlin on the gallows and tightens the noose.

Merlin: (shifts his gaze from Arthur to Morgana) (Goodbye princess, goodbye…my love…)

The lever is pulled, and he hangs to his death.

With tear in her eyes, Morgana yells out towards him while Lancelot, Captain of the First Legion, struggles to hold her in check. As Arthur looks upon the last moments of his friend's life, a single tear escapes from his eye and leaps on his cheek.

That very day, Camelot lost one of her sons, a friend, a lover, and gave birth to something new in return…

CAPITVLVM II

INITIVM FINIS[ii]

An eerie silence fills the air along with a sense of uneasiness, 'a person was hanged' one might say, but it was more than that.

The clamouring of the masses catches the King's attention as he was about to leave so he turns towards the corpse of his friend. After a brief moment, his eyes leap forward and flash with life and then – an explosion of obscure light fills the town square. Everyone present watches as though petrified and with gaping mouths, as Merlin's corpse begins to take on another form: black-plated armour wrapped around his body, covering every inch, rimmed with red gold and a dark ragged cloak covering the head and hiding the face, and on his head a crown of gleaming silver, written upon it 'Dhalsharrum'– 'King of Demons', in Old Dhalsarrian.

Arthur: It cannot be…

Lancelot: To the King! Everyone to the King!

The present knights and guards and the rest of the Knights of the Round Table, which were Camelot's elite force form a protective circle around his majesty.

Knight: Princess, hurry! 'Tis not safe here! (Extends his hand).

Morgana: Leave me be!

The armoured man leaps upon the wooden platform and turns his attention towards the king.

Arthur: Abaddon…

Abaddon: It's been a long time, Arthur, you've grown old.

Unfortunately, the King cannot find adequate words to utter so he only manages to produce incoherent mumbling.

Morgana: Merlin? (Approaches him slowly).

Arthur: Morgana, stay away from him! That is not Merlin!

Abaddon: Your father is right, young girl, the man you once knew is no more, now only I remain!

And he pulls out the jagged sword with runes running down the middle of the blade, decorated with a grotesque hand guard and holds it upward, shooting a pillar of energy towards the sky, announcing his arrival; the Dark King has come once more.

The pillar of light attracts the attention of all the seven kingdoms and their rulers face the windows of their castle for a better look; all knowing the meaning it bore, and they quake and shiver from the doom it foretells.

Most exited being the Demons of Dhalsarria. But they neither quake nor shiver but cheer the return of their once fallen king.

Knight: Oi, what in Bethor's name is that light?

Knight#2: I've no idea but it's coming from Camelot.

Fire Demon: It's the King! Our King has returned!

Fire Demon#2: We are saved! Our days of slavery are at an end! Long live Abaddon! Long live our King!

The rest of the vicinity catches on and the cheering spreads throughout like a pandemic.

Elf: Be quiet! (Hits the Demon that instigated the cheering) your shouting is grinding my ears!

Demon: Act high and mighty while you can, elven scum, soon your cities will burn, and your kingdoms will fall and that goes for every one of you scum! The Demon race shall rise again! A new dawn is upon us!

Elf: Silence! (Kicks him again) Demon filth! Know your place!

Werewolf: Pick him up!

Knight: Yeah, let's teach 'im some manners, boys!

The Werewolf proceeds to punch him while the knight is holding him.

Fire Demon: Guz Baltu Dhalatu[3]! Guz Baltu Sharru!

Despite being hit repeatedly, the Demon did not stop to chant that which means 'long live the Demons, long live the King' in the Demon tongue.

---

[3] Dhalatu – common plural of 'Demon'.

Even as he lay there battered and bruised on the street, he did not stop chanting.

At this point it should be mentioned that Dhalsarria, or Dhalsharri as it was called in their native tongue, was under military rule by the joint races who have divided the kingdom amongst themselves but still it was not unusual to see troops of different species mingle together like this.

At Camelot, Abaddon was now pointing his sword, Absharu, towards Arthur.

Abaddon: Hear my words, Arthur Pendragon, although I may not have my full strength, yet once I do, I will return, and Camelot will be the first kingdom to fall. Fortune turns Son of Dragons and now it is on my side.

As he prepares to abscond, the Princess makes a plea.

Morgana: Wait! Take me with you!

Abaddon: I told you, princess, I am not Merlin.

Morgana: Please! I don't want to stay in this wretched place!

Arthur: Morgana! Have you lost your mind, child!

Morgana: (she turns to him) You did this! You turned him into a monster! I hate you! I hate all of you!

Arthur: Morgana!

Abaddon: Let me have a look at you (he turns her face towards him slightly violently and peers into her eyes) Yes… I can see great promise in your eyes, you have the potential for great sorcery, it must be your Pendragon blood.

She does not know quite well why, but this pleases her, and she smiles.

Abaddon: Very well, I will allow you to accompany me, you might make a fine bride one day as well.

Morgana: Thank you!

Abaddon: But, if I as much as smell a treachery, I shall drive Absharu through your heart and feed your corpse to the crows.

Morgana: I will not, I promise.

Arthur: Morgana no! Morganaaa!

The rebellious Princess takes the Demon King's hand and they both vanish out of sight.

Arthur: Morganaaa!

Lancelot: My king…

Arthur: (grief-stricken) Betrayed… by my own child…

Lancelot: Your majesty, there will be time for grief, but now you must be stronger than ever my king, the people need a sound leader.

Arthur: Right…You're right…call a council of the seven at once.

Lancelot: Yes sire!

***

Somewhere outside of Londwyn

Abaddon: Looks like this is as far as I can go with my current powers. Still a surprising feat, as I would expect from the body of a sorcerer.

Morgana: Doesn't this put us in a spot? How will we escape? Surely, we cannot go on horseback, they will catch us.

Abaddon: Calm your mind princess, he should be arriving shortly.

Morgana: He? Who is 'he'?

Abaddon: You will see, once 'he' arrives. For the meantime we should find some place to hide, it may take a while until his arrival.

Morgana: How much is a while?

Abaddon: You pose a lot of questions princess; I only just resurrected and shouldn't like to be wearied down with them.

Morgana: My, you certainly have an attitude.

Abaddon: Come, let us find a more obscure place.

After what seemed to be two hours or so, a gargantuan figure lands near them, the blast of the shockwave sends the princess down on her bottom.

Morgana: That's…a Dragon!

Abaddon: So good to see you, old friend.

Argyros: And you as well, who's that twerp beside you, smells like a human.

Abaddon: That's because she is, this is Morgana Pendragon, daughter of Arthur.

Argyros: You did always like them young.

Morgana: Yes, I've heard the stories.

Argyros: Oh, they are not stories, they are real, every time he would conquer a race, he would keep the young and fresh girls for himself, sometimes younger even than yourself.

Morgana: That's disgusting…

Abaddon: I found it fun breaking the wills of young and defiant girls, it was my favourite pass time.

Morgana: I don't need any more details…

Argyros: Hahaha! And that brings me to my question, what makes you follow this degenerate Demon-King?

Morgana: I'd rather go with him than stay in that place…

Abaddon: The body I inhibit is that of her former lover who was unjustly sentenced to death, you know him, Merlin the Sorcerer.

Argyros: Merlin? Yet another weirdo it seems. Did you know that he is as old as the master?

Morgana: What?! Merlin? He couldn't be!

Argyros: (laughs) Oh, yes indeed.

Morgana: He did say he was older than he looks but I never imagined him to be **that** old!

Abaddon: It is true.

Morgana: Huh … well, at least going at it with other younger girls was not his past time.

Abaddon: That you know of.

Morgana: (gasps) How dare you! I will not let you slander Merlin's good name!

Abaddon: Alright, calm yourself, it was but a jest.

Morgana: One better left unsaid!

Argyros: Hahaha! I like this one, Abaddon. But be it as it may, he is no longer that man anymore.

Morgana: So I've been told and I don't care.

Argyros: Are you sure this is not some rebellious stage?

Morgana: No, I'm certain of it, this is my clear and rational decision.

Argyros: You really won't have any second thoughts and cry to go back to daddy dearest?

Morgana: No! I'm telling you! Are you daft?

Argyros: My, my, such fighting spirit, (leans his head down and looks at her) It seems that you're speaking the truth, I don't sense any malintent towards him.

Morgana: As I've been saying.

Abaddon: I also made it clear what would happen at the sign of treachery.

Argyros: Blade through the heart and feed her to the crows?

Abaddon: Indeed.

Argyros: Nasty business, sometimes they are half-dead when the crows start picking at their flesh.

Morgana shudders.

Argyros: In any case, I was quite excited when I felt your energy, I thought to myself 'the time has finally come'.

Abaddon: Not quite yet I still need to recover my full strength, once I do the carnage will begin once again.

Argyros: My bones ache for death and destruction.

Abaddon: All in due time my friend, all in due time.

Argyros: Come, let us go to my homeland for now, I'm sure the rest are dying to gaze upon you once again.

Abaddon: (climbs on his back) Come princess.

Argyros lowers his head once again so that Morgana may use it as a means to get to his back.

Argyros: Hold on tight! (He flaps his wings a few times and takes off to the skies).

The Black Dragon King Argyros, mightiest of the Dragons; natural disasters and machines of destruction. As we know, his kind fought alongside Abaddon and when his reign was over, they fled back to their abodes but not all; the Dark Dragons, Argyros' race fought to the last specimen, females included, hence no one to copulate with making him the last standing member of his proud breed.

After a while, somewhere over Viloth

Angel: (looking at a surveillance scrying orb) Sir, we are picking up a signal!

Angel Captain: What is it?

Angel: A Dragon, sir!

Angel Captain: A Dragon? Shoot him down!

Angel: Yes sir! Attention all units! There is a Dragon approaching our airspace! Take it down, I repeat take it down!

Angel: Sir…it seems that the creature is carrying someone… Shekinah have mercy…

Captain: What is it?

Angel: It is the Demon-King…and what looks to be a human girl.

Captain: Then we must take it down no matter what!

Argyros: Hold on we have company!

Abaddon: Lamasatu…

Morgana: What?

Abaddon: Angels!

The Angels begin to shoot magic missiles at them which Argyros evades by skilfully manoeuvring through the sky.

A couple of them intercept them from the front and shoot at them at once but the Dragon intercepts with a blast of his own and the clashing beams explode on contact.

Using his mass Argyros pushes through the line of Angels and flies on past them.

Angel: We mustn't let them escape!

They prepare for another volley, but Abaddon manages to cast 'Adaru[4]', 'Fear' on them and stops them in their tracks for couple of seconds.

Abaddon: That's all I can manage in my current state.

Argyros: It's more than enough!

More Angels begin to emerge from the towering spires, shooting at them.

Morgana: There is more of them!

Abaddon: Let's see what else I can do!

Focuses his energy and casts 'Bitranu Etutuu', 'Shell of Darkness', which grants the target immunity to projectile attacks for a set period.

Argyros: Brace yourselves. I'm about to go full speed!

He increases his flight speed and in mere moments makes it out of Celestia.

Morgana: That was exciting!

Abaddon: Exciting? There must be something wrong with your mind.

Morgana: How rude.

Abaddon: No one tells me how to talk.

Morgana: Humph.

Angel: They passed to Gehenna.

Angel#2: Should we give chase?

Angel: No, let the garrisons there take care of it.

Captain: Report!

Angel: They have made it to Gehenna, sir!

Captain: Damn it! Alert the army there! That Dragon must fall!

Angel: Yes sir!

The doors slide open, and another Angel comes in.

---

[4] Fear

Captain: (stands to attention) General Jomael, sir!

Jomael: I just received word of what happened, how are we standing.

Captain: The target made it to the Demon land sir, we alerted our armies there, that Dragon will fall.

Jomael: Make sure that it does or may Shekinah have mercy on us all.

Captain: Yes sir!

Celestia Minor, Dhalsarrian region ruled by the Angels

Angel: We just received report that a Dragon is flying over; we are to slay it at once!

Angel#2: A Dragon? Who cares about such a beast; let it pass, it's going to go back in his hole anyway.

Angel: We would if it didn't carry the Demon-King on his back!

Angel#2: By Shekinah!

Argyros: Incoming!

Abaddon: Angelic scum, they have made my homeland as their own…

Argyros: It's not just them, every race has a claim upon her.

Abaddon: They will pay, every last one of them.

Angel#3: Take it down!

Before they can fire however Argyros fires a bunch of missiles of his own at him that explode in their vicinity causing disarray.

Flying even faster, he finally makes it out of there as well.

Angel#4: They have made it to the Northern lands…

Angel#5: That is Dragon land, there is nothing we can do now…blast it all.

***

Jomael: Report!

Angel: … They escaped us, sir…the Dragon has made it past the Northern border into Drakhail.

Captain: Ahh!

Jomael: Curses! Incompetence! How hard it is to shoot down one Dragon!

Angel: If it makes any difference sir…it was the Black King.

Captain: That legendary one…

Jomael: Excuses! I don't care if it was Lugos himself! You had a simple task! Her majesty will not be pleased…I must inform her of our blunder now…idiots! (Walks away).

***

Argyros: We finally made it (makes a landing).

Abaddon: Ah, this place looks exactly the same as it did two hundred years ago.

Argyros: Well, we are not exactly builders you know.

Abaddon: Right you are.

The place where they landed is called Terebriz – 'The Dark Land', in the Draconic tongue. It was the home of the Dark Dragons but now only Argyros inhibits it. It is one of the four Dragonkin domains that constitute the greater land known as Draconia. Terebriz is just beyond the Dark Reach Mountains, a range that constitutes the natural border between Terebriz and Dhalsarria. The location in question more specifically was named Garaz Drakiz, meaning Dragon's Head. The name was given due to the tall, towering cliffs that surround the valley that in shape resemble the bony protrusions on a Dragon's head.

Three other figures soar through the sky and land on the nearby onyx cliffs. A Red and Blue Dragon, and a Snow Wyvern.

Argyros: It didn't take you long enough to come.

Unknown Dragonkin: We flew as fast as we could, it is a rare occasion after all.

Unknown Dragonkin #2: I had to see it to believe it, the Demon-King himself, alive and kicking, welcome your majesty.

Abaddon: I could say the same for you, Ignatos, Fulguros, my queen.

Ignatos: Heh, are we not kings as well?

Abaddon: Indeed, but you are no ladies.

Ignatos: Ladies? I see no ladies here.

Morgana: I'm a lady (her voice doesn't reach them, much to her frustration).

Queen: At least he knows proper etiquette.

Fulguros: Don't flatter yourself, Frigga.

Argyros: Don't start, you three, do you forget who stands before you?

Abaddon: Don't mind me, feel free to settle any scores between yourselves.

Argyros: Don't encourage them, these three fools might actually go at it.

Frigga: Surely you jest, we would never show such behaviour in front of our esteemed guest.

Morgana: What about me!

Ignatos: Hm? And who might you be, little one?

Morgana: Finally, you notice me! Hello! I am Morgana Pendragon, nice to meet you all.

Ignatos: Oh, I'm sorry, you are so tiny that we didn't notice you.

Morgana: But you notice him?

Frigga: He is not just anyone, it would be rude not to.

Morgana: Of course…

Fulguros: (leans down) Pendragon you say? Ahh yes, Arthur's daughter, is she your prisoner?

Abaddon: Hardly, more of a companion.

Frigga: For whatever purpose?

Abaddon: She decided to follow me on her own volition, therefore I will teach her the ways of magic so that she is not completely useless.

Morgana: Thank you very much, 'my king'; whatever happened to being nice to the ladies?

Ignatos: Oh dear! Are you going to let her talk to you like that? A mere Human!

Abaddon: She means nothing by it, don't you, princess?

Morgana: …Sure, whatever you say.

Frigga: So, you follow him knowing that you will be branded as a traitor to your kingdom?

Argyros: Her father had her boyfriend killed so now she's rebelling.

Fulguros: Just a phase then?

Morgana: It's not a phase! I realised that the ways by which we live are completely wrong! Innocents being executed just because some bogus evidence says so and my father, 'the king', instead of changing the stupid old-fashioned laws, abides them! Well, they can all go to hell as far as I'm concerned.

Frigga: Your father aside, what of your mother, don't you miss her?

Morgana: My mother is a stupid puppet, she does whatever she is told, she has no voice of her own, queen my arse, what good is being a queen when you have no say in any matter.

Ignatos: Such anger, truly this girl can be used to your advantage, I also sense great potential in her.

Morgana: The black one said that too, what sort of potential do I have exactly?

Abaddon: To become the greatest Sorceress that has ever lived.

Morgana: You really mean it?

Abaddon: I do.

She smiles.

Ignatos: Well, my king, since you are resurrected now, is it time to lay waste to the world once more?

Abaddon: That time will come Incinerator, but for that purpose I will need an army and to restore my generals, that's why I'm heading East.

Ignatos: East?

Abaddon: Indeed, my cousins there will provide me with the necessary shelter until I fully recover, including armies and vessels for my generals.

Frigga: Why not start here, in Baltia? We have the Giants, Orcs…

Abaddon: Orcs are one thing, but the Giants are not, dim-witted as they are, they are a force to be reckoned with and considering this pitiful state that I'm in, I don't have what it takes to break them.

Ignatos: You have us!

Abaddon: I appreciate it, but I can't afford any casualties among you, I will need you at your full strength for the war to come.

Ignatos: Hmmm…

Abaddon: Once I return, I shall obtain the might of the Northern races and build an army no one has ever seen before, Avalon will tremble in fear before my might even more than it did in the past! Everything and everyone will be crushed beneath my heel! (Unsheathes his sword and raises it upwards).

As if on cue, the Dragons raise their heads as well and let out mighty roars of triumph.

Morgana: (Incredible, to command respect and provide such inspiration for these beasts…I've never seen anything like this before).

Fulguros: I would love to stay and see you off, Dread One, however I must return, the little ones must be expecting food.

Argyros: You've become a doting parent I see (chuckles).

Fulguros: Well, the missus has fallen quite ill, and someone has to feed the children.

Frigga: Oh, poor thing, I hope it's nothing serious.

Fulguros: I haven't got the slightest of what's wrong with her.

Abaddon: Take me there, I will have a look at her.

Fulguros: You would do that? For me?

Abaddon: You have served me well, it's the least I can do to repay you.

Fulguros: How graceful of you, your majesty, I will never forget this.

Frigga: What a pleasant surprise, I didn't take you for the magnanimous type, sire.

Abaddon: Of course, I treat those loyal to me with kindness.

Frigga: That is good to know.

Abaddon gets on Argyros and helps the princess as well.

Frigga: Well, I will take my leave now.

Ignatos: As will I.

Frigga: It's been an honour seeing you once more sire.

Abaddon: You as well, Winter Queen.

Ignatos: Sire, when you're ready, the Fire Drakes shall fly with you once more.

Frigga: As will the Wyverns.

Abaddon: You have my gratitude; your loyalty will not go unrewarded.

Frigga and Ignatos bow their heads politely and fly off.

Abaddon: Lead the way, Tempestuous One.

And so, they fly off as well.

Argyros: I can't believe that worm Lindroz didn't show up.

Abaddon: I'm sure he will eventually, you know he likes dramatic entrances.

Argyros: That's what I hate about him.

Morgana: Who is that?

Argyros: King of the Wyrms.

Morgana: What's a Wyrm?

Abaddon: You'll see.

After some time flying, they reach high mountaintops that touch the clouds themselves, Kuruztoz Mantiz they are called in the Dragon tongue – Cloudtop Mountains, and it is the home of the Lightning Dragons.

Once they land, three cheerful young drakes come out of the big cave.

Fulga: Dad! Dad!

Furgon: Dad has returned!

Fulguros: Calm down now.

Drake: Uncle Argyros!

Argyros: Hey there Fulga, you've grown since the last time I saw you, you little devil.

Fulga: You think?

Argyros: I don't think, I know!

Fulga: Hooray!

Fulguros: How is your mother?

Fulga: She's asleep.

Fulguros: Good, go and wake her up, I bring someone who can help her.

Abaddon: (gets off Argyros) Greetings, little ones.

Furgon: A human?

Fulga: Can we eat him?

Abaddon: A human?

Fulguros: (shudders) Hold your tongue, boy! You are speaking to King Abaddon himself!

The two drakes startle and look around with sad eyes.

Fulguros: Sire, I beg of you to overlook this mishap! They are young and don't know what they speak off!

Abaddon: I am willing to overlook this but make sure it does not happen again.

Fulga: Forgive us, your majesty…

Abaddon: We all make mistakes, young one, I forgive you.

Fulguros: Truly your kindness knows no bounds… (bows his head).

Abaddon: Careful Fulguros, everything has its limits.

Fulguros: Sire (lowers his head even more).

Furgon: Can we eat this one then?

Fulguros: Neither are for eating!

Drake: Yes father…

Abaddon: Come now, take me to your mate.

Fulguros: Right this way, my liege.

Morgana: (So this is a Dragon's cave, I've only heard stories about them but to actually see one…)

Further inside

The Queen is laying on a heap of hay, sleeping, but breathing heavily. Abaddon stands beside her and places his hand on her body.

Abaddon: I see…she is suffering from internal bleeding; her stomach has been punctured.

Fulguros: That would explain the blood, it must be from those damn Great Oxen, I told her eating them whole is a bad idea.

Argyros: No wonder, those things have the horns the size of a human.

Morgana: (Just what kind of oxen do they eat?)

Abaddon: This should be easy to fix.

Morgana: I have a question, I was told that Dragons could regenerate, can't she use said ability to repair the damage of her stomach?

Fulguros: We Dragons may only regenerate lost limbs, internal damage however is a completely different thing.

Morgana: I see…

Abaddon casts 'Dark Restoration' which heals the target of any ailment. The Dragoness slightly opens her eyes but closes them again immediately.

Abaddon: Rest now.

She manages to mutter 'thank you, my king' and goes back to her slumber.

Fulguros: I can't thank you enough, my liege, thank you once again.

Abaddon: Right then, it's time we departed now, Argyros, Morgana, come.

Fulguros: Best of luck in your endeavours, sire.

Abaddon: Thank you, I appreciate it.

***

Outside, the ground begins to rumble and shake.

Morgana: (struggling to stay on her feet) An earthquake?

Argyros: I wish…

The ground erupts from beneath and a Dragon-like creature, lacking limbs, emerges with a loud roar.

Argyros: Lindroz… (growls).

Lindroz: Well, slap me some limbs and call me a Dragon, it really is you, Dread One (speaks with a loud and enthusiastic voice).

Abaddon: I see you're still fond of your loud entrances, Lindroz.

Lindroz: It's the way the great Lindroz rolls, haha. I came as fast as I could when I felt your presence.

Argyros: Not fast enough, you almost missed us.

Lindroz: Terribly sorry.

Abaddon: No worries, you came just in time.

Lindroz: Where are you headed then?

Abaddon: East.

Lindroz: East huh, sounds like loads of fun, I would ask if I could come with you, but I'm needed here.

Argyros: (We wouldn't take you anyway).

Lindroz: Got yourself a youngin there I see, old habits die hard, eh?

Abaddon: It's different with this one.

Lindroz: Sure, and I'm a Dragon, hahaha!

Abaddon: (sigh).

Morgana: Hello, my name is –

Lindroz: Don't know, don't care.

Morgana gasps.

Lindroz: Well, good luck in the East, Dread One, I will wait patiently for your arrival, then we can go wild on good ol'Avalon, hahaha!

Abaddon: Indeed we shall, old friend.

Lindroz: Until then! (Burrows back into the ground).

Morgana: He seemed…

Argyros: Silly? Ridiculous? Idiotic?

Morgana: All the above.

Abaddon: He may be an imbecile, but he is a valuable asset, nonetheless.

Argyros: I do agree on that one.

Abaddon: Come, let's be on our way.

Thus, they hop on the Black Dragon King and fly off to the East, slowly leaving behind the land of the Dragons and the continent of Baltia.

As you have seen, three types of draconic creatures inhibit the lands of Baltia. We have the Dragons of which three breeds exist; Fire, Tempest and Dark Dragons, there are also Water Dragons or Sea Serpents, but they live in the waters of the ocean to the south of Avalon. Then we have the Wyverns who inhibit the snowy mountains to the North, also called Ice or Winter Dragons by the races of Avalon, they are distinguished from their draconic cousins in the way that they do not possess front limbs and are smaller in stature.

And lastly the Wyrms, draconic beings that do not possess neither front nor rear limbs. Their land is known as Vurmuriz, Land of the Wyrms.

CAPITVLVM III

HATHASIA

Camelot, the Round Table, Council of Seven

On King Arthur's behest, the rulers of the seven kingdoms convene in Londwyn to discuss the newly arisen threat.

Arthur: Thank you all for coming on such short notice and I do apologise if I have taken you away from your busy schedules, but I am afraid that this matter cannot wait and must be addressed immediately.

Baldur: Aye, we've all sensed the vile energy that shot out from here.

Arthur: Indeed, it is as I feared, the bane of Avalon has risen once again. And even though I warned you of it, you decided not to listen and have dismissed me as a senile old fool.

Umbriela (Queen of the Angels): Now is not the time for 'I told you so', Arthur.

Arthur: I do not like saying it but, I told you so.

Umbriela face palms.

Now, the Queen of the Angels can easily be said to be one of, if not, ***the most*** *beautiful being in the entire world. Long, flowing, silver hair adorned her head, reaching all the way to her waist. Her face; as if sculpted in marble, perfect in every angle, her eyes; shining bright like two starts in the night sky, her lips; full and rosy. The complexion of her skin is white as snow and smooth as silk, with an ever so slight shimmer of light twirling beneath it. She is dressed in her regal armour, made of pure silver and white gold, inlaid with intricate blue design; it was more of a decorative piece rather than a battle suit. On her head sat a crown of shimmering white gold, with golden Angelic runes lined around.*

Cyril (King of Werewolves): Pointing fingers will do us no good, we must think of a way to handle this issue.

Cyril, the Werewolf King, was a rough-looking man, battle-hardened and stout. His hair is short and sharp, looking more like a wolf's fur than a normal hair. Square jawed, cowered with thick black beard that connects with his grizzly sideburns. He has high cheekbones and prominent, deep yellow eyes like a wolf.

His nails are black and sharp, and his body is covered in hair. He is definitely not one you could call handsome. He is dressed in regal clothing with no armour; emerald-green vest with golden buttons and a crimson velvet shirt, with a royal cape on top of all. On his head a silver crown. Like Arthur, he too was a prince when the final battle with Abaddon took place, succeeding his father, King Slavomir, after he was killed.

Umbriela: Well…the issue may be more difficult to handle than we think.

Urania (Queen of Faeries): Care to fill us in?

Urania, daughter of Queen Telubria of the Spring Court, elected as a Ri'ard – 'High-Queen', was of great beauty as well. Her hair is green, like the leaves of the trees in spring, going down to her shoulder blades. Her skin has a brown complexion like the tree bark, but it is smooth and not rough. Her ears; pointy, her eyes; verdant, radiant, and enchanting, her lips, unlike Umbriela's are reddish and thin.

Needless to say, her frame is small, smaller than any other major race of Avalon, but that adds a certain element of grace to her looks. On her arms and face she has decorative designs painted over, of glittering navy blue. She wears a long, almost transparent pale green dress; her wings, folded behind her, are highly decorated as well.

Umbriela: Shortly before arriving here I received a report from one of my generals that the Black Dragon has been spotted flying over Celestia, carrying Abaddon and…a human girl (looks at Arthur).

Arthur: …

Cyril: What is a Demon doing with a human girl?

Baldur: Never mind that, what of their fate?

Baldur, son of Ragnar, was as battle-hardened as Cyril and any other Dwarf for that matter. His rippling muscles were bulging as his arms were crossed before him. The Dwarves may be tiny, but they have the strength and the body to compensate for their shortcoming. His hair is short and bright orange, like burning flames, as is his long-braided beard that goes up to his chest. His nose is wide and bulbous, and his eyes tiny and sky blue. On him he has his dwarven regal armour, made of mithril steel and highly decorated; encrusted with all sorts of precious gems; the Dwarves were not shy in showing off their riches. On his head sits a tall, golden crown, that too encrusted with gems.

Umbriela: Unfortunately, my troops were unsuccessful in bringing them down therefore allowing them escape into Dhalsarria and ultimately in…Draconia.

Cyril: Pah! Incompetence!

Amra (Queen of Vampires): Such blunder is inexcusable!

Another female amidst the group of rulers, Amra too is on par with her fellow queens when it comes to beauty. Her own skin complexion is white, but unlike Umbriela it is paler, almost morbidly so, but that does not make her any less fair. Her hair is short and raven-black, going down to her neck, her eyes, blood red, with slanted pupils. Like Urania, her ears are pointy as well but unlike hers, Amra's are not that elongated. She too didn't wear any armour, but a regal dress instead, of cyan blue with quite a cleavage and tightened as well akin a corset, bringing her ample breasts to light. A ruby necklace decorates her neck and her head a three-pronged silver crown.

Umbriela: At least we tried!

Amra: If only your effort was more valiant.

Umbriela: How dare you!

Arthur: Enough! We did not come here to bite each other's throat!

Arthur's mighty voice silences the two queens.

Folduin (King of Elves): This should be of no concern to us, he cannot do much from Baltia; surely, he does not mean to invade us with the handful of Dragonkin that remain there.

Baldur: There is more to Baltia than Dragonkin; Orcs and Goblins infest those lands as well.

Cyril: Orcs and Goblins, savage primitives, they are as much as a threat as the flees that live on my Dire Wolf.

Arthur: Fools! Do you forget who we are dealing with here? He does not go there for the Dragons or Orcs he means to go East.

Folduin: To Hathasia…

Baldur: And then to the Demon lands beyond… (sigh).

Arthur: If he amasses the Demon armies of the East and with the combined numbers of Orcs and Goblins from the North it will be the doom of us all.

Cyril: I still see no reason for fear, we know very little of the Demons from the far East, who's to say they have more powerful armies than we do, eh? I say let them come, we crush them like insects.

Folduin: Lord Cyril is right, for now our fears are irrational, it is our fright of Abaddon what brings this uncertainty not of the unknown regions.

Urania: Abaddon is weak, fragile, it will take years before he regains his strength, and there is no sure guarantee that his kin from the East will be willing to lend them their aid. If you ask me, I think he's on a fool's errand, with delusional dreams of past grandeur.

Cyril: I agree, we have plenty of time to prepare our armies for an eventual assault and besides, things are different than from hundred years ago, this time we are united from the start!

General shouts of 'aye' fill the room.

Arthur: If we are to prepare, we best begin at once, our armies have grown dull from this time of peace, the old soldiers must be retrained and new ones trained, weapons and armour replaced with newer issues and upgrades.

Folduin: Agreed.

Folduin, second son of the Founding Elven King Singorin, who was slain in the Second Great War, at the battle of Pador na Undim, 'Fall of the Star', against the Angels. Most probably the fairest of all male rulers, as Elves were renowned for their stellar beauty in both their men and women. His hair: long and golden, going up to his lower back, with two long strands upfront going up to his chest. His eyes; glistering silver, and his skin complexion fair. He wears a regal armour made of gold and silver and a dark green undergarment. On his head is a beautiful golden crown with Elvish inscriptions.

Baldur: As usual, we will provide the materials and smithing.

Folduin: As will we.

Umbriela: And we the enchanting.

Arthur: Good, good, if everything goes as it should, Abaddon will regret his thoughts of former glory should he to cross us.

Baldur: Aye, only this time we'll make sure we thoroughly crush him, body and soul.

Arthur: May the Gods be with us.

All: May the Gods be with us!

Arthur: Unless anyone else wishes to speak then I shall regard this meeting finished.

Amra: I have a proposition.

Arthur: What do you propose, Night Queen?

Amra: We should send a spy to keep an eye on the Demon.

Folduin: A wise notion, however he is no fool, he will see through our ruse.

Amra: Not if I send one of my best.

Umbriela: It won't hurt to give it a try, would it? If it works, it shall be to our advantage.

Arthur: Then do it, but make sure it's the best of the best.

Amra: I would not have it any other way.

Arthur: In which case –

Baldur: Wait! There's still the case of the human girl that is accompanying the Demon.

Arthur: That would be my daughter…Morgana.

Everyone is appalled by this.

Baldur: A princess committing high treason? Now that's something you don't see every day.

Arthur: The fault lies with me; I sentenced my Court Magician to death which resulted in her lashing out against me and…leaving the kingdom.

Urania: To be young and in love…

Cyril: Daughter or not, she is still a traitor to your kingdom, and I expect you will treat her as a traitor.

Arthur: Of course, I have no other intention, whomever it may be a treason is a treason and it cannot be overlooked…although it weighs on me heavily and even more so on Guinevere, she is devastated…and blames me as well.

Umbriela: Perhaps a visit from one of my Hashmalim would elevate the grief.

Arthur: That would be much appreciated, thank you.

Umbriela: Of course.

Baldur: One more thing bugs me though…why would he agree to take her along?

Folduin: Is that really a surprise? He is known to be a deviant.

Baldur: Poor girl…

Arthur: …If everything is said and done then I suggest we end it here.

Baldur: That's all I had to say.

The others offer their silence which officially ends the meeting.

Arthur: Baldur! If you could remain for a moment, I wish to discuss some other things with you.

Baldur: Sure, what is it?

Arthur: It's about the ore proposal.

Baldur: Ah don't worry about it, we will be making the armature of the entire allied army anyway, so you won't be needing that manalith.

Arthur: Actually, it would still be a good idea to receive the agreed amount, I too have confidence in my smiths, and it would elevate some of your working stress as well. I only wish to help.

Baldur: It's fine really, we can handle it, Dwarves live for crafting.

Arthur: Perhaps I could triple your grain supply.

Baldur: I see what you're doing, you want to thin out the ore supply so that your armies are slightly more equipped than the rest under the guise of offering help.

Arthur: That is preposterous! I am appalled that you would even suggest such a thing.

Baldur: I may be many things, Arthur Pendragon, but a fool is not one of them, the ore supply remains as it is, you can keep your grain and your magic instructors.

Arthur looks at him in surprise.

Baldur: Good day to ya (leaves).

Arthur watches him leave, in bewilderment.

***

After flying for several hours, the trio at last makes it to the Sea of Sand, a desert wasteland which separates West Avalon from the Eastern side. As they are making their way, they fly over an outpost town in the middle of the desert. Their approach is noticed by the garrison army stationed there.

The soldiers are all wearing a light armour gilded with gold, on their heads they wear turbans and have their faces covered with scarfs to shield themselves from the sand and the scorching sun. As weapons they wield great spears with a golden tip.

Soldier: What is that thing?

Soldier#2: I think it's those giant lizards that they call Dragons, it's heading towards the royal city.

Soldier: We must alert his majesty, contact the Mystic right away!

The second soldier nods his head and heads inside.

***

Guard: My king, the garrison army of Sun'akhali is reporting that a flying lizard is heading this way.

King: A flying lizard, you mean a Dragon? Strange, Dragons do not come this far from the North unless… (he strokes his braided beard) Ah (smiles). Once they arrive do not detain them, instead see them inside, they shall be our guests.

Guard: Yes, my king (leaves).

King: Interesting…

***

Soon afterwards, they approach the royal city that is vastly stretched throughout the desert, with its ravishing spires and tall city walls.

Morgana: Wow! This must be the Royal City of the Men of the East.

Abaddon: Akhum, the capital of Hathasia, so you know about it.

Morgana: Only through what my father has told me, but seeing in real life it's…magnificent, it even looks better than Londwyn.

Abaddon: I'll have to agree on that one.

Argyros makes a landing, and they get off the Dragon. As soon as their feet reach the sand the guards cross their spears in a defensive manner.

Argyros: Do you think they will let us in?

Abaddon: Oh, I know they will.

The city gates open and out comes the guard from the palace. He murmurs something to the guards and they both remove their spears from the way.

The royal guard approaches and introduces himself.

Guard: My name is Marekh, on behalf of His Majesty, King Dharmat, I welcome you to Akhum.

Both Abaddon and Morgana slightly bow their heads as does Marekh.

Marekh: But I'm afraid we have not the space to accommodate for your mount, sir.

Argyros: It's okay, don't mind me; I'll wait outside.

Guard: It speaks… (murmurs).

Guard#2: Incredible… (murmurs).

Marekh: Are you sure? Perhaps we could make some arrangements –

Argyros: No, it's fine, I'm a Dragon, a little heat and sun won't kill me.

Abaddon: As he says.

Marekh: Very well sir, if you would follow me now.

Thus, they are led into the lavishing royal palace, with multiple side buildings attached to it making it look like a small town in itself.

The inner courtyard has a fountain with lion statues that spray water into it and the flooring is paved with glistering marble.

As they walk inside, the hallways are broad and spacious allowing for more free movement. The walls are filled with intricate lamps whose candles were currently put out as it was daytime.

Finally, they make it to the throne room, filled with beautiful decorations such as weapons and shields as hanging pieces, and walls painted pure gold. The whole place was practically screaming with richness.

At the throne was sited his majesty, King Dharmat whose real name was Marduk. Dharmat was the name undertaken by all kings in honour of the legendary king who established Hathasia. He is dressed in a royal garb made from velvet and soft linen, interwoven with gold ornate linings. The garb itself is of deep, turquoise green colour, and sapphire blue. On his head he wears a tiara, very ornate, encrusted with small gems and made of gold and brass.

His eyes are black in colour just like his hair and braided beard, and he has a light shade of eyeliner around his eyelids.

Dharmat: Welcome to Akhum, Dread Lord (he says spreading his arms).

Abaddon: Thank you for having me, Dharmat, which one is it now?

Dharmat: Currently I am the nineteenth (he says while smiling).

Abaddon: Ah, of course.

Dharmat: What brings you to these parts, Dread Lord?

Abaddon: Actually, my intention is not here at Hathasia, my goal lies farther east, beyond your kingdom.

Dharmat: And what possible business would you have with the – denizens of the Demon Lands?

Abaddon: As you see, I find myself in the need of an army so I thought that my kin here would be happy to oblige.

Dharmat: An army you say?

Abaddon: Well, I will need a force if I wish to restore my empire.

Dharmat: Ah, I guessed that that is your end goal.

Abaddon: Indeed, and as I find myself here, I would like to use this opportunity to ask assistance from you as well.

Dharmat: Indeed, however, this is a topic best discussed at a more appropriate location like the dinner table.

Abaddon: I graciously accept your offer.

Dharmat: Excellent, for now rest, have some wine, some fruits or some sweets, our cook makes the most exquisite sherbet.

Abaddon: Just some wine would do, thank you.

Dharmat: For your companion then mayhap?

Morgana: Some sherbet would be lovely, thank you.

Dharmat: Oh dear, how rude of me, how could I forget to inquire the name of such a lovely young lady.

Morgana: I am Morgana Pendragon, pleased to make your acquaintance (slightly bows).

Dharmat: Morgana of Camelot? I must say that this is the most unusual pair; what fate could've driven you to join with the feared Demon-King?

Morgana: (sigh) Must we do this with everyone we meet? It's so tedious having to explain it every time.

Abaddon: Let's just say that it was some unfortunate twist of events that led to this event.

Dharmat: Of course, I understand. Jamil!

At his behest a young man in his mid-twenties enters the room from the side entrance near the throne that is being covered by a red curtain.

The youngling has a fair skin with a darkish tan much like the king and every other man of Hathasia. He has a short but bushy black hair, and wears a short vest, and loose pants on his legs, and a high linen belt. On his neck he has golden rings, and a golden usekh collar covers his chest. He has piercings on both ears. His body is well built and hardened due to rigorous training.

Dharmat: This is my son, First Born Prince Jamil. He is a great admirer of yours.

Abaddon: Is he now? I would like to hear all about it at dinner.

Jamil: It would be my honour to indulge you, my king.

Abaddon nods politely.

Jamil: Allow me to show you to your chambers.

Abaddon: Lead on.

***

Abaddon: This is quite the lavishing banquet.

Dharmat: We have all sorts of delicatessens including of course our national dish (motions with his hand to the chair on the other side, opposite of him).

Abaddon: You didn't have to go to such lengths just for me.

Dharmat: Nonsense, we don't have guests of your stature that often in these halls.

Abaddon: You flatter me (sits down).

Morgana sits next to him on the side.

Dharmat: Did the lady enjoy the sherbet?

Morgana: Yes, it was quite tasty, thank you.

Dharmat smiles. Soon after, Jamil joins the table.

Dharmat: Maderwa kwoerda[5]? (Speaks in Hathasian).

Jamil: Widma swoerda[6]' they should be here any minute.

Dharmat: You will have to excuse my wife; she seems to be running late but she should be joining us presently.

---

[5] Where is your mother?

[6] With my sisters.

Abaddon: Of course, no worries.

Speak of the devil; they arrive just a few moments later.

Dharmat: Ah (gets up) allow me to introduce my lovely wife, Queen Azar and my two daughters Princess Bahar and Princess Ester. This is the Demon-King Abaddon from the West.

Abaddon: Ladies (gets up as well) pleasure to meet you.

He takes the Queen's hand but does not kiss it, much to her surprise and to the rest.

Azar: You as well, my king.

Dharmat: And this is Princess Pendragon of Camelot.

Morgana: My queen (bows).

Azar: My lady (bows as well).

After they sit down, the royal family looks at him as if expecting something which he finds confusing and so does Morgana.

Abaddon: Is something the matter?

Dharmat: Pardon me, Dread One, but surely you don't intend to eat dinner in that manner?

Abaddon: I don't see the problem.

Dharmat: It is a custom here that one should reveal his face in the presence of others, I didn't address this issue earlier as I thought you would unveil yourself by your own accord but I'm afraid I will have to insist now.

Abaddon: With all due respect, I prefer staying this way.

Dharmat: With all due respect, my lord, you are a guest here and as such it would be considered rude if you didn't abide by the host's customs.

Abaddon: …

Dharmat: …

Abaddon: Very well, if I must (takes off his crown and then his hood).

Everyone at the table is taken aback by his unexpected beauty, well defined face, dark, purplish skin, deep red eyes, with black sclerae, and long black silken hair. He also has pointy ears, and his whites are black instead. His pupils are slanted.

Azar: (gasps) By Mithras, what a comely face you have, must you keep it hidden in such manner?

Abaddon: No, I don't but I like how that looks, it makes me appear more sinister. As a king of Demons, I must keep appearances.

Azar: Right you are, my lord.

Abaddon: (forces a smile).

Morgana: I have to say that I prefer you this way.

Abaddon: I appreciate your preference princess, but I've no intention of changing my looks (takes a bite off the pigeon, revealing jagged teeth).

Morgana: Right…of course.

Abaddon: Now, on to business.

Dharmat: Ah yes, the issue of the army.

Azar: Army?

Dharmat: My lord wishes the aid of my army for his new imperial undertaking.

Abaddon: Indeed, as I find myself rather in a difficult situation.

Dharmat: However why would you need the help of someone like me? If you are going to acquire the aid of your kin to the East, I see no reason for the aid of my army.

Abaddon: The army of Hathasia has the best cavalry on all the continents, something my kin from both West and East, lack.

Dharmat: And what do I get if I let's say, accept your offer?

Abaddon: Camelot.

Dharmat: Oh?

Abaddon: I'm no fool your highness, I know that this empire had its eyes on the West for a very long time but it's impossible to invade with a single army. If you join me on the other hand, it will no longer be a farfetched dream. Therefore, allow me to reiterate myself, lend me your aid and in return I'll give you Camelot to rule on your own.

Dharmat: And the Princess has no objections to this?

Morgana: No, do with it whatever you wish.

Abaddon: There you go.

Dharmat: Of course, there is also the matter of **IF** we win.

Abaddon: There is no if, victory is assured.

Azar: Still a risky operation (looks at her husband).

Dharmat: What makes you so sure of success?

Abaddon: Let me put it this way, you know what I achieved with the Dhalsarrian army alone, now imagine that with the combined armies from the East and the North.

Azar: Still, I believe it should be discussed with the advisors.

Dharmat: (raises his hand in protest towards her) …Done.

Abaddon: (claps his hands) We have a deal then.

Dharmat: (lifts his chalice) To –

Abaddon: One more thing before we toast, we must seal this deal with a Blood Oath (produces a parchment written in the Common Tongue from a blue flame in his hand).

Dharmat: Is such a thing necessary? If nothing, it shows a lack of trust.

Abaddon: I know this may seem disrespectful however, I prefer not to leave things to chance, with this delicate matter I will need something more than your word.

Dharmat: (cynical smile) Of course.

Then, he produces a special pen with which he punctures his finger, and it absorbs some of his blood and he signs the document.

Abaddon: Would you be a dear and pass these on please? (To Ester).

The younger Princess passes it on until it reaches Dharmat, and he does the same and then it is brought back to Abaddon, after which he makes it disappear in the same manner as it came to be.

Abaddon: The deal has been sealed and there is no going back. I should warn you my lord that if you break this contract in any way it shall result in your death. The Blood Oath is unbreakable.

Dharmat: I would not dare to even think of such a thing, my lord.

Jamil: I think it's a great honour to be working with a king of your stature.

Azar: My son is a great admirer of yours.

Abaddon: So I hear; however, I didn't have the chance to know why.

Jamil: There is no one in the history of the continents that has achieved so much as you have. I've read everything about your conquests and method of warfare and the way you overcame Celestia with a blitz attack is purely ingenious. Also, one has to admire your first king as well, being able to singlehandedly unify the tribes of vicious Demons into one functional kingdom is unimaginable.

Abaddon: I wasn't aware that you were so knowledgeable.

Dharmat: It's all thanks to the books of our great historian Behrouz.

Abaddon: Ah yes, there was such a guy, I remember him now, he had travelled all the way to our homeland to learn more about us. Enthusiastic fellow, my father liked him I hated him however, he was too nosy for his own good. Of course, he only wrote what we allowed him to, you know state secrets and all that.

No response comes from the rest only awkward silence.

Dharmat: (clears his throat) My son is also an excellent swordsman if I may say so.

Abaddon: Is he now? Well, I would like to test his skills myself, perhaps a little sparring after dinner?

Jamil: I would love to, my lord.

Abaddon: Perfect (takes a sip).

***

Abaddon: You don't mind if I use my own sword, do you?

Jamil: No, of course not.

He produces Absharu.

Jamil: Wow…the Demon sword Absharu, may I hold it?

Abaddon: I would allow you but no, only a Demon may wield this sword; if it is handled by any other their soul will be devoured. It's to prevent it from falling in the wrong hands.

Jamil: Even so, such incredible craftsmanship…

Abaddon: One of a kind (smiles). Let's see how you hold against it, huh?

Jamil: I'm ready.

Abaddon: En garde! (Makes the first move).

They both show masterful skill; at the end however, Abaddon comes on top. He still gets an applause from his family, nonetheless.

Abaddon: Not bad, not bad at all, however there is still much room for improvement.

Jamil: I'm grateful for your patronage, my lord.

Abaddon: Hmmm (inspects his face up close).

Jamil is surprised by this sudden gesture. Abaddon feels Jamil's body with his hand.

His family members look at each other in wonder.

Jamil: My lord...?

Dharmat: Dread One?

Abaddon: Good...but not ready yet.

Dharmat: Is something the matter?

Abaddon: No, just talking to myself (moves away from Jamil).

This whole ordeal left Jamil slightly aroused.

Abaddon: King Dharmat, I thank you for your generous hospitality but I'm afraid I have to take my leave.

Dharmat: Leaving so soon? Surely you can stay for another night or two.

Abaddon: I didn't come here for vacation, there is still the matter with my kin that needs to be addressed.

Dharmat: Of course, and also a little piece of advice. The Demons of the East are a savage bunch and prone to violence hence their constant conflicts amongst each other, I would advise to proceed with caution.

Abaddon: I appreciate it but I'm more than capable to take care of myself.

Dharmat: I don't mean to imply otherwise but considering the delicate state you are in...

Abaddon gives him a look.

Dharmat reads the clue and refrains from saying anything further.

Abaddon: I'll prepare and take my leave, good night to you all.

Dharmat: Goodnight, my lord.

Abaddon: Morgana.

Morgana: Goodnight, your majesty (goes after him).

Abaddon: And Dharmat, makes sure your armies are well prepared, when the time comes, I will call for you.

Dharmat: Of course, I wouldn't have it any other way.

***

Morgana: This is such a nice place; do we really have to leave so soon?

Abaddon: As I said before, I'm not here for leisure, the sooner I secure the alliances of my kin the better.

Morgana: You sound so sure of yourself.

Abaddon: Should I have a reason not to? My name is greatly renowned throughout the world, they should be grateful for the opportunity to aid me.

Morgana: And what if they don't share your sentiment?

Abaddon: They will.

Morgana: But what if?

Abaddon: Agh, enough with your pestering, let's go.

She does a persiflage.

Abaddon: I heard that.

Morgana: Oops (fake smile).

***

Dharmat: Did you see the way he treated me? Subtly putting on airs in my home! **He** will call for **me? HE!** Who does he think he is? I am a ruler of a great kingdom, an empire! And he is the ruler of nothing, a king only in name! A husk of his former self!

Azar: Calm your nerves, my dear, and your tone, what if he hears?

Dharmat: Let him hear! I will not be intimidated in my own kingdom.

Azar: Well, there is nothing you can do for now, you made a Blood Oath, unbreakable (massages him in the nude).

Dharmat: There must be a way out, some loophole I can exploit.

Azar: We will find something, for now play his game and pray to the Gods that he wins.

Dharmat curses something incoherent.

Azar: Come (lays on the bed) and relieve your mind as we make love.

He goes to her.

And they make love while Abaddon sets his sight on a new region...

CAPITVLVM IV

FATVM CRVDELE[iii]

Onigashima, royal capital of the Oni

Abaddon and co. make their landing and as soon as they head towards the main gate, they are stopped by the two Onimusha guards, and the two that are on the stone walls draw their bows.

The Onimusha are a warrior type of Oni specialising in close combat using long swords known as 'katana'. The size of the sword may vary in shape and size depending on the warrior, some prefer bigger ones known as oodachi or shorter ones like the kodachi. There are also Onimusha who specialise in archery. However, the Onimusha are not exclusively limited to sword and bow, they also employ the use of pole weapons such as the yari or the naginata as is the case with the guards.

Their appearance is truly demon-like as they have two long horns protruding from their foreheads, long sharp teeth, and red eyes, although the eye colour may vary, it is generally red. They wear medium armour, sturdy and mobile at the same time, made of segmented steel plates. The Oni, or Ogres as they called in the Common Tongue, have an affinity to fire and can utilise it to enhance their weapons, dealing devastating flaming attacks.

Abaddon: At ease, brothers, we are not enemies.
Onimusha: Eh? What is this person saying?
Onimusha#2: I have no idea.
Abaddon: (Great, they don't speak Common).
Onimusha: Oi! Do you understand him?
Archer: I haven't got the slightest, mate.
Abaddon: (My Ogrian is utter nonsense but let's see what I can do).

Onimusha: Na wo nanore![7] I won't ask again!

Abaddon: Um…Waga hai wa Abaddon, um…Dhalsarria no ou… (introduces himself).

Onimusha: Abaddon? (Surprised).

Archer: Bullshit! Abaddon is dead! This guy must be an imposter!

Onimusha#2: Kisama! How dare you use the name of the great Demon-King so vaguely!

Morgana: What is going on?

Abaddon: I don't think they believe me.

Morgana: Maybe if you revealed yourself.

Abaddon: I don't think that'll help at all.

Argyros: This is why I hate dealing with ignorant barbarians, now what?

Onimusha: Let's restrain him.

Onimusha#2: Aa! (Proceeds to do so).

Argyros gets agitated and roars at the Ogres.

This causes them to prepare their weapons and stand on guard.

The archers however shoot their arrows at Argyros out of fright and agitate him even more.

Abaddon: Argyros! Calm yourself!

But it's too late as the enraged Dragon lunges forward with his huge maw and bites down on one of the archers taking a chunk of the wall as well.

Onimusha: Sound the alarm! Enemies at the gate!

The Bellman rings the bell, and it begins to reverberate throughout the city.

Abaddon: Stand back, Morgana! Things just got messy.

Morgana falls back to a safer distance.

Onimusha#2: Kakugou!

He attacks Abaddon with an overhead strike, but he manages to parry the blow with his gauntlet.

Then he draws Absharu and swings, but the Onimusha makes a swift retreat.

---

[7] Name yourself!

Abaddon: How dare…a lowly foot soldier like you, raise a blade on me, the great Abaddon!

Onimusha: Enough of your babbling! (Prepares to strike)

Abaddon: Nimu Anunuu!

He casts a sinister, dark aura that sows fear into the hearts and bones of his opponents, immobilising their movement.

The Oni feels as if the foulest malevolent creature has gripped them in his grasp and they begin to quake and shiver in fear.

Onimusha: Nanda kore wa…kono oura[8]… (drops his weapon).

The incoming soldiers are immediately affected by this spell and Argyros uses this opportunity to swipe them away with his tail.

However, a few of the Oni that arrived on the scene are unaffected by this. These much bigger and bulkier Oni are warriors of the Berserker class, ruthless and fearless. They do not wear much armour besides a breast plate, shin guards, and vambraces, depending on their sturdy bodies instead. The Berserks wield massive weapons like the tetsubo, axes and war hammers.

Abaddon: By Baal…

Argyros plants his left arm in front of Abaddon in a protective manner and lets out a menacing roar towards the assaulters.

Even though he is about hundred times their size the Ogres seem unmoved by his intimidation and ready their weapons while giving off battle cries of their own.

Argyros: These fools really intend to fight?

Abaddon: Looks like it.

One of the Berserkers leaps high into the air and means to slam down on Argyros' head, but he swipes him with his claw and slams him into the wall, but the Oni comes out unharmed. The others also prepare themselves for an attack and seeing no other option Argyros charges up a breath attack.

---

[8] What's this? This aura?

Abaddon: Don't! That's an order!

Argyros: I don't mean to stand idly and take a beating!

Oni: Shizumare![9]

The loud booming voice stops the Oni in their tracks. Abaddon breathes a sigh of relief.

Berserker: Tono[10]... (kneels)

The rest murmur 'it's the shogun' and kneel.

Tono: There better be a good explanation for you dimwits to interrupt my dinner!

Onimusha: Ha! Tono, this person here refused to give his credentials when asked and dared to impersonate our dear relative, King Abaddon.

Tono: **BAKAYAROU! THAT IS, KING ABADDON!**

Onimusha: Eh? I'm terribly sorry for my insolence, oh great one! I beg for your forgiveness.

Tono: Raise your head, soldier (stands behind him).

Onimusha: Tono... (does so).

Tono: State your name and position.

Onimusha: Hyozaburou...tono, city guard first division.

Tono: Hyozaburou of the city guard, first division, I can tolerate idiots, but I have no need of brainless shits like you (unsheathes his sword and decapitates him).

The rest do not even flinch as they saw this coming.

Tono: (wipes off the blood from his sword and sheathes it back) Now then, allow me to properly welcome you, Cousin Abaddon!

Abaddon: So good to see you again, Tetsuzaemon.

Tetsu: Give it here! (Embraces him, accompanied with a loud and cheerful laughter).

Abaddon: Energetic as always (returns the gesture).

Tetsu: And look at you, as if you've never died (he speaks Common with a heavy accent).

Abaddon: I wish I could say the same.

---

[9] Simmer down.

[10] Lord.

Tetsu: Ah! Small worries! (Smacks his back) You'll be back at full strength in no time, eh?

Abaddon: Hopefully.

Tetsu: Come! The night is still young, let us feast and drink to your arrival.

Abaddon: I already had dinner on my way here.

Tetsu: You stopped by the Human King, eh?

Abaddon nods in agreement.

Tetsu: Wine then! There is always place for a good wine!

Abaddon: Agreed.

Argyros: You can come out now!

Morgana: (steps out of her hiding place and comes forward).

Tetsu: Well I'll be, nice companion you have there eh? Hahaha.

Morgana: Our relationship is not like that.

Tetsu: I don't judge, little miss.

Morgana: It really isn't! I'm his apprentice! …even though he hasn't taught me anything yet…

Abaddon: In time.

Tetsu: An apprentice, eh? This little twerp? Doesn't seem like much.

Abaddon: Even though she may appear insignificant, she holds great potential.

Morgana: Oh, thank you 'master'.

Tetsu: Hahaha, I like this one, what's your name, little miss?

Morgana: Morgana, Morgana Pendragon.

Tetsu: Nice name, foreign though and her tan is much lighter than the Humans here, she must be from the West.

Abaddon: Indeed.

Morgana: You know him, but you don't recognise my name?

Tetsu: Should I?

Morgana: … (shrugs).

Tetsu: The little one has a sharp mouth on her (whispers to Abaddon) make sure she dulls it a bit.

Abaddon: It can't be helped, she is a princess, it comes with the title.

Tetsu: A princess you say? How did that come to pass?

Abaddon: That's irrelevant.

Tetsu: Right! Right! We've loitered around here long enough let's head to my castle!

Argyros: You go on, I'll just wait here.

Tetsu: Nonsense! You are a guest as well! I'm sure we can find some good accommodation for you, Mr Dragon.

Argyros: It's Argyros and I would be much obliged.

Tetsu: Oi! Kimi! Make sure Argyros-san is properly settled and well fed, ok?

Oni: Yes, my lord!

Tetsu: Hmmm (nods, extends his hand) after you.

And so, they head towards his castle. Unlike Dishum or the whole of Dhalsarria for that matter, Onigashima is a rather crude place, not having the grotesque and intricate splendour of its architecture. The structures are mostly built out of wood, stone and bricks and even though this may seem rudimentary, the buildings are still built in an advanced manner giving to them a certain beauty. This is due to the fact that the Oni are more of a fighters than builders.

And their shogun, Tetsuzaemon, can be described in the same manner. A crude looking person, with a stern face creased with a lot of wrinkles due to his age. Despite of this he still retains a sturdy and well-built posterior, wearing the royal armour made of brass and bronze with a tint of copper here and there to make it look more 'royally'.

His two pauldrons have the visages of two angry Oni carved into them which makes him look more menacing than he already is. On his legs he wears baggy pants and sandals. He has a white moustache spreading to the side and grizzly white hair. The complexity of his skin is seaweed green in colour.

***

Tetsu: Hahahah! (Laughing merrily)

Abaddon: So, about what we discussed on the way here…

Tetsu: Hai, the army, I must really think about this, and I will give your answer in the morning, how does that sound?

Abaddon: It sounds as if you're avoiding the topic.

Tetsu: Cousin, this is a delicate matter not a simple *'hai'* or *'iie'* question, I can't give a half-assed answer, now, can I?

Abaddon: Yes, I suppose you're right…

Tetsu: Now let's forget about such tedious matters and enjoy ourselves!

Abaddon: I believe I've enjoyed myself quite enough this evening and will call it for the night.

Tetsu: In which case you might want some female company eh?

Abaddon: Now that you mention it, that would be quite delightful.

Morgana: …

Tetsu: Oi! Onna wo mottekoi!

Upon his command a couple of Oni bring out several female ones and line them in front of the main table.

Tetsu: What do you say? Our women are quite the sight to behold are they not?

Abaddon: Yes, quite so, but I'm afraid they are too…sultry for my taste, I'd prefer something younger.

Tetsuzaemon dismisses them much to their disappointment.

The guys bring in the next batch, which is made of younger Oni female, which look like the equivalent of a twenty-year-old or so human female.

Tetsu: How about these lasses? Anyone catch your eye?

Abaddon: Not bad but still – younger.

Tetsu: (his face slightly sags down in disdain, but he manages not to show it) Bring in the slaves!

On his second command the boys bring in the third batch which consists of enslaved girls from the other Demon races native to the East, with the looks of 13-16 human years.

Abaddon: Perfect.

Some of the gathered in the hall begin to murmur but a quick stern look by Tetsuzaemon shuts them up.

Morgana: … Excuse me, I'd like to go to my room now as well, please (uncomfortable and sickened).

Tetsu: Oi Gozu! Show the lady to her room and don't you dare lay a finger on her, understood?

Gozu: Yes, my lord! (Escorts Morgana)

Abaddon: Goodnight princess. *She doesn't reply nor turn back.*

Tetsu: (groans) …

Abaddon: (turns his gaze back to the girls) hmmm… I'll take the one in the middle.

Tetsu: You! Stay! The rest of you back in the cells!

Abaddon finishes his wine and approaches the young Demon girl.

Tetsu: Mezu! With them!

Mezu: Sir! Right this way, lord Abaddon.

Tetsu: (What a crazy yarou, that's messed up even for me…)

***

Morgana: (lays on her bed and buries her face in the pillow) (Deviant… idiot…)

***

He touches her face, but she looks away in fright, her look seems dark and lifeless as if she has given up on life itself, her body is a bit roughed up, clear sign of mistreatment. The girl is well aware of what is to come and that almost brings her on the verge of tears.

Abaddon: Do not be frightened, my dear, I'm not going to hurt you.

She turns to him.

Abaddon: What is your name?

Girl: A-Asha my lord…

Abaddon: Asha, that is a lovely name, I am Abaddon.

Asha: Pleased to m-meet you…

Abaddon: (She doesn't seem to know who I am, good, I don't want her to become overwhelmed by my presence) (takes off his crown and hood).

Asha: (surprised) You are one of ours?

Abaddon: Close, I'm a Dark Demon from the West, you are of the Shadow ones, aren't you?

Asha: (nods)
Abaddon: That doesn't make us more estranged, does it not?
Asha shakes her head.
Abaddon: What a lovely girl you are (smiles).

He starts to take off his armour and clothing bit by bit until he is completely naked.

Abaddon: Come closer.
Asha: If my lord would have me…
Abaddon: That's why I picked you, didn't I? (Gentle smile).
Asha: (nods) R-right, forgive me…I'm not the smartest…
Abaddon: If I wanted smarts, I'd call for a librarian (slightly smiles) now…

Asha timidly approaches him.
Abaddon leans down to her height, lifts her chin, and kisses her. Asha returns the kiss, relaxes a bit.
As he kisses her, he takes off her ragged one-piece clothing and it falls on the ground, revealing her small naked stature.
Then, he breaks the kiss, takes her by the hand and leads her to the bed which is lit by the moonlight.

Abaddon: Don't worry, leave everything to me, I'll be gentle.

Asha nods, her ashen short hair slightly falling over her eyes.
He lays her down and gently kisses her neck and caresses the rest of her body, once she is prepared, he goes inside her and makes love to her whole the night long, having her from all sides and the young girl enjoyed it fully, having felt for the first time what is like to really be with someone.

***

It is morning and both are awake at this point.
Abaddon: Good morning.
Asha: Good morning my lord.
Abaddon: Last night was really enjoyable.

Asha: I'm glad I was able to please my lord.

Abaddon: Yes, you did good.

She smiles slightly.

Abaddon: Give me a kiss.

Asha leans over him and does so.

Abaddon wraps his arms around her as he kisses back.

After some time spent in each other's embrace, they lay back with Asha having her head on his chest.

Abaddon: Tell me Asha, what is the situation here.

Asha: …I'm sure you are aware that we are constantly fighting here…it's not a war but constant conflicts.

Abaddon: So I've heard.

Asha: My fate is a result of these conflicts…three years ago the Ogre's main army attempted a full-on invasion on Shilmatu[11], so they attacked my home city which lies on the border. Their attack came out of nowhere and they succeed in their attempt, destroying and sacking the city. No help came from the Royal Capital, the Zharum[12] had abandoned us deeming it better for them to have the city. The next day they took the women and children as slaves and brought us here while the rest marched forward, however, they were met by our army and driven off from our land and they've been at a stale mate ever since.

Abaddon: And what of the third faction?

Asha: I don't know much about them, they rarely come out from their underground kingdom.

Abaddon: Such a cruel fate…my people are suffering as well, enslaved by the abominable races of the West, but I will save them, every last one and restore my kingdom to its former glory, that is my goal, my purpose, for that I've risen from the dead.

Asha: Please, take me with you!

Abaddon: Sorry little one, I can't, I cannot allow any more distractions.

Asha: Please my lord I beg of you! I – I can't stay in this place anymore! (Tears up)

---

[11] Umbria in the Umbro-Stygian dialect.

[12] King in East Dhalsarrian.

Abaddon: I'm truly sorry, the least I can do is offer you relief from your misery.

Asha: That…would be fine as well.

Abaddon gets up from the bed and conjures up a dagger. Asha gets up as well and puts on her ragged clothing.

Abaddon: Are you sure you want this?

Asha: (nods) Please…

He approaches the girl and embraces her once more, and after a solemn moment he stabs her with the blade, and as she feels the dagger pierce her side, she clings her arms around him.

Asha: I'm glad…I got to meet someone as gentle as you at the end (smiles and a few tears escape her eyes as she closes them and passes away in his arms).

Abaddon: Sleep now, little one, sleep tight (one tear rolls down his cheek as well).

He raises her lifeless body in his arms and places her on the bed.

Abaddon: (gently caresses her cheek) Once I'm king again, I will put a stop to the fighting, this I promise you (kisses her forehead as he removes the dagger).

He decides to burn her body, not knowing how her remains will be treated by the Oni.

Then he silently proceeds to dress himself and leaves the room, going over to where Morgana is.

Abaddon: Good morning, princess.

Morgana: Morning…

Abaddon: You seem to be in a foul mood, did you sleep unwell?

Morgana: I slept just fine…

Abaddon: Is that so?

Morgana: And you? Did you have a good night? (Brushing her hair).

Abaddon: Can't say I didn't…

Morgana: Good for you then…

Abaddon: Do you hate me for it?

Morgana: No…but it doesn't make me like you more either.

Abaddon: Don't tell me you're upset about it? I reckon that's why you left in a hurry from the dinner as well.

Morgana: What does it matter how I feel, whatever I say you'll just dismiss it anyway.

Abaddon: Well, if you're not going to say anything hurry up so we can leave this wretched place.

Morgana: We'll leave when I'm ready.

Abaddon: Hurry up then!

Morgana: Don't you know not to rush a lady?

Abaddon: I don't have time for your frivolous business.

Morgana: Ugh! It's always 'me' 'me' 'me'! What about **ME?** You said you were going to teach me magic and we haven't even started with the basics!

Abaddon: Now is not the time!

Morgana: You say that all the time! When will it be?

Abaddon: Soon.

Morgana: Ugh!

Abaddon: Stop acting like a spoiled brat and get ready!

Morgana: No! Enough! I'm not your possession that you can simply order around and drag along with you!

Abaddon: Now you're complaining? You decided to come with me on your own! No one forced you to!

Morgana: And you accepted it!

Abaddon: Dammit!

Morgana: So you better start going on your word!

Abaddon: Or what? You'll go back to Camelot?

Morgana: …Idiot! (Grabs her dress and storms out the room).

Abaddon: Morgana!

Morgana: Stupid! …Fool! … Arse! I hate you!

Her voice echoes throughout the hallway as she moves away.

Abaddon: Baal, have mercy! This is why younglings are only fit for pleasure!

He exits the room and goes after her. He asks one of the guards and he informs him that she went to where the Dragon is settled.

Abaddon: (Agh! I'll deal with her later; I must see the king first).

***

Tetsu: Morning friend, did you have an enjoyable night?

Abaddon: … I did, but never mind that our talk is of priority now.

Tetsu: Ah yes…the army…hmmm… I have thought on this long and hard and I'm afraid I cannot help you.

Abaddon: As I thought…

Tetsu: You must understand the situation I'm in, things are different here, we are not united like in Dhalsarria. We could come under attack at any moment, and I simply cannot afford to spare my army for other dealings, I am truly sorry.

Abaddon: That is unfortunate indeed –

Guard: Tetsuzaemon-sama!

Tetsu: What is it?

Guard: I can't find the slave girl, sir! She must've escaped from Abaddon-dono's room!

Tetsu: Find her!

Abaddon: Don't bother looking for her, she's dead.

Tetsu: Dead?

Abaddon: I killed her myself.

Tetsu: Nani? Even if she has insulted you in any way, it is not in your place to punish her!

Abaddon: She didn't insult me, that girl was suffering, and I released her from the clutches of her wretched life.

Tetsu: She was my slave! You have no right to decide the fate of what is mine!

Abaddon: She choose that fate herself as well.

Tetsu: Abaddon-dono! You overstep your boundaries as a guest here!

Abaddon: I won't apologise for what I did; if given the chance, I would do it again.

Tetsu: Eihh! I have never seen such disrespect towards a host in my life! Is this the way of the West?

Abaddon: Let me tell you something 'friend'. I have kept slaves as well and paid no mind to how they are treated, but I have never physically abused the young ones! I've never raised a hand on them which is far from what you've done here! That girl thanked me and was grateful for the treatment that I have shown her!

Tetsu: Enough! You have your own ways of doing things and I have mine! I will not take any more insults to my honour!

Abaddon: (outraged) 'Enough'? I will not be silenced by some lowly barbarian!

Tetsu: Abaddon-dono! I have shown you nothing but friendship and hospitality since you arrived but no more! You are not welcome here any longer!

Abaddon: Good! I spit on your honour and hospitality!

Tetsu: Dette ikee! (Waves his hand)

Abaddon: Mark my words Tetsuzaemon, King of Ogres, I will come back, and our roles shall be reversed (storms out with his cape waving furiously behind him).

Tetsu: By all means, come back! Only next time I will show you the edge of my blade!

***

Argyros: What happened?

Abaddon: Not a word!

Argyros and Morgana look at each other in question and both shrug in the end.

Abaddon without a word gets on top of the Dragon and so does Morgana and they fly off for their next destination in silence.

***

Argyros: Is this it? There is nothing here.

Abaddon: It's down there.

He points towards a pathway that leads deep down into a precipice between two mountains.

Argyros: (sigh) I know the drill…I'll wait here.

Abaddon: You wait here as well.

Morgana: Whatever…

Abaddon heads towards the pathway that looks like stairs. The pathway keeps heading downwards and downwards…

Abaddon: (how long does this path take, I feel like I've been walking for hours).

As he's going down, he hears a sound and he stops, after a few moments the sounds get louder until finally a grotesque creature burrows itself out of the ceiling and comes down on Abaddon with a loud screech. He manages to fend of his attacker, but the creature attacks him yet again, so he is forced to stab it with Absharu and kill it.

Several of the same creatures emerge out of the ground and attack him but he kills them off with relative ease.

Abaddon: (These must be some lesser form of Demons, how annoying) (sheathes the sword and moves forward).

He keeps walking until finally he reaches a clearing with a large door at the other end.

Abaddon: (That must be the entrance, finally).

As he approaches it, he hears the same sound only on a larger magnitude this time and out from the ground emerges a skeletal Dragon, letting out a mighty roar.

Abaddon: A Skull Dragon huh, you must be the guardian of this place.

Even though the creature is a Dragon it is much smaller than the likes of Argyros.

Abaddon: Nimu Etutuu! (Casts it but it doesn't work) Nothing huh, since you're devoid of a brain so are you of fear.

The creature attacks him with his maw but Abaddon leaps backwards and evades the attack causing the Dragon to hit the ground instead.

Abaddon uses this opportunity to strike him with his sword, but it does not do him much good. The creature brushes the attack and goes in for another bite but fails yet again. Enraged, it rears up on its legs and fires a blast of necrotic energy from his mouth towards Abaddon, who manages to evade the attack but the blast from the impact still knocks him on the ground.

Abaddon: Getting pushed around by a lowly creature like you, how unsightly of me, let's fix that shall we? (Gets up).

Abaddon: Etu Kalu! (Casts 'Dark Restraint' which causes the creature to be held down by a pair of ethereal Demonic hands).

Abaddon: Let's see if I can pull this one off, Absharu: Enu Mashu: Kimiltu![13]

On his command the Demonic inscription that runs along the blade changes and the sword glows with a red aura, then with one mighty swing Abaddon completely destroys the Dragon, shattering it to tiny bits.

Abaddon: Looks like my powers are gradually returning, excellent.

The gate opens and a bulky looking Earth Demon emerges.

Demon: (looks around) Are you the one that destroyed the Skull Dragon?

Abaddon: (By Baal I have no idea what he's saying, I hope the king speaks Common) Um, me no understand, common, speak? (Makes gestures with his hands).

Demon: …?

Abaddon: CO-MMON, SPEAK? (Moves his hands again).

Demon: Co-mmon, little, you destroy Dragon?

Abaddon: Do you see anyone else beside me?

Demon: (scratches his head) Come, I take king, he speak better.

Abaddon: O-K!

Demon: Me dumb no deaf, no shout.

Abaddon: Sorry about that.

He takes him before the king beneath the earth.

The creature sitting before Abaddon did not look that much different from his kin to the West. He seems as if though he was made from earth. With green, earth energy showing from certain cracks throughout his body including his eye sockets. His stature is lean but sturdy, and he has long nails on his hands and feet, on his head he had two large, wide horns protruding from the sides and a crown made of roots and vine. As clothing he wears nothing but a ragged waist

[13] First stance: wrath.

cloth. His only armour is a pair of greaves and vambraces made of simple materials. On his face he wears a smug look.

The Demon speaks of something to him as he points to Abaddon.

King: My Subterran tells me you slew our guardian, well done.

Abaddon: Subterran?

King: That is our name, yes, we call ourselves Subterrans, Underearthers.

Abaddon: Hmm, alright. I'm surprised you kept such a thing as a guardian then again, I reckon you don't get much attacked down here.

King: Cheeky one aren't you, name yourself, brave traveller.

Abaddon: My name is Abaddon, King of Dhalsarria.

King: You're **THAT** Abaddon?

Abaddon: Ah yes, I get that a lot, don't let yourself be deceived by my looks oh king…?

King: Albunalich. King Albunalich.

Abaddon: Albunalich, though I may not look the part I can assure you that I am **THAT** very Abaddon you speak of.

Albunalich: Have you any proof to back up your brazen boasts?

Abaddon: I'm sure you've at least heard of the Demon Sword Absharu (presents it).

All present that look upon it gasp in awe.

Albunalich: So, it is true, tell me, what brings the famed Demon-King to our realm?

Abaddon: I've said this so many times that I dread of repeating myself, so I'll keep it simple, I need your armies to help me on my quest to retake Avalon.

Albunalich: I see… I sympathise with your plea fellow king, but I must respectfully decline.

Abaddon: You're not even going to ponder on it?

Albunalich: No.

Abaddon: No? (Boiling inside).

Albunalich: You see, I'm not interested in some grandiose conquests, I'm quite content with what I have. Besides, there's always the threat from the outside.

Abaddon: But I'm giving you the opportunity to make a name for yourself, you will be renowned and feared throughout the realms, the other Demon Kings will tremble from the mere mention of your name.

Albunalich: That sounds ever so appealing, but my answer remains the same.

Abaddon: …Are we not kin? We should help each other in times of need.

Albunalich: No, we are not, I don't remember being related to you nor do I remember any help coming from the West when we waged our wars here (leans forward on his throne).

Abaddon: … Let the past be the past, we can start to build our relationship from this point onwards.

Albunalich: You don't take no for an answer, do you?

Abaddon: I am really in a pickle here, I can't afford a 'no', not again.

Albunalich: Again? So, the others turned you down as well? I wonder why (smirks).

Abaddon: Mock me at your own peril, oh king.

Albunalich: Humph, before you say anything else I'd like to tell you that you're not the only one with a rare sword, oh king (pulls out a long, bronze blade with a large emerald as the centrepiece of the hand guard).

Abaddon clicks his teeth.

Albunalich: Titan Sword Balmung, a beauty, isn't it? (Smirks).

Now it would be adequate to say a word or two about these swords. Absharu, Balmung, and others alike are relics from an ancient age, long gone. It is believed that Absharu was crafted by Baal himself for one of his Abyssal Generals, and after the Gods left this plane of existence, he left it behind in Dishum's care. Ever since then it became a symbol of kingship in the Dark tribe. It was meant to be passed down to the eldest son when he would become king, but since his three sons all perished before any of them could claim the throne, it was left in the care of Demiurgos' father, a grandson to Dishum from his youngest son Baalpharzon.

Balmung was the blade used by Gai'ara, Queen of the Earth Titans, therefore it is infused with her magic to command the earth and plants. It was handed to Albunalich himself after she left.

Abaddon places his hand cautiously on Absharu's handle, ready to draw it at any moment.

Albunalich: Furthermore, I would like to add that I sense very faint magical energy coming from you, must be the many years of wandering as a spirit.

Abaddon: I warned you not to mock me (grips the handle).

Albunalich: Oh please, do make your move, I wonder who would come on top if we were to clash.

Abaddon: (Baal, give me strength…)

Without a warning, Albunalich leaps up in the air and comes down on Abaddon who blocks the attack in time with Absharu, causing a shockwave from the clash.

Albunalich smirks.

Abaddon: Kh! (Struggling).

Albunalich envelops Balmung with green earth energy and blasts Abaddon away who slumps on the ground. Then he swings the sword around and slams it in the earth, rending it asunder which causes an explosion to occur and launch Abaddon in the air, but the Underground King is not done yet as he magically causes a thorny vine to sprout out of the ground, grab Abaddon by the ankle and slam him back down with great ferocity.

Albunalich: The great Abaddon bites the dust (smirks). Does it taste good, 'great king'?

Abaddon: (props up on one hand and shoots a beam of light towards the ceiling from his sword).

Albunalich: Hm? (Looks at the light).

The light protrudes all the way up to the surface causing Argyros to notice it and take flight.

Morgana: Argyros, where are you going? Argyrosss…! Ugh! No matter what the species, men are always idiots!

After he gains appropriate altitude, Argyros shoots a concentrated breath attack that burrows deep into the ground to where Abaddon is, and crashes on the ground, exploding and knocking all around there off their feet.

Demon: What the hell was that? (In his language).

The Demons have hardly the time to collect their thoughts when Argyros comes crashing down from above, causing the ceiling to shake and smash some denizens with chunks of earth, while the rest are forced to cover their eyes from the protruding sunshine.

Albunalich looks in awe at the giant creature that just made an entrance, it was his first time seeing such a beast in person.

Argyros: Come on, partner, let's get out of here (he grabs him with his mouth and throws him on his back, then flies off).

CAPITVLVM V

DOMINVS MONSTRVORVM[iv]

Morgana: What happened?

Argyros: He got beaten up pretty bad.

Abaddon: I'm fine…

Morgana: You don't look fine!

Abaddon: What do you care? I thought you hated me.

Morgana: I don't…Ugh! You really are an idiot!

Abaddon: I –

He passes out and slides off Argyros' back, but Morgana holds him in place.

Argyros: What's wrong?

Morgana: He's slipping!

Argyros: Hold on! (Reaches on his back and sets him straight up).

Morgana: Thanks!

Argyros: No problem, kid.

Abaddon: Wha – (opens his eyes slightly but loses consciousness again…).

***

Abaddon little by little opens his eyes and slowly regains consciousness but he wakes up in an unknown environment.

Abaddon: Where am I…?

He is half-naked and wrapped with bandages around his torso.

Morgana: No, no, no! Don't get up! You need to rest (lays him back down).

Abaddon: I asked you a question.

Morgana: (clicks her teeth at his tone) We are at the castle of the Shadow Demon King.

Abaddon: So, we made it there?

Morgana: Shortly after you passed out, as soon as we landed, they were there; they must've seen us approaching.

Abaddon: Then I must speak to the king at once.

Morgana: No, you must rest, you mustn't overexert yourself in your condition.

Abaddon: Curse my own weakness…

Morgana: What happened down there?

Abaddon: I got defeated by that king…after he rejected my offer.

Morgana: Again huh…

Abaddon: You're right, I am an idiot… I don't know what I expected coming here, a stranger you only know by name comes to seek for your help of course you'll turn him down, so what if you're of the same race, you don't know him, you don't owe him anything…

Morgana: Indeed, it seems like a foolish notion, but you had no choice… (sighs) what will you do now?

Abaddon: The king of this place is my only hope…if he too refuses then I will have to rethink my stratagem.

Morgana: Do you have something else on your mind?

Abaddon: If they don't want to listen nicely then I'll have to beat them into submission.

Morgana: That's suicide! You couldn't defeat one of them let alone three!

Abaddon: Who said I'll do it alone?

Morgana: … Now I'm completely lost.

Abaddon: Don't sweat it; it's nothing to worry your pretty little head with.

Morgana: (gasps) Don't treat me like I'm some idiotic, peasant girl!

Abaddon: Tsk, I'm not you damned brat, I'm telling you that is not of your concern.

Morgana: …Fine!

Abaddon: Oh, to hell with this! (Casts Greater Heal wounds on himself).

Morgana: No! Don't waste your mana! Let it heal naturally!

Abaddon: I haven't the time to loiter around in bed (takes off the bandages).

Morgana: Could you for once stop being a stubborn fool?

Abaddon: No (gets up and walks away)

Morgana face palms and shakes her head.

***

The king's throne room

Abaddon walks in.

King: Already up and running I see, Sir Abaddon.

Abaddon: Don't take me so lightly Dumah, wounds like that are nothing to me.

Dumah, the King of the Shadow Demons wore himself elegantly, clothed in ornate exhibition armour with a red cape. His from is humanoid with a dark tone of skin, completely red eyes, and purple lips. The Shadow Demons are descendants of a group of Fallen Ones, Angels who have lost their grace after embracing the darkness of Baal. After their exile from Viloth, they've fled to the Eastern lands, mingling with the native population of Shadow Fiends, and establishing what is now known as Zhilmatu, 'Home of the Shadows', in the Dhalsarrian dialect of the East.

Dumah: Well, I'm pleased you are up and running. Perhaps we can talk about your predicament now.

Abaddon: My predicament is simple; I need you to lend me your armies.

Dumah: So your plan on reconquering Avalon is true then?

Abaddon: Yes.

Dumah: Hmmm…very well, I will help you.

Abaddon: Oh really?

Dumah: Yes; indeed, however, under one condition.

Abaddon: (I knew it) what is it?

Dumah: In return you must help me destroy the Oni and the Ground Dwellers.

Abaddon: Why would you want to destroy the latter? They hardly bother anyone from beneath the ground.

Dumah: Precaution. Who knows, one day they might decide to emerge and conquer us all, and I'd rather not have that happening.

Abaddon: Well, I'm afraid I can't do that; the other Demon tribes are pivotal to my plan.

Dumah: Pivotal? But they turned you down, humiliated you even.

Abaddon: How do you…?

Dumah: The little one told me.

Abaddon: Of course…in any case, I am not taking any risks this time, their armies will be well prepared, I can't afford to be defeated a second time.

Dumah: But you are the greatest Demon-King that has ever lived, when you regain your full strength, you'd be able to squish their armies like insects by yourself.

Abaddon: You overestimate me cousin, even my powers have limits, I am not an omnipotent deity.

Dumah: That is unfortunate to hear, I had hoped you'd accept my gracious offer. In which case you are free to stay here for as long as you like, rest, drink, fuck to your heart's content, you won't get any other help from me other than that.

Abaddon: And I had hoped that at least you will head my plea but here you are making demands instead.

Dumah: Are you familiar with the saying 'beggars can't be choosers'?

Abaddon: Beggar? You say others have humiliated me but here you are doing the same, it seems you have you mistaken my plea as a desperate call for help like I am some helpless peasant.

Dumah: Isn't that the case though? If you weren't desperate, you wouldn't be going from kingdom to kingdom seeking for help.

Abaddon: I ask for help not charity you piece of shit! You dare as the rest look down upon me from your high place at the throne! Well, I will not stand for this hubris!

The guards in the vicinity draw their swords on him but Dumah orders them to stand down.

Dumah: Then I suggest you take your leave, 'cousin'.

Abaddon: You and the two others like you haven't really seen the extent of my might, you take me for some weak, tiny existence clinging onto former glory but make no mistake that that is far from what I am, mock me all you want now but I will make sure it comes back to haunt you and the others like you.

Dumah: (claps) Such bold words, and true without a question, there isn't a shred of doubt in me that says that you are incapable of doing exactly as you say, and I'm afraid you have misinterpreted my words as taunts and mockery, that was not my intention, alas for someone as yourself in the position that you're in it's easy to mistake them as such, for I was merely stating the true circumstances of this unsavoury predicament. Perhaps it was my tone of voice as well that added to the confusion. In any case, please accept my humble apologies.

Abaddon: You keep talking, but all I hear is the sound of excrement pouring from your hole like the shit that you truly are! Have a nice day, until we meet again, and thanks for your hospitality (walks away).

Dumah: (his right eye is twitching from anger) Guards! Seize him! And throw him in the dungeons!

Abaddon: (Shit!) (Starts running).

Guard: Hey you! Stop! After him!

One of the guards jumps him from a side hall, but Abaddon manages to overpower and slay him with Absharu.

He uses his powers of teleportation to get to his room.

Abaddon: Come on! Time to go!

Morgana: On the run again! What happened now!

Abaddon: I and the king don't seem to see eye to eye, and I may have said some things I shouldn't have.

Morgana: Oh joy! What a surprise!

Abaddon: Shut your yapping and let's go! (Takes her hand)

In that moment, one of the guards breaks down the door.

Guard: Halt!

He envelops his sword in shadows and chucks them towards Abaddon. Abaddon teleports outside the castle along with Morgana.

Morgana: Okay, that's pretty cool!

Abaddon: Where is Argyros?

Morgana: At the entrance of the forest but it's pretty far, they might catch us.

Abaddon: Not if I can help it, hold on tight!

She clings onto him as instructed.

Then he transforms himself in a mass of dark cloud and travels onwards toward the edge of the forest.

Morgana: Amazing! You have to teach me how to do it!

Abaddon: All in due time.

Argyros: We're running again?

Abaddon: On the double (swings and tosses Morgana all the way up to Argyros' back).

Morgana: Wooow!

Argyros: You seem awfully cheery.

Morgana: Thanks to these awesome flights!

Argyros: (Kids, getting excited so easily).

Abaddon: Go! Go! Go! (Hops on as well).

Argyros: (builds up momentum and flies off) We've got to stop making this a habit.

Morgana: Tell that to mister sharp tongue over here.

Argyros: You really have a habit of pissing people off, don't you.

Abaddon: Only when they do so first.

Argyros: (sigh) Where to now? I'm pretty sure we exhausted our options here.

Abaddon: First we'll make a quick stop in Hathasia then we're moving on to Baltia.

Argyros: Back up north? What will you do there?

Abaddon: Something I should've done long time ago.

Morgana: Could you stop being cryptic and answer for once?

Abaddon: I'm going to build my own army.

Morgana: Okay…how?

Abaddon: That's something you'll have to see.

Morgana: Tsk.

Argyros: Can't wait to see that for sure.

***

Dharmat: King Abaddon, back so soon? Did you have luck on your journey?

Abaddon: Never mind that, I need to borrow your library and a dozen of your finest sword tutors.

Dharmat: For what purpose?

Abaddon: That is none of your concern.

Dharmat: But my lord, I thought we had a deal, a Blood Oath, are we not partners? Besides, I have a right to know what my tutors will be used for.

Abaddon: I'll build an army on my own then come back with it and bend the others to my will.

Dharmat: That means negotiations have failed, how unfortunate.

Abaddon: No matter, I tried asking nicely now I must exert force.

Dharmat: And…where will you find this army if I may ask?

Abaddon: Up in Baltia.

Dharmat: Baltia? But there is nothing but savage beasts there.

Abaddon: Savage beasts are all I need.

Dharmat: Very well, I will prepare your tutors, and, in the meantime, you are free to take whatever book you like, Hazir will show you to the library.

Abaddon: You have my thanks, Dharmat.

Dharmat: But of course, of course.

Hazir: Right this way, my lord.

***

Abaddon: (looks through the books on magic) (all of these are in Hathasian, curses…).

After searching for a while, he stumbles on some books that pick his interest.

Abaddon: (These are in…Elven? How did these books get here? Oh well, I guess that's the next best thing) (grabs a couple).

Then he goes on to search for books on smiting.

Abaddon: (slams the books in front of the old librarian) I'll be taking these, old man.

Librarian: (catalogues them without uttering a word) These need to be returned within a month.

Abaddon: I'll return them when I feel like it.

Librarian: You can't just…

Abaddon: Good day (leaves).

Librarian: Hey! Hey!

Guard: Give it a rest old man; do you even know who that is? That's Lord Abaddon.

Librarian: Abaddon the Demon? (Stretches out his head for a better look) He looks nothing like in the books.

Back at the throne room

Dharmat: Ah just in time, these are my finest sword masters in the entire kingdom.

Abaddon: Good, then we can be on our way.

Dharmat: Just a moment, take my son Jamil with you as well.

Abaddon: That won't be necessary.

Dharmat: He's very good with the sword as you have seen yourself, I'm sure he will be of great help to you.

Jamil: Please my lord, allow me to be of your assistance, I can assure you that I will not be a hindrance.

Abaddon: Fine, I'll take your word for it but if I deem you to be as such, I will send you straight back.

Jamil: Thank you so much! I promise that I will do my best to be of your service.

Dharmat: (I've never seen Jamil so excited about anything…)

Abaddon: Come, all of you, time is of the essence.

Dharmat: May I inquire of the duration of your absence?

Abaddon: As long as it takes my lord, as long as it takes.

Dharmat: (gives a meaningful nod) Have a safe journey, may the Gods be in your favour.

Abaddon: Amen.

***

Morgana: Took you long enough.

Abaddon: Do you ever stop complaining?

Morgana: Who are these men?

Abaddon: You already know the prince and the rest are tutors who will be coming along on our trip.

Argyros: Since when did I became public transport?

Abaddon: Come now, friend, this is of the utmost necessity.

Argyros: To you maybe.

Jamil: I get to ride a Dragon, how exciting!

Argyros: Don't get so uppity about it, brat, I'm not a damn attraction.

Jamil: Oh, pardon me, I meant no disrespect, it's just that this is my first time seeing a creature of your kind in person, I've only read and heard stories about you but to actually be able to ride on one…it's such a privilege.

Argyros: You're not just kissing my arse, are you?

Jamil: No, I wouldn't.

Argyros: In that case, all is well.

Abaddon: (whispers) Keep stroking his ego like that and you'll have him eating from your hand in no time.

Jamil: I –

Abaddon: It's just a joke boy (taps his shoulder).

Jamil: Right (smiles).

Argyros: What was that?

Abaddon: Nothing.

Argyros: (grunts and then lies down so that the others may climb his back) This is the last time I spend transporting other humans on my back, got that?

Abaddon: Sure, just fly off already.

Argyros grunts again before flying off.

***

Terebriz

Argyros: Could you explain to me now what we are doing back in my home?

Abaddon: We're dropping the princess off and gathering some more allies.

Morgana: Wait! What? You are not leaving me here alone!

Abaddon: I have no choice, the task I'm about to undertake leaves no place for distractions.

Morgana: Is that the only thing I am to you? A distraction?

Abaddon: Morgana! This is serious business! Everything depends on this one thing do you understand?

Morgana: I understand but I don't accept!

Abaddon: This is not up for discussion!

Morgana: You sound just like my father! I did not escape one just to end up with another Arthur!

Abaddon: I'm not having this fight again!

Morgana: You won't have to because I'm done with you! With all of this!

Abaddon: And where will you go? To Camelot? You'll be tried for treason!

Morgana: Better that than be treated like a nuisance!

Jamil: My lord, perhaps it would be a better idea to leave her at my palace, she would have a proper roof over her head and a warm bed, and my sisters would be delighted to have a new friend to play with.

Abaddon: With all due respect, Jamil, I don't trust your father, she would be safer here.

Jamil: But you are bound by a sacred contract, my father would be unable to take any underhanded tactic.

Abaddon: Even so, she would be safer here, amongst my true and trusted allies.

Morgana: (He...actually cares for my wellbeing?) ...Very well, I'll stay here.

Abaddon: Oh? No more tantrums?

Morgana: Tsk! No...but what am I supposed to do in the meantime?

Abaddon: (throws the books at her feet) I hope you can read High Elven.

Morgana: What are these?

Abaddon: Books on introduction to magic.

Morgana: (her face immediately lights up) (clears her throat and regains composure) Luckily, I was thought to speak High Elven due to father's regular dealings with the Elven nobles.

Abaddon: Good, then you're settled.

Morgana: Don't take too long, okay...

Abaddon: (places his hand on the top of her head) Don't worry, even if I do I won't leave you here (messes up her hair) stupid brat.

She gives him a hug.

Abaddon: Hey now, I don't remember us being that close and personal.

Morgana: Shut up (breaks the hug).

The two other Dragon Kings make their appearance as well.

Ignatos: Well look who's back, that was faster than expected.

Fulguros: And I only see a few humans but no army.

Abaddon: Well, the thing is... (goes on to explain the situation).

Ignatos: (sigh) We should've done that from the very beginning, there would've been no need for all that hustle.

Abaddon: What's done is done, now we move forward.

Ignatos: I can't wait to teach those pompous bastards a lesson.

Abaddon: Don't we all.

Fulguros: And the little princess is staying here?

Morgana: Unfortunately…

Fulguros: Not to worry, little one, I will send my youngins and the wife to keep you company.

Morgana: Really? You would do that?

Fulguros: Of course!

Morgana: Thank you so much! (Smiles).

Fulguros: Someone has to keep you fed as well.

Abaddon: (I completely forgot about that, best not to say anything.)

Morgana: Thank you.

Fulguros: Besides, a princess like yourself has no business in the rough dealings of us males.

Morgana: As you were…

Ignatos: Ready to fly, boys?

Argyros: I was born ready.

Thusly, after everything is said and done, the 'merry band' takes off to yet another destination.

Orcothrond, the land of Orcs

The land of the Orcs lies directly northeast of Ignariz, the fiery home of the Fire Dragons. To the south it borders Hathar, the northern province of Hathasia, and to the north it borders with Glaziriz, the snowy homeland of the Wyverns. It is a land of much forest and greenery to its north, but the south is mostly a barren wasteland. The land had received such scourging that it has not healed until this day. It is worth to note that this site used to be the once northern kingdom of Men, Arothyr. The Men of the North and the Orcs were often in conflicts, and after a seven-year war that ended in 1590 of the previous millennium, the humans expanded into their territory. The kingdom was destroyed in the year 1785 by a ferocious assault of the Dark Dragons. After its destruction the Orcs retook their lost lands.

Now as the three Dragons fly over, blackening the sun and throwing a blanket of darkness upon the land, the Orc commoners flee upon this sight of terror right as the trio opens fire decimating the village; a stream of fire, lightning, and dark energy turn the area into a barren wasteland. Word reaches the neighbouring capital town, and the Orc Lord of this tribe sets out to meet these aggressors himself.

He arrives with a small retinue before Abaddon's group.

The Orc Lord is huge and brutish with tribal tattoos all over his body making him look like a primitive savage and his brooding shoulders and wide chest make him look very intimidating. As clothing he dons a patchwork of iron and hide armour. He has pointy ears, tiny brown eyes, and a huge lower jaw with two massive tusks protruding upwards.

His head is bald and for decorations he has a necklace made of bones and a bunch of earrings on both ears of which one seems to be slightly chomped off. A large iron sword is hanging from his waist, and a simple waistcloth covers his lower parts. The colour of his skin is pale green as is the case with the other Orcs.

Abaddon: Do you speak common?

Orc Lord: Yes, little.

Abaddon: Are you the lord of this tribe?

Lord: (nods) Me master, Grough.

Abaddon: Grough, I am Abaddon, Demon-King of Dhalsarria, and your tribe belongs to me now.

As he speaks, the fire from the village rages in the background giving this meeting a sinister undertone.

Grough: We serve you?

Abaddon: Either that or you die by Dragon fire; the choice is yours.

Grough looks around and then at the Dragons, then proceeds to take off his sword, throws it on the ground and kneels. The other Orcs follow his example.

Grough: We serve great Demon-King now.

Abaddon: Rise.

They do as commanded.

Abaddon: How many warriors do you command?

Grough: Around 6,000.

Abaddon: That's not enough, what of the other tribes?

Grough: We war with other tribes, they enemies.

Abaddon: Not anymore, from this day forth all the other tribes are under my command as well.

Jamil: Send a messenger, tell them what happened here, should they resist, they will meet the same fate as this village.

Grough: Me serve king! No little man!

Abaddon: Do as he says.

Grough: Yes, king.

Abaddon: For now, I will need you to produce your finest champion and one of your best females.

Argyros: Are you going to do 'that'?

Abaddon: (nods) It's about time I brought one back.

Argyros: And what do you need the female for?

Abaddon: You'll see.

Grough: Come, me take you to big town.

The capital town does not seem any different from the village except the size; same primitive buildings made of clay and wood with hay rooftops. Thanks to the spacing between the constructs however, there is enough space for even the Dragons to walk around mostly unhindered.

The ruins of the old city of Caer Aradon could still be seen in the vicinity, some have even made homes in the more preserved portions of the forts.

Now as ordered, Grough produces his champion and female Orc.

Grough: This Grosh, he mightiest warrior.

Grosh, an Orc of equal size as Grough, is of the Warlord class of Orcs. They are the biggest and strongest amongst the Orc warriors, with a ruthless and fearless sense of battle. They wear massive full plated iron armour, and their weapon of choice is an equally massive flail that they can swing around with ease due to their monstrous strength and smash their foes to a bloody pulp.

Abaddon: Ah yes, he will do just fine. Next, I will need a statue carved in the image that I will describe to you and a young boy or a girl.

Jamil: My lord, what is it that you intend to do?

Tutor: It is the work of the Davian.

Abaddon: Yes, it is black magic; you don't have to watch if you don't want to.

Tutor#2: My lord…this goes against our beliefs.

Abaddon: My good man, I brought you here to be my aides not preachers, I told you that you are free to walk away during the ritual.

Jamil: I want to bear witness to this; I have read about these things in a book, and I want to see it up close.

Abaddon: Good lad.

Tutor: We will take our leave then, call us when we are needed.

Abaddon: Humans and their Gods…peh.

An hour passes and everything is prepared. Abaddon has drawn a magic pentagram and seated Grosh at the centre with the wooden statue of Baal looming over them. On each angle of the Tiamat Star a candle is placed.

Abaddon: (begins chanting in Old Dhalsarrian) Baalum Rabum Belum Niski Awatinum …

'Baal, Great Lord, Hear My Words …'

As he chants, a dark energy travels through the lines of the pentagram and lights up a candle once it reaches it. Once all the candles are lit, he calls for the young Orc boy who is being dragged against his will towards the centre. The two Orcs that are dragging him pin him down on the ground to keep him from struggling. Abaddon keeps chanting and once he reaches a certain point, he stabs the boy through the heart with an agla, and as his blood flows it fills out the lines of the pentagram, mixing it with the dark energy.

After all the lines are filled out, a vortex of necrotic energy forms from the circle around the pentagram and it shoots upwards letting out a terrible wallowing scream, then it descends downwards and goes into Grosh.

Jamil: This is…necromancy?

Argyros: He is a Necromancer, what of it?

Jamil: Nothing; I'm just…fascinated.

Argyros: You're one weird kid, you know that?

Once its fully inside him the same thing happens as when Abaddon resurrected inside Merlin's body; Grosh's appearance begins to morph into that of a completely different creature, his armour completely changes shape and instead of the rusty iron one it becomes one made of shimmering, obsidian steel and Demonic looking design with bladed spikes, same with the flail that now is a mace.

Abaddon: Welcome back, Alabashter.

Alabaster: My king, I'm grateful for the opportunity to serve you once more; this time, I will not fail you.

Abaddon: Arise, my fierce warrior.

Alabaster, the once general of the Obsidian Destroyers, rises on his feet, revealing a staggering and menacing stature, making the others feel unease and intimidation...

CAPITVLVM VI

NOVVM ORDO SAECVLORVM[v]

Grough: Who that?

Abaddon: One of my strongest champions.

Alabaster: The rest have not been revived yet?

Abaddon: Soon.

Alabaster: What is this place? Where are we?

Abaddon: This is the town of the Orcs; I'm going to use them for my new army.

Alabaster: That's right…we lost Avalon…but it will be ours once again, I swear upon my mace and our Lord Baal.

Abaddon: Patience Alabaster, patience, all things have an order to them, this is only the first phase.

Alabaster: Yes, my lord.

Argyros: Always eager to bash someone with that lump you call mace Alby old boy.

Alabaster: Lord Argyros, glad to see that at least you have survived.

Argyros: What can I say, I'm a kicker.

Abaddon: Now for the other stage, Ignatos, I'll need you to inseminate that female.

Ignatos: Huh?

Abaddon: Put your semen into her, don't make me repeat myself.

Fulguros: What are you planning, Dread One?

Abaddon: Something very interesting.

Ignatos: But in that little thing? Impossible!

Abaddon: She is twice the size of a Demoness, I'm sure she can take it.

Alabaster: Even just the tip is fine as long as you can do what is necessary.

Abaddon: Precisely.

Ignatos: Why don't you do it then? If you're planning on starting a new race, wouldn't it be better for them to have your blood?

Abaddon: Indeed, but I can't allow myself to lay down with such a beast, I still have my pride.

Ignatos: Get a kid then, that's how you like them, right?

Alabaster: Mind your tongue, Flame King! How dare you talk back to your master like that?

Ignatos growls.

Argyros: What's the big deal? It's a simple job.

Ignatos: I have a problem with putting my junk in others as well.

Abaddon: This is all for our cause, so grit your teeth and fall to purpose.

Ignatos: Oh alright, it's not like I have much of a choice,

Abaddon: And you don't.

Ignatos: Bring the woman.

Abaddon: Do it.

Grough: She says no want.

Abaddon: Tell her that I order it.

Grough relays the same in Orcish.

Alabaster: There are easier ways to do this.

Abaddon: (raises his hand) I don't blame her; these people are unaware of who is in charge here as of today (clears his throat).

He casts the spell 'Herald of Doom' which amplifies the sound of his voice in a 10 km radius. He casts the same spell on Grough as well so that his voice may also be heard throughout.

Abaddon: You will act as my translator.

Grough nods.

Abaddon: Everyone hear me!

The sound of his voice grabs the attention of everyone in the radius of the spell.

Abaddon: My name is Demon-King Abaddon from Dhalsarria! As of today, I am your king and all of you are my subjects! Whatever I say must be obeyed! My word is the law! I will appoint emissaries that will act as my spokespeople until I have mastered your language!

Their word will be as if my own! Insolence and insubordination will not be tolerated and the punishment for that will be your own lives! That is all!

Grough proceeds to translate as best as his understanding of Common allows him to.

As expected, there is general disapproval among some of the populace but deep down, they all know what it means to be in the presence of a Demon let alone a Demon King. The female Orc reluctantly complies after hearing this.

Abaddon: Tell the others to clear out, this is not some show.

Grough: Yes lord.

He shouts the same in Orcish and the common folk and warriors go back to their business.

The female Orc takes off her clothing and lies down on the ground.

Ignatos: Here goes nothing…

The gigantic Dragon takes his place above the Orc, somewhat frightening her and she fidgets on the ground. She starts to become even more uncomfortable when Ignatos produces his erect phallus.

Abaddon: Alabashter.

Without uttering a word, the behemoth Demon swings his mace and crushes both her legs to prevent her from fleeing. Screams of excruciating pain and anguish fill out the area.

Alabaster: Shut up! (Spreads out her legs for her).

Ignatos leans down as much as he can and goes to business.

He struggles at first, but he manages to insert at least the tip. Nevertheless, the friction and the sheer size of it cause her private parts to bleed.

Grough is not amused by what is happening with his kinswoman, so he looks away.

Ignatos: It's not working! I…can't finish like this.

Abaddon: Try inserting it a bit further.

Ignatos: Any further and she might break!

Abaddon: Do it.

Ignatos: Sorry about this… (strains and succeeds in penetrating some more).

The Orc is letting out screams mixed with pain, pleasure, rage...she herself might not be aware what to think at this moment. After a good amount of time, the act is finally over.

Abaddon: Excellent (walks up to the Orc and kneels down) you did well holding out, my dear, sorry about your legs, I couldn't risk you running away in the act (heals them).

Orc: Fuck…you (says in Orcish).

Abaddon: I'm going to assume that was a thank you.

Grough: …

Abaddon: Take her away.

Alabaster reaches out for her, but she slaps away his hand and gets up on her own.

Abaddon: If you try to do anything to the child, I will make sure you face a fate worse than death, tell her.

Grough relays that.

She spits on the ground, picks up her clothes and walks away.

Abaddon: Stay with her, if she tries anything, break her arms.

Alabaster: Understood.

Jamil: What happens next?

Abaddon: Now we wait and see if she conceives.

Jamil: And if she doesn't?

Abaddon: Then I move on to plan B.

Jamil: What is plan B?

Abaddon: You talk too much, Jamil, I don't like talkers.

Jamil: Apologies, my lord.

Grough: Come, me show you to rooms.

Abaddon: No, we'll set up camp here, for the work I'm about to do I will need to be out in the field as often as possible.

Grough: Me take materials then.

Abaddon: You do that.

***

Meanwhile in Camelot, the Tower of Sorcery

Arthur: (knocks on the door) Emrys, are you there?

Emrys: Yes! Come in sire!

Arthur: (enters) How is that thing coming along dear boy?

Emrys: It's going well sire; I am almost at the trial stage.

Arthur: Are you certain it will work?

Emrys: I'm sure of it, I followed every instruction to the letter and once it does, we will be able to produce our own materials, we will no longer have to depend on anyone.

Arthur: I hear many others have tried and failed.

Emrys: Many others did not have the great Merlin as their teacher.

Arthur: Yes…Merlin.

Emrys: Such a tragic thing…I still haven't gotten over the pain…

Arthur: Haven't we all? Give it time (puts his hand on his shoulder) the heart will mend itself.

Emrys: Thank you sire.

Arthur: (taps his shoulder while nodding meaningfully) …Keep it up and keep me informed.

Emrys: Of course, sire.

Arthur walks away.

Emrys: Ugh makes me sick every time I have to pretend I care, but no matter it's aaalll worth it (smirks).

***

Back in Orcothrond, the campsite has been set up.

Grough: What do with statue?

Abaddon: Put it in my tent.

He nods and proceeds to do so.

Abaddon: Once you are finished, I will need you to muster your entire army.

Grough: All of them?

Abaddon: Every single one.

Grough: Understood.

Jamil: What have you got planned this time?

Abaddon: What have I told you, Jamil?

Jamil nods apologetically and hangs his head in embarrassment.

***

The plain outside the city

Grough's entire army stands at attention before Abaddon.

Jamil: What is going to happen? Another ritual? (To Argyros).

Argyros: Just watch.

Abaddon: Tell them to kill themselves.

Grough: Lord?

Abaddon: You heard me.

Grough: I no understand… (perplexed).

Abaddon: It's not your job to understand but to do as you're told.

Grough: Yes lord (gives the order).

The Orcs look at each other in confusion.

Jamil: So, it is going to be another ritual, how exciting.

Fulguros: This kid is a weirdo.

Argyros: Kneis.[14]

Grough: Do it!

Having no choice, one of the Orcs takes out his sword and stabs his fellow soldier, instigating a chain of stabbing until all 100,000 fall dead on the ground into a lake of blood.

Abaddon begins to chant with his arms stretched out and a giant magic circle appears around the scene of carnage. After the spell is complete the rest watch in anticipation when one of the Orcs opens his eyes that are now completely white and gets up on his feet with a moaning cry. Necrotic energy oozes from them, the sight greatly terrifying Grough who has never seen anything like this before, he even takes a few steps back in sheer terror as his tiny eyes waver.

Jamil: Permission to speak, my lord…?

Abaddon: Granted.

Jamil: Are these things what they call 'Undead'?

Abaddon: Precisely, you just witnessed the creation of my Undead Knights.

Jamil: Incredible…my admiration towards you keeps on increasing ever more, my lord.

---

[14] I know.

Abaddon: My dear boy, this is only a fraction of what I'm capable off.

Jamil falls on his knees.

Abaddon: What are you doing?

Jamil: (pulls out his scimitar and presents it to him) My lord, from this day forward, I pledge my unconditional allegiance to you, from this moment you are my one and only king and I am your servant forever more, my life belongs to you.

Abaddon: Such admirable display of loyalty, I can assure you it won't go unrewarded.

Jamil: Thank you, my lord.

Abaddon: Now get up and stop embarrassing yourself.

Argyros snickers.

Jamil: …

Abaddon: Napashu! [15](Shouts in Dhalsarrian)

They stand at attention.

Abaddon: Labu! Etaku! Sadahu[16]!

They begin to march towards the city.

Abaddon: They obey well but their equipment is dreadful, show me to your blacksmith.

Grough: Yes lord (moves on).

At the smithy

The blacksmith immediately kneels when he sees them.

Abaddon waves his hand to signal that that is not necessary, so the Orc regains his former stature.

Abaddon: (pulls out the book of smiting he took from the library) Can you make something like this? (Points at the picture).

The smith looks at the depiction then at Grough.

Grough translates, and then the smith replies something to him.

Grough: He says maybe if know material.

He tells the materials to Grough.

Grough: (scratches his head in confusion) Me no understand.

---

[15] At ease

[16] Around! Forward! March!

Abaddon: (sighs) (damned savages, I need to learn their language as quickly as possible).

Abaddon tries to explain what the materials are in the simplest way possible with the help of miming as well and the message somehow manages to be conveyed to Grough, who then proceeds to relay it to the smith who shakes his head and says something to him.

Grough: He says he no know how to use material, he sorry.

Abaddon looks at the smith who shrugs his shoulders.

Jamil: Savages, I guess the only thing they are good for is battering iron.

Abaddon: Tsk…this is quite the predicament…Do you know how to write?

Grough: (shakes his head) No write, only talk.

Jamil: Great! They don't even have a writing system!

Abaddon: And it's going to take forever to teach them Dhalsarrian… Baal, have mercy (shakes his head) (closes the book impatiently).

Abaddon: How many smiths do you have?

Grough counts on his fingers.

Abaddon: Oh no, take your time…

Jamil face palms.

Abaddon: Patience boy, patience.

Grough: … Thirty, but he best.

Abaddon: Looks like I will have to borrow some of your father's smiths as well.

Jamil: I shall set off for Akhum immediately.

Abaddon: No need, I will see to it in the morning, I could do it now, but those two consecutive rituals took quite the toll, I only have enough mana for one trip.

Jamil: In that case, why not spend the night there?

Abaddon: No, I must remain here and attend to other matters.

Jamil: As you wish, my lord.

Abaddon: Come Grough, it's time for some language lessons.

Jamil: And what should I do?

Abaddon: Have the tutors start training the Undead.

Jamil: Is that a wise idea? Don't they listen only to you?

Abaddon: Tsk…Go and find Alabaster, have him give the commands.

Jamil: Does that mean that they only understand Dhalsarrian?

Abaddon: Yes Jamil, that's exactly what it means (says it with an irritated tone as he walks away with Grough).

Jamil: And where do I find him!

He pretends like he didn't hear him and keeps on walking.

Jamil: He can be a real arsehole sometimes… (sigh) I guess I'll start looking from here… (goes on).

Later that night

Abaddon: Thank you, Grough, that was very helpful, we shall continue again tomorrow (he says to him as he walks out of the tent).

Grough: Yes lord (walks away).

After he sees him off, he looks at the group of men who are having dinner around a campfire.

Abaddon: Jamil!

Jamil: (turns around) Yes, my lord?

He beckons him over with his index finger.

Tutor: What could he want now?

Jamil: I don't know, but best not to keep him waiting (finishes his bite and runs over to the tent).

Jamil: You called for me, my lord?

Abaddon: Take off your clothes (he himself is in a nightgown).

Jamil: My lord?

Abaddon: Your clothes, take them off.

Jamil: I don't understand…

Abaddon: Do not take me for a fool, Jamil, I know that you secretly crave me.

Jamil: My lord, I…my feelings towards you are purely ones of admiration I do not –

Abaddon: Shhh (puts his finger on his lips). It's okay, you can be honest with me.

Jamil: (looks down) It – it is as you say, my lord… I am attracted to my own sex…

Abaddon: It's nothing to be ashamed of, it's not a sin to follow your sexual desires.

Jamil: I am aware of that, it is also accepted in my kingdom, it's just... I didn't want my lord to think of me otherwise.

Abaddon: I don't judge, my sexual preferences are unorthodox as well (smiles).

Jamil: ...If I may be honest...ever since our sparring, I've been having sexual fantasies for my lord...

Abaddon: Then what are you waiting for – take off your clothes (whispers into his ear).

In a fit of ecstasy, he takes off his clothes and then they proceed to make out. After a few moments of passionate tongue exchange, Abaddon lowers Jamil downwards so that the former may give him oral pleasure. When this deed is over, they move on to the bed and they make love there.

Jamil: That was...incredible.

Abaddon: Let me make something perfectly clear here, Jamil, this is totally a no feelings attached affair, you understand that don't you?

Jamil: Yes, my lord, I understand completely.

Abaddon: Good, because I don't want this impeding our work.

Jamil: That is fine by me; a strictly physical relationship is more than satisfactory.

Abaddon: You really are a smart boy, if you keep up like that you'll get far.

Jamil: Thank you, my lord.

Abaddon: You can go back to your tent now.

Jamil: Can't I spend just this one night here...with you.

Abaddon gives him one mean look.

Jamil: Yes, of course my lord, excuse me (gets off the bed and dresses up) have a good night.

Abaddon: You as well.

Jamil throws one quick look towards him before exiting the tent. The others have already long gone to bed.

Abaddon: Why do I get the feeling I'm going to regret this...?

The following morning

Jamil: Good morning, my lord.

Abaddon: Good morning, Jamil, did you sleep well?

Jamil: Like a baby (slightly smirks) and yourself?

Abaddon: We Demons don't need to sleep.

Jamil: I wasn't aware of that.

Abaddon: Now you are and enough with the trivia; get to training the Undead.

Jamil: Yes, my lord.

Abaddon: That goes for the rest of you as well.

The other tutors get up from their seats and go to work as well.

Alabaster: Sire.

Abaddon: Alabaster, how goes the project?

Alabaster: No incidents so far.

Abaddon: Splendid.

Alabaster: I think she might be conceiving, it was faint, but I could sense another presence within her.

Abaddon: I'll look into it once I return from Hathasia.

Alabaster: What need from there?

Abaddon: Smiths, the ones here are incompetent and must be trained and educated.

Alabaster: What else is to be expected from such primitive beasts.

Abaddon: Alas, I need them for their brawn not brains (slightly smiles) you get back to the woman now.

Alabaster: One more question –

Abaddon: Do with her as you like; just make sure she stays alive.

Alabaster nods meaningfully and takes his leave.

Abaddon: Now then (focuses sternly and then vanishes in a cloud of darkness).

***

Akhum

Abaddon reappears before Dharmat.

Dharmat: (startles) My lord, you startled me.

Abaddon: Sorry, I didn't mean to do that.

Dharmat: What brings you here this time?

Abaddon: I find myself in the need of smiths, a couple should do.

Dharmat: Sounds to me like you're having trouble with those beasts.

Abaddon: If I didn't, I wouldn't be here, would I?

Dharmat: …

Abaddon: Now do me a favour, stop being a know it all and get me those smiths.

Dharmat: I would appreciate it if you did not address me in that manner in the confines of my home.

Abaddon: And I would appreciate it if you didn't test my patience.

Dharmat: …

Abaddon: Would you be so kind as to give the order or should I force it out of you?

Dharmat orders one of the servants to go and fetch the smiths.

Abaddon: See? Was that so hard?

Dharmat gives a displeasing and irritated shake of his head.

Abaddon: Let's have some wine while we wait.

Dharmat: (claps his hands and the wine bearer brings the drinks) Tell me, how is my son?

Abaddon: He's a cleaver boy; he'll make a fine aide one day.

Dharmat: I'm pleased to hear that.

Abaddon: You don't sound so pleased.

Dharmat: Oh?

Abaddon: You can cut that false façade, I know you dislike me, I've known since the moment I stepped foot in this palace.

Dharmat: In that case no, my lord, I don't like you at all.

Abaddon: Then the feeling is mutual.

Dharmat: Let's have a toast to that.

Abaddon: Cheers (raises his cup).

Dharmat: Cheers…

***

After a few hours, the servant returns with the requested smiths

Abaddon: Finally.

Dharmat: Gentlemen, this is King Abaddon.

Abaddon: Salutations.

They all bow courteously.

Dharmat: You will be going with him to the land of the Orcs and educate their smiths in the arts of crafting fine armaments.

Smith: But my king that is impossible, how are we to communicate with such creatures?

Smith#2: And are they even capable of learning such complex procedures?

Abaddon: They are capable enough; they may be primitive by our standards, but they are not dimwits. Besides, words are not required you need only show them how the procedure is done (he speaks in Hathasian).

Dharmat: You speak the language?

Abaddon: I do but I'm more comfortable speaking Common in situations where I don't have a full grasp of the language.

Dharmat: Understandable.

Smith: How long will this take? I don't mean to be rude…I ask for my family…they depend on my work.

Dharmat: Worry not, your families will be well provided in your absence.

Smith: Ohhh thank you, my lord, thank you.

Dharmat: You are my loyal subjects; it's the least I can do to repay you for your impeccable services.

They keep bowing their heads in gratitude.

Smith: When do we depart?

Abaddon: Immediately.

Smith: But we need to inform our families…

Abaddon: Dharmat will do that, since he is such a generous king, won't you, Dharmat?

Dharmat: But of course (smiles).

Abaddon: Then we can leave at once, gather around.

They do as their told and Abaddon uses his spell 'Greater Teleportation' to travel back to Orcothrond. This spell can only be used if the caster has previous knowledge of the location, he is traveling to which is why Abaddon could not use it before.

Once they are gone, Dharmat angrily tosses the chalice at the spot where they stood.

***

Dharmat: Lamar! …Where is that old fart! Lamar!

Lamar (the chief scholar): I'm over here sire! (Yells out from behind a stack of books).

Dharmat: For the love of Mithras, please tell me you have found something!

Lamar: Nothing I don't know already, my liege.

Dharmat: Agh! It's been a week now since I tasked you with this, yet you have not even the slightest clue.

Lamar: I am so sorry, sire, I'm doing my best…

Dharmat: Surely there must be something!

Lamar: I'm afraid the lore is perfectly clear, my liege, a blood oath may only be broken with the death of one of the parties…there haven't been any records of someone escaping its yoke.

Dharmat: If I have to endure that insufferable, bloated, wretch any longer than I should, then I shall take my own life!

Lamar: By Mithras! You must not say such fallacies, my lord! Taking one's own life is the gravest sin anyone can commit.

Dharmat: I'd rather burn in the Pit than be humiliated in front of my subjects!

Lamar: Oh…worry not, my lord. I swear on my life that I will find something!

Dharmat: You better or you'll find yourself at the receiving end of my wrath (storms out of the library)

Lamar: Gods have mercy… (continues flipping the book).

***

Back at Dhaldrog

Abaddon sets the smiths to task and he himself along with Grough and a couple of other Orcs go to where Rugha, the female Orc, lives.

Abaddon: Alabaster!

Alabaster: In a minute sire!

Grough: Good thing she no have man.

Abaddon: If you think that would've stopped him, you are dead wrong.

Grough: …

Alabaster: Sorry about that (exits the hut) I was engaged in some—

Abaddon: Not interested (holds up his hand then proceeds to enter).

Rugha looks at them with pure, unadulterated despise.

Abaddon: Don't worry, I'm here to see if there is any progress (walks up to her).

Rugha grabs her carving knife and swings it angrily at Abaddon.

Abaddon: (grabs it with his bare hand) I understand your pain and hatred but know that is for a greater cause (he speaks in some broken Orcish).

The others look genuinely surprised to see that he has taken up the language so quickly.

Rugha manages to settle down a bit and sits down.

Abaddon: (places his hand on her belly) You were right, it is starting to grow.

Alabaster: And now we wait for it to be born.

Abaddon: Don't be ridiculous, it will take years to finish what I'm planning; at that pace, I can't afford such luxuries.

Alabaster: Then…

Abaddon: Nigromancy, of course (begins to chant and dark energy seeps out of his palm and enters her womb).

As the spell goes on, her stomach begins to become more bloated, and she starts to feel pain. Grough moves a step forward but Alabaster grips him by the shoulder and he comes to a halt.

Once the spell is complete, Rugha is ready to give birth; however, instead of the conventional method Abaddon uses his magic to extract the baby from the womb. He takes out his agla and cuts the umbral cord.

Abaddon: It's beautiful (looks with awe at the newborn Orc-Dragon hybrid, then he takes a nearby rag and wraps the baby in it).

Rugha extends her arms towards him, asking to hold the baby. However, he completely ignores her and starts walking away.

Abaddon: I'm going to need a source of fresh and clean water, preferably a small pond, not a river, I need a still source.

Grough: Yes lord.

At that moment, whether it was rage, anger or just her motherly instincts kicking in, or a mixture of both, Rugha jumps up from the bed, grabs the knife and viscously throws herself at the man who was taking her child away. Abaddon did not even have to react, because before she could even deal the blow,

Alabaster swings his massive fist and hitting her with the back of it right in the face snaps her neck and her lifeless body slumps on the ground.

He continues walking unfazed and exits the hut as one of the Orcs turns around to look at the corpse briefly, but only ends up groaning it off as if trying to say, 'what was she thinking' and moves on.

Per his instructions, the Orcs find a small clean pond not far outside the town and take him there.

Abaddon: Yes, this will do. Hold it (hands the baby over to Alabaster).

Abaddon walks up to the pond, slices his own wrist, and lets the blood flow into the pond, then he chants and once he finishes the procedure, he orders Alabaster to dump the baby into the pond.

Alabaster does what he's told without a word.

Grough: … (Looks at Abaddon).

Abaddon: Wait for it…

Fulguros: Is it supposed to come out…?

Abaddon: Give it a minute.

At that moment a red scaly arm reaches out from the bloody pond and comes down at the ground, startling the onlookers besides Abaddon.

The creature hauls himself on shore, but his lower half remains in the water as it seems to be catching its breath.

Abaddon reaches out to it and pulls it out from the water and the sight is astonishing; a fully grown hybrid, having red scales, horns, tail, the eyes of a Dragon, and the humanoid and bulky build of an Orc, covered in the blood of a Demon-King, it is resting on all fours on the shore of the pond.

Grough looks with a gaping mouth.

Argyros: If that kid saw this, he would jizz his pants.

Abaddon: Oh, he'll have plenty of opportunities to witness this.

Ignatos: Come again?

Abaddon: (turns to them) We are far from over with this project.

Ignatos: (remains open-mouthed) Shit…

CAPITVLVM VII

QVID OMNES VOLVNT[vi]

Alabaster: Can this thing even talk?

Abaddon: Of course it can, it's an intelligent being.

Creature: M…as…

Alabaster: It's trying to say something.

Creature: Master…

Argyros: It looks like it recognises you as its master.

Ignatos: Do you have a name for these creatures.

Abaddon: They will be called Dragonborn.

Ignatos: Makes sense.

Abaddon: And this one shall be named Andrakos.

Creature: An…drakos…

Abaddon: You are a fast learner, that's right, you are Andrakos and you will be the captain of your brethren.

Andrakos: Cap…tain…

Abaddon: Mhm, come on, you must be hungry.

Andrakos: Hung…ry?

Abaddon: Stomach (places his hand on his stomach) empty.

Andrakos: Empty…yes.

Abaddon: We'll have to work on your articulation.

Andrakos looks at him even more confused.

Abaddon: Don't worry, you'll get there.

Abaddon: Alabaster, get him fed and sent off to train immediately.

Alabaster: Yes, my lord.

Andrakos: Alabas…ter.

Alabaster: I like this guy.

Argyros: I'm Argyros.

Fulguros: And me Fulguros.

Ignatos: And I'm Ignatos. I am your father.

Andrakos: Fath…er?

Abaddon: Don't overwhelm him with new information; you'll confuse him even more; he needs to adapt to his surroundings first.

Ignatos: He needs to know his own progenitor.

Abaddon: All in due time.

And so, they go back in town with Andrakos in tow; needless to say, the entire populace is looking at him with strange looks.

Argyros: Can it breathe fire?

Abaddon: It's only natural that he could.

Argyros: Maybe he didn't inherit that.

Abaddon: That remains to be seen.

Jamil: Lord Abaddon.

Abaddon: Ah Jamil, you seem in a hurry.

Jamil: The – (looks at Andrakos) Is…is that…?

Abaddon: Indeed it is, it's called a Dragonborn, and its name is Andrakos, it means 'Man-Dragon'.

Jamil: Incredible…truly remarkable… (approaches it and studies it from every angle) why didn't you call me for the birthing? I would've loved to see it.

Abaddon: You'll have your chance for the next one.

Jamil: Next one? Does that mean you'll create more?

Abaddon: Well, only one is not enough, is it?

Jamil: Yes!

Andrakos begins to feel threatened by Jamil's closeness and roars at him, startling the young man.

Abaddon: Easy now, easy.

Jamil: I guess I was too close…

Abaddon: He needs time to adjust; all of this is unfamiliar to it.

Jamil: Of course… (keeps looking at it) the semblance is more of a Dragon, but the build and body is that of an Orc…interesting.

Abaddon: That was the whole point, the destructive power and intelligence of a Dragon in one compact size.

Jamil: Your genius knows no bounds my lord.

Abaddon: I didn't get to where I am on power alone.

Jamil: Speaking of your powers, they seem to be returning at a remarkable speed.

Abaddon: So it seems…

Andrakos' stomach growls, interrupting the atmosphere.

Alabaster: Let's get you fed, big guy.

Abaddon: Now, you wanted to tell me something before Andrakos caught your attention.

Jamil: Ah yes, the other Orc leaders have arrived.

Abaddon: Excellent, take me to them.

Jamil: They are all waiting in Grough's castle.

Abaddon: Let's go.

As they walk Abaddon suddenly comes to a stop.

Jamil: My lord?

Abaddon: You go on ahead, tell them I will arrive shortly.

Jamil: Is something the matter?

Abaddon: Jamil, what did I tell you about talking too much?

Jamil: Very well my lord… (bows his head and continues).

Abaddon: Now then, how about you show yourself little mouse.

A hooded figure appears from beneath the shadows.

Stranger: As expected from Abaddon, how long have you known?

Abaddon: Since Onigashima.

Stranger: From the start huh? Then why didn't you act before?

Abaddon: Why? Because I can dispose of the likes of you at my leisure.

The stranger attempts to flee by returning to the shadows but Abaddon freezes them in place with his 'Aura of Despair'.

Stranger: Kh! (Struggling to move).

Abaddon: Let's have a look at you (removes their hood) a Vampire huh, I reckon Amra sent you to spy on me; sadly, you didn't do much of a good job.

Stranger: What are you waiting for? Go ahead, kill me.

Abaddon: Oh, I will, but first I'll have you tell me how much they know.

Stranger: I'm not telling you shit (spits in his face).

Abaddon: (wipes off his face and grabs her by the throat) That's okay, I have my own ways of finding out.

Abaddon: Ikuluru Lalatu.

He casts 'Soul Devourer', a spell unique to practitioners of nigromancy which enables the user to feast on the soul of the opponent, gaining its knowledge along with invigoration and restoration. The soul is being sucked from the orifices of the face, causing the body to spasm and lose all signs of life including colouration, in the process.

Abaddon: Thanks for the meal (tosses her body on the road) hmmm…so she has had them informed up until Shilmatu how convenient for me, even if they send another spy, it will be on a wild goose chase (smirks).

Abaddon: (Alabaster, I have an urgent task for you, come at my location at once).

Alabaster: (On my way my lord).

***

Alabaster: A Vampire?

Abaddon: Amra's spy.

Alabaster: Then they know we are here.

Abaddon: No, they know up to Shilmatu.

Alabaster: Looks like luck is on our side.

Abaddon: More like her own folly, probably she waited until she can give a full report on what we are doing here, thanks to that the fools at Avalon will believe I'm cooling my cock at Dumah's castle.

Alabaster: What do you want me to do with the body?

Abaddon: Oh, don't worry, I have the perfect idea for that.

***

Sanclunea, Lunaris

Igvalir (Amra's chief butler): You called for me, my queen?

Amra: Is there still no word from Nirvalena?

Igvalir: Nothing yet my queen.

Amra: Ugh! What is taking her so long? She should have sent a report by now.

Igvalir: Perhaps she was discovered?

Amra: She is one of our best covert operatives; she would not allow herself to be caught that easily.

Soldier: (rushes in) Lady Amra!

Amra: What is this insolence?

Soldier: Pardon the intrusion, my queen, but there is something you must see!

***

Amra looks in shock.

The sight is truly gruesome to behold; Nirvalena, skinned and crucified at the city's gate with a note stuck in her mouth.

Soldier: There is something in her mouth…a message?

Amra: (pulls out the slimy note that says 'next time send a better one') (crumples the note in rage) **ABADDOOONNNN**!

***

Abaddon: Gentlemen, sorry to have kept you waiting, I was delayed by some pressing matters…oh right silly me, you don't speak Common.

Bugrash: You'd be surprised to find out that that is false.

Abaddon: Are my ears deceiving me? You actually speak Common?

Jamil: Indeed, my lord, sir Bugrash here has a decent grasp of the Common tongue.

Abaddon: Well, if I had known, I would've come to your territory first.

Bugrash: That would change nothing, here we are despite that.

Abaddon: And how did that come to pass?

Bugrash: You mean my Common? I was fortunate to learn it from a certain man. Couple of years ago a group of bandits wandered into our territory and we captured them, one of them was a nice fellow named Timeon, out of curiosity I learned a lot of things about the ways of Men including their language.

Abaddon: Bandits wandering this up north? They must've been desperate to escape. You said 'was' what happened to him?

Bugrash: We ate them.

Abaddon: As expected.

Bugrash shrugs.

Ologh: So, this is that mighty king you're so afraid of? (To Grough in Orcish).

Abaddon: Yes, I am.

Bugrash: And you speak our language?

Abaddon: I try to learn.

Ologh: Where is his face? (He speaks only in Orcish).

Abaddon: Here it is (removes his crown and hood).

That leaves everyone to gasp in wonder.

Abaddon: Have I sated your curiosity?

Zog: He has a pretty face for a Demon, hahaha (he also speaks Orcish).

Abaddon: Is something funny?

Grough: He say you have pretty face, Demon.

Abaddon: Ah, yes, I get that a lot, I guess most expect to see a hideous face when they think of a Demon (slightly smiles).

Bugrash: I think that's understandable, no offence.

Abaddon: None taken…now that we've got trivialities out of the way, we can get down to business.

Bugrash: I think it would be best if I spoke on behalf of all.

Abaddon: If everyone agrees.

Bugrash: Yes, it was already settled before you arrived.

Abaddon: Go on then.

Bugrash: We understand that we are to serve under you.

Abaddon: I believe that the messages you received were perfectly clear.

Bugrash: They were but, that doesn't sit right with us.

Abaddon: It's not like you have any choice in the matter, it's either that or death and if you would prefer the later, I can grant you a swift and painless death, right here in this very hall.

Bugrash: …

Abaddon: Let me paint a picture for you, I have the kings of the three Dragon races ready to bring hell upon you at my command, and a Destroyer class Demon that can utterly crush your combined armies alone.

Guthug: What is he saying?

Bugrash translates Abaddon's words, and they cause some unrest amongst the five lords but still traces of scepticism linger on their faces.

Jamil: You would dare doubt the greatness of His Majesty?

Abaddon: Calm yourself boy, if they are still not convinced then perhaps a first-hand demonstration will finally put an end to this charade.

Abaddon: (unsheathes Absharu) Gentlemen, are you aware of what this is?

Grough: Sword?

Zog: So, what, we all have one of those, mine is even bigger, hahaha!

Abaddon: (smirks) that's where you're wrong, this is not just any sword you brainless buffoons, this is the Demon Sword Absharu handed down in my family for generations. Since your kind only understands force allow me to show you what real power looks like.

Jamil gets on the edge of his seat from excitement.

Abaddon: Absharu: Sanu Salu: Sharahu![17]

Same as the last time the runes along the blade change only this time the aura is dark purple instead of blood red. This ability of the sword multiplies Abaddon's magical powers manyfold. As a result, he gives off a tremendous amount of magical pressure that shakes the wooden construct. The Orcs get up on their feet out of fear as sheer terror seeps deep into their skin out of this awesome display of power.

Abaddon: (forms an orb of darkness in his other palm) Seen enough?

Bugrash: We yield! We yield! Please! No more!

Abaddon: (dispels the magic and the shaking stops) Do you understand now gentlemen just who it is that stands before you?

Bugrash: (takes one big swallow) we do…my king.

One by one they shout out 'king', 'king'. Abaddon smirks and sheathes back Absharu.

Jamil: (unable to contain his excitement) My lord! That was amazing! To be able to witness a display of power of that magnitude…I am truly blessed, Baal be praised!

Abaddon: No, you fool!

Out of the blue, Jamil is stricken with a terrible headache, and he falls on the ground squirming and holding his head.

Bugrash: What is happening to the boy?

---

[17] Second stance: pride.

Abaddon: He uttered the name of our God in reverence without being a follower. Other Gods don't like it if you praise someone else except your chosen one. Quick Jamil, take it back! Renounce what you said!

Jamil: I…aghhh!

The headache turns into a migraine that causes his eyes and other orifices on his head to bleed, he is unable to speak from the pain.

The pain keeps on intensifying as strange incoherent voices run around his mind.

Abaddon: Jamil! (Rushes at his side and tries to relieve his pain) go on, say it! Speak!

Jamil: I…take…it back…I take it back…just please make it stop! I believe! I believe in …!

As soon as he says that the pain subsides, however he still passes out from it.

Abaddon: Stupid boy! Your fanaticism will be the death of you (picks him up).

Bugrash: Your Gods are terrifying, makes me glad we don't have any deities.

Abaddon: As long as you do not anger them, the Gods are merciful.

Grough: Scary…me no say name…ever.

Abaddon: Probably for the best…you, take him to his tent (addresses one of the guards).

He approaches and takes off Jamil from his hands and carries him away.

Abaddon: (sigh) I would like to finish this meeting with my final instructions; all of you are to bring every last one of your smiths here, professionals from Hathasia will train them in the ways of proper smithing. And as for your armies I will send someone to begin their martial training.

Bugrash: But our armies are already equipped with that knowledge.

Abaddon: Mindlessly swinging your swords hoping it hits someone doesn't count for fighting. They need to be properly trained like real soldiers if they are to withstand the trials of the upcoming war.

Grough: War?

Abaddon: That's what all these preparations are for, war of such proportions that this world has never seen before, and I intend to win it, for that purpose all must be in impeccable order.

Bugrash: Yes, my king.

Abaddon: Good, you can expect these tutors as soon as possible, dismissed (takes his leave).

Ologh: Not only do we have to serve him, but we also have to fight his wars? This is madness.

Grough: I'd rather fight in a war that is not my own and maybe live another day than die a certain death.

Zog: I second that notion, brother Grough.

Guthug: We've been given a higher purpose! A chance to serve someone who goes beyond our comprehension! That person is not just a mere king but a God himself!

Zog: I wouldn't go that far.

Guthug: It's true! You saw it! You saw his power! He is a God!

Zog: He truly is powerful but to call him a God…

Grough: You may call him what you like but one thing is clear, that person lives on a completely different plane that ours and we are but lowly creatures destined to serve him.

Guthug: I shall erect a statue in his name in my town.

Zog: Are you insane?

Bugrash: Let him be, his mind has already been addled by his presence, he is a lost cause.

Grough shakes his head.

***

Meanwhile, somewhere else

Soldier: My king, I bring news from the Orc lands.

King: Speak.

Soldier: There are talks of a great Demon Lord, gathering armies in Dhaldrog. He also has three Dragons at his disposal, I saw them with me own eyes.

King: What else?

Soldier: The other Orc leaders have also gathered there presumably to fight under his banner.

King: If what you say is true then we must send an emissary to meet with this great Demon and offer him our services.

Soldier: Serve under his banner?

King: We would be fools to do otherwise, if we incur his wrath, we won't get away unscathed, besides this way he may reward us greatly for our services.

Soldier: But what if he refuses?

King: Hmmm…tell him we have many resources to offer if he finds himself in the need.

Soldier: I will depart at once, my liege.

***

Alabaster is standing in front of Abaddon's tent when he notices some commotion nearby. A group of Orcs seem to be dragging some sort of creature in the direction of the tent.

Alabaster: What's this about then?

Grough: We caught mangy Goblin at town gate.

Alabaster: Can you speak Common?

Goblin: Yes, my lord.

Alabaster: State your purpose.

Goblin: My name is Srank; I come on behalf of the Goblin King Iadvrim to seek audience with the great Demon that resides here.

Alabaster: Lord Abaddon is in the middle of his prayers; he cannot be disturbed.

Srank: I don't mind waiting my lord.

Alabaster: Very well, release him.

The Orcs unhand Srank after Grough orders them.

Srank: Savages (rubs his wrists).

Alabaster: I've only heard about your kind from stories, come, tell me more.

Srank: It would be my pleasure, my lord.

Alabaster: I am no lord, call me Alabaster.

Srank: As you wish Alabaster, sir.

Meanwhile, Abaddon is in his tent offering a prayer in front of the statue of Baal. It consists of kneeling before it and raising your arms towards his face as if begging and offering your woes. This position is done to show that you know your place as someone who is beneath his stature and but a humble servant.

Abaddon prays for success in his current dealings and for future ones to come. The prayer is sealed with a blood offering.

Baal, as you have seen by now is the chief deity of the Demon race. Most of them believe that he resides in the Abyss, namely the deepest reaches of the Earth. He is considered as the father of all Demons and there are several interpretations of their origins; some say that he singlehandedly gave birth to them all, dividing them into three clans, whereas some say that they came to be from the blood he spilled during the war between the Primordial Gods and the Titans that took place when the continents were as one, known as the Titanomachia.

Whatever the case may be, it is a generally held belief that upon their death all souls return to his side. He is also a tripartite deity consisting of three aspects Baalum Etutim, 'Baal of the Darkness', Baal Addadim 'Baal of the Storm' and Baalum Girrim 'Baal of the Fire.

It is Baalum Etutim whom the Dark Demons chiefly worship. To him they offer their prayers of wellbeing, prosperity etc. he is their patron and protector.

However, when a member of the Dark clan wishes to offer prayers to his other aspects as well, a statue of his tripartite nature is made as in this case. In this regard he is represented as a winged Demon having three horned heads, three pairs of arms and three tails. His symbol is the Mul Tiamatim, The Star of Tiamat – the Abyss, which is present on each of the foreheads of the heads.

Abaddon: (finishes his prayer and goes outside) What was all that racket earlier?

Alabaster: My lord, this Goblin wishes to speak to you.

Abaddon: A Goblin huh, speak then.

Srank: Oh, great and –

Abaddon: Spare me the lip service, tell me what you want.

Srank: A thousand apologies my lord, my name is Srank, a soldier in the ranks of the Goblin King Iadvrim; I am here to offer you our servitude.

Abaddon: That's noble of you but I've no need of it.

Srank: Ah we thought you might say that so my liege instructed me to tell you that we are prepared to provide you with any materials you may need, our mountains are very rich in natural metals especially manalith and onyx shards.

Abaddon: Hmmm…you do know how to barter.

Srank: Well besides fighters we are also skilled merchants believe it or not.

Abaddon: It's true that this area is particularly poor in the ore department…very well, relay to your king that I accept your offer.

Srank: Excellent my lord, excellent! The king will be most pleased to hear this news.

Abaddon: As you were.

Srank: My lord (bows graciously and takes his leave).

Alabaster: Was that wise? We already have more army than we need, training their ranks as well will take too much time.

Abaddon: No need for that, they seem more capable than the Orcs, besides they would serve a great purpose as fodder in the battlefield.

Alabaster: A wise move then my lord.

Abaddon: More importantly how's the boy?

Alabaster: Still unconscious, might I ask what happened?

Abaddon: In his excitement he foolishly praised our Lord Baal.

Alabaster: (sigh) Foolish indeed, a follower of Mithras has no place uttering his name.

Abaddon: Unfortunately, he had to learn the hard way.

Alabaster: (shakes his head) My lord, if you would excuse me, I have to go back to overseeing the Undead.

Abaddon: How are they coming along?

Alabaster: They pick up at a fast pace, same for the blacksmiths.

Abaddon: That it is good to hear, it would seem that our Lord's grace is in our favour.

Alabaster: Speaking of which, I believe it would be a good idea for me to offer a prayer as well.

Abaddon: You may use the statue in my tent.

Alabaster: Thank you my Lord, in that case I will see to that first.

Abaddon: Mhm.

Alabaster gives a polite nod and takes his leave.

Abaddon: (looks up at the sky) (I wonder how the princess is doing…).

***

Terebriz

Fulga: Hey, hey, Morgana, let's plaay!

Morgana: Sorry Fulga, perhaps later, I'm preoccupied with this volume now.

Fulga: You can read that later!

Fragora: Fulga! Stop being a bother to the princess; can't you see that she is busy now?

Fulga: Yes mother…

Fragora: I'm sorry, my children can be really bothersome at times.

Morgana: That's okay, I don't mind, it's just that I really need to get this down and…I am not understanding anything… (sighs).

Fragora: Let me have a look.

Morgana: I would but it's in High Elven.

Fragora: Ah I'm afraid I don't speak that language, perhaps if you translated it for me?

Morgana: Even if I did, could you really help me?

Fragora: (laughs) my dear child, we Dragons are magical beings, I would bring a shame to my race if I could not teach you a thing or two about magic and mana.

Morgana: Then why didn't you say so from the beginning? (Smiles).

Fragora: I thought you knew.

Morgana: (shakes her head) I thought that only applied to our patron deity.

Fragora: The White Dragon huh?

Morgana: You know about him?

Fragora: Only what I've heard from others since he is from an era long before mine.

Morgana: Is it true that he was part of a race of Light Dragons?

Fragora: Might as well be, since his description fits in.

Morgana: Wow so they really existed? What happened to them? Where are they now?

Fragora: Hahaha so many questions.

Morgana: Sorry, this is all really fascinating for me since we Pendragons are said to be his descendants, even our name means that, 'Son of Dragon'.

Fragora: It's nice that you are interested in your ancestry for one is nothing without history. Yes, it's true that they existed but unlike us they were a peaceful race, they didn't seek to destroy and kill like we do, and unfortunately their docile nature and love for peace was their downfall. They were destroyed by the much more vile and aggressive force, their complete counterparts, the Dark Dragons, Argyros' own kind. Or so it is said, I can't say for sure since I wasn't there. You're better off asking Argyros about it.

Morgana: Darkness swallowing the light…

Fragora: Very soon darkness will fall on these lands once more.

Morgana: Yeah…

Fragora: Does that frighten you?

Morgana: Not really, since I'm on the side where the darkness stems from.

Fragora: My sweet girl, are you sure that is the side you want to be on?

Morgana: More than anything (looks at her resolutely).

Fragora: (this child…) I see, but I suppose you know that once you step foot into the abyss it will swallow you whole, there is no going back from the dark side.

Morgana: I am well aware of that, and frankly…I don't mind it at all, does that make me an evil person?

Fragora: The line between good and evil is non-existent in this world; it is a label we ourselves decide to give to things based on our own perspective. If looked from the eyes of a fellow Camelotian, then what you are doing would no doubt be labelled as 'evil', but from your own perspective it is just. In the end it all comes down to our own personal belief of what it means to be 'good' or 'evil'.

Morgana: In Camelot we have this saying 'hero for others, murderer for another'. It goes well with what you're saying.

Fragora: Indeed, all summed up in one clever proverb.

Morgana: Then no, I don't think I'm an evil person, and I don't care how the others back at home see me, neither my father nor my mother. I am simply doing what is right for me and for that person.

Fragora: The Dread One?

Morgana: No…Merlin.

Fragora: Merlin? The Human Sorcerer Merlin?

Morgana: (nods). I'll find out who set him up and I will kill them, but slowly and brutally, like they deserve for what they did.

Fragora: And your father?

Morgana: …

Fragora waits in suspense.

Morgana: My father too (says it with a stone-cold look on her face).

Fragora: (So much hatred in such a small body, poor girl is already beyond saving, what cruel God would allow for such a thing or maybe…)

Morgana: What's wrong?

Fragora: Oh, nothing at all, I got slightly lost in my own thoughts ha-ha. Never mind that, tell me more about this Merlin fellow, what was he like?

Morgana: He…was the sweetest person I've ever met; he loved me deeply as I did too…

And so, the two spend the rest of the night talking about the man that once was…

CAPITVLVM VIII

SEMEN MALI[vii]

Back at the campsite, Jamil awakens from his sleep the following day

Abaddon: You are awake at last.

Jamil: Lord Abaddon? What happened? (Holds his head) the last thing I remember is me saying something I shouldn't have and then pain…immense pain.

Abaddon: You got carried away and you praised my God when you should not have, the other Gods don't take lightly to such blasphemy.

Jamil: …I got too excited…

Abaddon: Try to keep your temper under control next time.

Jamil: Yes my lord…I'm sorry I caused such an inconvenience for you.

Abaddon: No need to apologise, I don't hold it against you, but these are delicate matters, and you must be aware at all times.

Jamil: In that case I should like to convert! I want to become a follower of your Lord.

Abaddon: Did you not hear what I just said?

Jamil: I really mean this! Please my lord!

Abaddon: Your devotion and loyalty are clear enough Jamil; you need not go that far.

Jamil: But I want to!

Abaddon: You're not thinking rationally, the concussion must've addled your thoughts.

Jamil: I am very aware of my desires.

Abaddon: Boy, you are talking about renouncing your God and changing your faith! These are not trifling matters, I told you!

Jamil: I know! But this way I can serve you even more devoutly without being bound by my faith!

Abaddon: (sigh) …Even so it is still impossible, at least for now, only a priest may perform the ceremony of conversion.

Jamil: A priest huh…

Abaddon: So, I'm afraid your change of faith will have to wait, in the meantime remember whom you serve (turns to leave).

Jamil grabs his hand.

Abaddon: What do you think you're doing?

Jamil: Could you not stay…for a little longer?

Abaddon: I thought I made myself perfectly clear on the status of our 'relationship'.

Jamil: I know but…just this once.

Abaddon: Unhand me this instance, I am not one of your lover boys.

Jamil: (does it) Right…forgive me.

Abaddon: You're forgetting your place, boy.

Jamil: A thousand apologies my king…it won't happen again.

Abaddon: Make sure that it doesn't, or you'll find yourself without a hand.

Jamil: (nods humbly) …

Abaddon: (leaves) (sigh) (Looks like I made a terrible mistake…).

Alabaster: You seem down my lord.

Abaddon: Nothing serious Alabaster.

Alabaster: Little Jamil is giving you trouble?

Abaddon: More than I had hoped…he is talking of converting now.

Alabaster: Changing faith? I didn't know he admired you to that level; he's crazier than I thought.

Abaddon: I wouldn't call him crazy but too passionate for his own good. We spent one night together and now he's acting like he's in love with me, asking me to stay…

Alabaster: He even has such feelings towards you? Baal have mercy, are you sure it's wise to keep him around? If you'd like me to, I can take care of it nice and quick.

Abaddon: No need to go that far, he is a bright lad despite his unhealthy obsession with me and he'd make an excellent vessel for one of the generals.

Alabaster: I'm not sure anyone would want to be revived in the body of a freak.

Abaddon: It doesn't matter, does it? Only his body remains anyway. But perhaps you're right about the former notion, if by any chance he starts getting out of hand, deal with him.

Alabaster: Understood. On another hand my lord, I believe there is something or rather someone that could alleviate some of your stress.

Abaddon: Oh?

Alabaster: Follow me.

***

Abaddon: And who is that?

He refers to the female Goblin that is observing how the army trains.

Alabaster: Her name is Shelog, daughter of King Iadvrim.

Abaddon: The princess of the Goblins huh?

Alabaster: Yes, apparently, she came here to see the famed Demon King for herself.

Abaddon: Let's not keep her waiting then.

Alabaster: Ahem, Lady Shelog, this is my Lord Abaddon, king of Dhalsarria and master of the Orcs and Goblins.

Shelog: So, you are the one we are to call king huh, I must say you're not quite what I expected.

Abaddon: Don't you all? But sadly, I live to betray your expectations.

Shelog: Oh no, I am not disappointed, just slightly surprised, in fact I quite enjoy this sight better.

Abaddon: If this surprises you, then allow me to make that even grander (reveals his face).

Shelog: (shocked).

Abaddon: That look on everyone's faces never gets old (slightly chuckles).

Shelog: (blushes) (He is so handsome! Is he really a Demon?) …

Abaddon: My lady?

Shelog: (at loss of words) …

Alabaster: Oh dear, we lost her.

Abaddon: Snap out of it already (increases the tone of his voice slightly).

Shelog: Oh! Please forgive me I… I've never seen someone so…ravishing as you…my…lord.

Abaddon: Why thank you, I understand that this is somewhat of a shock to you but please do try and keep your composure; you are a princess after all.

Shelog: You're right such behaviour is completely inexcusable!

Abaddon: As long as it doesn't happen again.

Shelog: Of course!

Alabaster: How is she? Despite being airheaded she does seem nice enough almost like you want them, unlike the Orcs (speaking in Dhalsarrian).

Abaddon: She does seem a bit older for my taste, but she will do.

Alabaster: I'm glad you're not disappointed.

Shelog: Is that Dhalsarrian? It sounds so alien,

Abaddon: Never mind that, I would like it if you accompanied me to my tent.

Shelog: To your tent you say?

Abaddon: I'll be blunt; all of the work here has got me slightly pent up, so I find myself in the need of female company.

Shelog: A-are you asking me to share a bed with you?

Abaddon: Precisely.

Shelog: With all due respect my lord I am already promised to someone else…

Alabaster: You'd dare defy your master's wishes? Know your place!

Abaddon: Easy, Alabaster.

Alabaster: But my lord! I can't stand for such slander again!

Abaddon: Alabaster…you know my credo, right?

Alabaster: Apologies…

Abaddon: Now then, lady Shelog, you say promised, does that mean you still haven't been with this man?

Shelog: Correct.

Abaddon: In that case there should be no problem, am I right? (Extends his hand).

Shelog: Of course… I would be delighted to take you up on that offer (takes his hand).

Abaddon: Excellent (clasps it around hers).

Shelog: (Well, he is more handsome than Thrank can ever hope to be so no harm here, on the contrary I should be flattered, of all the females his majesty chose me! I mean of course between me, and those Orc brutes is not even a contest).

Abaddon: – Elog, Shelog? (Slaps her) Snap out of it, you brainless wench!

Shelog: (holds her cheek) I did it again…I'm terribly sorry.

Abaddon: Be quiet! You're really testing my patience here, girl.

Shelog: I'm so sorry! Please don't hit me again! (Shields her face).

Abaddon: Hold your tongue and move your legs.

Shelog: Yes, my lord… (walks on).

Alabaster: (In the end they are not so different from the Orcs…).

Jamil observes the situation from his tent, as Abaddon leads Shelog inside.

Jamil: (So…he would rather have a disgusting Goblin creature see to his needs rather than me, even though he said it's only physical…am I only good enough for one night?) (Squeezes the curtains on the entrance out of frustration).

***

Shelog: My lord…why did you ejaculate outside of me?

Abaddon: Do you really need to ask that? I can't allow my seed to be mixed with the likes of you.

Shelog: Y-yes of course…silly me…may I go now?

Abaddon: No, we will continue presently, I still have the stamina to go on.

Shelog: A-agin?

Abaddon: Is that a problem?

Shelog: No! Not at all! I'm still good to go as well.

Abaddon: Have a cup of wine to calm you down, and then we'll continue.

Shelog nods and proceeds to do as she is told.

Later that day

Alabaster: Jamil, where is Lord Abaddon.

Jamil: In his tent…

Alabaster: Still?

Jamil: Apparently…

Alabaster: What? Are you mad that it's not you in there?

Jamil: No…yes…

Alabaster: Haha well that's what Lord Abaddon is like, he does as he pleases.

Jamil: So he does…what do you need?

Alabaster: I'm here to tell him that a new batch of Dragonborn is ready for birth.

Jamil: I'll relay to him if you like.

Alabaster: That's ok I'll wait.

Jamil: Shouldn't you be overseeing the Undead?

Alabaster: Right back at you, shouldn't you be training them?

Jamil: I don't feel like it at this moment… (draws circles in the ground with a stick).

Alabaster: Listen boy, I don't like you but I'm still willing to give you a piece of advice since Lord Abaddon is fond of you.

Jamil: How generous of you, pray tell what is this advice you have?

Alabaster: Under any circumstance do not allow yourself to become a liability, if there is anything the master hates the most it's that, if he senses that you're straying too much that moment will be the end of you.

Jamil: Thank you, I will keep those words close to heart.

Alabaster: I'm not sure whether you're being sarcastic or not.

Jamil: I am not.

Alabaster: In any case, consider yourself warned.

Jamil: Mhmm…

Abaddon: Gentlemen (exits the tent) I expect there is a good reason for this dilly-dallying?

Jamil: I –

Alabaster: I came to tell you that the new Dragonborn are ready for birth my lord.

Abaddon: Jamil?

Jamil: I…I have no valid excuse my lord, I am simply feeling a bit under the weather.

Alabaster shakes his head.

Abaddon: Well instead of acting like a wounded virgin come and make yourself useful, our new guest has some trouble standing up.

Alabaster: I wonder why (chuckles).

Jamil: Yes, my lord…

Abaddon: And you; if you have nothing else to say then return to your post.

Alabaster: Yes, my lord (goes).

Abaddon: (goes to where the Dragons are).

Upon entering the tent Jamil is greeted with a gruesome sight, the Goblin princess lying on the floor, a drooling and mumbling mess, shaking, and quivering.

Jamil: What happened to you…? Not that I care (picks her up) come on, let's get you out of here.

Shelog tries to say something, but no words come out.

Jamil: Don't try to talk, you might hurt yourself (Lord Abaddon didn't tell me where I should take her) …

The expression on his face darkens.

He takes Shelog to the nearby river fooling the guarding Orcs that he takes her out to freshen her up.

Shelog: Th-this is not my room… (finally she says something).

Jamil: No, it's not.

Shelog: Then why take me here?

Jamil unsheathes his scimitar.

Shelog: Wh-what are you –

He proceeds to stab her through the gut.

Shelog: Why…? (Blood coming out of her mouth).

Jamil: You are in my way (pulls out the scimitar and pushes her into the running river, watching as the water takes her away).

He wipes off his sword and sheathes it back and then walks back.

The next day

Abaddon: Jamil, have you seen that braindead buffoon? I can't seem to find her anywhere.

Jamil: I…

Abaddon: Well, speak up, boy.

Jamil: I didn't want to disturb his majesty last night…

Abaddon: Spit it out already, did something happen?

Jamil: After you ordered me to help the princess, I thought it would be a good idea to take her by the river so she could wash herself and regain her consciousness; unfortunately, she was too unstable so…she fell into the river and drowned… I tried to save her, but I couldn't; the current had already swept her away…

Abaddon: … (slaps him) Never withhold such information from me again.

Jamil: I was going to tell you, my lord, but I –

Abaddon: Silence! Do you have any idea what you've done?

Jamil: I didn't account for that...besides, it's no big deal, it's just a mangy Goblin.

Abaddon: She was a princess! Now we risk the chance of her father calling off his alliance and we need those resources!

Jamil: We can take them by force...

Abaddon: Something I wanted to avoid at all costs! I was planning of using the Goblins as a vanguard!

Jamil: ...

Abaddon: Imbecile!

Jamil: I'm terribly sorry...

Abaddon: You being sorry won't bring her back would it! (Exhales) Come!

Jamil: Where are we going...?

Abaddon: To the river!

***

Jamil: What are we doing here?

Abaddon: Maybe the river didn't carry her that far, perhaps my Wraiths can retrieve the body so I can resurrect her.

Jamil: Will it work?

Abaddon: You better pray that it would.

He summons a Ghoul and orders it to search for the body. After a while the spirit comes back empty handed.

Jamil: Nothing huh...

Ghoul: Belu, ishu nipsu urimu.

Abaddon (dismisses the Ghoul) ...

Jamil: What did it say?

Abaddon: Jamil, how did the princess drown again?

Jamil: She um...bent down to have some water and when she got back up, she got dizzy and fell in the river.

Abaddon: You are not lying to me, are you?

Jamil: No my lord, I would never!

Abaddon: Right, then why did the Ghoul say that there is the stench of blood?

Jamil: Blood? I don't understand...

Abaddon: Let me explain it to you, Ghouls as undead creatures have senses of smell far different than any living creature, they can smell blood even if it had been cleaned or washed off.

Jamil: (shocked).

Abaddon: Now, with that in mind I'll ask again, what happened here?

Jamil begins to stutter and sweat profusely and the fact that he cannot read the expression on Abaddon's face because of the hood adds on even more to the pressure so he finally succumbs and falls on his knees.

Jamil: I'm so sorry, my lord! (Tears emerge from his eye sockets) I was overcome by rage and jealousy! When I saw you together with her, I was so frustrated I could barely contain myself! So, I killed her! I killed her with my own sword and threw her in the river! I'm so sorry! Please! I beg for your mercy (lowers his head on the ground).

Abaddon: (sigh) Jamil, Jamil, my sweet boy, for someone so clever, you are so dumb.

Jamil: My lord…!

Abaddon: Not only did you do something that goes completely against my wishes, but you had the audacity to lie directly to my face and make a fool out of me as well, instead of coming clean.

Jamil: It's because I didn't want my lord to be angry with me!

Abaddon: Well congratulations, you succeed in making me extremely mad.

Jamil: I will do anything to atone for my sin! Anything you say!

Abaddon: Look at you, you look like a snivelling brat throwing a tantrum, wipe your tears and man up.

Jamil wipes his tears and stands up.

Abaddon: (places his hand on his cheek and caresses it slowly) Such a shame you disappointed me Jamil, I expected better of you.

Jamil: My lord…?

Abaddon retracts his hand and takes a step back.

Jamil: (in confusion turns behind him) Alabaster when did you…

Abaddon: Rip his right arm.

The towering behemoth reaches out his left hand and grabs Jamil's arm.

Jamil: M-my my lord? N-no!

Alabaster: I warned you, didn't I? You couldn't just listen (applies pressure).

Jamil: Alabaster please…My loooo…agghhh! Aghhh! Please! No! Let me make it up to you! Let me atone!

Abaddon: Jamil, don't be mistaken, for those that serve me well, I can be akin a benevolent God but for those that don't, I'm a Demon of carnage.

Jamil: Nooo!

A crunch, a twist, a rip, a spray of blood and a lot of screaming.

Alabaster: Pitiful bastard.

Abaddon: (approaches him and kneels down) I'm not going to stop the bleeding; if you die from blood loss, it would mean that that was the extent of your worth, and if you do manage to survive and wish to keep on doing so, I suggest you learn to fence with your left hand (slaps his cheek and straightens up).

Abaddon: Oh, and one more thing, don't expect any more affection from me.

To Jamil those words dealt more damage than the pain of losing his dominant arm, for those words alone he dreaded not to hear in his lifetime and so he curled up on the ground and wept bitterly not from the physical pain but from the pain of losing his beloved patron.

Alabaster: Are you sure you want to let him off with just an arm?

Abaddon: Let him be, for him this is a punishment worse than death, losing the respect of someone you admire the most, but for now what's more important is how the Goblin King will react to this unfortunate news.

Alabaster: Should I have her guards relay the message then?

Abaddon: Please do, and make sure you tell them I had nothing to do with it; it was the work of a single individual and that he has paid the price.

Alabaster: Understood.

***

Iadvrim: What? I offer up my servitude and this is how he repays me? With the murder of my daughter! …Oh, my sweet Shelog…

Guard: To be fair, my king…the Lord did not order it…as I said.

Iadvrim: I don't care! It was still done by one of his men! He was careless enough to let that happen! And where were you?

Guard: We… (gulps) You see, my king…since the princess was with the Lord, we thought she is safe, so we were getting drunk with the Orcs…

Iadvrim: And you call yourself guards? Your duty is to protect her at all times you pea for brain nimrods! Off with your heads!

Guard: Can't we get a life sentence instead?

Iadvrim: Are you mocking me?

Guard: No, I –

Iadvrim: Grulk! Where is Grulk!

Grulk: I'm here my king.

Guard#2: Anything but Grulk!

Iadvrim: Teach these fools a lesson they'll never forget.

Grulk: Yes, your majesty (grins while smacking a giant club against his hand, then he proceeds to drag them away).

Iadvrim: Wolrim!

Wolrim: At your command sire.

Iadvrim: Prepare the army, we strike at the Wolfskins tonight.

Wolrim: Are we not under the servitude of their master?

Iadvrim: The deal is off! We'll show them what happens when they mess with us.

Wolrim: My lord, perhaps it would be unwise to instigate a conflict with such a powerful individual.

Iadvrim: We have to show them that we are not scared and in the worst-case scenario we have 'that'.

Wolrim: I see, I shall make the preparations then.

Iadvrim: He-he-he, they won't know what hit 'em!

Later that night, Wolrim's troops sneak up to Bugrash's town under the cover of darkness and using their nimble bodies they scale up the walls and start their attack.

Orc: We are under attack! It's a Goblin raid!

One of the Goblin archers shoots down the guard and he falls down, seeing this, another one of the guards rings the alarm bell.

However, it's too late as the Goblins already begin pouring from over the wall and attack the stationed guards, and while they are preoccupied with combat, a group of Goblins manages to overwhelm the guards manning the main gate, slay them, and open it so that the rest of the forces, most of which are Hobgoblins can storm into the town.

Hobgoblins are a mutated form of Goblins more resembling Orcs than Goblins themselves. They are bigger, stronger, and better fighters overall. According to Goblin tradition a battle royale tournament is held when there is a sufficient number of Hobs and the last one standing is made king. As there is no succession by birth right even the king's own son is not exempt from this trial. Another main component of the Goblin army is the Spider Riders.

These Goblins have tamed the giant arachnids that dwell within their mountain and use them as mounts which allows them to serve in the capacity of a cavalry. But what makes Goblins more formidable than Orcs is their technology, having access to rare, precious metals they are able to craft far superior weapons and armour. This, combined with their keen intellect, makes these creatures to be almost on par with the other more advanced races.

Meanwhile, Bugrash does his best to mobilise his army, but this proves to be difficult as the town is being more and more overrun.

Orc commander: My lord! We are not going to make it! This city is done for; at least you and your family must make it out alive.

Bugrash: You expect me to flee like a coward as my kin dies around me!

Orc commander: Please my lord; we'll do our best to secure you a safe passage!

Bugrash: No! I'd rather die amongst my people! But my family doesn't have to; make sure they get out of here alive!

Orc commander: Yes sir! (Leaves).

Bugrash: Raghh! Come on you little pieces of shit come and get some! (Grabs his battle axe and rushes out to meet them head on).

Orc: It's our Lord! Raghh!

Bugrash: Fight men! Fight to your last breath!

Orcs: Yaghhh!

This elevates their spirits, and they proceed to fight on even more fiercely.

A Spider Rider attacks him from behind with his spider that bites his neck but Bugrash is unaffected by this at all, he swings his axe around and embeds it in the stomach of the critter which lets out a squeaky sound but Bugrash doesn't stop there; he grabs the axe with two hands and using his monstrous strength he lifts up the arachnid along with its rider and slams it on the ground, crushing the

Goblin in the process. The creature keeps squirming, so Bugrash deals a coup de grace by bashing its head in, but the Goblin as well is still alive although bloodied, trying to crawl out from beneath his mount. As soon as he pops out his head Bugrash chops it off instantly.

As he was preoccupied with that, a swarm of Goblins rushes at him but he holds his ground and fends them off.

The fighting goes on and the Orcs fighting alongside him fall one by one, ultimately leaving him on his own. Huts around him are burning and the flames illuminate his weary face; mighty as he is he cannot fight alone.

Two Hobs jump him out of the flames, but he manages to fend off their attacks with one mighty swing of his axe.

One of the Hobs wielding a huge, two-hand sword, comes at him with an overhead swing but he shoulder-butts him and topples him down on the ground, blocking the other's attack with his gauntlet although the blade manages to cave it in.

He swings his axe at him, but the blade is unable to pierce the superior steel, giving the Hob a chance to smack him with his fist in his face and stagger him for a moment. Thinking he has the upper hand, the Goblin attacks, but Bugrash with a surgically precise swing cuts off his attacking arm right at the spot where it is the least protected. Then he picks up the Hob's sword and drives it through his screaming mouth, killing him.

Right as it seemed that Bugrash might actually pull it out from this predicament, a Goblin shoots a poison dart at him from one of the nearby rooftops. This Goblin is of the 'Trickster' class which specialises in fighting with underhanded tactics, like utilising poison as in this instance. Even though Bugrash is a big fellow the poison takes effect nevertheless and combined with the poisonous bite of the arachnid from earlier topples him on his knees.

The other Hob gets up and drives his great sword through his back, but even that is not enough to finish off this great warrior as he musters his strength and strikes with his axe through the unprotected part of the Hob's face, embedding it deep into his skull. Seeing as he is not going down, the Trickster shoots another dart and another until he no longer has darts to shoot.

Trickster: What's this guy made of? Just die already!

As if heeding his wishes, Goblin soldiers enter the area, led by Wolrim himself. The Goblin General calmly makes his way towards Bugrash while his troops try to take him down to no avail.

Even down on his knees, this fearsome Orc refuses to give in, swinging and swinging, killing every Goblin that dares cross the path of his axe until he no longer is able to hold it. With the clinging sound of the axe falling on the ground, Wolrim makes his last step towards Bugrash, now standing before him, longsword in hand.

Wolrim: We meet again, Bugrash.

Bugrash: Wolrim…I should've known it is you that leads the attack, you traitorous cur.

Wolrim: Come now, don't be like that, brother.

Bugrash: (spits on the side) My brother…died on the battlefield ten years ago.

It is becoming difficult for him to speak, and his vision begins to blur.

Wolrim: You should be proud of me, look; I made it to the rank of General.

Bugrash: I hope it was worth all the Orc lives it took to get you there!

Wolrim: They were, every last one, after all not only rank but I gained riches, knowledge, superior weapons, something I never could've had had I stayed here.

Bugrash: Spare me the pitiful gloating and kill me already.

Wolrim: (smirks) Shame, I wish I could've ended your life properly in a battle, but I guess I have to settle with this instead.

Bugrash looks at him with discontent.

Wolrim: Nice look, fitting for your end, but before I send you off, I shall impart you with the knowledge that after I kill you, I will go and have some fun with Rosha and then I'm going to kill her as well, but first I'll make her watch as I kill your young ones too (grins).

Bugrash smiles.

Wolrim: What's this? I thought you would be bursting with anger.

Bugrash: You may kill me, but I will die knowing that my wife and children are safe.

Wolrim: What?

Bugrash: They should be halfway to Grough's by now, and once they are, they will be safe for that person is there.

Wolrim: That Demon King…

Bugrash: That Demon King that you so foolishly angered by this act of war and believe me when I say you do not want to go in a war with him. You don't know this…but… (coughs up blood) but I witnessed his power first hand and it was only a small portion, but was enough to almost make me shit my pants (grins with blood on his teeth) so if I were you I would run, run like the wind as far away as possible lest I'd want to feel the full extent of his wrath…which you and your king will, and it will be…the last thing you…do.

The enraged Wolrim stabs him through the throat finishing him off.

Wolrim: Send a party of Goblin Riders to hunt down Rosha and the kids, bring them to me alive!

Goblin: Yes sir!

Wolrim: (looks down at the corpse of his brother) As if I'm supposed to be scared; even we have something terrifying up our sleeves (snickers).

Just what could be this 'thing' they keep referring to…?

CAPITVLVM IX

POTITOR DOLORIS[viii]

After some while chasing after them, the Spider Riders manage to gain on Rosha and her young ones, but as fortune would have it, they were already nearing the entrance to the town of Dhaldrog. The posted archers take notice of this pursuit and go on to shoot the pursuers, but the Goblins manage to deflect the oncoming missiles and while the Orcs take the time to reload, one of the Riders hurls his spear at the Dire Wolf that is carrying the mother and children and gravely wounds it, but the beast keeps on running relentlessly.
One of the Orc archers uses this moment and succeeds in hitting his mark, taking out the said Rider. This moment of triumph is nothing to rejoice at for the party of Riders numbers at least a dozen and soon the others ready their spears as well.

Archer: Lady Rosha is in trouble! Someone go and intercept her quick!

Alabaster: What is the trouble? (He asks in Orcish as he has been picking it up as well).

Archer: The wife of Bugrash has a party of Goblins on her tail, there's too many; we can't shoot them all in time!

As this exchange of words is going on, the vile Goblins succeed in slaying the Dire Wolf and it topples on the ground along with its host.

Goblin: Quick! Grab them!

The archers release a volley of arrows, and some do hit true however it is not enough as some of the Riders get their hands on the family but, when all hope seems lost for them, Alabaster in one mighty leap finds himself before the Goblins, knocking them off their feet with the force of the shockwave.

Goblin: What the hell was that?

Goblin#2: More like who! Look! A Demon!

Goblin: Kill him!

Now the Goblins that still have their spears in hand throw them at Alabaster, but they deflect off his armour like tiny darts.

Goblins: Our weapons have no effect!

Leader: Don't falter! Charge!

They are speaking in the Goblin tongue which to the normal ear would sound like a gaggle of angry children.

And so, they lead on their mounts and charge at the behemoth of a Demon that is standing before them, alas to their own peril.

Alabaster swings his mighty mace that is more akin of a hammer and mows them down like a farmer mowing grass with his scythe. So great is his force that nothing is left of them but mangled bodies. Those that manage to survive attempt to flee but his innate trait 'Dreadful Presence' prevents them from doing so and thus they stay frozen in fear. They fall to the mercy of his mace Halnadu; it is mercy indeed for it is a swift death they are granted as he takes to the air once more and comes crashing down like a furious thunder, smashing them into oblivion, armour and all, leaving behind only a smudge of blood.

One of the spiders still wriggles on the ground half dead but is soon laid to rest by the heel of his mighty grieve, and so big is his foot that he crushes the creature almost whole.

Rosha: Ohhh thank you, stranger, thank you (she says in tears, hugging her young ones tightly).

Alabaster: Can you walk?

Rosha: Y-yes.

Alabaster: Then follow me.

And so, he takes them before Abaddon so that she may tell of what happened, unto him.

Abaddon: Good work.

Jamil: Who is this person?

Abaddon: Did I give you permission to talk?

Jamil: No, my lord…

Abaddon: Then hold your tongue.

Jamil: Yes, my lord…

Abaddon: Answer the question.

Alabaster: Her name is Rosha, apparently, she is the spouse of Bugrash, she had a party of Goblins pursuing her.

Rosha: My lord, I am forever grateful to your man for delivering me from a certain death (still distraught).

Abaddon: Calm yourself, tell me what happened, why were Goblins pursuing you?

Rosha: Oh, my lord… (wipes her tears and tries to calm down).

The little Orcs are crying and weeping as well adding to the confusion.

Abaddon: Jamil, get these kids out of here and give them something to calm down.

Jamil: Yes, my lord…come on children.

However, they begin to cry even more at the idea of being separated from their mother.

Rosha: It's alright, children, go with the nice man, mama will be with you shortly.

They give consent and go on with Jamil whom Rosha thanks and he gives a polite nod.

Abaddon: Now, tell me everything in the calmest manner.

Rosha: It is horrible, my lord…Goblins…they attacked suddenly, without any warning, their numbers were great and they almost immediately took over the town…our troops had not the time to prepare…my husband bid Hrugh to take me and the children to safety…I would not leave him but he insisted and assured me that he too would soon follow but…(tears come to her eyes yet again and she covers her mouth to prevent herself from crying, she swallows bitterly and keeps on) …I'm most certain that he has met his demise and now lies dead amongst the rubble of our once city… (ultimately, she can no longer hold on and bursts into tears once more).

Alabaster: So they really attacked, fully aware of what their actions will wrought.

Abaddon: If they were counting on it then they are going to get it; my wrath that is. Alabaster, gather the Dragons and take Andrakos with you, teach them what it means to make an enemy out of us.

Alabaster: Finally, my body has been acing for a proper fight (grins widely beneath his helmet).

***

Argyros: We are going on the offence against the Goblins, huh?

Ignatos: Pitiful bunch, they don't stand a chance.

Fulguros: You don't even need to come, just the three of us will make a quick work of them.

Alabaster: No, this is a perfect opportunity to stretch out a little, it would be a shame to miss out, besides it's on Lord Abaddon's orders.

Argyros: I understand that, but why is **he** coming? (Turns to Andrakos).

Alabaster: It will be good for him to gain some battlefield experience, besides—

Argyros: Orders, I get it…

Ignatos: Hop on sonny.

Andrakos: Sonny…?

Ignatos: It means son, now hop on.

Andrakos: Son…

Fulguros: Aw, he seems glad.

Ignatos: Shut it!

Now both Andrakos and Alabaster mount Ignatos and Argyros respectively and they are off to 'Khazan Ainul' or the Iron Mountains which is the dwelling place of the Goblins. It is not a large stretch of mountains, but it is a part of a larger chain which makes up the northernmost point of North-East Baltia.

Now Andrakos as a warrior does not wear any armour thanks to his draconic genealogy but he does have his dominant arm protected with a pauldron and a gauntlet and he also wears waist and shin guards. Despite having the ability to regrow lost limbs, a battlefield is an unforgiving place, and should he lose his arm or leg it may cost him his own life for he may not have the time to regenerate.

In the meantime, Wolrim was growing restless at the lack of news.

Wolrim: Still nothing?

Captain: No sir…

Wolrim: (grunts) Then it's safe to assume that she has made it to this Demon King…fuck! We have no time to waste any longer, order the troops to fall back we are going home.

Captain: Yes sir!

Wolrim severs Bugrash's head and takes it with him as a trophy.

As the Dragons make their way towards their destination dawn breaks upon them and the blood-red rising sun shines as a dark omen.

Alabaster: There, that's the place.

Argyros: That is one enormous range of mountains, reminds me of our own lands.

Fulguros: Getting homesick?

Argyros: Nah! Just reminiscing a little.

Alabaster: Let's do this; open fire!

Now the Dragons rear their heads backwards and spring them forth, spewing destruction upon the mountain, however the attacks seem to explode in thin air.

Andrakos: That is…strange.

Alabaster: There seems to be some sort of magical barrier around it.

Ignatos: I didn't know Goblins can utilise magic.

Alabaster: Me neither, but it may be the work of some magical artefact, they are merchants after all.

Argyros: That would make more sense (grunts) what are we to do about it then? If Abaddon was here, it'd be no problem.

Alabaster: That is true, but you are forgetting something very crucial, my friend, I wasn't the commander general of the Destroyers for nothing.

Argyros: (snickers) I see.

Alabaster: Just fly me over the topmost point and I'll do the rest.

Despite the attacks not getting through, the tremors of the impact are still felt like a mighty earthquake at the Goblin's lair.

Iadvrim: So, they are finally here huh, no matter, as long as we have that barrier, they cannot do anything, amass the armies! We will meet them outside with our full force!

Wolrim: With pleasure, your majesty!

Argyros flies up at the very top and Alabaster stands atop of his back and takes the mighty Halnadu off his waist, the runes along the weapon light up like flares and then the Demon takes his leap and when he reaches a certain point, he swings down his mace. Now to the naked eye it may seem as if he is hitting the air but lo! The barrier gets shattered under the might of Halnadu, for that is the sole purpose of the unit called Obsidian Destroyers – to destroy.

Their prime ability 'Destruction' not only allows them to inflict massive physical damage upon anything they hit, but it also grants them the power to break through any sort of magical obstacle, making barriers such as this meaningless.

As he now falls, Argyros swoops in and he falls atop his back.

Argyros: Nice work!

Alabaster: That was nothing.

Goblin: Sir! The barrier has been breached…nay! It was fully destroyed!

Iadvrim: Gah! Then deploy it again!

Goblin: We only have one charge left! If they break it down again…

Iadvrim: Do it!

Ignatos: Let's give it another go!

He spits out a massive fireball, but it is once again deflected by the barrier.

Ignatos: Again?

Alabaster: No problem, I just have to take it down again.

Ignatos: These little shits are really getting on my nerves.

Alabaster: Wait, do you hear that?

Argyros: Hear what?

Alabaster: Footsteps.

Argyros: looks like they finally come out to play.

Ignatos: Let's give them a warm welcome.

As soon as the Goblin army rears its ugly head from the foot of the mountain, the Dragons open fire and bring ruin upon a number on them. However, they do not falter, and they are ordered to shoot at the Dragons with some sort of special bows that allows them to reach up to the height they are at.

Wolrim: Keep shooting!

The arrows deal no damage but are enough to annoy them and prevent them from firing.

Ignatos: You little! (Charges up a fire ball but an arrow gets stuck in the inside of his mouth causing him stinging pain) (Roars loudly).

Wolrim: Take that you worm! However, it's quite strange that there are only flying lizards around here, where are their armies?

At that moment, Alabaster comes crashing down on the ground like a meteor from the sky.

Wolrim: You must be the General, where are your troops?

Alabaster: There is no one else but me.

Wolrim: A one-man army, huh?

Alabaster: I am all that it takes to deal with the likes of you, sending an army would smear the name of my great lord.

Wolrim: Awfully confident, Mr General, no matter how strong you are you can't face all these numbers by yourself.

Alabaster: I'd like to prove you wrong (tightens his grip on Halnadu, the 'Pain Bringer').

Wolrim: Charge!

The whole host of Goblins pours onwards like a swarm of bees upon the lone behemoth, unbeknownst that they are rushing into certain death. The first of the soldiers come down with their weapons on him but their steel shatters and breaks from his magical armour, it will take more than high quality steel blades to pierce the armour of a Destroyer.

Once they are taken aback by this revelation, Alabaster swings Halnadu and mows down the Goblins before him as if he was swatting flies. Torn off heads and limbs fly off in every direction, guts and blood fill the battlefield as this monster swings his powerful mace. Three Hobs charge at him at once, but before they can even reach him, he hits one of them and blows his upper body clean off him in a burst of guts, blood and flesh. The second one meets the same fate, and the third one gets squashed like a pancake; their inferior armour cannot hope to withstand the mighty blows of the 'Pain Bringer'

More keep on coming and more keep on meeting the same fate, until finally Wolrim takes it upon himself to challenge him but is met with a swift end; Alabaster grabs his sword and breaks it in half with his bare hand and rams the broken off shard through his skull.

The soldiers begin to panic at the loss of their commander and some turn to flee but instead to safety they run straight in the jaws of death, as the mighty Dragonborn who has been fighting all this time as well, meets them with dragon fire and burns them alive in their suits of armour.

Some of the Goblins out of desperation throw themselves at Alabaster and try to find an opening and stab through his armour, but their struggle is in vain as there are no gaps in the Destroyers' armour for they are fully covered in it. So, with a mighty twist and turn he shakes off the pesky vermin off him, however one of them has managed to latch himself firmly and keeps on stabbing out of frustration resulting in the breaking of his steel. Now Alabaster grabs him whole, for his arm is as big as his torso and crushes him like a walnut.

The air around them grows heavy with the stench of blood and it is filled with the sounds of bones breaking, bodies being splattered and the screams of pain and anguish of these unfortunate sods.

Faced with this triple threat, the Goblins face nothing but certain doom; however, some do manage to escape the desolation and bring word to their king.

Goblin: My king! It is hopeless! Our numbers are dwindling by the second! If this goes on, we will be completely annihilated!

Iadvrim: How many men?

Goblin: That's the thing, sire…it is but one person, a single Demon with the might of a whole army in his one swing!

Iadvrim: What?

Goblin: He is simply too powerful! We cannot hope to defeat him, even Wolrim fell like it is nothing.

Goblin#2: I saw him squish a Hob like he was a watermelon!

Goblin #3: Not only that, sire! There is also a strange creature that resembles a Dragon, but it is bipedal and is about the size of a Hob!

Iadvrim: Enough! I heard enough!

Jaqrakhal: (comes in wobbling) Sire, perhaps it would be most wise to surrender and reinstate ourselves in his servitude.

Iadvrim: Silence you old fart! As if he would accept us graciously like last time! No! I shall not surrender as long as we have 'that'.

Jaqrakhal: Sire! Wielding that could prove more dangerous than what we are facing outside!

Iadvrim: Be quiet! …I've made up my mind, I'm going to waken it! And they'll see that we are not pushovers! (Retreats to the furthest depths of the cavern).

Jaqrakhal: Sire wait! Sire! (Wobbles behind him)

Goblin: Everyone keeps saying 'that', 'that' but what even is that?

Goblin#2: Don't ask me; I don't have the faintest idea.

Now Iadvrim reaches his destination, and there is some figure encased in what would seem a crystal casing. Below the crystal, there is a space for the embedment of a jewel. He reaches in his royal gown and produces said jewel, which is a pure white amethyst with tints of blue light, and he sticks it within the socket. Now the jewel begins to radiate with a bright blue colour, the same as the crystal. Once this is done, the light of the amethyst flows into it and the casing begins to break, accompanied with great tremors that can be felt even outside.

Argyros: What the hell?

Alabaster: This doesn't bode well…

The crystal completely shatters and the mysterious figure bursts forth.

Iadvrim: Oh, right! (Points the jewel on the top of his sceptre towards him) I command you to bend to my will! Heed my words for I am your master!

The jewel glows and the glow reflects in its eyes and they become bright red themselves.

Iadvrim: Aahaha! Now go forth mighty spirit! Destroy that wretched fiend!

Jaqrakhal: My king…ohhh!

Iadvrim: You're too late, you senile buffoon, I already released him and now he's ready to do my bidding.

Jaqrakhal: Sire! You are tangling with forces beyond your comprehension, you cannot hope to control such a being!

Iadvrim: All he needs is to destroy that Demon, after that I'll throw him back in the crystal!

Jaqrakhal: Oh, dear me…

Outside, violent winds begin to blow from the mountain and swirl into one place out of which the being is formed and finally takes physical shape.

Andrakos feels the threat it poses and bares his teeth at it as do the three Dragons.

Goblin: What is that thing? A foe! A friend?

Goblin#2: I don't know, man!

Goblin#3: This shit is becoming too much for me to handle! Let's get the hell out of here, boys!

And so, the present Goblins drop their weapons and run as fast as they can towards the entrance of the mountain.

The being pays them no mind as it is focused on Abaddon's party.

Now this creature is of the strangest complexion. It has bracelets made of stone with ancient inscriptions on its wrists and ankles. Its hair is made of vines, and it has moss covering some parts of its body which is made of stone, and it also wears an armour made from tree bark. An aura of wind is constantly swirling around it, waving its long hair.

Alabaster: This is no good, that's an Oread!

Argyros: A what?

Alabaster: Spirit of the Air, they are servants to Boreas and serve as guardians of the mountains.

Ignatos: Then why the hell did it allow Goblins to infest its mountains all this time?

Alabaster: I don't know, but I do know that I have to take it down.

Ignatos: Can you do it?

Alabaster: I can try.

Alabaster jumps high in the air, reaching the spirit and swings with his mace, however the creature will have none of this, and erects a magical barrier, but as we have witnessed so far it has no effect on Alabaster and he breaks through, but the creature is able to stop his mace with its bare hand and with its other hand blasts him back on the ground with a burst of wind.

Argyros: This thing is quite powerful.

Alabaster: I'll say…

Ignatos and Fulguros fire a blaze and lighting stream at it, but they are not able to reach the creature due to the barrier of wind that surrounds it.

Now Andrakos tries to do something, and he too leaps at the spirit but to no avail, as the Oread sends him on the ground with relative ease and constrains him with vines that sprout from the ground, but when they prove ineffective due to the Dragonborn's inhuman strength, he completely entangles him in vines, and he falls flat on the ground.

The Oread now uses the same vines to try and take away Halnadu from Alabaster, but the Demon is no pushover and uses this against him as he pulls the spirit to him and hits him with a punch in the face. The spirit's face seems to crack but it immediately mends itself, then it cleverly uses its hair to entangle Alabaster's hand and then does the strangest thing – mushrooms begin to sprout from the crust on its back and it releases spores out of them, spreading them throughout the air with its wind magic.

Argyros: Be careful! Those shrooms are poisonous!
Alabaster: Poison has no effect on me.
Argyros: But you're not dealing with normal poison, are you?

Alabaster uses his enormous strength to break free from the vines of the spirit, but they simply reattach to the rest of its hair and hold him back in place again. Now the creature seeing that the Demon is struggling to break free, produces more vines from the ground as he did with Andrakos and strengthens its hold on him. With one of its hands, it produces a cloud of the spores and uses wind magic to make it circle around Alabaster's head, and him having holes on his helmet for his eyes becomes dangerously exposed to them.

But the Dragons will suffer none of it, and Argyros lunges forth with his maw and snaps the vines in two, and Ignatos slaps the spirit away with his tail before it has the chance to regrow them again.

Fulguros takes his chance and fires a lightning bolt at it but the spirit regains its wits rapidly and quickly erects a wall of stone that halts the bolt, while Argyros comes in from the side to try and snap it with his jaws, but the creature swiftly moves out of the way and with its stone magic creates a giant stone hand that grabs the Dragon by the maw, pinning him down on the ground.

Now the other two Dragons seeing their brethren's predicament, spring forth to his aid but the same fate befalls them as well, as two hands erupt from the ground and hold them down. This spirit is no fool, knowing that such measures will not hold the creatures in place, so he creates additional stone giants to keep them locked in place.

The entangled Andrakos becomes enraged and wriggles around in an attempt to break free, so the Oread makes some sort of flowers to sprout from the vines that are entangling him and puts him to sleep with their pollen.

Argyros: (manages to free a portion of his maw so that he may talk) Alabaster run! We can't beat this thing by ourselves! Call the Master!

Alabaster: You can't ask me to turn back and run like some coward!

Argyros: We have no other choice! This is not the time to act on your honour!

Alabaster: I said no!

The Demon grips his mace and springs forth into action, with his strength he finds himself before the trapped Dragons and with a mighty swing destroys the Giant that was holding Argyros and the stone hand as well, then proceeds to liberate the other two as well.

Argyros: Thanks! I owe you one!

Alabaster: You don't owe me anything.

Now the Oread seems deeply upset by this and with its magic it creates all manners of woodland creatures to attack them. However, the behemoth steps forward, breaks them with his mace one by one, and begins to make his way towards the spirit. The spirt keeps sending animals in his way that explode in a flash of green light when destroyed.

When it sees that this is doing it no good, it also sends spheres of rotating wind at Alabaster as well, to accompany the animals, but the Demon is like a juggernaut and cannot be stopped, it even tries to entangle him with vines yet again to no avail. With all of its attacks in shambles, it finally calls upon the winds of the mountains to blow and halt Alabaster in his track but that does him no good as well as the Demon is braving through the gale.

Now seeing as the Demon is almost inches away from it, it dons itself in a huge armour made of stone, making it the same size as Alabaster and rushes at him. It strikes him with its fist straight in the face, but the Demon is hardly fazed, he goes on to retaliate with a punch of his own, but the spirit blocks it with its palm and headbutts him instead.

He swings his mace, but the Oread blocks again, this time with its lower arm and since the mace was unable to completely break the stone, it becomes embedded, and the stone starts to encroach around it. Seeing this, Alabaster quickly pulls the mace away.

Alabaster: (That's no ordinary stone).

As he was contemplating this, he begins to realise that wherever the spirit hit him, that place has petrified. Speaking of which, now the spirit grabs his right arm and begins to petrify it. Quickly, he switches Halnadu to his left hand and the runes on the mace lit up again and he smashes the stone armour off the spirit's left hand, thus halting the petrifying process and he proceeds to smash it in its torso and sends him flying a few metres away.

At that moment, the jewel that is controlling the Oread begins to flicker, causing the creature to become disoriented and hold its head in pain.

Iadvrim: What is happening?

Jaqrakhal: It would seem that the jewel is giving out!

Iadvrim: Agh! How long does it take that insufferable idiot to finish off one Demon! (Groans and taps the jewel angrily).

Alabaster: That's odd…

Argyros: What's wrong with it?

Alabaster: I don't know, but I could've sworn I saw his eyes change colour for a moment, from red to cyan.

Ignatos: It might be controlled.

Alabaster: In that case…!

Iadvrim: Work, you piece of junk! Work!

The jewel flares up even brighter causing the spirit to regain its composure, but a little too late as the Demon comes swinging down at him with great fury, busting its stone armour completely with a thunderous strike. He takes another swing but since it does not have much momentum behind it, it only blows half of the left side of his head when he hits, and it falls on the ground seemingly lifeless. This causes the jewel to shine even brighter until it ultimately bursts into thousand pieces like fireworks.

Iadvrim: Nooo!

Jaqrakhal: What now, sire?

Iadvrim: We must flee! To the tunnels beyond and away!

Jaqrakhal: Just the two of us? What of the others?

Iadvrim: Screw the others! We are already done for! We need to save our own skins!

Jaqrakhal: And what of the gold…?

Iadvrim: The gold…no time for that! We need to go! Now!
Jaqrakhal: We must make haste then!

***

Argyros: Is…is it dead?
Alabaster: I don't know (kicks the spirit with his foot).

The spirit's right eye lights up with life yet again, but this time it is its normal cyan colour. This slightly startles the group, so they take a few steps back.
Its bashed part regrows itself and the spirit gets up on its feet with no problem.

Fulguros: Was it a good idea not to finish it off?
Alabaster: We are about to find out.
Oread: (exhales) Finally, I am back to my former self, ye have my gratitude, strangers.
Alabaster: What happened to you?
Oread: I was being enthralled by a powerful magic.
Ignatos: As we thought; how did that come to pass?
Oread: Many years ago, I was trapped in a crystal cage by an evil spirit that invaded my mountain, it must have been the same fiend that created the device that controlled me…and now as I have been freed from both imprisonment, and thraldom, I must defeat that spirit and chase it off my mountain, will thou lend me thy hand?
Alabaster: I'd gladly do so but whatever was inhabiting your mountain is long gone, it is now infested with Goblins that dwell within its deeps.
Oread: Goblins thou sayest?
Alabaster: Indeed, I doubt you need our aid in dealing with such vermin.
Oread: It is as thou sayest, I must tend to this matter at once, but before I go, will ye tell me your names?
Alabaster: My name is Alabaster, and these are Argyros, Ignatos and Fulguros, Dragon Kings of their respective kind, and this one is Andrakos.
Oread: What a strange creature, never before have I laid mine eyes upon such a specimen, I want to say it is an Orc yet it resembleth a Dragon as well…

Alabaster: It's a new race, a crossbreed between the two, my master calls them Dragonborn.

Oread: And who is thy master, might I ask?

Alabaster: Abaddon, King of Dhalsarria.

Oread: Abaddon? I know not that name but from what thou sayest, I judge him to be a Demon.

Alabaster: It is as you say, and what do they call you, spirit?

Oread: I am called Ormazd, spirit of Chairn Nagol[18].

Alabaster: Ormazd, I would like to ask a favour of you, if I may.

Ormazd: If it is within my power then I shall gladly accept it.

Alabaster: Your mountains are quite rich in all sorts of ore, materials we need to craft our armour and weapons; therefore I would ask permission of you to excavate it.

Ormazd: As a token of my gratitude, ye have my permission.

Argyros: I was sure you'd protest.

Ormazd: I am but a spirit, my domain are these mountains, I do not trouble myself with the dealings of outsiders as long as it does not affect mine abode.

Alabaster: I give you my word that we will do no harm to it and only take what we need.

Ormazd: As the saying goeth: 'no harm, no foul'.

Alabaster: In that case, we bid you farewell, great spirit.

Ormazd: May the blessings of Lord Boreas be upon thee.

And so, they take their leave towards Dhaldrog.

Argyros laughs.

Alabaster: What's so funny?

Argyros: You talking politely, it was my first time seeing you in that light.

Alabaster: Well, I thought it would put us in a more favourable position if I didn't come off as a brute.

Ignatos: And it worked.

Fulguros: I think it would've worked either way, the fella simply wanted to repay the favour.

Ignatos: Yeah well…it even gave us its blessing; I didn't know an acolyte of Oxylus could do that.

Alabaster: Boreas is a neutral God; he'd allow Baal himself to live on a mountain as long as he did well by it.

---

[18] Iron Mountains in Spirit Speech.

Ignatos: Speaking of which, I wonder what will happen to those Goblins.

Argyros: Who cares?

Fulguros: I certainly don't.

And they all laugh at that remark but the same could not be said for the Goblins. As Iadvrim and Jaqrakhal were making it towards the exit tunnels in the back, they get intercepted by Grulk, the executioner.

Grulk: Where are you going, sire?

Iadvrim: Grulk! Get out of the way, you big lump!

Grulk: You don't mean to escape all by yourselves, do you?

Iadvrim: Move! That's an order!

Grulk: No! You brought the wrath of a monster and the mountain upon us! You ruined us! And now you want to save your own arse!

Iadvrim: How dare you speak to me like that? I am your King!

Grulk: You are no King, you are a coward.

Iadvrim: I don't have time for your insubordination! Either move or die by my blade! (Unsheathes his sword).

Grulk: So be it! (Does the same).

Jaqrakhal: Oh, dear me…

Lo! A thunderous voice makes itself heard throughout the mountain; it is the voice of Ormazd.

Ormazd: Harken ye who dwell within these caverns! Make yourselves scarce from my mountain lest ye feel my anger!

Jaqrakhal: It's the voice of the spirit…

Iadvrim: Oh, great spirit! I beg for your mercy! Do not chase us away for we have nowhere to go!

Ormazd: Nay! Had ye the decency to ask for my permission and for that of my Lord I would have considered, but ye have kept me imprisoned and used me against my will to bring harm upon others!

Jaqrakhal: I told you; you shouldn't mess with these forces sire!

Iadvrim: Silence you fool!

Jaqrakhal: …

Iadvrim: Please oh great spirit! We promise that we will do no harm to these mountains or to your great self! Take pity on our souls! These caverns have been our home for so long and we've grown quite fond of them, it would sadden us deeply if we were to leave.

Grulk: Why do you care? You were about to leave anyways!

Iadvrim: Fool, if we can get the protection of this spirit those Demons won't be able to touch us! (Speaks in a lowered voice).

Grulk: I see!

Ormazd: Save thine words for I will hear none of it! Such is the punishment for the disrespect thou hast shown me! Leave now or I shall do it myself!

Iadvrim: Oh, Great Spirit –

Ormazd: Silence! This is thine final warning!

Iadvrim: Well, screw you, we are not leaving!

Jaqrakhal: Sire, this is not the time to be stubborn!

Ormazd: So be it!

Now a great tremor can be felt within the caverns, as a giant volcano like protrusion emerges from the topmost peak of the mountains and strong currents blow and gather all the remaining Goblins into one place and finally, they are ejected from the caverns as would lava spew forth, and thus the sky is filled with screaming Goblins as they tumble down the mountain side; some survive but some meet their doom from the high fall. Those that manage to survive are forced off Khazan Ainul, as they called it, and must look to other places to call home.

Jaqrakhal: Now what sire…?

Iadvrim: I don't knooowwww!

CAPITVLVM X

INIMICVS INIMICI AMICVS[ix]

Iadvrim: Wait, I just thought of an idea, yes, yes, yesss.

Jaqrakhal: What is it, sire?

Iadvrim: We go south.

Jaqrakhal: South? To Avalon?

Iadvrim: What else is south, you old fart?

Jaqrakhal: It – (sigh) (why bother?) I understand, you mean to sell our knowledge of the enemy.

Iadvrim: Indeed, the enemy of my enemy is my friend.

Jaqrakhal: And the others?

Iadvrim: We'll pick those up as we go on, the rest will have to fend off for themselves, I don't intend to scour the entire mountain for stray Goblins.

Jaqrakhal: Yes, quite right…off we go then.

Iadvrim: Off we go (snickers).

***

Back at Dhaldrog, Alabaster was relaying to Abaddon the events that transpired.

Abaddon: We are quite fortunate this Ormazd was so kind as to let us use the mountain to our advantage, I would've hated to get into a scuffle with an Oread.

Alabaster: He was a tough opponent indeed but a far match for you, I reckon, my Lord.

Abaddon: Of course, I only meant it would be a waste of my time. And what of the Goblin King? Please tell me you disposed of him.

Alabaster: I'm afraid not…

Abaddon: (sigh) I would expect a miss like this from Jamil but not from you.

Alabaster: My lord?

Jamil: If I may speak, my liege.

Abaddon: You may.

Jamil: Frankly, I would not have let him escape as he has valuable information on our plans, should he relay that information to some unfavourable bunch, the result would be most unsavoury.

Abaddon: Hear that, you brooding dimwit? He has valuable information and you let him go!

Alabaster: I…didn't think of that at the time…

Abaddon: It's because you don't think! You just smash things! Apparently, that's the only thing you're good at!

Jamil secretly smirks.

Alabaster: My deepest apologies, lord, allow me to make amends!

Abaddon: Gather the Dragons! Comb every inch of the land until you've found that weasel! And pray that you do or so help me Baal!

Alabaster: Yes, my lord! (Rushes off in a hurry).

Abaddon: I'm dealing with idiots…

Jamil: That's quite unfortunate, my lord.

Abaddon: How goes your retraining, Jamil (suddenly cuts him off).

Jamil: So far so good, my lord.

Abaddon: Stop adding 'my lord' to every sentence; it's annoying.

Jamil: Yes, my – (stops himself)

Abaddon: Come, let me see your results.

And so, they exchange a few blows but needless to say Jamil is easily bested.

Abaddon: Not good enough, you have one month to perfect it, otherwise I'll take your other arm and you'll have to hold a sword with your teeth (walks away).

Jamil throws his scimitar on the ground in frustration.

Now Abaddon climbs the highest hill in the vicinity and chants a spell and crows, ravens and snakes begin to gather about him, circling above and crawling below.

Abaddon: Go forth my loyal subjects, look for this creature, do not stop until he is found!

And the creatures go forth to do his bidding.

Few days pass and there is neither strand nor sound from Iadvrim much to Abaddon's displease.

Abaddon: …

Jamil: He is cunning, he knows these parts better than we do, it should be easy for him to evade our gaze.

Abaddon: Even the gaze of the crows and snakes I sent! Curse him! And curse your stupidity!

Alabaster: …

Abaddon: I have no choice now, I must hasten the process of forming the army, Jamil, tell Grough to send word to the other Orc Lords, tell them to meet me with their entire armies at Karazdhur Plain.

Jamil: It will be done.

Abaddon: In the meantime, I'll go see your father.

Jamil: To gather more magicians, I presume?

Abaddon: You presume correct (sighs, then switches to Dhalsarrian) I assume he is making his way to Kururi Ulu Rabiri[19], those two kingdoms are the closest to these regions.

Jamil: My lord I –

Alabaster: I would say Kururi is more probable my lord, it is a straight line down south from here.

Jamil realises he is not the one being addressed and hangs his head low.

Abaddon: Tell me, how long do you think it will take him to reach Kururi? What are your estimations?

Alabaster: Hmm … it is hard to say. From what I've seen by scouting with the Dragons the terrain is treacherous, filled with dense forests where it would be easy for one to get lost. On top of that there is a vast range of steep hills separating this region from Kururi, each filled with wild beasts.

Then we would have to consider the weather conditions. We are getting into autumn which means heavy rains and strong winds, the road will be muddy and hard to follow, not to mention it would be dangerous to travel under trees with a thunderstorm above your head. Traveling under such conditions would definitely set one back. Taking all of that into consideration I would say roughly around two months, perhaps three.

---

[19] Nidvelir or Elviun.

Abaddon: That is a good analysis, Alabashter, you can really use your brain when you want to. Let us say it takes Aratam Shinu[20] then, it would be another aradu to march back here with an army. So, that gives us around three months total to prepare …

Jamil feeling left out, not being able to understand the conversation, leaves to do his task with a sense of immense frustration.

Alabaster: Can it be done?

Abaddon: Who do you think you're talking to? For now, keep on training the knights as you were.

Alabaster: Yes, my lord (bows and leaves).

As he walks away one could see that he is walking with a limp, as Abaddon jammed his sword in his foot, completely severing the front part as punishment.

***

Dharmat: What need brings you here yet again, oh Dread One.

Abaddon: I'm in the need of magic users that are willing to dabble in nigromancy.

Dharmat: I'm afraid our religion does not tolerate black magic.

Abaddon: This is not the time for piety Dharmat, the hour is great and I'm in much haste.

Dharmat: You are asking of me to behest my sorcerers to renounce their fate and join your Dark God, I cannot and will not do it.

Lahar: My lord! My lord! I –

He comes rushing down in the throne room all exited and huffing but stops himself when the king gives him a scornful look and he takes notice of Abaddon's presence.

Lahar: I…found that book you were looking for (starts sweating nervously).

Dharmat: Excellent Lahar, I will see to it after I'm done with my guest.

Lahar: Yes…of course, pardon my rude entry… Lord Abaddon (bows to him).

Abaddon: And what is this book you were so eager to say that you found?

Lahar: It is uh…a book about sacramental rights (nervous smile). The Festival of Feasts is upon us you see, and my lord wished to conduct an ancient

---

[20] Two months.

ritual that has not been practiced for a long time so he…asked me to find this book.

Abaddon: Festival of Feasts?

Dharmat: It is the time of the year when we honour our Lord Karthas for all the bountiful provisions he has blessed us with, with a magnificent feast, you are welcome to attend.

Abaddon: Thanks for the offer but I have more pressing matters to attend to than stuffing my face like some pig.

Dharmat: (a single nerve pops up above his eye) That's too bad, it's a rare chance to taste all the fine delicatessens Hathasia has to offer.

Abaddon: Like I said, I'll pass.

Dharmat: As you wish (signals Lahar to leave the room).

Lahar does so.

Abaddon: Now about my need, I could go to more unpleasant ways to make you give me what you want should you not heed my words nicely.

Dharmat: Tell me, do you always resort to threats when you can't get what you desire?

Abaddon: I hate to stoop to such uncouth behaviour, but my need drives me and I'm not beyond employing such measures, uncouth as they may be, so I say again, I need some Sorcerers that are willing to dabble in bloody nigromancy. Surely there are at least a few wretched souls that are curious about it.

Dharmat: I'll see what I can do although I'm not making any promises.

Abaddon: Order them if you must, I need them ready by the morrow am I understood?

Dharmat: Perfectly.

Abaddon: Good (vanishes).

Dharmat: Pawar a kora[21]! Aghhh!

***

Dharmat: Lahar!

Lahar: I'm here my lord.

Dharmat: I'm guessing you made that blunder earlier because you found something of use!

Lahar: Indeed, my lord, indeed!

---

[21] Son of a whore.

Dharmat: Ah! Praised be, Mithras! What is it? Speak, man!

Lahar: (opens the book) This was written in a very ancient language, so it took me quite some time to decipher it. It mentions of a being known as 'The Judicator'.

Dharmat: Judicator, some kind of a judge?

Lahar: It is called many names one of which we should be familiar with, Namhur.

Dharmat: Namhur? The God of Justice.

Lahar: Yes, although as it is described here, I would say that it is some sort of a deity presiding over pacts and various other agreements.

Dharmat: Does it say of a way to summon it?

Lahar smiles pleasingly. Dharmat returns the smile.

And so Dharmat summons Tharmut, his most skilled Mystic to perform the ritual of summoning. A Mystic is the Hathasian equivalent of a Wizard, and a Wizard is someone who is exceptionally favoured by mana. Now mana is the source of magic in this world, everybody possesses it, even the smallest creatures but not all are graced equally by it.

Wizards are individuals that are born with remarkably high affinity towards mana, hence their innate talent for magic casting. The females are called Witches. Those that are with high mana affinity, but not as much as a Wizard, are called Sorcerers. Wizards and Sorcerers that specialise in a certain field of magic are called Mages. A Mage can also be someone who has less mana affinity than both the Wizards and the Sorcerers but possesses at least one of the elements.

'Magician' is the umbrella term used for all types of magic practitioners. There is a certain type of magician that channels their power from the planes of the Gods, through their faith: these are called Avatars. Avatars are the Human variant of the Dhalsarrian Warlock.

Tharmut performs the ritual, and the being makes an appearance; its skin is pale white, and its body is slim. It wears a long-sleeved gown, with ornate designs made out of gold and the gown itself is lilac in colour. It wears a tall judicial hat on its head and its face is veiled. In one hand it holds a set of scales and in another a grotesque mallet. Blue flames dance around its feet.

Judicator: Who dares summon me? (It speaks with a sinister and hoarse voice).

Dharmat: I do (he steps forward).

Judicator: And who might you be, mortal?

Dharmat: King Dharmat XIX, ruler of Hathasia.

Judicator: Name your grievance.

Dharmat: I entered a blood pact with the Demon-King Abaddon, and I wish to retract from it.

Judicator: One does not break away from a blood pact lest one of the parties involved perishes; liberation only comes with death or when the pact is fulfilled.

Dharmat: I already know that! But…I had no choice but to agree! If I didn't, I wouldn't have gotten Camelot!

Judicator: It sounds to me that you are just another foolish mortal that got way in over their head and now wants to weasel their way out of it. You reap what you sow, puny man.

Dharmat: Please, I'm begging you, there has to be a way.

Judicator: I shall review this pact.

Dharmat: Thank you.

Judicator: Be silent! Bring forth document number 0422108.

It speaks to one of the strange, undead cherub-looking creatures that accompanies it, and the creature produces the pact and holds it before its face.

Judicator: I see, it says here you are promised the rule of this Camelot kingdom in exchange for your help.

Dharmat: Correct.

Judicator: And judging by your desperation, the pact has not been fulfilled yet.

Dharmat: Yes.

Judicator: Are you aware of the fact that a failure to comply with the conditions stated here will result in death?

Dharmat: He did mention that.

Judicator: Then you have nothing to fear; once it is fulfilled, you shall be freed of the Blood Oath.

Dharmat: You don't understand! I can't wait that long! I can't stand him! We were supposed to be partners, but he is treating me like I'm his subject, making all sorts of demands and threats should I not comply!

Judicator: It is you who does not understand, puny man! (The flames at his feet grow more intense, startling Dharmat) the laws of the Universe do not work and bend on the will and whim of mortals! The only way out is by either fulfilment or death!

Dharmat: Death! (A slight glimmer of hope sparks in his eyes but then dies out in the same moment) …but…but I cannot kill him…he is too powerful …and he has my son…

Judicator: Thank you for wasting my time with your frivolous regrets! This will go in your records! (Slams his mallet down) The pact stands! And should you waste my time again, I shall have your soul!

Dharmat: You have my sincerest apologies…great Judge.

Judicator: Foolish mortal, this is why you do not deal with Demons! Let this be a lesson to you (vanishes in a spiral of blue flame).

Dharmat: (hangs his head in silence) …Tharmut…

Tharmut: Sire?

Dharmat: …How do you feel about nigromancy?

Tharmut: It certainly is a unique form of magic, and I am interested in it from an academic perspective, but I would dare not practice it for it is most foul.

Dharmat: Being interested …will suffice…this is an order; gather your men and have them ready by the morrow…you will be going to the land of Orcs in the North.

Tharmut: That is where the Lord Abaddon is…my king you don't mean to –

Dharmat: Did you not hear me? It is an order! If you value your lives, you will heed my words!

Tharmut: My lord… (bows and heads out).

Dharmat: Leave me…

Lahar: Sire…

Dharmat: **Leave!!**

Lahar bows and heads out as well, slightly stumbling due to being startled from his shout.

When Dharmat spoke he did not sound confident and kingly as he usually does, that was the voice of a man in defeat, a man who has consigned himself to the great wheels of destiny.

In Orcothrond, Abaddon addressed the other Orc Lords and told them that their armies will be converted into Undead for the war effort, even though they were displeased they ultimately conceded as he convinced them that due to the unfortunate turn of events the remaining Orc army will not suffice.

The next morning came, and Abaddon went to Hathasia to collect the Mystics. And then he tutored them in the art of nigromancy and they, having no choice but to obey, unwillingly mastered this art. Two months passed, the season shifted to that of autumn and the weather was dark and gloomy, filled with much rain. In that that the Hathasians Mystics underwent rigorous training in the arts of nigromancy with Abaddon. Already being magicians of a high calibre, and with his relentless and strict instructions, they had managed to master this form of magic to a very high level, sufficient for the task at hand, and more.

With the help of his new Nigromancers Abaddon managed to produce thousands of Dragonborn, fully grown and armed.

An armour gilded with gold was made for Andrakos, to distinguish him from the rest of them, fitting for a turtanu.

But he was not the only one fulfilling his machinations; Iadvrim through thick and thin had made it to Nidvelir, the home of the Dwarves, alone, for Jaqrakhal fell along the way to a pack of Dire Wolves. Now these wolves were spies of Abaddon as he had employed every fell creature in the Northern lands to search for the Goblin King and so word reached him of his passing into Dwarven territory.

Abaddon: So, he has made his way to Nidvelir, that weasel. You, make sure these wolves are well fed and rested, they deserve it (he addresses one of the Orc servants and he complies).

Jamil: This is troublesome, how do you think they will respond?

Abaddon: Knowing Baldur, he will push for an assault but I'm sure Arthur will be against it, paranoid as he is, ultimately it will be on the collective vote of the council.

Jamil: We are not ready, if they attack with their full force, we won't be able to repel them, and all of this effort would've been for naught.

Abaddon: Let's pray it doesn't come to that (sigh) if only I was at full strength again…

Jamil: You mean you still need time? I could've sworn you're already at your peak.

Alabaster: A power as great as the master's does not return so easily, if I had to reckon a guess, I would say he is still at sixty percent.

Abaddon: And you would be right…I don't yet have the power to repel the seven rulers at once.

Jamil: Then we are all but doomed…

Abaddon: You worry too much boy, a time for worrying will come should that come to pass.

Jamil: … I will prepare the army for an assault.

Abaddon: You do that.

Jamil nods and leaves.

Abaddon: Come, let me heal your foot, I can't have you limp in a battle.

Alabaster: My lord (presents his foot).

Abaddon: (heals it with 'Medium Healing') There.

Alabaster: Thank you my lord.

Abaddon: Go and call Guthug here.

Alabaster: At once (leaves).

After a while he returns with Guthug in tow.

Guthug: You called for me your lordship?

Abaddon: Guthug, it's time for you to fulfil a greater purpose.

Guthug: Ah music to my ears your lordship! How I longed for such an opportunity! I will do whatever you ask of me.

Abaddon: Good, Alabaster, make the preparations.

Alabaster: Yes, my lord (leaves).

***

In Andvelir, the capital of Nidvelir the council of the seven is taking place and all besides Baldur are present there in holographic shapes.

Baldur: Ladies and gentlemen, I call upon you in times of urgent need with news you must all hear.

Arthur: This news better be worth the time you are taking away from our preparations.

Baldur: Believe me you will want to hear what this wretch has to say.

Cyril: What wretch?

Baldur: Bring the knave in!

Upon his command, two guards enter and throw Iadvrim before them.

Folduin: A Goblin? What is a Goblin doing in your kingdom?

Baldur: He came all the way from the Iron Mountains to deliver me this message; speak!

Iadvrim: My name is Iadvrim great Lords and Ladies, as the venerable Baldur said –

Folduin: Cut the pleasantries and get to the point, we haven't all day.

Iadvrim: Right, I bring ill tidings from the North, the Demon Lord is amassing the Orc armies in Dhaldrog, crafting superior weapons and armour, and teaching them to fight. Not only that, but I also hear he is crossbreeding them with the Drakes, creating abominable creatures that breathe fire, and fight like Orcs!

Umbriela: Crossbreeding Orcs and Dragons? That's unheard of! Alas…it sounds like some foul machination he would attempt.

Arthur: This is getting more dangerous than we feared…to be able to utilise those primitive savages in such a manner…ingenious and most terrifying.

Urania: Hold on just a moment! How do we know this creature speaks the truth?

Iadvrim: I have no reason to lie your highness, he is the reason I stand before you in such manner, in exile and homeless, I offered him my service, but he repaid me with the death of my beloved daughter! And then he came on me with his Infernal Monster!

Urania: If what you say is true then we are indeed in dire straits…no doubt he means to use these armies to force the allegiance of the Demons in the East.

Baldur: Which is why I propose a full-on assault, a pre-emptive war if you will, strike the iron while it's hot!

Amra: I agree! I want to make him pay for what he did to Nirvalena.

Cyril: What are you all so afraid of? Is this not what we have been preparing for almost a year? This new threat means nothing, I say we meet him in an open battle like we planned to.

Baldur: No! Who knows what other devilry he has up his sleeve? If we wait, it will be the end of us!

Arthur: I agree with Cyril, we should focus on bolstering our defences as we were.

Cyril: (nods) We've beat him before we can beat him again, as I've said before, this time we are ready!

Umbriela: I agree, we shouldn't risk the loss of troops before the great storm, we don't know how much his own strength has returned, we might be sending our men to early graves.

Baldur: That's why we as rulers will go as well! If he is at half strength better for us! It will be easier to kill him!

Urania: No, we cannot afford the loss of a king or queen before the war, it will ruin the morale of the people.

Amra: I've heard enough! You are all cowards! Fear has gripped you so hard that you would rather sit behind your walls and wait for the wolf to come at your doorstep!

Arthur: Tis not fear but common sense, no good will come of weakening our fighting forces now.

Amra: Then we hit him with everything we've got! Send forth all legions!

Arthur: Think rationally! We yet lack the numbers for such an undertaking! It is better to crush the enemy all at once than fail and give him a chance to regroup and retaliate while we are weak and defenceless.

Amra: Lack the numbers? Surely you jest!

Arthur: Do you know so little of war you stubborn girl? Numbers alone don't win battles! Have you ever been to the Northern lands? I should think not! In fact, none of you have! You would be sending your men into certain doom!

Amra: Guh!

Folduin: Arthur speaks wisely, the unknown terrain works against us as well, therefore I am also against this pre-emptive war.

Arthur: It is decided then, no need to take a vote.

Baldur: You are making a mistake!

Amra: Spineless bastards all of you!

Iadvrim: Ahem! (Gains the attention of all) I may be of assistance there (smirks).

Baldur: (grins) What say you now?

Arthur: Tsk! I'm still against it! I will not be sending any men.

Folduin: Then I propose the following, since Baldur and Amra fancy themselves brave and bold, let them lead on the attack!

Baldur: Fine by me! My legion of Dwarves is more than I require!

Urania: Baldur! It is madness!

Baldur: I care not for your words! Amra, will you have my back?

Amra: The Vampires shall lend their assistance, Lord Baldur.

Baldur: Excellent! We will go down in the annals of history as the heroes that saved Avalon!

Cyril: I am almost tempted to join you, but I'd rather save my full strength for what's to come, I am sorry, but I will not be aiding you.

Amra: Just sit back and leave everything to us.

Arthur: Such brashness, such brazenness; you would imperil us all.

Baldur: Remember this, Arthur, you will be thanking us!

Arthur: Pah!

Umbriela: I pray for your success; may the grace of Shekinah be upon you.

Urania: And of all the Deities of Nature.

Cyril: Let Myeseczka allow you to fight with the strength of thousand wolves.

Folduin: And may the light of Solarion ensure that your paths are never darkened.

Arthur: You will receive no blessings from me.

Everyone looks at him scornfully.

Arthur: ...May Lugos bestow you with longer life... (says it unwillingly).

Iadvrim: I would say my blessing as well but I'm afraid we have no Gods.

Baldur: No need, we've received more than enough, I thank you, my friends, and I assure you that we will not fail your good will.

Arthur: Before I go, let me ask you something, creature; in your dealings with Abaddon did you see a human girl, young one, she would be around seventeen of age?

Iadvrim: Oh, I'm afraid I don't know, sire, I never stepped foot in Dhaldrog you see...

Arthur: Is that so...never mind then.

Iadvrim: This girl, is someone dear to you?

Arthur: She is my daughter.

Iadvrim: Sorry to disappoint you, the dealing went through my middleman Srank, and he didn't mention anything about a human girl.

Arthur: Pity...well, thank you anyway for your valuable information.

Iadvrim: Of course, it was my pleasure, sire.

Arthur: ... (disconnects).

Umbriela: Such a shame of what happened to her, she was a lovely girl.

Folduin: Indeed, my son was quite fond of her, they were good friends, it saddens me deeply that they shall not be able to share laughter together once more…

Urania: Once this evil is defeated her senses shall be restored and she will see the errors of her ways.

Baldur: Ay! Poor girl or not she's still a traitor and she should be dealt with accordingly.

Folduin: If the people of Camelot are wise, they will forgive her out of her young brashness; if not, I am more than willing to take her under my own wing, my son would be delighted as well.

Baldur: That is not your decision to make, Folduin.

Amra: Hah! Enough already, who cares about one little girl, as long as the queen lives, he can make many more; come, we have more pressing matters at hand.

Folduin: How can one harbour such feelings towards an innocent child? Does your heart not ache at all?

Amra: Why should it? She is no daughter of mine.

Urania: You need not reason with her; your words are wasted on a creature of the night.

Amra: What's that supposed to mean?

Urania: Like you don't know.

Amra: You tiny little bitch, how dare you? I have goodness in my heart as any of you!

Urania: And you are great at showing it too.

Cyril: Ladies, ladies, it's unbecoming of you to fight among yourselves, such petty trifles do not suit women of your stature.

Urania: Humph (disconnects).

Umbriela: Oh dear… (does the same).

Folduin and Cyril do the same, leaving only Amra.

Amra: That little…!

Baldur: Calm yourself, Amra, your focus is needed elsewhere, don't let the Faery's petty taunts get to you.

Amra: You speak justly (exhales) … You! Goblin! Can you draw us a map?

Iadvrim: But of course, my lady, we are not savages like those barbaric Orcs.

Amra: Good, get to it then, I have my armies to prepare, I will get back to you as soon as I'm ready.

Baldur: Alright.

Amra disconnects.

Baldur: Now I'll show those spineless idiots that the Dwarves are the best warriors!

Meanwhile in Dhaldrog

Abaddon: I welcome you back, Malgarashu.

Malgaras: It is an honour to be back Belunum.

Alabaster: I'm glad that we will be able to stain the battlefield with the blood of our enemies together yet again, Ahu[22]

Malgaras: As am I Alabashter Ahu.

Jamil: So, this is another one of your generals, my lord?

Abaddon: Malgaras here was the *turtanu* of my Doombringer legion.

Jamil: What a peculiar name.

Abaddon: They are called like that for a reason.

Jamil: I would love to hear it if you would be so graceful to tell me.

Abaddon: I will leave that to Malgaras as you acquaint him with the vicinity.

Jamil: Yes, my lord, this way, master Malgaras.

Abaddon: You are free to join them as well Alabaster.

Alabaster: And what will you do my lord?

Abaddon: I will be right back (vanishes).

Malgaras: Coming?

Alabaster: Right behind you (goes on).

***

Fulga: And then –

Morgana: Why did you stop?

Fulga: It seems we have a visitor.

Morgana: (looks up) Abaddon!

Abaddon: Hello princess, did you miss me?

She smiles.

And she immediately throws herself in his arms and he too embraces her...

---

[22] Brother.

CAPITVLVM XI
BELLVM PRAECAVTVM[x]

Morgana: Took you long enough, you big oaf!

Abaddon: That is no way to talk to your benefactor.

Morgana: Benefactor my arse, you left me here for two months!

Abaddon: Stop being a brat, I was busy!

Morgana: Humph!

Fragora: My, my, this child is an energetic one.

Abaddon: I hope she's put that energy into good use.

Morgana: Of course, who do you think I am?

Abaddon: Actions speak louder than words, show me what you've learned.

Morgana: Watch closely (she places her hands in a circular motion and produces a magical sphere).

Abaddon: Materialisation, one of the basics, good, now let me see you utilise it.

Morgana contracts the sphere into one of her palms and releases it in a form of projectile, causing a dent into one of the rocks.

Abaddon: Good, very good, expulsion. I see you've mastered the basics.

Morgana: Took me quite a while but now it's a piece of cake.

Abaddon: That's the easy part; the hard is yet to follow, you need to choose which path to take.

Morgana: Right, there is that.

Abaddon: Just so you know, I'm only versed in nigromancy and necromancy I can't teach you any other forms of magic.

Morgana: That's too bad because I wanted to be a Fire Mage.

Abaddon: Fire? Why fire?

Morgana: Because I want to burn everything.

Abaddon: That's not ominous at all.

Fragora: …

Morgana: You got a problem with that?

Abaddon: No, as long as that is what you truly desire.

Morgana: It is.

Abaddon: Well, there are pyromancers within my fire brethren, but they are under occupation so that's out of the question. I guess Ignatos could teach you something but in the end, it is all up to your elemental aptitude.

Morgana: Elemental aptitude?

Abaddon: Yes, we are all attuned to one of the primal elements, for instance my clan is of the dark one, the Angles are predisposed to light and so forth.

Morgana: And how do we decide that?

Abaddon: With this (produces a glass like stone with no colour) this is a special stone called 'The Arbitrator'.

Morgana: I've heard about this stone from Merlin.

Abaddon: Then that saves me the trouble of explaining what it does.

Morgana: I just have to pour my mana inside and it will glow accordingly.

Abaddon: Precisely.

Now, last time we talked about mana and how it affects us all. This time let us talk about magic. There are seven main elements that exist in this world and every from of magic is a subsidiary of a certain element. They are: Fire, Wind, Water, Earth, Lightning, Dark and Light. As Abaddon said, those like him are predisposed to darkness therefore they are able to utilise forms of magics such as nigromancy, and so forth. But even those who are predisposed to one element can use others as well, should they awaken it. They are in no way limited to their predisposed one.

Other examples of magic such as psychokinetic abilities fall in the Wind element for they are connected with the mind and Wind is associated with wisdom and the mental. Magic such as strengthening magic falls under the element of Earth and so forth. Now Wizards and Witches can utilise any form of magic since they are greatly predisposed to mana, and therefore possess affinity to all the elements at once. Since Sorcerers are less favoured by mana than Wizards, but still to a great degree, they usually possess affinity to two or three elements. Those that possess only one element go on to become Mages.

Now the case of the Human Wizard is unique only to them and it does not manifest in other magicians of other races. This is the way of nature balancing things out when it comes to racial traits. All the races have inherited some divine trait of the Gods in different measures. The Demons have their unnatural stamina, the Dwarves their unmatched mason skills, the Vampires have their superhuman speed and so on, while the Humans have their unparalleled Wizards.

Now Morgana pours her mana into the stone and after it receives enough quantity, it glows light blue.

Morgana: Oh!

Abaddon: Congratulations, you are a Lightning Mage.

Morgana: Wait, it's changing colour…

Abaddon: Well would you look at that, you have Dark element also.

Morgana looks up at him.

Fulga: (as I thought, darkness laid in this girl from the start…)

Morgana: That's wonderful! That means I can learn magic from you!

Abaddon: Indeed, however I'm afraid it will have to wait.

Morgana: What do you mean?

Abaddon: It means that you'll have to stay here and learn how Lightning works from Fragora.

Morgana: No! Not again!

Abaddon: Listen to me, there is a chance that war may come to me sooner than I thought, it's safer for you to stay here.

Fragora: War? What are you saying, Dread One?

Abaddon: Come, I'll tell you everything…

***

Morgana: That's awful…

Abaddon: Now do you understand? The enemy knows of my position, and I can't tell in how many numbers they will strike.

Morgana: So, you mean to tell me that you may lose?

Abaddon: There is a certain chance that it may come to pass. If they release a full-scale attack, then I'm afraid victory is all but lost.

Morgana: No! That can't be!

Abaddon: We are not ready…the Dragonborn I have are not enough to take on the entire force of Avalon.

Fragora: Then I must mobilise the others, we will fight with you to death or glory.

Abaddon: Thank you Fragora but even that will not avail us, without the other Demon armies I can't win even if Dharmat would ride out to my aid. And I am not yet at full strength to repel the other rulers.

Fragora: Like I said, we are with you to whatever end.

Abaddon: And I don't intend to just roll over and die, if we are going down, we will take as many of them as we can.

Fragora: Damn right!

Abaddon: Morgana…if anything should happen to me…you're in charge.

Morgana: Don't say that! Stop raising flags!

Abaddon: I must think of the worst outcome.

Morgana: B-but! Why me? I don't know anything about leading!

Abaddon: Don't worry, you are a strong girl, and you will have Jamil and my generals at your side, even Argyros, all of them will be of your help.

Morgana: Why would they follow someone like me? I'm a nobody to them…just a human girl…

Abaddon: (takes off his crown) I leave my crown in your care, with this no one will dare question you.

Morgana: You're placing a big burden on my shoulders… (her eyes tear up).

Abaddon: I know but I can't think of anyone else more worthy.

Morgana: I can't …I can't do this…I can't!

Abaddon: Listen, if I entrust this to someone else there will be chaos, my people have done it in the past and will do it again. You as my confidant, my protégé have the most right to wear this, only you can act as a deterrent amongst the three clans. You are strong, Morgana, believe more in yourself.

Morgana: Alright…alright…I understand…

Abaddon: Kneel.

Morgana: Kneel?

Abaddon: You know what kneeling is, right?

Morgana: Tsk, of course, I know! I just don't –

Abaddon: Can you do as I say without any further comments?

Morgana: Okay. Okay, I'll kneel… (does so).

Abaddon takes out Absharu and taps her on both shoulders.

Morgana: (surprised).

Abaddon: And now I pronounce you Princess Regent of Dhalsarria.

Morgana gasps from disbelief.

Fragora: Oh, dear me, such an honour!

Abaddon: Arise, Mistress Morgana.

Morgana: By Bethor's beard, I can't believe you did that…

Abaddon: Now it's official, and Fragora here is our witness.

Fragora nods.

Morgana: I don't know what to say! This is…

Abaddon: You have to promise me one thing; if I perish, you must set out back to the East and convince the others of joining with you in an assault of Avalon, tell them that they will be next if nothing is done, surely that will stir them to action.

He takes both of her hands.

Abaddon: I entrust my dream in your hands.

Morgana: I promise! I won't let you down! You have my word.

Abaddon: Good, good, I must return now and see to the preparations.

Morgana: (hugs him) Thank you so much for this, it means a lot to me.

Abaddon: You don't have to thank me; it was only natural.

Morgana: Can I try it on?

Abaddon: Go ahead.

Morgana: (puts it on her head) Well? How do I look?

Abaddon: It might be a little too big, but it fits you well.

Fragora: You look like a true queen.

Morgana: A queen in the need of a bath, I reek, haven't had a bath in a week.

Fragora: Well, you were the one who refused to bathe until you mastered that move.

Morgana: Touché.

Abaddon: (slightly chuckles) I'm going now.

Morgana: Wait! I want to give you something in return as well.

Abaddon: What could that possibly be.

Morgana: You'll have to come a bit closer.

Abaddon: (leans down a bit) Is this good enough for you?

Morgana: (takes off his hood) It's perfect (gives him a kiss).

Fragora: Oh dear!

Abaddon: I kind of saw that coming.

Morgana: Shut up! (Slightly blushing).

Abaddon: Say princess, you don't hate me?

Morgana: Hate you? What for?

Abaddon: I took over Merlin's body.

Morgana: ... I see nothing wrong with that, you gave Merlin a second chance, if you hadn't done that, he would've been fodder for worms by now...even if you're not Merlin himself ...you are still trying to do something grand with his former body...even if you're not Merlin himself, I still – (stops herself).

Abaddon: Now I'm going for real, and if Baal wills it, I will return for that crown.

Morgana: Wait!

Abaddon: You have something else you wish to give me?

Morgana: As a matter of fact, I do (gives him her own crown).

He takes it.

Morgana: Now you have to come back and return it to me.

Abaddon slightly smiles and hangs the crown on his waist.

Morgana: Farewell...

Abaddon: Farewell princess (vanishes).

Fragora: You were going to tell him, weren't you?

Morgana: Now is not the time for that, come, take me to the lake before you set off to your task.

Fragora: For that you must climb up first (lays down).

Thus, Fragora leads Morgana to the lake so she can take a bath. There, she takes a look at her own reflection in the water.

Morgana: It really does suit me (smiles).

Fragora: Wait for me here I will be right back.

Morgana: Don't worry, I'm not going anywhere.

Fragora flies off.

Jamil: My lord, you are back.

Abaddon: As you can see, how go the preparations?

Jamil: Everything is proceeding as it should.

Abaddon: Good, where is Malgaras?

Jamil: He is having ale with Alabaster at the local tavern.

Abaddon: What's the matter? You don't drink?

Jamil: I hate the taste of ale.

Abaddon: Pansy.

Jamil: Not only that…they started talking in Dhalsarrian and I felt left out so I left…

Abaddon: Then perhaps you should start learning the language since you serve me.

Jamil: I would if someone would teach me.

Abaddon: I'll tell Malgaras to do it, Alabaster wouldn't like that idea.

Jamil: I thought maybe…

Abaddon: You thought what?

Jamil: … Nothing.

Abaddon: Exactly. Now take me to this tavern.

Jamil: But my lord, beer is not a suitable drink for a person of your stature.

Abaddon: Do they have wine?

Jamil: No.

Abaddon: I thought so but no matter, I don't like the taste of ale either but I'm not beyond drinking it and I need a drink, come!

Jamil: Um sire?

Abaddon: What is it?

Jamil: What happened to your crown?

Abaddon: You'll find out.

They head to the tavern where Abaddon meets up with the two other Demons.

Malgaras: Your highness (bows).

Alabaster: Sire (bows).

Abaddon: Greetings you two. Master! Two rounds of ale! (In Orcish).

Master: Coming right up my lord (in Orcish).

Abaddon: (ignoring Jamil he switches to Dhalsarrian) Listen very closely, in the event of something happening to me in the upcoming battle, you are to follow Morgana's orders.

At the sound of Dhalsarrian, Jamil's heart sinks again and he clenches his teeth in frustration.

Jamil: What about Morgana … my lord?

Alabaster: Who is this 'Morgana', my lord?

Abaddon: (ignoring Jamil) She is the girl that travelled with me up to my coming here, I left her in Terebri on Garazu Drakizim, for her safety.

His frustration grows and so he gets up to leave.

Jamil: If my lord would excuse me, I will go tend to the army.

Abaddon: No, I will not excuse you, sit down.

Jamil: With all due respect, sire, but I cannot understand a word you're saying!

His tone attracts gazes from other patrons.

Abaddon: Sit down, and **do not!** Raise your voice at me.

Jamil: (timidly sits down) My apologies … I let my frustration get the better of me.

Abaddon: That's why you need to sit. Don't you know? Listening is the best way to pick up on a language.

Jamil: Yes … of course …

Alabaster chuckles at the way Jamil is treated.

Malgaras: Sarrunum, you would entrust the rule of our people to a human girl?

Abaddon: She is not just any girl. She was a princess of Camelot, and she is loyal to me, she obeys my will and I have made her Princess Regent of Dhalsharri.

Malgaras: Outrageous!

Abaddon: Remember your place, turtanu!

His voice voices like a mighty thunder throughout the tavern startling the other guests as well.

Malgaras: Forgive me my lord I was overcome in the moment (bows deeply).

Alabaster: Yes, forgive him, he just came back from the dead and seems to have forgotten who is sarru here!

Malgaras bows even deeper, his head almost touching the wooden table.

Abaddon: Raise your head, and do not ever speak out of turn again am I clear?

Malgaras: Yes, my lord!

Abaddon: Good, and my decision is final, all of you are to aid her in her rule, no exceptions.

The two of them utter 'yes, your highness' unanimously.

Abaddon: One more thing Malgarashu, Jamilki Dhalshanum Lamati.

Malgaras: As you wish Sarrunum.

Abaddon: Jamil, I just told Malgaras that he is to tutor you in Dhalsarrian. I will check your progress monthly, and I pray that it goes better than your fencing.

Jamil: Understood my lord …

Abaddon: Good. Master, another round!

Master: Right away, my lord.

In two weeks' time, the armies of Dwarves and Vampires, fifteen thousand strong, are ready to cross the border into Orcothrond, the land of Orcs.

Word reaches Abaddon through a raven that was patrolling the borders.

Abaddon: So, they've come, and faster than expected. Alabaster! Muster the legions! The time has come!

Abaddon: At once!

In a matter of minutes, the army is prepared and marched outside the city. Abaddon turns around on the hill overlooking the plains and his armies of Undead and Dragonborn lay spread out, ready, and hungry for blood.

Abaddon: The hour is upon us when the enemy comes knocking on our doorstep! Their numbers may be vastly superior to ours, but we will not falter…

Another raven comes gawking, Abaddon stretches out his hand and it lands on it.

Abaddon: Talk to me…

The raven relays the message and flies away.

Abaddon: Baal be praised, his mercy is with us…My messengers tell me that the army of the enemy is made only of Dwarves and Vampires!

The soldiers, including the three generals shout out in praise.

Abaddon: Our Lord Baal sends us his grace!

The Demons start shouting 'Guz Baltu Baal!' which means 'long live Baal' and the rest follow, resulting in a cacophony of praising that echoes throughout the area.

Abaddon: My army! My soldiers! They think that they are enough to subdue us, destroy us! But we will show them the folly of their ways! There will be no mercy! They will fall on our swords and break against our shields! Today we stain the land with the blood of those that oppose us! To war!

Again, they roar with the shouts of victory, and they march on to battle chanting, and this if what they chanted, in Dhalsarrian.

'Sarrunum Ashtushum Dektunu
Karbu Belutu Beluu
Hatapu Alattunu Ishatki
Errenki Irrii Imbii
Batakuneru Lamashtam

Kamakuneru Eliu Abarrii
Daamkuneru Shamu Burumu!'

Translated in the Common Tongue it would be as follows:
'We fight for our King and God
Blessed be the reign of our Lord,
Sacrifice we make in blood
By the entrails of Dwarven scum.
Vampires, we'll tear apart
Pile their bodies up high,
Blot out the sun and the sky!'

Filling the air with the clanging of armour as well, as the Dragons circle the skies above.

***

Baldur: We will rest here.

Amra: Rest? There will be no rest!

Baldur: We've been marching five days straight; the men are exhausted we deserve a short break!

Amra: We are already into enemy territory, and you want to take a break, are you out of your damn mind?

Baldur: Relax! According to the Goblin the enemy does not know about this forest region.

Amra: You would trust this creature?

Baldur: We have no choice, besides, not all are monsters with unlimited stamina like you.

Amra: Fine! But only an hour! No more!

Baldur: An hour is more than we need.

Amra: Good, set camp!

***

Amra: I don't like this place, there are too many ravens and crows flying around, it makes me feel uneasy.

Baldur: You're scared of few birds? And you call yourself a queen?

Amra: Not scared I just don't like them; they are bad omens.

Baldur: Not only scared but superstitious as well, ridiculous.

Amra: Don't you believe in anything?

Baldur: Aye, I believe in my axe.

Amra: Primitives…

Baldur: I'll have you know that –

Amra: Shh! Be quiet!

Baldur: What is it?

Amra: I heard something.

Baldur: Hah! Not only scared and superstitious but paranoid too! Yer a riot lassie!

Amra: Silence you old fool! There it is again! A creaking amongst the leaves…

Baldur gulps and takes his axe.

After a suspenseful moment one of the Dwarves falls on the ground, screaming...

Baldur: Enemies! To arms!

As the rest gather their weapons, a shower of needles comes raining down from the treetops taking out a number of Dwarves and Vampires alike, sowing disarray amongst their ranks and lo! Amongst that confusion a band of Goblins descend upon them. These are the remnants of the Goblin army that Iadvrim left behind. A few days back, led by Grulk, the Goblin champion, they had made their way to the gates of Dhaldrog and pledged their allegiance to Abaddon once more, and thus he tasked them with garrisoning the regions where the enemies would be most likely to pass.

The Goblins manage to cut down a few Dwarves, exploiting the gaps in their armours on an expert level, jumping them in groups or doing so individually.

With the Vampires they have no such luck since these creatures use their monstrous strength to fend them off with ease, cleaving them with their blades or bare hands and feasting on their blood.

But the Goblins are persistent and nimble creatures, and they succeed in taking out few with the assistance of their mighty Hobgoblins.

Amra orders her mages to raise a barrier and they form a cocoon of blood around them, fending off any other attackers, allowing them to dispatch the ones inside with ease. The Stonemasons, which is to say the Dwarven mages, help in this by creating Golems of stone that heavily bash the tiny Goblins.

Baldur himself has cut down dozens of Goblins including three Hobs with his mighty axe Sundrian which means 'Sunderer' and Amra with her sword Sangcroue, 'Bloodfang'.

Everything seems fine for a moment when the roar of a creature disrupts the solemn silence.

Baldur: By Fafnir's beard, what is that?

Amra: I have no idea but be on your guard, whatever it is it doesn't sound pleasant.

Baldur: Well, let it come! This Dwarf hasn't had his fill of skulls to bash!

The ground begins to shake beneath their feet when the creature begins to approach closer and closer, and finally reveals its visage; it is none other than Grulk, the new leader of the Goblin army but not Grulk as he was before; with his magic, Abaddon had changed him into a Bugbear, a creature more evolved than a Hobgoblin, bigger and much stronger, with razor sharp teeth and glowing red eyes, ghastly green fur all over his body, donned in heavy magical armour and magical great axe with Dhalsarrian runes on it. But he was not alone for with him he had dozen other Hobs who had undergone the same treatment, all armed with great weapons like clubs and maces.

Amra: What are those horrid abominations?

Baldur: Don't ask me; I've never seen anything like it in my whole life!

The Bugs come down on the barrier with great furry and shake it, the Mages work their blood magic, and the cocoon produces sharp spikes that stab at them, but their armour and thick bodies avails them, this infuriates them even further and they smash like the breaking of thousand lightnings, ultimately breaking it asunder and a swarm of Goblins comes rushing in.

The joint armies meet them, and the clash begins once more, filling the forest with the sound of steel and screams.

To aid them in this clash, Amra's Phantomancers, Vampire Mages specialising in the art of summoning wraiths and other ghoulish creatures from the Netherworld, the plane of their God, Noctis, summon a band of shadowy, spectral wraiths that assail the Goblins. Them being incorporeal gives them an edge against the Goblin's weapons, enabling them to rush in unharmed and kill them by invading their bodies. Some of the more experienced Phantomancers call forth a number of Soul Wraiths. These spirits of horrendous countenance with torn lips, long, wretched, limbs and nailed, gnarled fingers, wearing spectral, torn hooded cloaks, each carry a lantern in which they store the souls they steal from their victims. These wraiths inhibit the Everdark, a place of everlasting darkness where Noctis, the God of Vampires, resides within the Netherworld.

With spectral chains they attack the onrush of Goblins and yank their souls from their bodies. The lesser Goblins take fright at the sight of these apparitions and waver, but the fearless Bugbears trudge on.

Thuri, Baldur's cousin rushes at one of the Bugs and exchanges a few blows with it before being overpowered and flung on the ground, and the Bug being thrice his size cuts him in half with his axe which is the size of his body.

Grief-stricken, Baldur charges at the beast, swinging Sundrian, and the beast swings his axe as well, and when they meet the latter breaks under its magical might. Baldur swings again and cleaves the Bug's legs in half, right at the knees and it falls flat on the ground, screaming from the pain. Baldur takes a third swing and splits its head open, spilling the brain all over the woodland floor.

Amra is also locked in a struggle with a Bug, stabbing with Bloodfang through an opening in the armour but the creature's tough skin holds the strike, and it knocks her down on the ground. Now this Bugbear wields a massive club and slams it down upon Amra even breaking the ground with the impact but lo! Amra turns into blood and splashes all around; it turns out that Amra was in fact a 'Blood Clone' and the blood wraps around the Bug and holds it in place, giving the real Amra a chance to strike from its rear and cut its head clean off with one mighty strike.

Seeing his comrades go down so easily by the hands of these great rulers of races, Grulk lets out a wild bellow, signalling the last horde of Goblins to come rushing in. But this time it is not only Goblins that come in the fray, but Mountain Trolls as well, fully armoured and armed with war hammers. Together with another group of Bugbears they hit the Dwarves like a tidal wave sweeping them left from right, bashing their heads and breaking their bodies.

The Vampire fighters however, despite suffering great casualties as well, hold their ground much better, dispatching the Trolls with their swiftness, evading their strikes as graceful as the flow of water, and striking with deadly precision. One of the Vampire captains stops a hammer of a Troll with her bare hands and kills the creature by piercing its throat with a blade made of blood, using it as an extension of her own sword for she could not reach it herself.

Amra: At this rate, we'll be overrun! There may be more!
Baldur: Leave it to me! Hiyah!

He takes a mighty leap into the air and comes crashing down with Sundrian, using the magical power of the axe to rend asunder the ground beneath the Trolls and Bugbears and sends them falling into a dark abyss.

At that moment Grulk steps up and challenges Baldur.

Grulk: I will kill you, tiny Dwarf (he grunts).
Baldur: Come then!
With a mighty bellow, he comes at Baldur.
Baldur: Dheur un yeor![23]

And they clash, Grulk's axe being empowered with a powerful magic will not be undone so easily so he holds his ground. He manages to strike at Baldur but lo! His royal runic armour shields him from damage and Grulk's axe bounces off as if it had struck rubber. The enraged Bugbear attempts to knock him on the ground but is unable due to the armour's protection, so Baldur chops off his leg and Grulk staggers but miraculously does not fall on the ground and keeps on fighting even with one leg.

On the contrary, it is as if his maimed state grants him more power and he fights with more vigour. As his attacks become more ferocious, Baldur finds himself overpowered by Grulk's might and not only that, his axe works its magic and it breaks the protection on Baldur's armour making him susceptible to attacks and Grulk with a mighty swing, slashes him across the chest but the mithril mail underneath halts the blade from reaching his skin.

Amra dispatching a few remaining Goblins comes to his aid by trying to stab him in the back, but the attack is reflected due to the magic on the armour, and she only succeeds in distracting him and he turns and grabs her by the throat.

---

[23] Death to you!

Amra: Filthy scum! How dare you touch me!

Now the blood vessels on her face pop up and her eyes become bloodshot, then with her left hand she grabs the arm that is holding her and rips it clean off, then with the other she pierces straight through his heart leaving a gaping hole. Grulk lets out a sad sounding moan and slumps lifelessly on the ground.

Baldur: Thanks, I owe ya one.

Amra: Can't even handle a mere creature like that, how pathetic.

Baldur: That was no ordinary armour and weapons it had; Abaddon's foul magic was infused into them.

Amra: All I'm hearing are excuses.

Baldur: Pah!

Amra: Whatever the case, they sure did a number on us…

Baldur: They knew we were coming…the vermin set us up…I'll have his head when we get back!

Amra: This is what we get from trusting a lower lifeform…

Baldur: Let's count the dead…

Amra: No, we need to move, we can't stay here.

Baldur: Aye…yer right lassie…by the looks of it my light infantry took the most beating…

Amra: We didn't pass so lightly as well…come we'll leave all this behind, no time to pack.

Then, yet another mighty roar tears through the air, even shaking the trees themselves.

Baldur: Now I recognise that one…

Amra: Dragons… (as she looks up at the sky).

CAPITVLVM XII

SPIRITVS DRACONVM ET POTESTAS DAEMONVM[xi]

Amra: Dragons! Brace for impact!

Baldur: Shields up!

Upon his command, the Dwarves of the heavy infantry raise their shields above their heads.

Flammos (second in command of the Fire Dragons): Set their flesh on fire!

And so, the flock of Fire Drakes spews forth the burning inferno from their bodies, setting aflame trees, animals, and ground alike. The fire begins to rage around the invading armies and some of the soldiers fall victim to the scorching blaze. Dragon fire is no ordinary fire, hotter than any flame that exists in this world, second only to the infernal flames of the Fire Demons of Dhalsarria, it burns the flesh within seconds, leaving only piles of ash behind.

Their runic armours provide protection to some degree, but they do not grant full immunity and so, many fall.

Baldur: Keep up those shields!

Amra: Fall back! Fall back! Mages, cover us!

The Vampire mages erect their barriers of blood again which manages to grant them safe cover, but the Fire Drakes are not the only ones in flight; the Wyverns under Frigga's command set forth their icy breaths and freeze the blood, and the lightning breath of the Lightning Dragons breaks it with its destructive force leaving them vulnerable to attacks.

Baldur: Bloody Drakes!

Amra: We are almost at the edge of the forest! March forth!

Baldur: Stonemasons!

The Dwarven Stonemasons use their stone magic to provide more cover for the troops. Granted, stone does not make much difference here but this is no ordinary stone, but one made of magic that repairs itself upon receiving damage.

Frigga: The Dwarves think they are safe beneath their stonework! Prove them wrong!

All at once, the Wyverns release an attack that makes it seem as if a massive blizzard has fallen upon the area, turning everything around into icicles. Then quickly, the Fire Drakes spew their scorching flames and from that quick overheating the stone expands and breaks, leaving the company vulnerable yet again. Some are even flung on the ground by the sheer impact of the stone breaking.

After the excruciating assault they finally make it out of the woods and into a clearing. As soon as they reach it, the Dragonkin disperse but do not retreat entirely.

Amra: They felt back huh, since we are on an open field, they are being more cautious but no matter; open fire!

The Mages begin to shoot magical projectiles out of their staffs and Vampiric archers retaliate with their blood arrows.

Baldur: Defensive towers!

The Stonemasons erect stone towers around the ranged units, granting them protection and elevated ground for better shooting. Phantomancers summon more Shadow Wraiths to their cause. They however cannot invade their bodies like with the Goblins, for the Dragon's hide repels all form of outside magical influences. So, in order to make up for this the Wraiths seek for an opening when the Dragon opens his maw, to strike, or more cleverly they insert themselves through their nostrils.

This causes the Dragonkin to fly to higher altitudes in order to avoid being attacked, but this makes them unable to return the attack; now they will have to be more careful as they approach.

Amra, unaffected by the Dragonkin's tactic, climbs one of the towers and stands at the top of it, then using her own blood magic she produces a gigantic bow and arrow and shoots the missile hitting one of the Fire Drakes and taking it out. As the Dragon's scales are harder than any steal and fend off magical attacks the only way to despatch them is to aim for the folds where their scales overlap; this is their only weakness, and the reason why they are so feared and are so formidable as it requires pinpoint precision to strike,

Baldur: Raise the towers! Let's take the fight to them!

And now the Stonemasons increase their size, granting them better range.

Flammos: The wretches are starting to fight back! Take down the towers!

One of the Fire Drakes spews continuous fire, burrowing into the foundations of one of the towers but its regenerative properties keep it at bay, and he is struck down before he can make it collapse.

Seeing as this will not avail them the Dragonkin gain momentum and ram their gigantic bodies into the towers breaking them apart.

This does prove effective and one by one the towers begin to fall on the ground.

Amra: Accursed lizards!

She flings her sword at one of the Dragonkin and kills it, then retrieves it with her psychic powers.

Frigga spots her atop the tower and releases her wintery breath upon her but Amra shields herself with blood magic. She flings her sword again at her, but the Wyvern protects herself by turning her backside where the scales are tougher, and the blade bounces off her pale scales.

She continuously attacks her using her psychokinesis, but Frigga skilfully dodges her attacks and retaliates with her breath, freezing the sword in mid-air.

Now Amra sends out psychokinetic waves towards Bloodfang and with them she shatters the ice, and it returns to her hand. However, this creates an opening for one of the Wyverns to slam into the tower and bring Amra down.

As she is falling; however, she channels the powers of the night god Noctis and gains bat wings that allow her flight. Using this ability, she clashes with the Queen of Wyverns.

Frigga parries her attacks with her talons but this in turn makes it more difficult for her to fly as Wyverns do not possess front limbs. Thus, she begins to use her feet and tail instead which proves much more effective.

Amra: Why fight a lost cause? Join us and avoid death, it's still not too late.

Frigga: Save your breath, bloodling, you'll never get me on your side, I swore an oath, and I will take it to my grave!

Amra: Then die!

She lunges with her sword, but Frigga spits an icy saliva on her face that freezes over and renders her blind, then proceeds to turn her frozen solid. Now she swings her tail in order to try and shatter her, but Amra breaks free from the icy prison and grabs her by the tail and using her devilish strength swings her around and tosses her towards the ground. The force behind the attack was so fierce that Frigga is plummeting towards the ground at an alarming rate.

She tries to regain her altitude but to no avail as it also left her groggy like a child after a coaster ride. Amra uses this opportunity to strike at her and pierces her bloody with Bloodfang, putting an end to her existence, and thus the Winter Queen of Graziriz was no more.

Wyvern: She killed the Queen! The Queen is dead!

Glauros (second in command): That one is dangerous! Fall back! Fall back!

Flammos: Stand and fight you cowards!

The Wyverns begin to retreat on Glauros' command.

Fire Drake: Captain! What should we do?

Flammos: Urg! Fight of course! Fight till your last breath!

Amra spots Flammos and rushes towards him however she is intercepted by the flaming breath of a couple of Dragons but using her psychokinetic powers she creates a force field around her that shields her from the fire, and she presses on.

Flammos: Come on then! Raargh!

Flammos rushes as well and attacks with his mighty talons, and Amra parries with Bloodfang. Having front limbs, the Fire Drake is doing better at holding on against Amra as he can use the scales on his arms to block, if necessary, which makes it frustrating for Amra.

Amra: I'm willing to make the same proposition I did to that Wyvern, fight for us and live.

Flammos: And I'll tell you the same thing she did; up yours, bloodsucker!

Amra: Stubborn lizard! Why fight for that Demon? You owe fealty to no one.

Flammos: It's not about fealty, you dumb cunt, it's about honour and respect!

Amra: A force of destruction talking about honour and respect? I never thought I'd see this day, does this have to do with that oath that Wyvern mentioned?

Flammos: 'That Wyvern' had a name – Frigga! And yes, it has to do with that, when Abaddon first came, we gave our word to fight for him. He didn't even use force, all he had to do is appear and show us his power and that moment we knew he is a person we can stand behind. He told us 'Fight for me and I'll see your desires fulfilled', and that's all the reason we needed.

Amra: If you did it for him you can do it for us as well, once we defeat him his dreams of reconquering Avalon will be shattered and scatter like dust in the wind.

Flammos: (chuckles) Defeat him? Shatter his dreams? What a joke, if you truly believe that then you really are a dumb cunt, you are nothing compared to him, farts in the wind is what you are, we burned your world with that person once and we will be by his side when he does it again.

Amra: You will die before you can lay your eyes on such fate!

Flammos: Will I?

Amra: Join your comrade in the next world!

Just as she was going to rush him, Tonitros, Fulguros' eldest son strikes Amra with his lightning breath from behind her as she was distracted by her conversation, and now Flammos seizes the opportunity and rakes her with his flaming talons, setting her arm ablaze.

Overcome by agonising pain she cuts off her arm before the flame can progress any further and then she reforms her arm.

Amra: You will pay for that!

Now Tonitros comes at her, but she evades his attack with the swift movement the Vampires possess and reappears behind him, grabs him by the tail and slams him into Flammos.

Seeing the pinch their leaders are in the rest of the Dragons fly in to assist them, but they fall under Amra's blade instead. Soon the land bellow was stained red by the blood of the fallen rulers of the skies.

Tonitros: She is too powerful! We must retreat!

Flammos: No! I will not run like those cowardly Wyverns!

Tonitros: We've done enough! There is nothing much else we can do!

Flammos: I will fight!

And now Flammos spits out a fireball of gargantuan proportions right at Amra's direction but with her powers she redirects it right back at him and he topples down on the ground with a mighty slam.

The troops bellow cheer and rave at their seeming victory over the Dragonkin but it is short lived when the loudest roar ever heard so far rends the sky and the air. Unlike the ones before this one shivers the skin, freezes the blood, and rattles the bones. All turn towards the source of this monstrous bellow.

Tonitros: He's come… (he whispers).

The Black Dragon King has finally arrived in his full glory; his wings blackening the sun and his mighty roar parting the clouds and shaking the earth beneath. And wherever he goes, Abaddon follows.

Now his mighty bellow is accompanied by the chanting of the Demon King's army that rises on the horizon and these two sounds are the only thing that can be heard among the grave silence.

And the remaining Dragons rejoice adding their own bellows in the cacophony of cheering.

Baldur: Stand your ground, lads! The real battle begins now!

Amra flies down to join her troops as well.

'Deur un ur inimur!' 'Death to our enemies,' yell out the Dwarves as they get themselves in position.

The Dragons now fly over to the other side to join the oncoming army.

Soon, the armies of Abaddon, numbering 20,000, align themselves opposite of their enemies, a few miles away, roaring and slamming their armours and shields.

Abaddon lands with Argyros at the helm, and when he does, tremors are sent throughout the ground that are felt all the way on the opposite side, making them slightly lose balance.

Now, Abaddon pulls out Absharu and raises it high in the air.

Abaddon: Nadunim Damunum!

Bring me their blood! He yells and places his hand forward signalling the charge and they descend into battle.

Amra: Volley!

And her archers release a volley of blood-thorn arrows but none of the opposing army falls.

Amra: What devilry is this?

Baldur: Those are not Orcs…they are Undead!

Amra: Another detail that weasel left out!

Baldur: Aim for their heads! Cut off their heads! Chargeee!

And their armies rush on and so they meet halfway, and the clash begins. The sound of steel clashing against steel now fills the air instead.

The Vampiric Hemomancers release a volley of magic projectiles from the newly renewed towers and now Argyros takes flight. He flies past by and with one mighty mouth beam brings them down again, causing them to crash down upon the armies of Dwarf and Vampire.

The Undead Orcs prove themselves as formidable opponents against the tinier Dwarves, with their big stature and unholy strength. Especially the Orcs from the Warlord class who possess the bulkiest bodies of their brethren. They come down with their giant flails, breaking both shield and armour.

One of the Orcs even picks up one Dwarf and bites his head clean off, basking in the fountain of blood that ensues and drinking it as well.

But the Dwarves are a feisty bunch and will not be undone so easily, especially those of the medium and heavy infantry of who the former come in, with mightier armour and weapons and cleave at the Undead Orcs.

Guts and blood from both sides spill on the floor, brain matter and goo as well stain the earth. The stench of blood very soon runs rampart turning the air rancid and heavy to breathe. But these are warriors and to warriors the stench of blood is like the fragrance of roses.

The mighty medium infantry by cleverly using their runic weapons rend the magic armour on the legs of the Undead, bringing them to their knees and looping off their heads.

However, these are not a mindless rabble but trained knights, soon adapting to the situation and anticipating their leg strikes.

To make matters worse from behind of the Orc vanguard now come in the Red Dragonborn with their fire breath, led by Andrakos.

They use their draconic strength to topple the Dwarves and boil them alive, as their weapons shatter and break upon contact with their scales.

Andrakos fiercely brings down his foes, one by one be it by chopping, stabbing or burning, there is simply no stopping the first Drakeling.

Now come the Blue ones, spawns of Fulguros with their breaths of destructive lightning, easily breaking the runic protections of the Dwarves and with their enchanted hammers breaking their bodies.

Finally come the Black, produced from the loins of Argyros himself, the mightiest of the Dragonborn, need no weapon but their bare hands to rend asunder the armour of their foes and bring them death.

Thus, the vanguard of the enemy army is easily overrun but this is far from over; now the mighty Skelthuz Bhregor, 'The Ironhides', the heavy infantry of the Dwarves, make their way with their broad shields in testudo formation keeping at bay the breath attacks of the Dragonborn.

As soon as they get to a favourable distance, they break formation and, with their runic spears, unleash hell upon the Drakelings.

Now these are not ordinary runic spears, but ones especially equipped with destructive Earth magic that is perfect for piercing magical armours and since their scales do not possess the same sturdiness as their fathers, they too suffer at their hands.

Nevertheless, they hold their ground through sheer numbers, but the Dwarves push them back little by little.

The Black ones release another assault of their dark breathes at one of the units, but they quickly assume testudo formation again and shield themselves.

But this time they get the idea of concentrating their fire power into one point and by doing so they overwhelm the shields of the front row, and they break under the pressure and by the impact of the blast they are thrown backwards disrupting the formation.

One of the Undead finds himself there and with his sword strikes one of the Dwarves from the back causing him to fall forward, adding oil to the fire and they topple over each other.

By the time they gather themselves it is too late as the Orc jumps atop the pile and sinks his teeth into one of them, and then the surrounding Dragonborn join him as well, gorging and feasting on the flesh of the fallen Dwarves.

But the Dwarves are not alone in this battle, and so their Vampiric comrades join the fray to help them out.

These swift and nimble creatures have no problem bypassing the Orc's and Dragonborn's hefty fighting style, trained as they may be, and send them to their graves, be it by jumping over them and striking from behind, or by evading their strikes with zigzag movements.

Thus, with their help the rate at which they push back increases.

But their charge is put to halt when the behemoth Alabaster makes his entrance. Coming in from the rear, Halnadu in hand, the giant Demon is ready to unleash the wrath of Abaddon on those that oppose him.

A number of Vampires rush him at once but their weapons shatter when they connect with his armour, and with one mighty swing he mows them down, however Vampires have the tedious ability to regenerate as long as their heads or hearts remain intact, but this comes at the cost of their own blood, so they have to be careful. Due to this, some survive the onslaught and this time rely on their pure physical strength to take down Alabaster but that too will not avail them for the 'destroyer' magic placed upon him will not be undone so easily, and they find themselves with twisted and broken knuckles and arms.

Now with his left hand he grabs one of the Vamps and uses him as a weapon against another one using the former to bash the latter's head into a bloody pulp and still proceeding to swing the one like a weapon, hitting the rest as well as they were too horrified to even act.

Thus, they find themselves on the ground, battered by their own brethren as Alabaster slams the mace into the ground and sends out a surge of mana that branches out beneath the earth, exploding beneath the fallen Vampires, turning them into mush.

The Dwarves of the Skelthuz Breghor strike with their spears at Alabaster but even their magic breaks against his armour and they find themselves unarmed.

Haldanu, the 'Pain-bringer' smashes their shields like they were made of plywood and then smashes their bodies as well.

To add to their despair another terror appears: Malgaras the Doombringer.

Now Malgaras is dressed as follows: on his head he wears a hood that completely covers his face much like Abaddon and this is part of a hooded cape which is ragged and black like night. On his head he also wears a helm in the semblance of a ghastly crown with Demonic runes across. On the rest of his body, he wears a light black armour with Demonic motifs on the pauldrons and breast plate, and black clothing. His weapon of choice: the partisan, Salmu Deberu, 'Black Doom.'

Now the reason why these Demons are called Doombringers is because of their special ability; the curse Deberu, 'Doom'. Whenever one of them strikes the flesh of an opponent with their weapon they apply said curse, and if the opponent deals a mortal wound to a Doombringer the effect is reversed, and they perish instead. Truly a fearsome ability, and extremely rare as well. The curse only manifests within certain Demons of the Dark tribe through atavism, passed down by the spilled blood of Baal. Thus, theirs was an elite infantry unit.

As if this was not bad enough, Andrakos comes as well from another side of the battlefield and so the three commanders are ready to fight side by side.

Using 'Shadow Step', Malgaras moves swiftly like a shadow and wreaks carnage amongst the ranks of the enemies.

The heavily armoured Dwarves cannot hope to match his speed and they fall prey to his partisan for Salmu Deberu pierces any protection.

One of the Vampire squads hope to match him in a contest of speed but the swiftness of the 'Shadow Step' will not be undone and they end up being skewered like shish kebab. The captain of said squad now stands against him. He goes in for a swift jab with his own spear, but Malgaras anticipates his strike and evades by moving to the left and counters with a jab of his own. He reacts timely and moves out of the reach of the spear, but the tip grazes his cheek, nonetheless.

Captain: You have skills I give you that but when it comes to spear fighting, I am unmatched in my unit.

Malgaras: Doesn't matter how good you are, your luck's run out when you ran into me.

Captain: Don't look down on me!

Being a new member of 'The Twilight Twelve' an elite Vampire unit, fills him with confidence. He rushes at him, and they engage in a speedy clash of spears. For a moment it seems as though they are on equal footing however the captain uses his vampiric strength to overpower Malgaras, stunning him for a bit which gives him the chance to go in for a kill.

Another one of the captains shout out to him in a desperate attempt to prevent him from dealing a deadly blow 'Maeglir don't! He is a Doombringer!' but it is too late as the new green captain has already stuck his spear through Malgaras' head. The moment those words reached his ears he knew that he made a royal mistake...

Malgaras: Fool, die now.

Maeglir's heart stops and he dies turning to ash.

Bad news for said captain as well as he left himself open causing Andrakos, who was his foe to get a hold of his sword and snap it in two, and then end his life by cleaving his head off.

However, this is a battlefield and here there is no room for one-on-one duels, and thus a Dwarf with his axe means to embed it into Andrakos' skull but luckily for him, Alabaster reacts in time and smashes the Dwarf to a pulp from behind.

Alabaster: Keep all four open!

Andrakos: Sorry...

Alabaster: Next time I may not be here to save your arse.

Thus, with the three powerhouses present, the armies of Abaddon turn the tides and begin pushing back even more than before.

Even the efforts of the Phantomancers who act as support in the background do not bear any fruit, as they are thwarted by the Hathasian Mystics, now trained in dark magic which they use to wrestle control over their wraiths and use it against them.

Meanwhile on another side, Baldur is doing some head splitting on his own with his trusty axe. Now he means to use Sundrian and have spires of earth to gorge his foes, but little does he know that there is another fearsome foe on the battlefield. Dagon, the commander of the magic unit whom Abaddon revived using Tharmut's body, uses his magic to nullify the attack.

Baldur: What in the…?

He tries once more but it ends up with the same result. This enrages him and with a mighty leap he goes to face Dagon.

He may be physically weak, but his magic compensates more than enough for that shortcoming, and he uses his ability to repel Baldur with a surge of a magical wave.

Frustrated, Baldur orders his troops to take down the magic caster, but he erects 'Duru Isatuu' a wall made from the infernal flames of the Abyss that turns everyone to cinder should they dare pass through it. Not even the runic armour of the Dwarves is able to sustain them, and they perish an ashen death.

The Vampires however try to brave through with their regenerative ability, but only manage to come to the other side burned and mangled making them easy pickings for Dagon who delivers the coup de grace with eldritch bolts.

Using nigromancy he conjures up an Abyssal Golem and sends it forth to battle Baldur. The creature attempts to smash him with his massive fists, but the Dwarven King takes the hit and remains unscathed and using the power of Sundrian makes a quick work of the beast turning it to a pile of rubble.

Now Dagon conjures up even more Golems only this time they fire magical blasts from their eyes.

Baldur's armour keeps him safe, but the force from the blasts knocks him around nevertheless; a ranged fighter is the worse opponent for someone such as himself.

Dagon grabs a hold of Baldur using 'Dark Restraint' and these ethereal Demonic hands hold him with a firm grip and he cannot get free. His axe falls on the ground and Dagon casts it aside with magic.

The Golems close in on him and ready to fire their blasts from point blank, however Amra arrives in the nick of time, jabbing 'Bloodfang' into the eye of one of the Golems causing its head to explode.

Using her swift movement, she jumps from one Golem to another, despatching them then she severs the ghastly arms and frees Baldur.

Baldur: Thanks, I owe you my life.

Amra: Don't thank me yet, we are far from safe.

Dagon: It has been hundred years since I last saw your faces and it makes me glad, I see them yet again so I can exact my revenge for my king.

Amra: Don't get ahead of yourself, Warlock, you are talking to the Queen of Vampires.

Dagon: You are no one to me.

Amra: That's what you all say, before biting the dust!

Using her blood magic, she casts 'Roses d'Sang', which creates a bramble of crystalline roses with razor sharp thorns that entangle around the target and rip him to shreds.

But Dagon uses his magic to nullify the effects and then casts 'Vampire Bane' on Amra, and she falls on her knees in agony and chokes on her own blood as it starts to gush out from her orifices as well.

Baldur: Amra!

Dagon: Merlin is not here to save you this time.

Some of her own mages realise the pinch she is in and cast magical projectiles towards him to disrupt his magic, but he erects a protective barrier with his staff and shields himself.

Baldur: You're forgetting I'm here as well!

Dagon: So?

Baldur means to break the ground beneath Dagon's feet and throw him off balance, but the cunning Warlock momentarily dispels the barrier, and casts 'Binding Darkness' which creates a patch of darkness that slows down anyone caught inside it, preventing them from moving freely.

Amra holds her own through sheer willpower, but her consciousness is beginning to slip gradually, and when all seems lost something comes swiping in and flings Dagon in the air and onto the ground, disrupting his channelling of the 'Vampire Bane'

He looks up and sees a Dragon made from crystallised blood.

Dagon: A Bloodforge Dragon huh, in that case…

He uses his necromancy to summon a Lichdrake and have it deal with the Bloodforge.

Amra: You're just in time, any second longer and I would have been on the doorstep of my ancestors.

Carogin (commander of the mage squad): My apologies for not arriving sooner your highness.

Baldur: Aye, I could've used you when he was flinging me around.

Carogin: Apologies to you as well, Lord Baldur.

Baldur: Don't sweat it, laddie, any help is better than no help.

Dagon: You fools must think I am some fodder since you converse so freely in my presence.

Carogin: Not to worry, Master Warlock, I will deal with you shortly.

Dagon: You? Deal with me? Do you have any idea to whom you are speaking that way?

Carogin: A spectre of the past who has no business amongst the living.

Dagon: Impudent wretch! Behold my power!

He raises his staff in the air and casts 'Unholy Impaler' which creates several magic circles in the sky that continuously rain down piercing bolts of dark energy.

Carogin erects a higher level of the 'Blood Cocoon' to shield them from the bolts, but it shatters under the might of the spell nonetheless and two more come raining down, but the company manages to move away in the nick of time.

Some Dwarf and Vampire warriors rush at him at once, but Dagon erects a four-sided version of the 'Duru Isatuu' and turns them to cinders.

Carogin: I've never seen a Warlock so powerful before.

Baldur: Aye, Dhalsarrian Warlocks are nothing to sneeze at, luckily, we had Merlin last time but this time…

Carogin: You have me.

Baldur: No offence lad but that is not really reassuring.

Carogin: None taken (slightly smiles) my lord, my lady, I will cover you, you must get close to him and deal the final blow.

Amra: We are counting on you, Carogin!

Carogin: Go!

They rush onwards but suddenly they are blasted back by the appearance of a black smoke that comes crashing down from the skies.

The smoke takes shape as they are all watching aghast, and out of it he comes; Abaddon the Demon-King.

Dagon: My king (kneels).

Amra: Abaddon…

Carogin: So that is him huh…how frightful…

Abaddon: We meet again Amra, Baldur.

Baldur: Not that I am pleased about it (grips his axe).

Abaddon: Of course, no one should be pleased when they rush to their deaths.

Amra: It's over, Abaddon! Your deranged ambitions end here!

Abaddon: No, my dear queen, the only thing that will end here is your life…

CAPITVLVM XIII

POMIS DISCORDIAE[xii]

Abaddon: Dagon, I leave the small fry to you.

Dagon: Of course, my lord, I will make quick work of him.

Amra: Carogin run, save yourself, he is not an opponent you can beat on your own.

Carogin: With all due respect, my queen, I cannot possibly let the two of you handle such monsters on your own and besides, I cannot bring such a shame upon myself as fleeing.

Dagon: You should listen to your queen little Vampire, run, run while you still can.

Carogin: Yet you continue to mock me, I will make sure you regret it.

Abaddon: Now then, time to snuff out the flames of your life.

Baldur: Ya ready lassie? (Firmly grasps his axe).

Amra: Ready as I can be.

Drops of sweat roll down their faces.

Abaddon: (raises his sword) Absharu: En –

Amra: I won't let you!

She attacks him instantly, but he blocks the attack.

Abaddon: You recognised the ability and acted fast; impressive.

Amra: Of course! How can I forget!

He pushes her away, but she comes rushing back in and a high-speed sword fight ensues. Baldur can only watch as they move swiftly along the ground akin instantaneous flashes of light and bids his moment for striking.

They stop for a second and he seizes this opportunity and jumps at Abaddon, however the latter stops his attack with his bare hand and throws the aghast

Dwarf right into Amra, then he shoots an eldritch blast at them, but Amra protects them with her psychic barrier.

Meanwhile Carogin casts 'Clouere d'Sang' which creates a field of bloody spikes, but Dagon uses a patch of darkness to lift himself in the air and avoid the attack.

Carogin responds by creating wings of blood and creates a blood sword and because he is versed in close combat as well goes in to face Dagon.

Dagon casts 'Vampire Bane' on him but instead of making him choke on his own blood like he did to Amra, his wings and sword shatter and he falls on the ground on his own spiked field.

Dagon: There are other ways of using this spell, you see.

Carogin dispels the field and heals his wounds, now he is finally beginning to see what makes this Warlock so frightening.

But Dagon will not wait, and while Carogin is too busy tending to his own wounds, he casts 'Dimtu Sakhaltuu', 'Tower of Torture', which creates an obsidian spire to erupt from the ground and impale Carogin and it keeps goring him as it ascends in the sky becoming akin a Demonic tower. Once it reaches a certain peak it stops, and chains with spiked ends protrude from the spire and embed themselves into his flesh and chain him to the tower.

Then he casts 'Shade of the Colossus' and the ground splits open and from it rises a shadowy titan. He is so big that only his upper body reaches the heaven above while his lower body remains in the ground.

Now the Colossus raises his giant arm and brings it back down and Carogin can do nothing more but watch in terror and fright as this massive object is nearing him, throwing a huge shadow in the process and crushes him onto the ground along with the tower as we crush sandcastles on a beach.

Nothing remains from the smashed Carogin except a few specs of blood on the ground. The people in the vicinity get affected as well, being knocked over by the massive shockwave that ensues. Once its task is done, the colossus retracts back into the ground and the ground closes and restores itself back to normal.

Baldur: By my beard… (as he was watching the whole thing transpire).

Amra: That's why I told you to run…fool.

Casting spells left and right takes its toll on Dagon, and he collapses on the ground from exhaustion, holding on to his staff for support.

Dagon: Looks like I went a little bit overboard with that last one…

Abaddon: You did well, Dagon, fall back, that's an order.

Dagon: You don't have to order me, your majesty, I would have done so regardless…

He turns into darkness and retreats from the battlefield.

As soon as he is out of sight Amra attacks Abaddon with Bloodfang but he blocks the attack again, now she infuses her strength into her other arm and means to deliver a punch, but he stops that attack as well, the powerstone on his pauldron lighting with purple light.

Abaddon: You're forgetting that you are not the only one with superhuman strength.

Then he proceeds to hit her in the abdomen with his knee and slams her face into the ground by grabbing her by the back of her head.

Now she infuses her strength throughout all her body making her veins pop up all around, and her skin turns reddish, and she pushes him away with raw power.

Baldur joins in and they both attack him at once, he creates a sword of darkness and with it he parries Amra's strikes while he parries Baldur's with Absharu.

Some of the remaining soldiers nearby think to seize this opportunity and strike him from behind, but he casts 'Aura of Despair' on them, and they fall frozen in place.

Malgaras appears using 'Shadow Step' and despatches them in one strike.

Malgaras: We will hold back any nuisances, my king.

Abaddon: Most appreciated.

In the middle of their clash, Amra manages to get a clean hit on his face with her full power, staggering Abaddon a bit then she throws herself at him, grabs him by the waist and throws him way up in the air, then she sprouts her wings again, jumping after him. He regains his posture and fires a couple of eldritch blasts at her which she redirects to the ground with her psychokinesis, then she reaches him, and an airborne clash ensues. They fiercely exchange blows and since it is so tightly packed both do not have the opportunity to cast spells.

But at one point Abaddon enhances Absharu with the 'Wrath' stance and shatters Bloodfang, making Amra wince in frustration.

Baldur: Lassie!

He flings Sundrian at her and she grabs it and in a swift instant manages to get a blow on Abaddon's torso and then she uses the momentum to strike him with a furious barrage of slashes.

Abaddon murmurs something and Absharu changes colour, but Amra is too busy driving him towards the ground that she does not notice. Ultimately, she finishes with a powerful slash that sends Abaddon crashing down, but she does not stop there; her eyes flare up red as she uses her psychic powers on a higher level to gather the weapons of the nearby fallen soldiers and creates one massive, bladed cluster, sending it to crash down on Abaddon like a cascading waterfall of thousand blades. The impact creates a cloud of dust, and everything lays silent for a moment.

Baldur: Did we get him? (Asks expectantly).

The dust settles and Abaddon raises unscathed, covered in dark blue aura.

Amra: He's unharmed!

Abaddon: Absharu: Enu Rebu: Egutu.[24]

This fourth stance upgrades his defence and durability to unimaginable levels making him impregnable to all attacks be it physical or magical.

Abaddon: Last time it took all seven of you and you barely managed to kill me, did you really think that just the two of you had any hopes of winning?

They both wince.

Baldur: Tsk…

Abaddon: I see, you thought because I am not yet at my full power you might have a slimmer of a chance of winning, but you failed to realise that I don't need my full power to deal with the likes of you.

Amra casts 'Torber d'Sang' which creates a waist high bog of blood to stuck Abaddon and uses her psychokinesis to immobilise him completely.

Amra: Baldur now! (Throws Sundrian back at him).

---

[24] Destroyer sword; fourth stance: sloth.

He catches it and rushes onwards with a mighty war cry.

However, Abaddon will not be undone by this, and he breaks free from Amra's telekinetic binds.

Abaddon: Absharu: Enu Shalshu: Akkilu![25]

This time, the sword glows with a cyan coloured aura, and begins to drain the mana from the surrounding area, causing the bog to shrivel and deplete and not only this it also sucks in the mana from Baldur's Sundrian, turning it into a useless, normal axe. The same goes for his own personal mana as well and he falls on his knees from exhaustion, Amra as well loses her wings and falls towards the ground, but she manages to land on her feet safely although she immediately falls on her knees as well from the loss of strength.

Amra: Mierde…! Fuck! (Falls on the ground completely)

Abaddon uses his 'Shadow Step' and sweeps past Baldur, cleaving him in half and ending his life.

Amra: Nooo! (Strains herself to get up on her knees).

Abaddon: (approaches her) It is the second time we face each other Amra, and twice you fail.

Amra looks at him full of scorn.

Abaddon: It would be such a shame and a waste to let someone like yourself perish here; there is no need for you to die this time, I could use you in my ranks.

Amra: Heh…how ironic…I said the same thing to your Dragonkin before I killed one of them.

Abaddon: I see…but it doesn't have to be the same way for you.

Amra: You're asking me to betray the people with whom I've built peaceful relations for the past one hundred years…people who trust me… something you cannot possibly understand, can you, Abaddon.

Abaddon: … Tell me, where will that trust go if you go back defeated and broken?

She looks at him with confusion and angst.

Abaddon: They will laugh at you and scorn you, especially that old fart Arthur since no doubt he was the one most against your going.

Amra's eyes begin to waver.

---

[25] Third stance: Gluttony.

Abaddon: Admit it, there is nothing left for you, look around; your men and women are almost completely wiped out.

She does so and her eyes fill up with images of death and carnage, broken bodies and broken swords, endless blood soaking into the land, Abaddon's hordes rallying up what remains of both armies accompanied with their screams of anguish and an immeasurable sense of dread befalls her.

Abaddon: And those people you deem friends secretly despise you, you know this, don't you?

The scene of the council where she got into a squabble with Urania comes to mind.

Amra: No…you're wrong! The only one that spoke up was that wench Urania!

Abaddon: One speaks what all inwardly think, they cowardly sent you off to your doom instead of rallying up all their forces and standing to fight against me.

Amra: If that came to pass…we would not be having this talk.

Abaddon: Indeed, but it didn't because they are not your friends, and only care for their own survival every single one of them, they only stick together because it is convenient for them but when the bough breaks, none are willing to take a risk, so they pushed on the responsibility to you.

Amra: No one made us! We made that choice on our own, we could've stayed and fought with the rest but we… (winces).

Abaddon: In that case they could've invoked the power of the treaty to force you into submission, but they gave their consent, I bet it was Folduin that made the final push, wasn't he?

Amra: How do you know…?

Abaddon: I'm no fool, Amra, I've seen many things while I roamed the land in my spirit form, I know how they work.

Amra: …

Abaddon: I'm guessing what they really thought is that at best you'd defeat the weakened enemy and if not, at least you'd deal a significant blow to his forces, and they would also get rid of a nuisance in the process.

Amra: Again, with that? You're just trying to twist my mind! I won't fall on your poisonous words! Not again! Never again! It has been two hundred years, but my heart still has not mended from the blow you dealt me!

He looks her deep in the eyes.

Amra: Say something damn you!

Abaddon: Amra, you are creatures of the night, you were meant to be in the darkness with us from the start, there is no place for you in their world of 'light' (extends his hand) join me and I will give you everything.

Amra: (spits in his hand) Don't sell me off so cheaply! I told you! I won't fall for your words!

Abaddon: (shakes off the spit) Let me paint you a picture then, there are two ways this can transpire; one: I kill you and then reanimate your corpse to do my bidding like a mindless puppet or, two: you consent to serving me willingly, what's it going to be?

Amra: (grunts) You truly are despicable…

Abaddon: I know, and I take great pride in it.

Amra: … I have one condition though, if I'm going to serve you, it will be as a queen.

Abaddon: Sorry but that position is already taken.

Amra: You have a spouse?

Abaddon: Perhaps.

Amra: …

Abaddon: Not to worry, you will serve as one of my commanders, an honourable position for a woman of your stature.

Amra: And what makes you think I won't betray you?

Abaddon: Oh, after I'm done with you, that thought will be forever banished from your mind.

Amra: What do you mean…?

Abaddon: Take my hand and find out.

She does so although reluctantly and then she screams out in pain as an unimaginable surge of power rushes through her entire being. A magical pentagram with purple colour appears beneath their feet, as Abaddon is chanting something. A dark purple aura with black undertones shoots up from beneath Amra, the Demon King was working his nigromancy; it was the same ritual he used on Grulk to transform him into a Bugbear.

Once finished, Amra had obtained greater power than she ever had but had become something entirely different as well, a Lamia; a vampiric creature with snakelike properties, granting her access to a whole new set of abilities.

Abaddon: Arise anew, my Lamia.

Amra: What is this power? (Still not used to it) I've never felt anything like it before…

Abaddon: I unlocked your dormant potential, evolved you into a greater being.

Amra: I feel…amazing.

Abaddon: You're welcome.

Amra: My king! (Kneels down) I'm forever in your service!

Abaddon: And I gladly accept it (smirks beneath the hood).

Malgaras: This new look suits you better (approaches).

Amra: I remember you, you're that Doombringer – Malgaras, correct?

Malgaras: Correct, it has been such a long time Lady Amra, I hope we can get along this time.

Alabaster: (comes up as well all covered in blood) Welcome aboard, just make sure you don't displease our master.

Amra: Not to worry, I mean to repay this favour in full.

Abaddon: (Oh how easy it is to sway the hearts of people with this opium called power) (snickers in his mind).

He looks around and he spots the corpse of Frigga and starts to walk towards it.

Abaddon: (places his hand on her head) Rest in peace, my beautiful queen, your winter ends here.

Argyros: (flies down) You won't revive her?

Abaddon: No reviving for this one, she deserves a proper burial.

Flammos: A proper burial? Her kin fled like mangy curs!

Abaddon: But she fought till the end.

Flammos: Pah!

Ignatos: Show some respect, you ingrate! This is no ordinary Wyvern!

Flammos: My king!

Ignatos: Don't 'my king' me! Apologise right now!

Flammos: Yes, your highness (does so in Draconic).

Argyros: I don't mean to pry but is it a wise idea to include her killer amongst our ranks?

Abaddon: I have more use of one Lamia than a hundred Wyverns.

Argyros: Granted.

Soon the remaining Dragons gather around her corpse as well to pay their respects.

Abaddon: I'm going to take her body back to Glaziriz and pick up someone else on the way as well, you tell Alabaster to march the troops back to Dhaldrog.

Argyros: Aye, aye sir.

Abaddon: But before that…

He raises himself up in the air with darkness and spreads his arms, then he casts his necromancy after which a giant magical circle, as big as the whole plain emerges and lo! The corpses of the fallen soldiers begin to rise.

Abaddon: Now return to the earth before I summon you next.

And so, they sink down in the magic circle and it contracts to one point and disappears, after which Abaddon disappears as well with his Greater Teleportation.

Argyros: Orders from the king! We are marching back.

Alabaster: All right you lot! Back to the city!

His voice booms aloud as if blown from a trumpet and the troops line up and begin marching.

Malgaras: Still, we butchered your men and those of your allies and you are going to join us with no problem?

Amra: I do have a problem and I grieve for my people, but I like this power even more.

Malgaras: I see… (typical person drunk on power, how pitiful).

Thus, Abaddon takes Frigga's corpse back to Glaziriz and word reaches Fragora about the upcoming funeral.

Morgana: What was the matter?

Fragora: We must go to Glacinia, child.

Morgana: Must we go now?

Fragora: I'm afraid so, it is an urgent matter.

Morgana: More urgent than my training?

Fragora: Right now, yes.

Morgana: Why? What has happened?

Fragora: We must pay our respect to the fallen queen.

Morgana: Frigga is dead? Oh no… (means to ask about Abaddon but does not have the heart to).

Fragora: He is there as well.

Morgana: (smiles) Then we must not keep them waiting, it would be rude to show up late at a funeral.

Fragora: Are you sure it's not because you want to see him?

Morgana: Shut up!

Fragora: (chuckles) Climb on, child.

She does so.

Meanwhile in Glaziriz, many Dragonkin have gathered to send off the Winter Queen.

Morgana: Abaddon!

Abaddon: Princess!

She immediately gives herself in his arms.

Morgana: You're back! Thank goodness!

Abaddon: Now is not the time, we talk later.

Morgana: Of course, sorry…

Lindroz: Ah, the twerp, heard you've been training in magic over here, how's that going?

Morgana: So far so good.

Lindroz: Good, good.

Morgana: She really is dead then… (looks at her corpse) what a shame…such a beautiful creature, laid to rest.

Abaddon: That is the nature of war, I'm afraid, you win some you lose some…

Glauros (lieutenant of the Wyverns): Your majesty, if you would do the honours.

Abaddon: Gladly.

He uses strands of darkness to gently lift up her corpse and place it inside the massive tomb of ice, to rest in peace with her forefathers.

All gathered lower their heads in respect and give a moment of silence.

While this is ongoing Fragora takes Morgana under her arm to shield her from the cold.

Abaddon: Here lies Frigga, Queen of Wyverns, Mistress of ice and snow, ruler of Glaziriz, daughter of Friggos, may her soul rest in peace until she is one with the mana once more (speaks in Draconic).

'Rest in peace glorious Frigga,' say the Dragonkin unanimously at the end of the rite. When everyone begins to go their way, Abaddon addresses Glauros.

Abaddon: You stay, I want to have a word with you.

Glauros: As you wish.

He stays, knowing of what is about to happen.

Morgana: What about me?

Abaddon: You go back with Fragora to Dragon's Head; I'll come as well after I'm done here.

Morgana: Or I could just wait?

Abaddon: I don't want you freezing in the cold.

Morgana: Alright, I'll be waiting (smiles a little).

Fragora: Come child.

Lindroz however also stays behind and seems a bit lost in thought.

Abaddon: What's the matter, old friend?

Lindroz: ... I should've been there...I could've watched her back.

Abaddon: It's not your fault, we could've been burying you right now as well.

Lindroz: It's not an excuse...I let Grindos die and now...

Abaddon: You're still hung up on that?

Lindroz: I never forgot it...how could I? I left her to fight alone and now Frigga as well...

Puts his hand upon his body in a comforting manner.

Lindroz: Beautiful Snow Queen...gone forever...if only we were born of the same race...

Abaddon: Some things are simply not meant to be.

Lindroz: If only fate was more merciful... (turns to Glauros) you are her second in command, aren't you? Where were you? What were you doing?

Glauros: Do not try to shift the blame on me, Lord Lindroz, we had our hands full as well!

Lindroz: You let your queen! Your leader! Die! (Roars).

Abaddon: Calm yourself, friend, let me handle this, now go before you do something you'll regret.

Lindroz: My only regret is staying behind like a coward...I will kill the one responsible for this, mark my words.

Burrows himself underground and disappears out of sight.

Abaddon: Now then, how should I handle your little episode?

Glauros: My king, I –

Abaddon: No excuses, I heard what happened from Flammos, fleeing in the midst of battle…

Glauros: I will give no excuses, my liege, I only did what I deemed was right for the survival of my kind, we were being overrun –

Abaddon: You know what I'm hearing, Glauros? Excuses.

Glauros: …

Abaddon: Tell me, how many of the Dark Dragons remain?

Glauros: Only Argyros…

Abaddon: Only Argyros, and why is that?

Glauros: Because…they fought till the last one.

Abaddon: Which is the opposite of what you did.

Glauros: With all due respect, your majesty, a lot of the other Dragonkin fled that time as well! Yet I see them not scorned!

Abaddon: Do not patronise me, Wyvern, my body was dead, but my spirit was there, I saw what happened that day! Only a handful returned while you did so with two hundred strong! It's simple! You saw your queen die and you got scared!

Glauros: Forgive me, Graz-Rahiz[26], for not waiting my kind to face near extinction before deciding to retreat; while I serve you, my loyalty lies to my own people!

Abaddon: And thanks to that, many good Dragons died.

Glauros: They had a choice, and they chose to fight on…

Abaddon: They chose to believe in their king!

Glauros' eyes widen in surprise as he is hit with the sudden realisation.

Abaddon: What hurts me the most is not because you fled but because you didn't believe in me! The others knew I would come, and they fought on! They believed in their king! And I did come! Moments after you turned tail! I came!

Glauros: Rahiz mi[27] … (icy tears sprout in his eyes, lowers his head) I have wounded you deeply! I humbly beg for your forgiveness…On my life I swear I will not bring such a disgrace to your honour once more…

Abaddon: You all whine and beg to be forgiven after the deed is done well no more, no more forgiveness from the King of Demons.

Glauros: My king…?

---

[26] Great King.

[27] My King.

Abaddon: You have proven yourself unworthy of your fealty, now I must find your worth anew.

Glauros becomes stunned and confused.

He screams in pain as Abaddon reaches his hand and envelops him in dark energy; he performs the same magic he did to Amra and morphs Glauros into a humanoid knight with armour out of Wyvern scales and fur, a shield and an ice sword and a pair of wings on his back.

Abaddon slightly slumps over from exhaustion but stays on his feet.

Abaddon: You will lead the Wyverns from now on, and henceforth shall be called Kushsanu[28].

Kushsanu: (kneels) Yes, your majesty, your wish is my command, and I will obey until my lord relieves me or death takes me.

Abaddon: Well said, now go! And make your presence known to these spineless cowards.

Kushsanu: As you command! (He flies off).

Abaddon: I better get back and get some rest…I'm spent…

Vanishes and reappears at 'Dragon's Peak' and sits down on a rock as soon as he arrives…

[28] Winter Knight

CAPITVLVM XIV

CANTVS IGNIS ET GLACIEI[xiii]

Morgana: You're finally back! ...what's wrong?

Abaddon: Nothing, just a bit tired is all, this is what I get from working three days straight (sighs) once I recover some of my mana, I'll be fine.

Morgana: Idiot! Why must you always exert yourself?

Abaddon: Because there are things that only I can do.

Morgana: You need to take better care of yourself!

Abaddon: I said I'll be fine; now cease your nagging!

Morgana: Humph! In any case, I'm glad you're back alive and well.

Abaddon: I'm glad to be back (reaches to his waist and takes off her crown) I believe this belongs to you.

Morgana: And this to you (smiles and places his crown back on his head) it looks so much better on you.

Abaddon: Well, it was crafted for my head (slightly chuckles).

Morgana: (chuckles as well) May I...

Abaddon: Go ahead (taps his lap).

She shyly fidgets because he guessed her purpose and does as he bid her.

Morgana: This armour is a bit hard.

Abaddon: It's armour, it's supposed to be hard.

Morgana: I know but it's quite uncomfortable...

Abaddon: You could always sit on the ground.

Morgana: No! No! It's fine.

Abaddon: Then quit complaining.

Fragora: Look at you two, how adorable.

Abaddon: What's that supposed to mean? Do not treat us like some prepubescent couple.

Fragora: I wasn't!

Abaddon: Make yourself scarce before you anger me any further.

Fragora: I was going to anyway, no need to be rude about it, my king (takes her leave).

Morgana: (chuckles at the scene) Sorry (mouths it out).

Fragora gives her a wink before entering the cave.

Abaddon: (sigh) The attitude on these Dragons, dear God…

Morgana: Don't mind her.

Abaddon: What's the matter with you? Do you have a fever or something? (Notices her red cheeks).

Morgana: What? No! I'm perfectly fine.

Abaddon: Your face is all red, don't tell me you feel embarrassed about your position.

Morgana: Not at all…speaking of which, why did you allow me to…

Abaddon: Why? You seemed somewhat eager, so I thought I'd grace you with this privilege.

Morgana: Privilege you say?

Abaddon: Of course, I don't allow just anyone to get so close to me.

Morgana: (hearing this makes her extremely happy) Could you…remove your hood? Talking to you like this up close is most unsettling.

Abaddon: You didn't seem unsettled so far.

Morgana: Just do it! …please?

Abaddon pauses for a moment then does so.

Morgana: There, much better (smiles).

Abaddon: Say princess, you meant to tell me something before I left but you didn't, could you tell me now?

Morgana: N-now? (Her heart starts racing).

Abaddon: Did I stutter?

Morgana: You don't have to be rude about it.

Abaddon: I can be as I please.

Morgana: Then I'm not telling you.

Abaddon: You don't have to.

Suddenly, she acts out of impulse and kisses him on the lips.

Morgana: There, I said it.

Abaddon: You said you weren't going to.

Morgana: But I did.

Abaddon: (smiles) Oh princess, princess, you are in love with me, aren't you.

Morgana: You say it like it's a bad thing…

Abaddon: I don't blame you, I'm handsome, charming, well-mannered…when I please, it's natural that you'd feel infatuated with me.

Morgana: Infatuated? No! What I feel is more than that!

Abaddon: Tell me princess, how long have you spent time with me? About two weeks all together? Can a person really fall in love with someone in such a short period of time?

Morgana: (springs up from his lap) It's more than enough time!

Abaddon: You sound just like a naïve girl that has been struck by the handsome prince and thinks she loves him.

Morgana: What I feel is real! It is not a phase!

Abaddon: You don't know me, the real me, you don't know the things I've done!

Morgana: Killing and feeding to the crows, so you've told me.

Abaddon: Hearing and seeing are two different things!

Morgana: So what? We all have our demons!

Abaddon: Morgana **I am** a Demon!

Morgana: I don't give a damn about what or who you are! I care about the person inside!

Abaddon: … Was your love for the young Sorcerer so shallow that you'd forget about him and so easily throw yourself at the man that took over his body!

Morgana: (slaps him) How dare you! I loved Merlin with all my heart, and he is still dear to me but that doesn't mean that I am not allowed to fall in love again! And I do love you! Do not treat me like a common whore!

Abaddon: Why? Why would you? Is it because I treat you nicely, is it because I want to keep you out of harm's way and all that, is that it? Well let me tell you something princess, I don't do it out of love I do it because you are of use to me!

Morgana: You think I don't know that? That's the first thing you said when you took me with you, that I may be of use to you and I intend to do so, and I am fine with you not loving me, but you cannot ask me to do the same!

Abaddon: …You would stick by my side even after hearing this?

Morgana: My life is bound to yours now, there is no going back for me, your fate is my fate, and I will not part with it, not until I burn those responsible for what happened with these two hands and even after that…I will still stay by your side.

Abaddon: There really is something wrong with your head…

Morgana: It's called love.

Abaddon: Love, love, love, you're making me puke…

Morgana: You've never been in love before?

Abaddon: No, love has no place in my affairs, such a frivolous thing holds no meaning.

Morgana: You're lying.

Abaddon: You're calling me a liar?

Morgana: Yes, I am, I don't believe that you're doing it completely out of need, why go so far for one girl, I'm sure there are plenty of others with more potential than me.

Abaddon: That's what you think, I just hate wasting good potential.

Morgana: Whatever makes you feel better your highness.

Abaddon: You really have a sharp tongue for one so young.

Morgana: I was raised that way.

Abaddon: Props to Arthur then.

Morgana: That's the only thing he did right by me…

Abaddon: Don't be a fool Morgana, I'm telling you, I'm acting nice only to assuage you and make you feel better, what good it would be for me if you got angry and ran away.

Morgana: I don't buy it for one second.

Abaddon: Oh, please even if I did, it wouldn't be in a bratty child like you.

Morgana squints her eyes at him.

Abaddon: What's with that look.

Morgana: I really can't believe you, the great Demon-King, unable to be honest about his feelings.

Abaddon: For the last time there are no feelings! You are really starting to get on my nerves, girl.

Morgana: Why don't you just admit it? You care for me! Admit it! Admit it!

Abaddon: Alright I do! But it's far from being 'love!'

Morgana: Humph (smiles smugly) doesn't matter it's still something, a step towards it if I may say.

Abaddon: You are such a teenager.

Morgana: Not denying it.

Abaddon: (sighs) Go now, leave me alone I need to rest for a while, go practice your magic.

Morgana: Once you do, are we going to leave?

Abaddon: Not yet, I have one more errand to take care off here, further up north.

Morgana: What's there?

Abaddon: The land of the Giants.

Morgana: I get to see Giants next? Nice!

Abaddon: Not you, you're staying here until I get back.

Morgana: Oh no! I'm not staying behind again!

Abaddon: It's one thing after another with you!

Morgana: You left me here for half a year you're not leaving me again!

Abaddon: If it's about the Giants, you'll get to see them after because they will be coming with us.

Morgana: What?

Abaddon: You heard me, I'm marching them to Orcothrond and then to the East from there.

Morgana: Oh, then you could've said so in the first place.

Abaddon: Just go…please?

Morgana: Humph, males can be so daft sometimes (walks away).

Abaddon: Sometimes I really wonder why I keep her around… (sighs).

Fragora: Don't worry, child, he's not ready yet.

Morgana: With that attitude, I wonder if he'll ever be ready…

Fragora: You're still young, you have time.

Morgana: There's a limit to how young I can stay.

Fragora chuckles.

Morgana: Fragora, do you know whether he has had any love interests in his life?

Fragora: You think he's lying about it?

Morgana: I don't know, maybe…maybe something awful happened, and he doesn't want to talk about it.

Fragora: Oh, I don't know child, you're better off asking Argyros that, he was closest to him after all.

Morgana: Maybe I will…

***

Abaddon: Now then, I guess I should head out.

Thus, after a short rest, he gets up and using 'Greater Teleportation' vanishes towards the land of the Giants.

The land of the Giants is called Torenheim in their language, and it is separated into three regions: Niflheim, meaning 'Home of the Chilling Mist' the dwelling place of the Frost Giants, creatures made out of pure magical ice which is thicker and sturdier than normal ice; Surtrheim, 'Home of Surtr', the land of fire and home to the Fire Giants who are made out of molten rock and hot lava; and finally Fjalldorfheim, 'home of the forests', the home of the Mountain Giants, creatures of human appearance only much, much bigger.

Foremost of these lands is Niflheim.

Strong blizzards, thick snow, and ice plague it, even more fierce than the ones in Glaziriz. Thanks to this rough terrain, no other creature can dwell within, even the Wyverns would have trouble flying amidst these ferocious storms. To help him endure this cold, he has wrapped himself in the pelt of a dead Wyvern, further enchanted for extra protection against it.

Now the King of these Giants is Ymir, biggest and mightiest of them all, being able to freeze the land over wherever he steps foot and his magical ice club Isulfur, 'Ice wolf', has the ability to produce ice even in the hottest of places.

Word came to him that Abaddon is here, and he agreed to see him.

Thus, Abaddon was led into his palace made out of ice and snow, decorated with beautiful ice sculptures, and Ymir himself was seated on an enormous throne of ice, laced with intricate designs and symbols. Abaddon greets him and bows out of courtesy, looking like an ant compared to an elephant as he stands before him.

Ymir: What brings Abaddon, King of Demons, before the mighty Ymir yet again?

Abaddon: Great Ymir, I came once to seek your aid and now I come again with the same purpose, lend me the might of the Frost Giants in my conquest.

Ymir: So, it is again that you would seek Ymir's help in your wars Demon King, Ymir has made his intentions clear the last time and will repeat the same answer, the Frost Giants will not fight in wars that are none of their concern.

Abaddon: I'm afraid that answer will not satisfy me this time, the last time I let you go but not again, I will have your allegiance by force if I must.

Ymir: Is this how your people ask of favours? With threats?

Abaddon: Whatever is necessary, so I ask of you to reconsider.

Ymir stands up, his head now touching the ceiling of the palace and points his glassy eyes towards Abaddon.

Ymir: Let us step outside, we shall settle this in combat.

Abaddon: I'd rather not kill you before the actual fighting starts.

Ymir: Tiny king thinks he can beat Ymir?

Abaddon: I don't think, I know I can.

Ymir laughs with a booming voice.

Abaddon: (This idiot seems unaware of my might; if I do fight him, I might accidentally send him to the afterlife).

Ymir: Ymir is the strongest there is, no one can beat Ymir.

Abaddon: How about I fight someone else instead?

Ymir: Hmmm (scratches his beard) very well, you will fight Laufey, Ymir's son, he is weaker only to me.

Abaddon: I accept this challenge.

Ymir: Call for my son, tell him a challenger awaits (he instructs one of the Giants).

It should be noted that Ymir spoke in the language of the Giants and Abaddon did as well for he is well versed in it.

And thus, they stepped outside on the frozen field, Abaddon and Laufey standing against each other and the other Giants nearby in order to spectate this battle, cheering on one of their leaders.

Abaddon: You won't hold it against me if I end up sending him to an eternal slumber, would you?

Ymir: No; if he ends up dead, it will mean that was the extent of his skills.

Abaddon: Glad to hear it.

Laufey: I will crush this tiny Demon like an insect, yahaha!

Abaddon: I wouldn't count on it (unsheathes Absharu and activates the 'Wrath' stance).

Laufey takes a swing with his own club, but Abaddon blocks the attack using Absharu, much to the surprise of the other Giants.

He takes another swing, but Abaddon uses 'Blink' to move out of the way and he ends up hitting the snow.

Abaddon: (This bloody snow is making it hard for me to move, I guess 'Blink' is my only option).

And no wonder since the snow reached up to his waist. But then another idea comes to his mind; he uses his magic to propel himself in the air and hover above the snow.

Abaddon: Ah, much better.

With a loud shriek, Laufey swings at him, but Abaddon effortlessly blocks again, he keeps on swinging, but every attempt is thwarted.

Now when he was going for another swing, Abaddon thrusts the sword into the club and shatters it to pieces, causing the Giants to wow in awe.

Abaddon now uses 'Jaws of the Abyss' which produces strands of darkness with snapping jaws that bite down and subdue the target. The size of the jaws varies depending on the mana input in the spell so Abaddon makes them extra big so that they may seize the Giant.

However, Laufey will not be stopped by this, so he uses his own magical powers and uses 'Glacial Bellow', which grants him the ability to freeze his targets with just his voice, and the ice magic of the Giants being very ancient and powerful one is able to freeze darkness itself. Thus, the infernal jaws become frozen and shatter.

Abaddon: (Incredible, he was able to freeze the shadows with just his voice, looks like the magic of the Giants is more powerful than I expected, I cannot afford to be lax, better end this fast).

Laufey: Look! He is so frightened by my might that he cannot move, hahahah!

Ymir: You fool don't let your guard down!

Laufey: Don't worry dad, this next one will be the last.

He leans forward and a magical circle appears before his mouth, and he fires 'Ice Cannon' at him which freezes everything in its path indiscriminately.

Abaddon: (Here is my chance) Absharu: Enu Hamsu: Nasinu[29]!

Absharu shines with a light blue aura and Abaddon points it in the incoming blast and the blast disappears.

Everyone looks aghast, Laufey the most, wondering what the hell just happened to that huge ice blast.

---

[29] Fifth stance: Avarice.

Abaddon: I believe this is yours.

As Laufey looks at him with a puzzled and dumbfounded look, Abaddon extends his left hand towards him, causing a magical circle to appear before it and fires the blast back at Laufey with double the size and purple black in colour as opposed to its clear silver white.

Laufey ends up stricken by his own magic and his body gets completely blown to bits, large chunks falling onto the deep snow.

Abaddon: I guess I win.

Taking a moment to process what had happened, the Giants finally burst out in cheers this time aimed towards Abaddon.

Now allow me to explain what really happened; the Avarice stance of Absharu allows Abaddon to absorb any form of magical attack and throw it back at the opponent with doubled force. But because Abaddon's attribute is Darkness, the nature of the attack and its effect changes accordingly as we saw with the 'Ice Cannon'

The King of the Frost Giants claps his massive hands, and the sound reverberates throughout in the form of a mighty echo.

Ymir: Brilliant! Well done! An excellent display of skills! Ymir has witnessed your power and it surpasses even that of Ymir himself.

Abaddon: Thank you (this idiot just saw his son get blown to oblivion before his eyes and the first thing he does is congratulate me; by Baal, just what sort of creatures are these?).

Ymir: Ymir acknowledges you as a mighty king and so the 'Fristoren[30]' will join you in battle.

Abaddon: Now that is the answer I have been seeking.

Ymir: What would you have us do?

Abaddon: I would have you gather your forces and have them ready for marching, we will be heading to Orkenheim after I settle my business with the other Giant tribes.

Ymir: You wish to see Surtr and Brundig and ask for them to join your cause as well?

---

[30] Frost people.

Abaddon: Indeed, I do.

Ymir: Ymir advices against that, Surtr's folk are very stubborn and hotheaded they will not yield, neither will Brundig's folk but because they are hermits and live secluded in their mountains.

Abaddon: I told you; I will use any means necessary.

Ymir: Even so I would still advice against employing the Fjalltor[31], they are not fighting people they only wish to live in peace.

Abaddon: No, every creature counts, I intend to hit Avalon with all the force I can muster, and I will do so.

Ymir: If you wish it so then be it, although it saddens me deeply.

Abaddon: Believe me Ymir, if I don't do this now there will be no dawn for the rest of you, if I end up losing the war the forces of Avalon will descend upon the other races with great fury and uproot them from this world.

Ymir: Ymir is not very familiar with the ways of those beyond our borders, but if you say so then it must be so, and we must avoid a grim future for us all.

Abaddon: For that end I will need a guide for I have never been to the lands beyond Niflheim therefore I can't use my 'Greater Teleportation' spell.

Ymir: Ymir will take you to the border of Surtrheim but will not traverse yonder for its fires are too intense for even Ymir to handle as it is vice-versa, which is how we've kept the peace between our two tribes.

Abaddon: Makes sense, and you have my gratitude for offering to be my guide great Ymir.

Ymir: Ymir offers because he knows these lands better than anyone, therefore Ymir is aware of a shortcut that will lead us straight at 'Helgrind'.

Abaddon: Lead the way then.

And he hops on his shoulder, and they go on their way.

Ymir takes him through a frozen tundra which was hidden out of sight by numerous hills which made it really difficult to locate if not by the guidance of Ymir. Once they pass it, they end up traversing across a wide ravine which brings them straight before the 'Helgrind', 'The Gates of Hell'. The gates were made of iron and were black. They were wedged between the two ice-covered cliff sides and were as big as a Giant. There was no handle to open them for they could only be opened from the inside. Their top was adorned with spikes, curving upwards. No Giant kept watch for there was no need; as Ymir said, the fires in

---

[31] Mountain people.

Surtrheim burn so hot that even his own kin could not endure them. Any other foolish enough to pass beyond them would be turned to cinder in a matter of seconds.

Ymir: This is as far Ymir goes, Demon King.

Abaddon: This far is well enough, I'll take it from here.

Ymir: Ymir wonders, will you be able to withstand the scorching inferno that awaits beyond these gates?

Abaddon: Don't worry about me, I have the blessing of Baal and with it the protection of the Heldur[32], it will keep me safe from their harm for no flame is hotter than the blue flames that burn in his domain.

Ymir: Then Ymir will bid you farewell for now at least.

Abaddon: Go, and make sure your Giants are ready.

Ymir: I wish you luck with your negotiations (he turns and heads back).

Abaddon: Who needs luck when you have power… Oh great Baal, grant me your divine protection and I shall grant you a hundred sacrifices (he says in Dhalsarrian).

And an aura of blue flames envelops him and swirls protectively around him and he ditches the Wyvern pelt.

Thusly he enters through the gate, and nothing could prepare him for the sight at hand for it was more intense than he had hoped.

Smouldering embers dot the landscape and obnoxious fumes that reek of sulphur fill the air making it difficult to breathe. The skies above are covered by clouds of ash and ash falls all around like a black snow. The heat was so intense that it made the vision blurry and caused migraines to occur. The land was barren and scorched, devoid of all lifeforms. Fiery geysers erupt here and there along the way, shooting high up in the sky. Lakes of bubbling lava fill the land as well, and in the distance a massive volcano would erupt violently producing the aforementioned elements and spewing scorching magma and lava. This place was the true embodiment of the word 'inferno'.

As he walks, the land sizzles beneath his feet but he was protected, though he has to cover his mouth as to not breathe in the ashen air.

Abaddon: I reckon that volcano is where Surtr resides.

---

[32] Abyssal Flames in Giant.

And he was right, Surtr the King of the Fire Giants had made that volcano his own abode, Ralekgruve, 'The Searing Pit' it was called, and he makes his way there.

Baal's blessing made it possible for him to make it there unharmed and he enters inside, facing no resistance along the way which again he found it not strange at all for the Giants were convinced that none could enter let alone travel through the land.

In the middle of the volcano there is a lake of lava like the ones outside but since this one was inside it; it was hotter than any other and despite the protection of both the blessing and his magical armour, Abaddon notices that the surface of his plating gives off a slight steam.

Then the lake begins to bubble and boil as the volcano shakes and Abaddon presumes it would erupt again but instead of rising to the surface, the lake splashes open, spraying some of the magma on him, but it simply glosses him over due to the Abyssal flames.

What comes out from it is a being the same size as Ymir, with its head almost reaching the mouth of the volcano. Its body was made of molten rock, and veins full of lava instead of blood flowed throughout it and its eyes burn bright. That is Surtr, King of the Fire Giants, and once he spots Abaddon, he reaches for the giant sword that was set propped against the side of the volcano by the lake and sets it ablaze.

Surtr: Who dares enter my domain, speak now or face my wrath!

Abaddon: I am neither friend nor foe, I am someone who would have your allegiance.

Surtr: You come here and make demands of me? I will put you in your place, puny man!

He comes down at him with his flaming sword, but Abaddon is left unharmed.

Surtr: What is this? No living creature can go unharmed when faced with my terrible fire!

Abaddon: That may be so, but it is no ordinary fire that guards me.

Surtr: (looks closer at him) A coating of blue flames? I have never seen nor heard of such flames before, what sort of devilry is this?

Abaddon: It is the Heldur, a subject of my Lardur ed Godur, Haldar[33], it is through his blessing that I am shielded from the harms of this land.

---

[33] Lord and God, Baal

Surtr: So that is how you were able to make it all the way here. Who are you, little one?

Abaddon: My name is Abaddon, son of Demiurgos, King of Demons and Master of Monsters.

Surtr: Helertoren ed Skrimtoren[34] you say, then you must be from the lands down south.

Abaddon: Indeed I am.

Surtr: It is my first time meeting someone like you, do all of your kindred command this beldur[35]?

Abaddon: No, not all, there is only one race of my kind that is able to freely utilise them, our first king was of this race, perhaps you've heard the name Magdabulgu.

Surtr: Magdabulgu…no, I'm afraid not, we don't get news from the outside world, with how isolated we are.

Abaddon: There is, nor ever was someone as powerful as him in controlling the beldur.

Surtr: And for what purpose would the kindred of such being with their protection as well want my allegiance for?

Abaddon: Fight for me, so that I may conquer the world.

Surtr: An enticing notion, I always wanted an opportunity to shower the world in the flames of Surtrheim and make it snow black ash.

Abaddon: Then this is a chance you must take for the sake of your ambition.

Surtr: Yes indeed, I will show everyone the might of Surtr! One swing from my sword burns down mountains! With two I can burn whole cities, with three I can turn an entire country to cinder and ash! All will fear me and tremble, my name will be etched in the annals of history and songs will be sung of my terror in the times long past my life!

Abaddon: And all that can be yours if you march out with me.

Surtr: As someone who wields the favour of a flame that I cannot hope to grasp and as someone who is willing to unleash me upon all I am inclined to follow your lead, Abaddon, son of Demiurgos.

Abaddon: (smirks beneath his hood) (If I had known that it would be this easy to persuade him, I'd have come here before, it is my own folly for believing that he would be the same as Ymir).

---

[34] Demons and Monsters

[35] Blue fire

Abaddon: Although, I was led to believe that you are stubborn (hot headed you are I'm afraid).

Surtr: You make sound arguments, no need for spite here.

Abaddon: Fair point, now all that remains are the Mountain Giants.

Surtr: Hah! You would call upon them to fight? Cowards, the lot of 'em! They do not have what it takes to go to battle, they would rather live in peace with their trees and birds! Sometimes I wonder if they truly are Giants.

Abaddon: I will have their allegiance one way or another, I need all the forces I can muster.

Surtr: If you must have them follow you, just threaten that I will burn down their homes and forests, that will surely set them off.

Abaddon: An interesting proposition.

Surtr: Or better yet, I accompany you personally.

Abaddon: No need to trouble yourself; I can manage on my own.

Surtr: It is no big deal, I always wanted to give those cowards a piece of my mind.

Abaddon: You're not one of action, are you?

Surtr: Um…

Abaddon: Are there any other things you wished you've done that you haven't?

Surtr: … I can't think of anything else at the moment.

Abaddon: (Which means there probably are, what a dimwit…).

Surtr: …

Abaddon: You can stop thinking now, let's get a move on.

Surtr: Right…

Abaddon: (Is he still thinking about it? Good grief…).

Surtr: How long is that protection going to last you? Because unfortunately, even though we are on good terms, I am unable to make my heat burn less for you for this is how nature created me.

Abaddon: It should last long enough until we finish our task.

Surtr: If that be the case then I shall place you on my shoulder, Abaddon, son of Demiurgos.

Abaddon: Just Abaddon is fine…

Surtr: You want me to call you 'Just Abaddon'?

Abaddon: No, you nimrod, just call me by the name 'Abaddon'.

Surtr: Oh, alright then, that makes more sense.

Abaddon: (By Baal I am dealing with braindead halfwits, I hope at least that these Mountainous ones have some descent brains in their skulls…)

Surtr: Does your sword have a name?

Abaddon: Yes, it does, it's called Absharu, it means 'The Destroyer' in my language.

Surtr: A fitting name for a sword, mine is called Oeskbreidur it means 'One Who Brings Ash'.

Abaddon: That fits as well, considering your nature.

Surtr: Then we are of the same mind.

Abaddon: Oh joy… (…I wonder how Father and Mother are doing, I wonder if they are still amongst the living…Oh great Baal, protect them, protect everyone, don't let another soul die until I save them all, and I will, the day of reckoning is nigh…).

And so, Surtr takes them eastward towards the land of Fjalldorfheim.

CAPITVLVM XV

TERRA MAGNORVM[xiv]

Thus, they reach the end of the border of Surtrheim and before them lay a forest with firs almost as big as Surtr which allocated the natural border with Fjalldorfheim. As the Giants of these lands were tame people there were no gates or guard posts of any kind for they believed that the rest would not pick any fights or cause them trouble as it was unwarranted.

Abaddon: I've never seen such tall trees before in my life.

Surtr: This is my first time seeing any kind of trees, are they all this big?

Abaddon: No, most trees are of normal size, yet again they are only normal by our standards so you could say there isn't any set norm for normal in this world, it all depends on the perspective and the background of the one that is making an observation.

Surtr: Huh?

Abaddon: Never mind, carry on.

Surtr: You talk funny sometimes.

Abaddon: (That's because you're too dumb to understand).

Surtr: These trees are in my way!

And so, he swings Oeskbreidur and with one fell swoop burns away the nearby trees and clears up a path, however due to the nature of the flames the other trees are set ablaze, and a forest fire erupts around. But the duo did not care and pressed on unfazed and as Surtr walked the greenery beneath his feet was set ablaze as well leaving a trail of massive footprints etched in the scorched earth.

The raging blaze catches the attention of a couple of Giants who were out in the forest to gather wood for their lunch, and they start yelling out in panic.

Giant: Look! The forest is on fire!

Giant#2: Over there! An Eldurtor[36] is approaching! We must warn the others!

One of the Giants pulls out a gargantuan horn and blows it, warning the others in the village one of whom rings the emergency bell that rings with the sound of thousands church bells.

The blast from the horn was so powerful that it shook the trees themselves and scared off a couple of local birds who were as big as a Giant's arm and those arms were big.

Some of them kept shouting 'the others are coming' and they all hurried to gather what they can and evacuate the village.

These Giants are akin ordinary villagers; they are herders, farmers, smiths, communal people that live in settlements also akin to human villages, and their homes are giant huts. They wear clothing made of the fur of wild animals and they make footwear and belts out of their skin. Their appearance is also very human like except they have much more hair on their bodies and their skin is thick.

On their heads, they have big and bushy beards and eyebrows as well, and they have big round black eyes. Their women are comelier however, lacking the excess hair on their bodies. It is also worth noting that they are as not as big as the Frost and Fire Giants but a few heads shorter. Each village has a village chieftain but the chief of them all is Brundig who lives in a big hall in the centremost and grandest village called Mitdur which means 'town in the middle'.

The reason why they are called Mountain Giants is not because they live on mountains but because their area is a heavily mountainous one having a mount almost on every turn.

Abaddon: What was that sound? It sounded like a horn.

Surtr: Some of them must have noticed us and used it as a warning sign.

Abaddon: Which means there must be a village nearby, it would be bad for us if they manage to evacuate before we get there, we need to get at least to one Giant and have them reveal the location of their leader; make haste, Surtr!

Surtr: I will run as fast as these legs of mine allow it.

---

[36] Fire people.

Now he gives a thunderous bellow and picks up the pace, sprinting forward and toppling down every tree along the way.

The ground beneath him trembles as if it is being stumped by the hoofs of countless horses and the crowns of the evergreen trees shake and shiver, dropping their pines on the ground.

Just as the local Giants are making efforts to evacuate, they spot the oncoming Surtr in the distance and feel the tremor that is accompanying him.

Giant: They are here!

Giant#2: It is only one of them!

Giant: Doesn't matter, one is bad enough, we aren't going make it!

Chief: We must hold him off here and allow at least the women and children to evacuate!

Giant#3: It's impossible Chief! We aren't strong enough! We'll be slaughtered!

Chief: Would you rather die along with your families?

Giant#3: …

Giant: The Chief is right! We may not be warriors, but we are still Jotnar – we are strong!

Thus, they cheer themselves on and go to grab any tool they can find to use as a weapon – from chopping axes to grates and shovels.

Chief: Come on!

Abaddon: Looks like they are willing to sacrifice themselves in order to allow their families to escape, how foolish.

Surtr: I will deal with them in an instant!

Much to the Giants' surprise, however the women stand their ground as well.

Giantess: Come on! We are not cowards! Let us stand with our men! If this Eldurtor is allowed to reach Mitdur we will all be killed regardless, so if we are fated to die anyway let it be amongst our husbands!

And the Giantesses let out war cries and grab whatever they can find for a weapon.

Chieftain: Hildegard what are you doing? You must protect the children!

Hilde: I am, Dyorn, here with you!

Dyorn: Foolish woman, the lot of you!

Surtr: They actually mean to oppose us?

Abaddon: Make sure you let one of them live.

Surtr: Skuldig![37]

Surtr: Findsttu eldur min pathur!

He yells out 'feel the power of my flames' and stabs his sword in the ground, and through his magic he sends out a powerful blazing wave that scorches the earth and sets the whole village along with the Giants on fire. The huts burn down in an instant and not even the Giants' thick skin will avail them from the searing pain, and they fall down, one by one, in screams of agony, reduced to cinders. These poor souls never stood a chance.

Now using his magic again, Surtr recalls the flames from Dyorn the Chieftain who falls on the ground only badly burnt, but on death's door regardless.

Surtr kneels near him so that Abaddon may address him, but the half-dead Giant spoke first.

Dyorn: Why…what have we ever done to you? In what way have we grieved you to deserve this injustice, oh great Eldurtor?

Abaddon: It was never our intention to harm you, we only wished to speak, it's you who assumed the opposite and took a hostile stand against us, so if you want to blame anyone blame your own harshness, Giant.

Dyorn: And who might…you be?

Abaddon: That's of little concern at this point, tell me what I need to know before you draw your last breath.

Dyorn: … You didn't even give us a warning …instead you attacked mercilessly.

Abaddon: Sadly, I don't take kindly to those that draw their weapons on me and furthermore I find myself at wits end of my goodwill.

Dyorn: Your way of talking and speech betray you…you are not from these parts…are you?

Abaddon: I'm the one asking the questions here.

Dyorn: …You burned my village to the ground, and you turned my people to lumps of coal…you could at least do me a courtesy and let me find out who is responsible for this…

Abaddon: My name is Abaddon and I come from Helheim.

Dyorn: Ah so you are a Helertor…yes…I have heard stories of your people…

[37] Understood.

Abaddon: As you can see, I am very real, and I've told you who I am now you tell me what I need to know.

Surtr: Speak, cur! In what hole does your king hide?

Dyorn: Never… (passes away).

Abaddon: …

Surtr: Insolent…! Raghhh! For that, I shall burn this land until no tree nor house is left standing!

Abaddon: No, that way we risk burning down other villages as well and I need all the Giants I can spare.

Surtr: Then how do you suppose we find him? This land is vast; it will take days.

Abaddon: I have my ways.

And he works his black magic and waits for someone to hear his call. After a few moments of silence, the nearby trees begin to jostle and the giant shrubbery to rustle and out of it comes out a creature unlike ever before: a giant black wolf with size going up to Surtr's waist.

Wolf: Are you the one that calls me?

The Great Wolf speaks, and as he speaks his deep yellow eyes burn bright.

His fur seems ruffed up and it appears that he has multiple scars around his body.

Abaddon: A giant talking wolf, I never expected a creature like you to answer my call, then again considering we are in Giant's land it should be of no wonder that the animals are of this stature as well.

Wolf: Mind your tongue, halfling! This is no ordinary animal that stands before you! I am Fenris Wolf! Master of these forests!

Abaddon: A mutt with an attitude, it is you who needs to mind their tongue, 'friend'.

Fenris: My fangs and teeth are sharper than any blade, and I would have no problem prying you open from your armour like a turtle from its shell, ripping you apart! (Growls)

At this moment, Abaddon silently casts 'Nimu Qulumuu', 'Aura of Dread' which is the second to highest of his spells of fright, and Fenris being a fierce but simple animal is easily affected and becomes overcome by a dreadful sense of despair, causing him to shiver and whine like a tiny, frightened mutt.

Once he judges that he has had enough, Abaddon dispels the spell.

Fenris: My apologies for speaking out of turn, you must be some powerful Wizard.

Abaddon: Close, I'm a Nigromancer, a Black Wizard if you will but also, I am more than that, I am a mighty King of Demons.

Surtr: And I am –

Fenris: I know who you are, Surtr Ashbringer.

Surtr: So, you've heard of me, good.

Fenris: Everyone's heard of you, and fears you, for good reason as well; just look at what you've done to this village.

Abaddon: You knew we are here?

Fenris: I picked up the scent of his fumes ever since you stepped foot in this land.

Abaddon: That far huh?

Fenris: Don't underestimate my sense of smell, it's thousand times better than that of a normal creature.

Abaddon: Astonishing, are there any more like you?

Fenris: There are many, but our numbers have dwindled due to our oft skirmishes with the Giants.

Surtr: What trouble have you with those peace lovers?

Fenris: Do not let their seemingly peaceful way of life fool you, they can be savage warriors if the need arises.

Surtr: Hahaha oh yes, we have seen how savage they can be!

Fenris: Seize your laughter, you fool! These are but normal villagers you've encountered, the folk of Mitdur are of different sort, they are fighters through and through! Not only that, but they are also wielders of powerful magic that they use to make their weapons stronger.

Abaddon: The way Ymir spoke; I was led to believe that all these folk are peaceful and hate fighting.

Fenris: The Ice one is a fool and knows not of what he speaks! It may have been so in the past but now that is changed. I complain about it, but my kin have a big part in it…many years ago we began attacking their villages and eating their young. Now these Giants may prefer to stick to their farms, but no one can sit still in the face of such danger. So, their jarl made it so that their magic would be used to protect them, and they have imbued it in the form of sacred runes in their blades and use them to smite us.

Normally, our hides are resistant to physical attacks but there is nothing even I can do against such force and so they drove us off into the darkest reaches of the woods. Many of my kin fell prey to starvation because they were too frightened to step out when food became scarce…it is a sad fate.

Abaddon: Nothing sad there, Fenris Wolf, you reap what you sow; had you stuck to your hunting grounds in the woods, this fate wouldn't have befallen you.

Fenris: It is as you say, Black Wizard, but we are creatures of prey, it is in our blood to hunt and the flesh of young Giantlings is so tasty and juicy, nice, tender, and full of blood (drools as he says this).

Abaddon: I understand, that's the law of nature, the weaker falls prey to the stronger. My name is Abaddon, by the by, and I may be of your assistance.

Fenris: Does that mean you have come to rid the Giants of their pathetic existence?

Abaddon: (On the contrary, the pathetic ones are you.) Not quite, I am here to enlist them in my army for my war effort and hearing they are in fact capable fighters makes the reason all more worthwhile.

Fenris: They will never agree to partake in such violence, but something tells me you do not take no for an answer.

Abaddon: And that something is right on the point.

Fenris: That is good to hear, that would mean this land would be free of their pest and me and my kin will be able to hunt and roam freely.

Abaddon: I wouldn't count on that either.

Fenris: Whatever do you mean?

Abaddon: I'll have you fight for me as well.

Surtr: Hah!

Fenris: Me, fight for you? To what end?

Abaddon: To an all you can eat buffet.

Fenris: That sounds enticing but I must respectfully decline, I do not believe that is something worth risking my life over.

Abaddon: Have you ever tried Dwarven meat?

His ears perk up.

Abaddon: Elven? Human?

Now he is drooling, and his eyes are flashing.

Abaddon: All of these delicatessen can be yours if you but walk out of here with me.

Fenris: You have me convinced!

Abaddon: (Simpleton).

Fenris: But that would mean we would have to fight alongside these detestable Giants!

Abaddon: Indeed, and you wouldn't be the only one, many of the factions in my army hate each other and would not be caught dead working together but they have no other option because I, the future king of this world says so and whatever I say, goes.

Fenris: The law of the strong…right, I believe we would be able to set aside our differences for the sake of good meat.

Abaddon: Good boy, now take me to where the jarl is.

Fenris: It would be my pleasure.

And so, they reach Mitdur under the guidance of Fenris Wolf.

The sight that awaits them is quite different than the rest, the town was surrounded by a large fence, as high as the Giants themselves. Most likely this was done so to keep the wolves at bay when they were more of a threat, and it has stood there ever since. Despite of its height however, Surtr and consequently Abaddon, who was perched at his shoulder, could see over it and have a look at the wooden houses inside and the grand hall that stood in the centre. The town had dirt roads as well and they all lead towards the hall. The entire town was built in a circular manner so if one would look at it high above it would look like a giant disk in the middle of a valley.

Fenris: This is it, the town of Mitdur.

Abaddon: Seems different than that village, fitting for a capital.

Fenris: It is no capital, more of a stronghold if you will. These people do not have the sense of kingdoms, so you could say that Brundig is no king either.

Abaddon: That's why he is called jarl instead.

Fenris: Correct.

Abaddon: We call those 'lords', depending on the country he could be anointed with a certain title like an 'earl', for example.

Fenris: Your way of doing things confuses me.

Surtr: Me as well.

Abaddon: It's nothing to worry about.

Surtr: I don't think they are aware of our presence.

Fenris: Leave that to me (he takes a deep breath and releases a deep howl).

His howling alerts the denizens and again the loud alarm bell is sound. Inside the hall, Brundig is deploying his men to arms. They put on their bronze plating and brandish their bronze, battle-axes. Since they were peace-loving people, they have not moved on from the bronze production of armaments.

Brundig: I didn't think they are brazen enough to come all the way here again, let's teach them a lesson boys!

And with great shouting they storm out of the gates, but they are surprised when they see only one wolf and a Fire Giant.

Brundig: Fenris! (Grunts).

Fenris: Brundig! (Growls).

Brundig: Where is the rest of your foul kind?

Fenris: Have you no eyes? It is only me and these two here.

Brundig: I only see this Eldurtor here.

Fenris: Look closer, up on his shoulder.

Abaddon: Greetings.

Brundig: Oh, 'tis a tiny man that speaks our language, are you some kind of a Gnome from these parts?

Abaddon: I beg your pardon?

Brundig: A Gnome, you know…tiny people, they live underground…

Abaddon: Never before have I heard of such creature, and I don't appreciate being confused as one!

Fenris: Fool! This is no Gnome! He is a mighty Wizard King!

Brundig: A Wizard that is a king? There is no such thing! You must take me a fool.

Fenris: Because you are!

Surtr: You are both fools! He is neither a Wizard nor a Gnome he is a Helertor from the south! A king from Helheim!

And the Giants begin to murmur amongst themselves.

Brundig: Helheim is real? I thought it only existed in the stories we used to scare our children…

Abaddon: You use our existence as bedtime stories for your brats? I never thought I'd live to see such humiliation!

Brundig: You must understand, we mean no disrespect, we know nothing of the world beyond our borders nor do we care to know for it doesn't concern us.

Giant: Um jarl, I'm pretty sure they are the ones responsible for the fire and the burning of that village, I don't think you should be speaking with them so friendlily…

Brundig: Right! So, it was you huh?

Abaddon: (Idiots! Idiots all of them! Every last one! How was this person even made jarl?) Enough of these sideshows! I'm here on serious business.

Brundig: And what makes you think we'll do business with those that brought so much pain to our people?

Abaddon: I'm afraid you're absent choice.

Brundig: Is that so? Well, I say there is always choice!

Abaddon: Before you do anything stupid, I suggest you take a moment and think of those who are dear to you and the rest of your kind, what fate would they suffer should you act brashly.

Brundig: Only a coward would use the lives of innocents in their dealings!

Abaddon: You call it cowardice I call it leverage.

Brundig: What would you have me do?

Abaddon: Fight for me and I will spare the civilians.

Brundig: You would drag us into conflicts that do not concern us, you are a cruel man, sir king…

Abaddon: I'm no man, jarl, I'm a Heletor and cruelty is what we do, but then again, we all have one inside of us, be it a man or otherwise, do we not?

Brundig: I suppose you're right…you must be driven by great need to come all the way here…however I must ask compensation for the lives lost in that burning.

Abaddon: I believe me allowing your people to live is compensation enough, jarl.

Brundig: …

Giant: You mustn't let him coax you, jarl!

Brundig: Be silent, Snori…

Abaddon: Do we have an agreement?

Brundig: (looks at Surtr and his flaming sword, at Fenris and his gnarling snout then back at Abaddon and with a heavy heart extends a hand) Aye…we do.

Abaddon: Excellent, shake his hand for me, Surtr.

They shake hands, Brundig's hand slightly sizzles from the heat.

Brundig: But if we are to go to battle, we will need better armour and weapons.

Abaddon: Of course, you will be provided with the proper equipment.

Brundig: …

Abaddon: Cheer up, once all is over, I will let you return to your homeland, all you have to do is survive.

Brundig: And survive we shall.

Abaddon: Now gather all your able-bodied men, we leave at once.

Brundig: How will we pass? We can neither brave the scorching inferno to the west nor the harsh cold to the south.

Abaddon: Leave that to me.

Fenris: It should be also mentioned that we will be working together.

All the Giants yell out 'what?' in unison.

Abaddon: I suppose that wouldn't be a problem.

Brundig: It is a problem! They are our archenemies!

Fenris: You as well! But I am willing to overlook it for the delicious buffet!

Brundig: Of course! You are an animal! One has to offer you a good chunk of meat and you'll wag your tail like a housedog!

Fenris: Why you! I ought a –

Abaddon: Silence! There will be no fighting amongst yourselves!

As he yells, he releases his aura, and they freeze in place.

Abaddon: Go at once!

Brundig: Yes! Right! Come on boys.

Abaddon: Baal, give me patience…

Fenris: Who is this Baal?

Abaddon: He is our deity.

Fenris: Why would you believe in such nonsense? Gods do not exist.

Abaddon: You didn't think I existed yet here I am.

Fenris: That maybe so but you are still a denizen of this world, to believe in a higher existence out of this plane is foolish. We are all made by mana, there is all there is to it, neither God nor Devil has any part in it.

Abaddon: I won't hold it against you, nonbelievers are always sceptics until proven wrong.

Fenris: You're saying you are able to convince me otherwise?

Surtr: Take a look at the flame that surrounds him, it is otherworldly, 'Heldur' it is called.

Fenris: Truly beldur does not exist here but it is nothing more than wizardry I reckon. Tell me, have you ever seen this God of yours?

Abaddon: The Gods can't take physical form therefore they can't directly make themselves known to us but some of our priests are able to communicate with them on a spiritual level and even borrow power from them.

Fenris: Doesn't that mean that they are siphoning energy from the source of mana itself?

Abaddon: Hmmm, and what about the Titans? It is said they were given birth after the spilling of the Creator's blood by his children, the Gods.

Fenris: Fables and fairy tales, utter nonsense.

Abaddon: For a wolf living in this backwater place, you sure are sharp.

Fenris: I may be an Ulfur, but I am no simpleton, I understand how this world operates, call it natural instinct or whatever.

Abaddon: I think we'll be able to get along quite well.

Fenris: As long as you don't try to convert me.

Abaddon: Nonsense, we've never once tried to force our beliefs on others.

Fenris: Only your rule it would seem.

Abaddon: That's more important.

Fenris: Heh, well I will go and gather my pack and return here.

Abaddon: I will see you presently in that case.

Fenris: I will try to be as quick as possible.

He says that and dashes forward towards the woods.

Abaddon: Are you okay, Surtr? You seem absentminded.

Surtr: I was trying to fathom the meaning of your conversation, all this talk about Gods and mana is confusing to me.

Abaddon: Don't try too hard; you might damage your brain.

Surtr: You're right, that would be quite the tragedy.

Abaddon: Yes…it would (sigh).

A few hours pass and out comes Brundig with all his fighting men and from what Abaddon can reckon there are about a hundred of them.

Brundig: Here we are, all we can gather.

Abaddon: What of the other villages?

Brundig: (shakes his head) They are just ordinary people they will be of no use to you, these boys here know how to properly wield an axe.

Abaddon: I guess you will do then.

Fenris also arrives with the packs of Giant Wolves.

Fenris: We are ready.

Abaddon: Very good, we can move now.

He casts 'Mass Teleportation' and a massive, magical circle appears on the ground, encompassing the entire area where they were standing. The next moment they are teleported to Orchotrhond.

The bunch are astounded and perplexed, never having witnessed such a feat before, exclaiming things like 'incredible', 'unbelievable', 'unreal'...

Brundig: What sort of magic is this ...?

Abaddon: It is a spell called 'Mass Teleportation', the highest level of the 'Blink' spell. It allows me to transport as many people or objects I may choose to a destination of my choosing. Amazing, is it not?

Fenris: Amazing is an understatement, with this you could easily transport armies from one place to another without having to march long distances.

Abaddon: Yes, that is quite convenient, unfortunately it is also quite taxing. Now I'll do the same with Surtr's and then Ymir's people.

Now he uses 'Greater Teleportation' to get him and Surtr to Surtrheim and he orders him to gather his kind as well. Once that is done, they are transported to the plains of Orcothrond as well and the Frost Giants too and ultimately all three races find themselves face to face for the first time and a loud general conversation erupts between them.

Abaddon: I'm sure you all have a lot to talk about, so I'll leave you at that while I make the final stop.

Ymir: More are coming?

Abaddon: Oh yes, many, many more.

With those words, he vanishes back at the land of the Dragonkin to muster the remaining of Baltia's army of beasts...

CAPITVLVM XVI

AFFECTVS DIVERSI[xv]

Back at Garaz Drakiz

Morgana: Welcome back, again.

Abaddon: Don't be sassy or I won't take you.

Morgana: Does it mean you're ready then?

Abaddon: Once all the Dragonkin assemble, we are leaving.

Fragora: I'll go make the call then.

Abaddon: Much appreciated; however, you can leave Glacinia to me.

Fragora: Understood.

Fulga: Are we going to a new home?

Abaddon: No little one, you and your brothers are staying here with mommy.

Fulga: But I want to see daddy…

Abaddon: You will…just not now.

Fulga: Promise?

Abaddon: …I'm sorry, I'm not in a position to promise you that.

Fulga: (her eyes widen and water) Are we going to burry daddy like Aunt Frigga…?

Abaddon: I can't promise you that either, no one's future is safe in a time of war, even my own.

Fulga: …I don't want daddy to die, mommy will be sad…I will… (stops herself and weeps).

Morgana: There, there (picks her up and pats her) don't cry, I'm sure you'll see your daddy and your daddy wouldn't want to see you cry now, would he? Dragons are strong and mighty, and they don't shed tears, do they?

Fulga shakes her little head.

Furgon: Why is sister sad? Did something happen to dad?

Abaddon: Your father is fine, everyone is fine; there is no need to worry.

Furgon: Then why is she crying…?

Abaddon: She cries because the future is unsafe…and things we are unbeknown of frighten us and make us sad, but we need not weep, for it may also hold moments of glory.

Furgon: I don't really understand but I know crying is no good.

Abaddon: It's not a sin to cry, little one, we are all allowed to shed tears when the time is right.

Fulga: I get it, I won't cry, it's not the time.

Morgana: That's right, how smart you are.

Fulga smiles with a toothy grin.

Abaddon: (*sigh*…poor innocent souls) … (averts his gaze and focuses on something else, using telepathy to reach Glauros) (Glauros, can you hear me?).

Glauros: Yes, my lord, I hear you.

Abaddon: (The time is ripe, assemble everyone and come meet me at Dragon's Head.)

Glauros: Thy will be done, my lord.

With that, all were notified. Fragora flew around the other lands of the Dragonkin sending them the message with a distinct bellow, one that said, 'it is time to sortie, war is coming'. And all heard her call and flew from their dwellings, others dug beneath the ground and came to gather at the once home of the Dark Dragons.

Seeing them all gathered fills Abaddon with hope and a feeling of potency rises within him and he begins to address them all with his mighty voice.

Abaddon: My winged and non-winged brothers and sisters you are all gathered here for one purpose and one purpose alone, and that is to lend me your aid as you once did, so that we may restore our place as rulers of Avalon! I know how long you've waited for this hour, the hour when we wreak our vengeance to those that brought to ruin and end our glorious reign! But I ask you to wait just a bit longer and stave your hunger for death and destruction. One year! One year is the time I need to fully restore my former powers, it may even take less than that, and when that happens, when I'm fully able to breathe in the air of my prime, the hour will fall upon us to fly out and tell the world: we are back!

And then loud roars fill in the entire area, passionate and energetic roars of triumph and victory long craved. The sound was so loud that it would rupture one's ears but nevertheless Morgana stands tall and proud with a satisfying smile on her face amidst that draconic cacophony for she felt pleasure and not dread.

Abaddon pulls out his sword and creates the rift one more so that the Dragons may pass.

Abaddon: For now, we move to a new land so that we may join the rest of our brothers in arms! Onwards!

Now they flood the portal as they go through one by one.

Morgana: What is that?

Abaddon: A space rift, it connects Dragon's Peak and Orcothrond. It is a teleportation spell of the highest level.

Morgana: You can even do that much? Incredible!

Abaddon: Oh, I can do much more than that, just wait and see.

Morgana: You never cease to amaze me.

Abaddon: Glad I can provide high quality entertainment.

Morgana: I didn't mean it like that.

Abaddon: I know, I'm simply messing with you (slightly chuckles).

Morgana: …Dummy (mumbles).

While this was going on, elsewhere a blood eagle was making its way back to Andviler. Since there was no word from his father, Haldur, son of Baldur has beckoned Luzira, Amra's little sister and second in line to the throne to work her magic and assess the situation, as she too was equally worried.

Luzira looked much like Amra, one could say they were almost identical, but they were not twins, though people easily confused them when at a young age. Unlike Amra however she wears her hair long, and combed, making it smooth and strait, and it was long, reaching up to her waist. Her figure was slim and gracious, and at the moment she was wearing a long, velvet dress of deep crimson. The dress covered her chest area, going up to the base of her head. She had the same, bright red eyes as Amra, inherited from their mother. Her name she got after her grandmother on her mother's side. Usually, it was the custom for the older sister to inherit the name, since the matriarchy was established, however her mother, Gizela did it out of spite to her own mother, and named Amra after their father's mother, leaving the second child to bear her name.

Haldur looked like a younger version of Baldur, only his beard was shorter and grizzly, and his head was bald. He was dressed in royal vestments decorated with many jewels, and he had a long, royal cape of emerald green, with the family crest at the back.

Once the eagle returned, it perches itself on her shoulder and whispers the goings on of the battlefield.

Iadvrim was present as well because he wanted to know what fruits his knowledge of the terrain had born.

Haldur: What news?

Luzira: (sigh) It says the field was barren, devoid of any body or weapon.

Haldur: So, it is just as I feared, they have been defeated… (slams his fist in anger).

Luzira: Not only defeated but it would seem that that wretch Abaddon has acquired the bodies of the dead to use as his foot soldiers.

Iadvrim: Defeated? But that's impossible! I told them of areas only known to us Goblins!

Haldur: And look what good it brought us! My father is dead because of you! You might have been leading them to a trap all along!

Iadvrim: I have done no such thing your highness I swear on my life! I don't know how this could've …happened… (he comes to a sudden realisation).

Haldur: What is it? Speak!

Iadvrim: It must have been some of my kinsmen…they have joined hands with the Demon and told him everything…it's the only explanation.

Luzira: This is what you get when you betray your own, you get betrayed in return.

Iadvrim: I'm still innocent here!

Haldur: Doesn't matter! Your actions are what brought this misfortune upon us!

Iadvrim: That is not fair! I shared my knowledge with you! Without my map they would've perished even sooner!

Haldur: Silence!

Iadvrim: …

Luzira: The fault lies within us as well; we should've sent our own scouts to map out the area instead of relying to vermin.

Iadvrim: What you shouldn't have done 'my lady' is start a war with the Demon to begin with! What hope had you of winning when only one of his men has the strength of hundreds of yours!

Luzira glares at him.

Iadvrim: Agh! I was a fool of ever going against him and for what? A dead daughter! Idiot! You can make as many as you can, but you can't remake your kingdom! ...Khazan Ainul would still be mine...

Haldur: You can regret your decisions in the afterlife.

Iadvrim: Huh?

Haldur unsheathes his short sword and severs his head which tumbles on the floor while his dead body falls over on the table.

Haldur: I release you from your service (wipes the blood off and sheathes it).

Luzira: And good riddance (licks a bit of the blood and then spits) disgusting.

Haldur: (snaps his fingers) Clean this mess up.

A couple of his servants come in and remove the corpse while the others clean the blood from the table and the floor.

Haldur: We must notify the others.

Luzira: Mhm and organise our coronation ceremonies, good thing I planned in advance.

Haldur: You already suspected her to be dead?

Luzira: What other option is there? The Goblin was right, we had no chance from the start.

Haldur: (sigh) I begged my father not to go but the stubborn bastard wouldn't listen, his own pride mattered more than the voice of his own son.

Luzira: I advised my sister against it as well, but she wouldn't listen to reason, same as your old man, she was too blinded by rage and I don't blame her, we've known Nirvalena since we were children, losing her was like losing a sister. I was enraged too but I knew better. If only mother were alive, she might have talked some sense into her.

Haldur: A broken heart is not easy to tame, it makes us do foolish things sometimes at the cost of our own lives...

Luzira: Breaking ours in the process...what a nonsensical way to go...we should fight for the living not to avenge the dead...and certainly not broken bonds... (she says that last part with a lowered tone).

Haldur: That's very clever and very true…that's why we need to be better and think of the future.

Luzira: To be honest, I don't believe that there is any future for us.

Haldur: You don't believe we can win this war?

Luzira: No…I don't, and when Abaddon wins, it won't be like last time, he is going to kill us all, every last one so that no one else will rise up against him, it's going to be a genocide.

Haldur: You can't say for certain! I refuse to believe that there is no hope! If we go by that defeatist attitude, we might as well give up now!

Luzira: Cast aside your idealistic thinking for a moment and think rationally Haldur, think of the time two hundred years ago, think of what Abaddon achieved only with his own army from Dhalsarria and the fire breathing lizards form the North. Right now, even as we speak, he moves to amass armies beyond our borders, armies of which we know nothing, neither their strength nor numbers.

Haldur: Aye we do not, but we've confirmed that they will not cooperate with him.

Luzira: They refused him because he was weak, but he won't be weak for long, each passing day his power returns to him and when he is fully restored, he will have their allegiance, heck! He may not even wait that long.

Haldur: We must hold faith, Luzira! When we, the leaders lose faith is the time when we are defeated for real.

Luzira: Our people won't survive on faith alone, Haldur.

Haldur: What are you suggesting? You don't mean?

Luzira: I've already made up my mind…when I'm crowned queen, I will lead my people to the East.

Haldur: Luzira! What you speak of is treachery!

Luzira: It's not treachery, it is common sense!

Haldur: He's brought nothing but death and suffering to us! He killed your sister, my father!

Morvene: I despise Abaddon as much as you but it's the only way! It's the only way we'll survive! Like I said, we must fight for the living!

Haldur: This is madness! You cannot do this! The others won't allow it!

Luzira: Then the others will have to kill me if they wish to stop me! My decision stands and my people will stand with me!

Haldur: You would turn your back on your brothers and sisters with whom you've built strong relations! You would betray us all?

Luzira: Don't mistake my intentions for betrayal! I love all of the races dearly, but I refuse to let my own people get slaughtered, and if you are any wiser than your father, I suggest you do the same!

Haldur: You wound me, Luzira! You wound me deeply…

Luzira: I'm sorry…but I will not die in vain like my sister (stands up and leaves).

Haldur: I curse you, Luzira! I curse you!

At the same time in Camelot

Arthur: Emrys! I hear you asked to see me personally.

Emrys: Sire! It is finished sire! I did it!

Arthur: Is it…?

Emrys: Yes, it is finally complete! Behold! The Philosopher's Stone! *He holds up a big lump of a crystal-like stone with a strong red colour.*

Arthur: Does it work?

Emrys: I haven't tested it yet, that is why I called for you, I wanted you to have the honours of the first trial.

Arthur: Good thinking, my lad, hand it over.

Emrys: (gives him the stone) Here sire, a normal pebble.

Arthur: Right, what do I do now?

Emrys: Just touch it with the stone.

He does that and the stone begins to glow and after a few moments lo and behold! The pebble turns to gold.

Emrys: It works! Oh, Gods it works!

Arthur: (stutters) Magnificent! Ohhh my dear boy, this changes everything!

Emrys: I'm well aware, sire.

Arthur: Now all we have to do is mass produce this and our kingdom will be self-sustainable, no longer will we have to rely on those filthy Dwarves for ore (looks at him) it is able to produce it, is it not?

Emrys: By tweaking its properties, I should be able to make it transmute materials into manalith, yes.

Arthur: This is the single most significant discovery in the history of Camelot, nay! Of whole Avalon I daresay.

Emrys: And you would be right sire, countless magicians have tried and failed, not even those of Hathasia, the birthplace of alchemy have succeeded.

Arthur: None must know about this, this must be used and produced in utmost secrecy.

Emrys: Indeed, why should others share in our hard-earned labour, if they want it, they can make it of their own, if they can that is (laughs).

Arthur: Yes, yes, for now make this one so that it may produce manalith and put it to use immediately.

Emrys: Right away, sire; however, I am still bothered.

Arthur: By what?

Emrys: Won't the others grow suspicious if we suddenly cancel our trade with the Dwarves?

Arthur: Of course, we will keep the current trade only for pretext, but we will lower our grain supplies in return and if they make a fuss about it, we will offer them to lower their export as well.

Emrys: Your cunning knows no bounds, sire.

Arthur: When you've lived as long as I have, you learn to do things in a certain way.

A knock comes on the door.

Arthur: Enter!

Guard: There is a meeting of the council sire, the others ask for your presence.

Arthur: I will be there presently.

The guard bows and leaves.

Arthur: It is probably about the campaign, there has not been any news until now so maybe something was discovered.

Emrys: I hope the tidings are well.

Arthur: If it be by the will of Lugos, then they may as well be.

Emrys: Amen.

Arthur: Amen. I best not linger any longer, I shall leave you to your work and I expect great results again.

Emrys: I will not fail you, sire.

Arthur: Mhm (nods and leaves).

At the round table.

Arthur: Haldur my boy, I pray you have good tiding for us.

Haldur: If only the Gods were so merciful, I come bearing the illest of tidings.

Folduin: So, they have passed…

Haldur: Aye…unfortunately both armies were wiped out, none survived…

Arthur: I knew it! I told them! Did I not tell them?

Urania: Yes Arthur, we know, you do not have to shout it.

Umbriela: Such a tragic fate…both were good people but too stubborn in their own convictions.

Cyril: If only they listened to our council…now our armies are nothing but weakened.

Arthur: If –

Folduin: Pardon the intrusion but aren't we a member short? Luzira should be here.

Haldur: That is the other thing, Luzira means to betray us.

Arthur: Say what?

Urania: What do you mean betray us?

Haldur: Exactly what it means, she wants to join the enemy.

Cyril: Outrageous! To whatever end?

Folduin: I understand your anger, but I also understand where Luzira is coming from and I do not blame her, she has lost her sister and it causes her to lose faith in our cause.

Haldur: Aye, she thinks that joining Abaddon is the only course of action for survival, she thinks we have no chance of winning.

Arthur: That is no reason to go to the other side, does she not realise that she will be partaking in the slaughter of her sworn brethren?

Folduin: I have no doubts she does, but the love for one's own kin outweighs the love for others.

Umbriela: How can you justify this? I too understand her but that is no reason to abandon us! Now is the time when we must be the most united than ever before! We must fight together if we want to have any chance. Joining with a seemingly overpowering enemy sure is easier than confronting them but it doesn't make it the right answer.

Haldur: Well said, my queen, I tried to persuade her to no avail, she is fully convinced that she is doing the right thing.

Arthur: Then you know what must be done.

Haldur: …

Urania: Arthur Pendragon! Surely, you're not suggesting…

Arthur: We cannot allow her to join with him, the risk is too great.

Folduin: Indeed, our list of allies grows thinner, but assassination is not the answer.

Haldur: She herself said that if we wanted to stop her then killing her is the only way.

Arthur: There! Even she has accepted her faith which means there will be no consequences, we kill her and let her cousin ascend to the throne instead.

Umbriela: I am appalled by this! To be able to endorse the murder of a fellow monarch is unheard of! And you are doing it with a straight face at that!

Cyril: It's ignoble as well!

Arthur: Oh, spare me the moral talk! We must think of our survival here! It already hangs in the balance as it is we cannot be adding more weight on the other side!

Haldur: Personally, I'm against it as well but if we have no other option then…

Umbriela: Haldur, not you too!

Haldur: Well, if you have any better suggestions, your majesty, I'm all ears!

Umbriela: …

Arthur: Let us take a vote, those that are for say 'aye', aye.

Haldur: Aye…

Cyril: Nay!

Umbriela: Nay.

Urania: Nay.

Umbriela: That's two to three, you lose.

Arthur: Folduin still has not cast a vote.

Umbriela: It doesn't matter at this point.

Arthur: Yes, it does. Folduin my friend, you know what I say to be true even if you are against it, make the right choice.

Folduin: I understand but I am sorry, I will have to say nay.

Arthur: Then you've doomed us all (disconnects).

Haldur: … (disconnects as well).

Umbriela: Don't feel guilty, we've done the right thing, we'll find a better solution to this.

Urania: I sure hope so (disconnects).

Cyril: It was the noble thing to do, we can't allow homicide amongst our own ranks.

Umbriela: Indeed…farewell Cyril.

Cyril: Farewell my queen (disconnects).

Arthur: Damneg yid[38]! Pacifists every last one!

Thomas (his personal aide): What troubles you so, my king?

Arthur: The unwillingness of the others to get their hands dirty for the sake of this realm.

Thomas: 'Tis a shame the others do not share in your wisdom.

Arthur: 'Tis a shame indeed, therefore I must take matters into my hands, Thomas, call for Ser Damian and tell him I have a very important mission for him.

Thomas: At once, my lord.

***

Damian: You called for me, my king?

Arthur: Damian, I have a very important mission for you of the utmost secret nature.

Damian: Whom do I need to kill?

Arthur: Luzira of Sanclunea

Damian: Lady Luzira? Is she not Lady Amra's sister?

Arthur: Amra is no longer with us, therefore Luzira is moved to very unsavoury actions, ones that would put us all at jeopardy, she needs to be stopped.

Damian: I reckon no one is to know of this?

Arthur: Indeed, do it discreetly and quietly, leave no trace behind.

Damian: It shall be done, my lord.

Arthur: Do not fail me, Damian, Camelot depends on it.

Damian places his fist upon his heart as a formal greeting and vanishes.

Ser Damian Orwell is the head of a secret organisation of knights who deal in espionage and assassinations, known as 'Fran Duach', 'Black Crow'. They are highly trained and skilled individuals, able to despatch even the most formidable targets without fail. This order was first founded by King Bethor I, First King of Camelot, in the year 2002, when the kingdom was formed out of the divided Thyrodyn. It is one of the oldest order of knights in the realm of Men, having existed somewhat over a thousand years.

---

[38] Damn them.

Meanwhile in Orcothrond

Abaddon: It fills my heart to see all these races joined here under one banner.

Morgana: It's incredible, Giants, Dragons, Orcs…it's like I'm living in a Faery tale.

Abaddon: More like an old epic really, Faery tales are not so grim.

Morgana: It depends, I read one about –

Surtr: Lord Abaddon.

Abaddon: What is it, Surtr?

Surtr: I simply wanted to express my gratitude for this opportunity, thanks to this I was able to meet my other kin for the first time, it brings me much pleasure.

Abaddon: I'm glad you like it, friend.

Surtr: I like it a lot so thank you.

Abaddon: Nothing to thank me for really, I'm only doing this for my own gain.

Surtr: That matters not to me.

Abaddon: Aren't you a ray of sunshine.

Surtr: … I do not understand that reference.

Abaddon: Never mind, run along now.

Surtr: Oh? And who is this tiny creature?

Abaddon: That's Morgana, she's a human.

Surtr: I've never seen a 'hooman' before.

Abaddon: Not 'hooman'; Human.

Surtr: Human…

Morgana: What is he saying?

Abaddon: He's thanking me for bringing him here and he wanted to know who you are.

Morgana: Oh, and what did you tell him?

Abaddon: That you're an Imp.

Morgana: An Imp? How rude!

Abaddon: Relax, I'm kidding.

Morgana: Those jests of yours need to stop!

Abaddon: Let me think about it hmmm…

Morgana: Well?

Abaddon: The answer is no.

Morgana: Ugh! Unbelievable!

Abaddon: Oh, don't get your knickers in a twist, in some sense you are an Imp to him.

Morgana: Humph! (Walks away).

Surtr: What a strange creature… (walks away).

Morgana: Stupid Abaddon and his stupid jokes! He thinks he's so funny, well let me tell you something mister! You're not! Ugh!

Amra: Who are you talking to?

Morgana: Ah? (Blushes) N-no one… (surprised) Lady Amra?

Amra: Greetings princess, long time no see.

Morgana: Wh-what are you doing here? …What happened to you?

Amra: As you know we lost our little skirmish, but Lord Abaddon was graceful enough to pardon me and awaken the true me.

Morgana: 'Lord' Abaddon? The true you? What are you on about?

Amra: I'm a Lamia now, dear, and I'm bound to his will as my gratitude.

Morgana: So, you are on our side now.

Amra smirks.

Morgana: That's assuring to hear, you'll make a fine asset.

Amra: And you my sweet princess, I can hardly believe that you'd be here on your own volition.

Morgana: A lot has happened, and I've made up my mind.

Amra: Your father is worried sick about you.

Morgana: Oh, is he now? Humph, I couldn't care less.

Amra: I'm sure your mother feels the same.

Morgana: Didn't you hear me? I do not care.

Amra: You really don't care, do you? My, my, whatever has befallen you sweet child? You used to be such a nice and lovely girl.

Morgana: Life and reality fell on me, like a ton of bricks, made me realise some things I wasn't aware of before.

Amra: That things aren't really what they seem?

Morgana: Yes, something like that.

Amra: May I ask what your purpose is here?

Morgana: I'm a Sorceress in practice.

Amra: A Witch? How impressive.

Morgana: No not a Witch, Sorceress.

Amra: Isn't it the same thing? I never quite understood the difference.

Morgana: A Witch is – ugh never mind it's too bothersome to explain.

Amra: Leave it, why don't you show me what you can do.

Morgana: Watch (focuses and then releases a bolt of lightning, shattering a nearby rock).

Amra: Needs more practice but well done nonetheless, so your attribute is lightning huh.

Morgana: And darkness, but Abaddon needs to teach me that and so far, he's been nothing but busy…

Amra: Shame you're not water, I could've showed you some tricks.

Morgana: I didn't know you were water attribute Amra, can I call you Amra?

Amra: …Of course (smiles dryly) well my blood magic is water attribute, so I do know a thing or two.

Morgana: Hm it's no big deal, darkness is much better anyway.

Amra: You don't say…

Morgana: I do say, if you've seen the things Abaddon can do then you should know.

Amra: … I think I'm going to take my leave now, good day to you.

Morgana: Good day Amra (walks away).

Amra: (walks a few steps then suddenly stops and turns towards her) Morgana!

Morgana: (stops and turns) Yes?

Amra: Are you…his queen?

Morgana: What?

Amra: When I agreed to serve him, I wanted it to be as his queen, but he said that place is taken, are you…the one?

Morgana: (surprised but tries to hide it) … Yes, yes, I am.

Amra: I see…in that case congratulations, you are the second most important person here.

Morgana: Thank you (smiles pleasingly and walks away again).

Amra watches her walk away and then bites her lower lip allowing blood slightly to trickle from it.

Morgana: (rushes back to Abaddon) Am I your queen?

Abaddon: My queen?

Morgana: Am I? (Excited).

Abaddon: I don't remember us getting married.

Morgana: Then why did you say to Amra that that place is taken?

Abaddon: Who said that it was you?

Morgana: (stunned) What?

Abaddon: I never said it's you, did I?

Morgana: Are you telling me there is another girl? You said you've never loved anyone!

Abaddon: I lied.

Morgana: (shocked) I swear if this is some kind of a joke again…

Abaddon: It's not.

Morgana: (on the verge of crying, covers her mouth) How could you lie to me about something like that, how can you be so cruel?

Abaddon: I'm a Demon, get over it.

Morgana: Bastard! You…I hate you! (Runs away).

Argyros: Now, why did you lie about something like that?

Abaddon: You know why.

Argyros: Not every woman is like her, Abaddon.

Abaddon: Don't patronise me.

Argyros: I wasn't, I'm only expressing my thoughts.

Abaddon: Then stop expressing them.

Argyros: (sigh) As you wish 'my lord'.

Alabaster: Was that the young lady just now?

Abaddon: Yes.

Alabaster: I wanted to meet her in person.

Abaddon: Don't worry she's not going anywhere; you'll get your chance.

Alabaster: More importantly my lord, when do we leave?

Abaddon: On the morrow.

Alabaster: Understood.

Abaddon: I need to take care of something now, excuse me.

Alabaster: My lord (walks away).

Abaddon: (goes to where Lindroz is) Lindroz.

Lindroz: Dread One! What can I do you for?

Abaddon: We need to talk.

Lindroz: What about?

Abaddon: About Frigga's murderer.

Lindroz: You know who it is?

Abaddon: I do, as a matter of fact they are right here, amongst us.

Lindroz: Frigga's killer…is here? Who is it? Tell me!

Abaddon: Why don't I show you instead.

He contacts Amra through telepathy and she gets there shortly.

Lindroz: That's the one, huh?

Amra: What's this about then, my lord?

Lindroz: You're the one that killed Frigga!

Amra: Frigga? I don't know who that is.

Lindroz: The Ice Wyvern!

Amra: Oh her, yes, I did, but the way you're saying it, it's making me look like a common murderer! This is war, Great Worm, and people die, loved ones, close ones, no one is exempt, it's just how it is, we can be sad about it but getting angry and pissed off won't change the fact they are dead, so get over yourself.

Lindroz: Say what you will, I will have your blood!

Abaddon: No one will be having anyone's blood, there will be no bloodshed amongst comrades.

Lindroz: Comrade? Her? Never! And you, Dread One, how can you betray me, us, like this! Allowing the killer of one of our own, one that has been our enemy for centuries to join our ranks!

Abaddon: Amra is right, there is bound to be casualties in war.

Lindroz: That's what Frigga is to you? Another casualty? How dare you!

Abaddon: How dare I? How dare you! I care deeply for those that serve me well, Frigga included! If I didn't care I wouldn't have buried her with all honours I would've turned her into a zombie instead!

Lindroz: …

Abaddon: And you're right, Amra was our enemy, but she's a powerful individual and I am not beyond utilising those, foe or otherwise. I will use any means necessary to win this war, even if it means getting the murderer of a dear friend to my side.

Lindroz: It's just one person, you don't need her! You already have enough strong individuals; one vampiric cunt won't change a thing!

Abaddon: My decision stands.

Lindroz: I can't work with her! I refuse to accept her as one of our own! If she stays then I'm leaving, and if I leave my kin leaves with me.

Abaddon: Leave? You don't get to leave; you swore an oath, and you would see it broken?

Lindroz: You make me do this.

Abaddon: No, we will settle this in another way, I will give you the chance to kill Frigga's slayer.

Amra: My lord?

Abaddon: It will be a duel, I will grant you a humanoid body for one day only and you will fight her, if you manage to win you will get your revenge but if you lose you stay, agreed?

Lindroz: I accept.

Abaddon: Amra?

Amra: Fine by me, as long as I can kill him in return.

Abaddon: Then it's settled it shall be a fight to the death.

Alabaster: Now this is interesting.

Malgaras: I haven't seen a death match in ages.

And then Abaddon uses his magic and turns Lindroz into a Wyrm Knight much like he did to Glauros although this one is a temporary transformation.

Abaddon: Ready, begin!

Now the two warriors rush at each other, weapons in hand and the clash begins...

CAPITVLVM XVII

NOX MEMINI[xvi]

Morgana is being approached by Jamil who would rather be here than observe the match.

Jamil: Why does a fair lady such as yourself weep like so?

Morgana: Jamil? (Wipes her tears).

Jamil: Hello princess, I do wish our reunion was in a lighter mood, mind telling me what troubles you?

Morgana: It's that stupid Abaddon…he lied to me…

Jamil: Yes…our lord tends to do his work rather cruelly; I can personally attest to that (shows her his missing arm).

Morgana: Good lord! What happened to your arm?

Jamil: It was my fault really, I was foolish enough to wrong him and this is the result…he also treats me no more than a common servant, which hurts me more than my missing arm.

Morgana: What did you do to warrant such cruel punishment?

Jamil: I killed the Goblin Princess in a jealous fit of rage which caused us to enter a conflict with her father, making us lose a considerable amount of the Goblin hordes.

Morgana: Dear me, you're lucky to be alive, but more importantly, why would you be jealous of that princess?

Jamil: You see I…I have feelings, amorous feelings towards him and he wouldn't give me the attention I so much crave for…instead he settled with that creature despite having already spent a night with me.

Morgana: You mean you and him…?

Jamil: (nods) although for one night…and he said no feelings attached but…

Morgana: Then we are in the same boat…

Jamil: You too?

Morgana: No, no! I mean we didn't…do…that I – I um confessed my feelings and he said he doesn't feel the same which I thought it was a lie, but it turns out… (feels her throat clog up) he…has… (on the verge of crying yet again).

Jamil: You mean to tell me he has another one, like a proper woman?

Morgana: (nods) He has a spouse, a queen… (tries to hold her tears).

Jamil: (covers his mouth in disbelief) … He's never mentioned her before…not even a name, nothing…

Morgana: And he had the audacity to make me princess regent of his homeland when he already has someone else, I guess it was only temporary until I wage his war in case, he perishes…

Jamil: And liberate his home and…spouse…that is too cruel.

Morgana: I knew he was vile, but this is just…

Jamil: Let us speak to the Dragon, I'm sure he knows something.

Morgana: I don't think he would tell us anything.

Jamil: But it is worth a try.

Morgana: …I suppose you're right (wipes her eyes).

Argyros: Hey kids (leans over them surprising them both).

Morgana: Argyros!

Argyros: I came to see how you're doing; I really didn't like the way Abaddon treated you earlier…

Morgana: You were worried about me? Thank you so much (snivels).

Argyros: You look pretty hurt…

Jamil: Can you blame her?

Argyros: I suppose not…

Morgana: Tell me Argyros, who is she?

Argyros: That's a bit…

Morgana: At least tell me her name.

Argyros: I'm sorry, it's not really in my place to talk about it, it's best if you hear it from Abaddon himself, I'm sure he will tell you when he's ready.

Morgana: Right, I'm sorry, I shouldn't put you in such awkward situations.

Argyros: I understand, but I also want you to understand that he has his reasons as well, I'm not trying to justify him it's just…

Morgana: Mhm…it's okay.

Argyros: Anyway, I'm going to head back and finish watching that duel, if you would like to join me?

Morgana: Not really in the mood for a bloody contest, thank you.

Jamil: I'll stay with Morgana if that's ok (turns to her).

Morgana: (nods) I appreciate it.

Jamil: Don't mention it.

Argyros: Well in that case I'll leave you two youngsters alone, see ya around (walks away).

Morgana: See you…

Jamil, did you know that this land here once used to be a human kingdom?

Jamil: No, I didn't, but that would explain those old ruins I have seen all around, it does not look like something an Orc would build.

Morgana: Would you like to hear more about it?

Jamil: Of course, I love learning about the histories of our world, especially these parts since they are rather poorly attested.

Morgana: According to our annals, the son of the King of the First Men, who was born in the aftermath of the Titanomachia, had seven sons. They came to be in the land which we now call Nidvelir.

Jamil: The Dwarven Kingdom.

Morgana: Yes, but back then it was uncharted territory. Now five of the seven sons travelled southward and founded the land they called Thyrodyn, 'Land of the Men', and established there the Pentarchy. Two of the brothers travelled up north where they founded Arothyr, 'Land of Arathur' named after the older of two brothers, who was their leader and later king. Legends say that the blood of the Gods and Titans was strong within him.

He waged many wars with the Orcs, and it is said that he had killed many, all on his own, and wrestled them out of their lands. The kingdom was rich and prosperous and did much trade with others, but it was met with a tragic end. The Black Dragons came and destroyed them, bringing their civilisation to an end. There were no survivors, and their cities were reduced to ruins.

But their vestiges remain in the form of teaching. You see, they were very close with the Drow, the Dark Elves that live in the north of Elviun, and so their magic was much advanced, especially lunar, and starlight magic. They heavily weaponised it and developed devastating spells which they used to defeat the Orcs, who were savage and primitive. That knowledge at least was preserved, and it is still taught at the academy.

Jamil: That is truly fascinating. However, little good did that knowledge do against the Dragons it would seem.

Morgana: Don't be ridiculous Jamil, you know Dragons cannot be harmed by magic.

Jamil: I know, that is why I meant it as a jest.

Morgana: Well it was poorly delivered.

Jamil: Let's speak no more of it.

In the meantime, the duel between Lindroz and Amra is well underway.

Lindroz, whose equipment includes a one-handed axe and a buckler, takes a swing at Amra, who parries with her gauntlets. Due to her already exponential physical strength which was furthermore amplified by her transformation she fights using her bare hands.

After she parries the swing, she goes for a punch which Lindroz blocks with the buckler but the recoil from it leaves him a bit staggered.

Since Lindroz is not used to having limbs, he has a hard time adapting to them which leaves him at a disadvantage, but his draconic instincts keep him in the game, nonetheless.

Amra: All you've been doing is wildly swing that axe and block, you bore me.

Lindroz: Wench!

He rushes at her, but Amra effortlessly steps out of the way and trips him on the ground. This brings out a chuckle out of the spectators.

Abaddon: This is hardly a match.

Malgaras: She is toying with him, it's painful to watch really.

Amra: I think it's about time I put an end to this charade.

She pulls out her new weapon; the bow and arrow and takes a shot at him. Now these arrows are no ordinary ones but infused with Amra's new magic and are able to petrify anyone they pierce. In addition to this Amra can infuse these arrows with other types of venom like poisonous or corrosive one, all of which are part of her serpentine arsenal. But before the arrows can hit their mark Lindroz straightens up and spits yellow, sulphuric fire that corrodes the arrows in mid-air.

Then Abaddon casts Etu Erur, 'Dark Awakening', at him which increases ones fighting capabilities as long as they are a servant of darkness.

This causes a black aura to ooze from Lindroz' body and his eyes glow red.

Lindroz: What did you do to me?

Abaddon: Evened the odds.

Lindroz: Undo this spell at once! I want to beat her with my own strength!

Amra: At least this way you'll be able to put up more of a fight, stop complaining.

With a loud roar he rushes at Amra, swinging his axe but she dodges by leaping in the air and shoots an arrow while airborne, however Lindroz deflects it with the buckler, then reaches out with his hand, grabs Amra by the ankle and slams her on the ground.

While she is groggy on the ground, he spews his sulphuric breath once more, but she defends with a psychic barrier, however the breath is so potent that it melts the psychic layer and seeps inside, causing trouble to Amra who did not expect this.

Having no other option, she puts down the barrier and uses her speed to get away from the corrosive cloud then she casts another new spell of hers unknowingly, in her moment of ire but it has no effect on the Wyrm.

Amra: (What was that?)

Lindroz: I don't know what you were trying to pull but it won't work.

Amra: Then how about this?

She uses 'Mind Waves' to directly assault his mind, incapacitating him by causing him severe headaches and forces him on his knees.

Then she uses her swift movement to close the distance and with her enhanced punch shatters the front piece of his armour and he falls on his back from the force.

Now she stands atop of him with her bow drawn and pointing at his throat.

Abaddon: That's enough!

Amra: You said I can kill him.

Abaddon: I changed my mind, after all both of you are more worthy to me alive than dead.

Amra: Heh, you didn't have the intention of letting us kill each other from the start did you?

Abaddon: I had to motivate you somehow.

Lindroz: You truly live up to your name Dread One.

Amra: (gives him a hand) You did well, for a worm.

Lindroz: … (takes it) Being praised by a bloodsucker makes me sick so save it.

Amra: And here I was nice enough to give you a hand.

She lets go of his hand and he falls back on the ground, making the others laugh.

Argyros: You're a sore loser!

Lindroz: Bite me! (Picks himself up)

Amra: Is there a place here where one can get a good drink? I'm parched.

Abaddon: That's a good idea, let's all go for a drink, you as well.

Lindroz: … Fine, I lost so I have no right to complain.

Argyros: Are you sure it's a good idea to go drinking while that Qalasu[39] is sad and hurt (says it in Dhalsarrian)

Abaddon: I didn't know you cared so much.

Argyros: It's just…she's a nice girl, loyal, she adores you, she deserves to be treated better.

Abaddon: I didn't ask for her adoration.

Argyros: (sigh) If you're going to be that way then there is no point talking, enjoy your mead.

Abaddon: That's my intention (walks away).

Argyros: (You fell for the wrong person dear girl)

Lindroz: By the way, this body is pretty convenient, I am way more efficient in battle like this, is there any chance I can keep it?

Abaddon: Oh really? I thought you didn't like other powers.

Lindroz: That was meant for that power up of yours.

Abaddon: You don't have to excuse yourself.

Lindroz: It's not an – no, I won't be roped in into your shenanigans.

Abaddon: (chuckles) Good to see at least someone catching up to my witty humour.

---

[39] Young girl

Lindroz: Because I know better.

Abaddon: Hmmm in that case, I suppose I could grant you the power of polymorphosis.

Lindroz: I would appreciate it.

Abaddon: Come see me after our outing, we'll get it done.

Lindroz: Will do (looks on ahead at Amra) just so you know, I'll never forgive her.

Abaddon: I know, and I don't expect you to, the only thing I ask of you is your cooperation not forgiveness.

Lindroz: That I can give you.

Abaddon: Then let us renew our oaths over a mug of ale.

Lindroz: I've never had one of those before.

Abaddon: You'll love it…

Lindroz: What's wrong?

Abaddon: Nothing, you go on ahead; I'll come join you shortly.

Lindroz: Alright.

And so, he walks on following the rest as Abaddon stays behind and vanishes shortly after.

Jamil: Lord Abaddon!

Abaddon: Leave us.

Morgana: Stay.

Jamil: Um…

Abaddon: Don't make me repeat myself, boy.

Jamil: Yes, my lord (takes his leave).

Morgana: What do you want? Came to shower me with your lies again?

Abaddon: No, I came to invite you to join us at the tavern, it'd be a great opportunity to meet the others as well.

Morgana: Thank you but I'm not in the mood for drinking.

Abaddon: Why not? It's better than sulking here all by yourself.

Morgana: I wasn't by myself; Jamil was keeping me company.

Abaddon: I hardly think Jamil is adequate company.

Morgana: Well he's certainly better than you, at least we have one thing in common.

Abaddon: So he told you about his grievous misdeed, he's lucky he still has his head attached to his shoulders.

Morgana: I'm surprised you didn't feed him to the crows.

Abaddon: I was going to feed him to the wolves, but I thought that there might be some use of him still.

Morgana: In any case I'm not going, sorry but I don't feel like being around you at this point.

Abaddon: And what good would being angry at me do to you?

Morgana: I have a right to be angry, besides, I'm a human being my emotions don't work on a switch you know.

Abaddon: Emotions will only drag you down, learn to own them.

Morgana: Emotions is what makes us human, there is no harm at letting them loose in a while.

Abaddon: And look what that has done for you.

Morgana: I don't expect a cold-hearted bastard like you to understand.

Abaddon: Oh, I understand, more than you know, more than you know… (becomes absentminded for a moment).

Morgana: Hm?

Abaddon: (shrugs it off) Never mind, I'll be at the tavern now, do come join us if you change your mind.

Morgana: Wait!

She shouts out after him, but he's already gone.

Morgana: … (Argyros' words come to her mind) … (What are you not telling me?)

Later that night

There is a theatrical play playing at the Royal Theatre in the capital of Sanclunea, Lunaris, and all sorts of nobles have gathered to see it, Luzira included.

The leader of the Crows, Ser Orwell, has infiltrated the establishment as well using his illusion magic which allows him to completely mask his presence making it as if he is not there at all. Being a master at this art it is highly difficult for even the most trained sensors to sense his presence. Thus, he has earned the nickname 'Phantom' for he slips in and out before anyone can even realise what had happened.

Now he seeks out Luzira in the VIP longue and once he spots her, he makes his move. When he gets into a favourable range, he pulls out a hidden blade from beneath his cloak, which is attached on a leather bracer using a particular mechanism.

Luzira: (Have you come to kill me?)

Damian: (Telepathy huh, so you were able to sense me despite me using my most advanced magic, as expected from the Royal Family.)

Luzira: (You may mask your appearance and mana, but you can't hide the smell of blood no matter what you do, not from me.)

Damian: (Knowing why I'm here makes my job a lot more easier.)

Luzira: (Do you expect me to just roll over and die? Sorry but I have no intentions of leading my people to a slaughterhouse.)

Damian: (That's why you mean to betray everyone and join with the enemy?)

Luzira: (I don't have to explain my reasoning to an assassin.)

Damian: (Neither it is my job to preach my views to my targets, so I'll have you retire here.)

He goes in for the throat, but she grabs his hand and flings him forward. Once he hits the ground his spell becomes undone and his body is now visible, causing an uproar in the longue.

Guard: An intruder!

Guard#2: Protect the princess!

Damian, whose eyes are covered with a mask, smirks, and disappears akin a projection.

Luzira: A body double?

In that moment, the real one emerges from the ground and jabs her in the throat! She tries to regenerate but for some reason it does not work so she desperately tries to stop the bleeding with her hand.

Damian: It's futile to struggle, that blade was dipped in Pit Spider venom, you'll be dead in seconds.

Guard: Get him!

They try to grapple him, but he slips away from their grasp and disappears.

Luzira: The blood…it won't stop flowing…

Now it begins to leak from her mouth as well.

Guard: Lady Luzira has been hit! Take her to a medic now!

General panic ensues as everyone begins to flee the theatre in terror.

Luzira's consciousness begins to fade, and she collapses into the arms of one of the guards as he is hurrying to get her to a mage.

Now these Pit Spiders are truly strange beasts, these massive arachnids that are native to the wilderness of Camelot like to bleed their prey dry before consuming them. Hence their venom is meant just for that; once stung, it paralyses the target's mana flow and causes extreme haemorrhaging which leads to full exsanguination of the body. They do this because for some reason their bodies are unable to digest the blood of other creatures.

Sadly, it becomes too late for Luzira, and she perishes on the way to the Court Magician...Arthur's devious ploy bears fruit.

Back at Dhaldrog

Morgana decides to visit the tavern after all, entering a bit shyly for she is a bit intimidated from all the shouting.

Morgana: (My, what a vulgar place.)

Abaddon: Well, well, look who decided to show up.

Amra: Tsk (murmurs from beneath her drink).

Abaddon: What made you change your mind?

Morgana: I decided to stop feeling sorry for myself and have a drink instead.

Alabaster: Great decision, this way we get to meet the girl that almost became our queen ahahaha.

Morgana: For a limited time at least (looks at Abaddon).

Amra: (Hm? Wait a minute so she is not his queen?)

Alabaster: What do you mean there is –

Abaddon: (Say another word and I will have your head).

Alabaster: Nothing…

Morgana frowns.

Abaddon: Don't mind him he's had a bit too much to drink.

Alabaster: That's right, I don't know what I'm saying ahahaa.

Now that his helmet was down one could see that Alabaster was not some big, ugly brute. Quite the opposite his face was rather comely, with high, prominent cheekbones, squared jaw, and deep, verdant eyes. His hair was short and black.

Amra: (There is definitely something going on here, I need to find out what).

Morgana: (Weird…) In any case, I'm Morgana Pen – I guess it's just Morgana now; pleased to meet you.

The rest name themselves and their status as well.

Morgana: So, you are all great functionaries then.

Alabaster: And strong too, I can take out an entire army by myself.

Morgana: That is preposterous, no one is that strong.

Malgaras: You haven't seen him fight; he really could do it.

Morgana: So you mean you could beat Ser Lancelot in a duel?

Alabaster: Who is that?

Morgana: He is the current captain of the Knights of The Round Table.

Lindroz: Back then it was…what was his name, Hedgehog?

Malgaras: Hedwig.

Lindroz: Yeah, that's the one, the one with the missing right eye, now that was a warrior through and through.

Morgana: Ser Hedwig Godwyn? I know of him, he is from the line of Ser Godrick ap Godwyn, the First Captain of the Round Table and the most famous Paladin of Pyrhas! They called him the 'Red Lion'.

Alabaster: Now that is someone I would've loved to fight!

Abaddon: He almost singlehandedly won the *Kyryadol.*

Morgana: But he was bested by Ser John in the final duel.

Abaddon: Not really it was a team effort. I've read your annals.

Morgana: But Ser John did most of the fighting.

Abaddon shrugs.

Alabaster: Hedwig too was a Paladin of Pyrhas.

Morgana: That position is hereditary in his family.

Malgaras: If I remember correctly, it was Carmox that fought and slew him, right?

Alabaster: Yeah, good old Carmox.

Dagon: Speaking of her –

Morgana: Her?

Dagon: Yes, she was a *Dhalka,* a Demoness, not only males fill our ranks you know, we aren't sexists.

Morgana: What was she exactly?

Dagon: Well, she was like these two over her except that she led the Abyssal Knights, and she herself was a Knight of Baal.

Amra: Ugh that unit huh…brings back bad memories.

Morgana: What is a 'Knight of Baal'?

Dagon: She knows what I'm talking about.

Amra: You could say they were Paladins of Baal. They were a nightmare, gave us a lot of trouble, easily one of the most elite units out there. Abaddon trained them well (throws a glance at him).

Morgana: Wow, why haven't you resurrected her yet?

Abaddon: I haven't had the opportunity of finding a good vessel for her.

Morgana: Well, you brought back the others using Orc bodies, why not her as well.

Abaddon: I would if it weren't for herself. Carmox was an extremely proud Demoness, a true nationalist, if she found out I brought her back in an Orc body she would send herself back in the otherworld.

Morgana: That makes sense then…in any case you have been through a lot, I'm sure you have loads of stories to tell.

Amra: Oh, we could sit here and talk about the old times the whole night.

Morgana: Why don't we then? I'd love to hear more of what you have to tell. *They all laugh at this.*

Morgana: What's so funny? I was being serious.

Amra: My sweet child, it's just that you are but a young girl you couldn't possibly last the whole night, I'm sure you'd fall asleep halfway.

Morgana: (blushes slightly) I've had my fair share of late nights, don't sell me so short!

Dagon points his staff at her.

Morgana: Hm?

Dagon: Remove sleep! There, problem solved.

Morgana: What did you do?

Dagon: I took away your need of sleep, now you are like us.

Morgana: That is a useful spell, I wish I knew that when I had to study all those algebra volumes…

Alabaster: Everyone wait!

Everyone looks at him in confusion.

Alabaster: I didn't get to answer your question.

Morgana: Right, we kind of derailed from that one…well please do.

Alabaster: The answer is yes, I could beat him, in fact I could beat the whole of 'The Table' or better yet, you could throw in the Archons in the mix too and I could still beat them.

Amra: Now you're overreaching, clearly your drunkenness speaks for you.

Alabaster: I'm sober enough to know my own strength.

Malgaras: You're definitely speaking out of your arse, there is no way you could beat 'The Table' and the Archons combined.

Alabaster: Just send them my way and I'll send them straight to hell, you'll see.

Laughter ensues.

Morgana: Was that the group of elite Angyles?

Malgaras: They are the ones.

Morgana: Then your claim is definitely out of your arse.

Laughter again.

Alabaster: No, it's not! And don't you mean 'Angels' not 'Angyles'?

Morgana: No, I mean 'Angyles' that is our word for them.

Dagon: He's so drunk that he forgets that even Camelot has its own language.

Alabaster: I don't think I've ever heard Camelotian clearly before, unless you count the insults they hurled at me on the battlefield.

Abaddon: That doesn't count.

Alabaster: If my lord says so then it must be so.

Laughter.

Alabaster: Go on then, say something.

Morgana: Like what?

Alabaster: Anything, whatever comes to your mind as long as it's a coherent sentence.

Morgana: Ummm… 'Adryf es hwyr y hart es' (smiles).

Alabaster: What does it mean?

Morgana: It's an old proverb, it means –

Amra: 'Home is where the heart is.'

Morgana: Yes, that's correct (smiles cynically).

Lindroz: You speak the language?

Amra: I speak all the languages, a ruler is required to be versed in the speech of their allies, excluding Dhalsarrian for obvious reasons. Although, I speak it (looks at Abaddon again).

Morgana notices these glances she has been throwing at him and finds it quite curious but decides not to bring it up.

Lindroz: That sounds like a real pain in the arse, besides what's the point when you all can speak Common?

Amra: Proper courtesy and etiquette but I wouldn't expect a worm from the North to understand such values.

Lindroz: Are you calling me dumb?

Malgaras: Don't get excited, you know you are.

Laughter.

Morgana: Whereas I can only speak High Elven and Common, I never got to learn the other ones…

Abaddon: Nor to worry, once we are done there will be only one language spoken in Avalon.

Morgana: I better start learning it then.

Alabaster: I could teach you if you'd like.

Dagon: You? Haha, you could not teach a child to tie its boots let alone a complex language such as ours.

Alabaster: …You're probably right.

Dagon: Do not fret girl, I can help you out in that sphere, you will need it if you are about to learn the dark arts anyway, which I can also teach you in place of our great king.

Morgana: Really? You would do that for me? Thank you so much!

Dagon: It's the least I can do.

Morgana: There, another burden is off your chest, my lord.

Abaddon: What did I tell you about being sassy?

Morgana: I don't know, you say many things it's hard to keep track.

Abaddon: Tsk…

Malgaras: First time seeing someone talk at the king like that and not get a cold warning.

Morgana: First time for everything.

At that moment Andrakos enters the tavern and yawns with a loud roar causing everyone's attention to turn on him.

Andrakos: Hello everyone (waddles inward).

Lindroz: Blimey…is that?

Abaddon: First of the Dragonborn.

Even Kushsanu who has been silent and kept to himself this whole time, looks up at him.

Andrakos: I am so sorry, my lord, it seems I've fallen asleep otherwise I would've joined you sooner.

Lindroz: Lindroz; nice to meet ya lad.

Andrakos: Greetings (inspects him closely) I've never seen you before, are you a new one?

Abaddon: Not at all, since he's not a Dragonborn to begin with.

Andrakos: Makes sense, what are you then?

Lindroz: I'm a…what am I? A Wyrm Knight I guess?

Andrakos: What is a Wyrm?

Amra: A worm with scales.

Lindroz: There you go with that 'worm' 'worm' again! Cut that shite out already!

Amra: No.

Lindroz bares his teeth at her.

Abaddon: Calm yourself, don't make a scene here.

Lindroz: Tsk…

Abaddon: And I'll have you stop antagonising each other in my presence or otherwise, or else, do I make myself clear?

Lindroz: Yes, Dread One.

Abaddon: Amra? Am I clear?

Amra: Yes, my lord.

Abaddon: Good, I'm all for banter but let's keep it friendly.

Malgaras: And there it is.

That brings out a few chuckles.

Andrakos: I'm sorry friend are you same as him?

Kushsanu: …

Lindroz: Why don't you speak up? You've been sitting like a mute there the entire time.

Kushsanu: There is no need for words, I only speak when my lord commands me.

Lindroz: Aren't you a fun one.

Abaddon: You can speak whenever you want if you wish so, Kushsanu, you are not a dog with no will.

Kushsanu: Your will is my will, my lord.

Abaddon: In that case, my will is for you to speak up freely.

Kushsanu: As you command.

Alabaster: You need to loosen up! Don't be so uptight! (Smacks his back).

Kushsanu: I would advise you to refrain from such action in the future.

Alabaster: Whatever…party pooper.

Lindroz: Was Glauros always like this?

Dagon: Whereas I did not know him personally, I would say that the transformation has triggered a change in character.

Amra: I'm still the same.

Dagon: In your case it was more of a metamorphosis, shedding your skin to become something more advanced whereas in his case it was a more of a full transformation, a transmutation if you will.

Amra: I see.

Malgaras: Leave it to a High Priest of Baal to explain the arcane ways.

Dagon: I would put a shame upon my title and myself if I was not able to explain that at least.

Malgaras: Cheers to that.

Morgana: I would love to hear more about the arcane ways, my father always said it wasn't in my place to know about that because 'I'm a princess', but I know his true reason was that he didn't want me getting closer to Merlin.

Dagon: You and that Sorcerer were in love?

Morgana: Yes, but my father was strongly against it, all because he wanted to marry me to one of the nobles.

Dagon: As are the human ways (takes a sip) whatever happened to him?

Morgana points at Abaddon. And all eyes fall upon him.

Dagon: My lord! Then when you said that you had found a suitable body…

Abaddon: It was Merlin's.

Dagon: No wonder your magic was on such a high level.

Abaddon: I was quite in luck actually, praised be Baal, he happened to be scheduled for execution due to treason.

Morgana: Which he didn't commit.

Dagon: Humph, it is simple to find out the truth of whether someone has committed a crime or not through magical means, and as far as I remember that young boy had an extraordinary skill in the psychic powers, which begs the question that perhaps Arthur wanted him dead.

Morgana: No…no even my father wouldn't go that far.

Amra: Well, you said it yourself, he was against you being together and this way he would be able to get rid of him, pretty convenient wouldn't you say?

Morgana: …No, I refuse to believe that; it must've been because our laws are so outdated that they wouldn't have accepted magic for investigation and presenting proof…

Amra shrugs.

Abaddon: Let's avert ourselves from such gloomy topics and regale her our stories as we promised.

Dagon: Right you are, sire, such mood downers have no place on a table of festivity (takes a drink) in which case I would like to start off with a tale of my days as a young Warlock.

Alabaster: No one wants to hear your boring stories, old man.

Dagon: Old man? I'm only a thousand years old! Have you no shame? Calling me old!

Everyone laughs.

Morgana: I would like to hear it, Sir Dagon.

Dagon: Oh please child, call me Dagon, no honorifics needed with this Warlock.

Morgana: Dagon it is then (smiles).

Dagon: This was a very long time ago, before I was even initiated to be a High Priest, at that time I was fresh out of magic school…

And so, he goes on to regale his tale and thus they spent the night, drinking and entertaining young Morgana with stories of the past.

The next morning, the news of Luzira's death had spread throughout the entire kingdom of Sanclunea and its citizens were in an uproar, especially her cousin Priscilla.

Butler: My lady, calm yourself…

Priscilla: How can I calm myself when my cousin is dead! Again!

Butler: The situation requires you to be at your utmost –

Priscilla: Shut up! What of the culprit?

Butler: Nothing yet, we are still looking.

Priscilla: Then look harder! We must find him! Do you know how it would make me look if he is not found? People will think I killed her to get to the throne!

Butler: The timing is quite terrible indeed…

Priscilla: You don't seem much affected by this development, George.

George: Pardon my rudeness my lady but I serve you, not your cousins, and I believe that you are the right person for the throne, and nothing else would give me the greatest pleasure but seeing you sit upon it, adorning the royal crown.

Priscilla: You wouldn't happen to have anything to do with this, would you, George?

George: I would never…

Priscilla: (squints) You're dismissed.

George: My lady (takes his leave).
Priscilla: …

Meanwhile back at Orcothrond, Abaddon was rallying up his forces and preparing them for the long march East.

And then there they were, the surviving Orc Lords were at the head of their respective armies for they have learned rudimentary Dhalsarrian and were able to give commands to the Undead Orcs. And before them stood Alabaster, Amra and Malgaras as Turtanim, 'those of general office'. Beside them stood the army of the Dragonborn with Andrakos at the helm. Behind them all, walked the three races of Giants, and before all flew the Wyverns led by Kushsanu and the Dragons led by their kings.

Lindroz and his kin burrowed beneath the earth; and at the very front, at the head of this massive army flew Abaddon atop Argyros and Morgana and Dagon were with Ignatos and Fulguros and thus began the march before the great march.

CAPITVLVM XVIII

TVBA MIRVM SPARGENS SONVM, COGET OMNES ANTE THRONVM[xvii]

Back at Avalon, there is an emergency meeting regarding Luzira's assassination.

Umbriela: I'm sure you all know why we are gathered like this again.

Urania: Yes, despite our agreement on the last meeting, Lady Luzira was murdered regardless!

Umbriela: And we all know who was responsible for this heinous act.

Urania: Well? What do you have to say for yourself, Arthur?

Arthur: Me? How dare you accuse me of such an act?

Cyril: Don't play the innocent card, Arthur, we know it was you.

Folduin: Or it could have been your likeminded ally.

Haldur: Now yer accusing me?

Folduin: One of you has to be the culprit, no one else knew about Luzira's intentions.

Arthur: Who said that it was about that? Perhaps her cousin has done it to claim the throne, it is pretty convenient timing.

Folduin: And perhaps you have aided her in that regard considering you were the one that suggested that she should be placed at the throne.

Arthur: Now you are accusing me of colluding with the Vampires?

Folduin: Are you?

Priscilla: I can assure you I had nothing to do with the murder of my cousin nor have I been conspiring with him (she joins the meeting surprising them all).

Umbriela: Lady Priscilla?

Arthur: This is a private council! How dare you barge in uninvited?

Priscilla: Last time I checked Baldur not Haldur was king of the Dwarves, yet here he stands.

Arthur: He was called in his father's stead.

Priscilla: And why wasn't I called?

Arthur: Because…

Priscilla: You didn't want to face me; I'd expect that from you but not from the rest.

Umbriela: Indeed, we should've called for you, but first we wanted to sort things out before making contact.

Priscilla: Well, let's sort them out, together, and you can start by telling me why my dear cousin is dead.

Arthur: Perhaps some of the factions supporting you, did it?

Priscilla: Nonsense, we value our rulers despite who they might be, we would never stoop so low to uncouth deeds such as assassinations.

Arthur: That's not how your grandmother felt when she overthrew King Ethion II and established a matriarchy.

Priscilla: That was in the past, now it is different. And he deserved it.

Arthur: Mhmm.

Urania: If you're innocent as you say you are then you'll have no problem undergoing the 'Trial of Purity'.

Arthur: You would summon 'The Judge' on me?

Urania: You have nothing to worry about if your claims are true.

Arthur: No! I will not be put on trial like a common criminal!

Umbriela: I believe you don't have a say in this matter, of course, Master Haldur will have to undertake it as well.

Folduin: What will it be, Arthur? Will you confess here amongst your peers or embarrass yourself before the Gods when your lies are laid bare.

Arthur: You want me to confess? Fine! I confess, I did it! I was behind her assassination!

Umbriela: There! Was it so hard? You could've spared us the trouble and confessed from the start! Instead, you tried to weasel your way out of it! What happened to you, Arthur? You used to be so noble.

Arthur: What happened you ask? I became wiser, nobility will not keep our people safe! When we first made the peace treaty, we swore to uphold that peace and that is exactly what I did!

Priscilla: By killing my cousin? She had done nothing wrong!

Arthur: Nothing wrong? She meant to abandon us and go to the enemy!

Priscilla: No! That is not true! Luzira would never do that!

Arthur: You think too highly of your cousin, go on, what are you waiting for? Tell her!

Priscilla: Lady Umbriela, tell me it is a lie…

Haldur: 'Tis the truth, milady, she said it herself, I was there personally.

Priscilla: Why would she do that…?

Haldur: Why? Is it not obvious? Because she was afraid, afraid of losing! She believed it to be the only way of saving your people.

Arthur: And she had every right to be afraid, Abaddon's armies are growing by the day while we bicker amongst ourselves! We have the Gods to thank that he does not strike us now! … Had Luzira led your people to join his cause it would have been over for us, at least this way we still have some hope.

Pricilla: I understand how you feel but killing her was not the answer!

Arthur: You all say that, yet you failed to provide better solutions! We have no time to waste! I only took the initiative of what was already on our minds.

Cyril: You have no right! No right to decide for the rest of us, Arthur!

Arthur: If I had left it to the rest of you, we would be an ally short right now!

Umbriela: Enough! Enough…(sigh) Arthur, we understand that your intentions were just and for the sake of our peace, but you still acted against the will of the council, you can't just take matters into your own hands like that!

Arthur: What are you going to do? Ban me from the council?

Umbriela: No, but I notion for you to be stripped of your right to vote.

Arthur: That is absurd!

Umbriela: I'm sorry, you can't be trusted.

Urania: I second the notion.

Folduin: I as well.

Cyril: As do I.

Haldur: … I refrain from voting.

Umbriela: Haldur!

Haldur: …I cannot vote against him…for I was thinking the same thing.

Priscilla: (gasps) You too?

Haldur: I'm sorry, milady (gulps heavily) it had to be done…

Arthur: At least one of you sees reason.

Folduin: Be silent, Arthur.

Umbriela: Then, by the majority of the votes, you are hereby stripped from your voting right.

Arthur: Hah! What does it matter, my voice never counted for much anyway.

Urania: That's because you were always too radical.

Arthur: It's called being reasonable.

Urania: Foolish is what it is.

Priscilla: Can we stop squabbling like little children and figure out how to deal with the mess you created? What am I to tell my people? How am I to face them?

Arthur: You will address your people and expose Luzira for what she was, a traitor. If need be, we will all attest to that.

Priscilla: But she was assassinated without a just trial, the people will not like that.

Arthur: No problem, we will offer up a scapegoat, it is simple enough.

Umbriela: You got it all figured out, haven't you, Arthur?

Arthur: As any **reasonable** person should.

Priscilla: I do not have a choice, do I?

Arthur: No, you do not.

Priscilla: I better go and make the arrangements then…

Haldur: As do I, my brother is arriving tomorrow for the coronation.

Arthur: And you will take his place in Dhalsarria?

Haldur: It hasn't been decided yet but most likely yes.

Arthur: In that case, we better prepare suitable tributes.

Haldur: You don't have to trouble yerselves my brother isn't keen on material goods.

Folduin: It should be a suitable gift regardless.

Arthur: I will be off then.

Urania: Arthur, you're walking on thin ice here, you best not give us another reason to doubt you.

Arthur: No, of course not, good day (disconnects).

Cyril: (growls) If he was lying about that, who knows what else he is hiding.

Urania: Well, we can't exactly spy on him, it would be a breach of the accords.

Cyril: He already breached the accords when he went against our decision.

Folduin: We cannot stoop to his level; how will it make us look after we have reprimanded him for his actions.

Umbriela: Folduin is right, we must be better people.

Priscilla: Not if the person comes to us themselves.

Umbriela: What are you suggesting?

Priscilla: On the day of Ivaldi's coronation, Arthur surely will come with a retinue. At that moment I will enchant one of his servants and have him divulge any relevant information to us.

Urania: Ingenious.

Umbriela: But if he finds out he will not take it lightly.

Urania: If he does, he has no right to be upset after what he pulled.

Umbriela: I suppose you're right.

Priscilla: Good, it is decided then.

Urania: Indeed.

Priscilla: With that I bid you farewell until next time, ladies, gentleman, goodbye (disconnects).

With that the council disbands and everyone retreats to their own abodes.

Hence three days pass. Priscilla made a public address to the Vampire people, revealing her cousin's true intentions and instead of protesting the people were glad and the support towards her was even more solidified. On the day of Ivaldi's coronation as it was agreed upon, Priscilla used her psychic powers on Thomas, Arthur's personal aide and enthralled him. Meanwhile Abaddon was making his way across the northern borders of Hathasia and towards Onigashima. At one point they stop, and he uses 'Mass Teleportation' beyond the borders of their kingdom. Suddenly they pour in and destroy the outpost town in a matter of minutes, then they move on towards the capital which is not far from the borders.

An Onimusha is on watch duty looking through his spy glass when he spots the advancing army.

Oni: An army that big is heading this way and we haven't received reports form the borders? Unless…they've trampled them all…yabee! I have to tell the Lord!

And so, he rushes towards the palace, headfirst.

Oni: Tonoo!

Tetsu: Nani goto ja[40]?

Oni: Tono kiitekudasare[41], it is Abaddon-dono…

Tetsu: So, he's come back, just like he said.

---

[40] What is the matter?

[41] Please heed me.

Oni: That's not all…he has a massive army in his toll, at the pace they are going they should reach us in no less than thirty minutes!

Tetsu: Nani? Gun wo atsumero! Sensou ja[42]!

Oni: Hai!

Thus, the Oni army assembles as much as it can and marches out to meet Abaddon.

Abaddon: Halt!

Argyros gives off a loud roar signalling to the rest to stop marching.

Then Abaddon blinks off him on to the ground and steps up to face Tetsuzaemon. The place where they meet is a vast, grassy clearing, with a thick, deciduous forest on the right side, that went up a hill, one of many in a long chain.

Tetsu: Abaddon, I did not expect us to meet under such circumstances.

Abaddon: You brought this upon yourself, Tetsu, all of this could've been avoided if you agreed to help me.

Tetsu: So, you bring war upon us.

Abaddon: I don't wish to war with you, surely there is a way to settle this like normal gentlemen.

Tetsu: I already told you; I will not lend you my help, and need I remind you that you are banished from this land.

Lindroz polymorphs into a knight and steps up.

Lindroz: So, this is one of the knaves that refused to kneel huh?

Tetsu: Knave?

Abaddon: Stand down, Lindroz, that's an order.

Lindroz: Why? Just give me a few minutes with him and I'll make him bend the knee.

Tetsu: This is beyond rude!

Abaddon: Lindroz! I will not say it again, stand down!

Lindroz: As you wish, Dread One. Consider this your lucky day Ogre.

Oni: Bureimono! Haji wo shire![43]

Tetsu: Hold your ground!

Oni: But tono!

Tetsu: Eiighh!

He stands down.

---

[42] Assemble the army! It is war!

[43] Insolent wretch! Have some shame!

Abaddon: Tetsu, this is your last chance to join me quietly otherwise I will be compelled to use force.

Tetsu: I refuse, I will not bow down to you.

Abaddon: So be it, Dagon!

Dagon: (materialises before them) Belunum[44]

The Oni immediately reach for their weapons.

Abaddon: Adurtu Gerrukki Batartuni Hasatti?

He says, 'Do you remember the village we passed on the way?'

Dagon: Annu.[45]

Oni: Tono, just give us the signal!

Tetsu: Matte! Something is wrong…

Abaddon: Shukki Abatu.

He says 'destroy it' unto Dagon who points his staff towards its direction, and he utters an incantation.

Oni: Nani wo itteoru?[46]

Oni#2: Wakaranu[47]…tono what should we do? Give us the sign.

Tetsu: He's casting a spell! Sasenu![48]

He unsheathes his Oodachi, the Demon Sword Muramasa and swings towards Dagon but Abaddon blocks the strike with Absharu.

Tetsuzaemon gnarls.

Suddenly, the skies above become dark, and the clouds go heavy and loud with thunder and a whirling mass appears in the distance towards where Dagon is holding his staff.

Oni: Tono! Over there is Sagahara, my family is there!

Tetsu: Kakaree![49]

He gives the signal, and the Oni are ready to enter battle, but they are stopped in their tracks when Dagon finishes the incantation and the sky above the village opens, a layer of five magical circles appears high in the air and a ray of unholy energy shoots through the layers down to the ground. The next

---

44 My Lord.

45 Yes, certainly.

46 What is he saying?

47 I know not.

48 I won't let you!

49 Charge!

thing they see is a mighty explosion lighting up the skies with a bang so loud the present here can hear it loud and clear as if it exploded near their feet.

Oni: It can't be…in just an instant … (falls on the ground, grief-stricken).

The light from the explosion is so intense that it slightly illuminates them as well.

Oni: Nogame…Gouki… (breaks down in tears) Kisamaa! Yurusanu[50]!

Tetsuzaemon is still looking towards the scene of the explosion, unable to move nor talk, as if he was devoid of all of his senses and is unable to stop the Oni soldier who rushes at Dagon with his katana drawn and engulfed in Oni fire.

Oni: Shineee[51]!

Before he even has a chance to get to a striking distance, Dagon clenches his right hand, and the Oni explodes into chunks of meat splattering all around him.

The rest like Tetsuzaemon just stand there and watch blankly, still processing what has happened before them, but one thing was very clear, if they go to war with Abaddon now, they will all die.

Abaddon: Now that was only the magic of my Warlock, imagine what **I** can do.

Tetsu: (turns to him with a vacant look in his eyes, covered in the blood and viscera of his fallen soldier) I accept your offer (gulps) …Onigashima is yours.

Oni: Tono! We can't just give up! We must avenge –

Tetsu: Yield!

Oni#2: Tono, we will fight to the bitter end!

Tetsu: Yield I say! Or do you want to end up like poor Ootomo, guts and blood on the ground!

Oni#2: We are warriors! We do not yield or bow down to anyone!

Tetsu: (turns around and decapitates the Oni himself) Anyone else has a problem, open your bellies right now!

Silence fills his ranks.

Abaddon: A wise decision.

---

[50] Bastard! I won't forgive you!

[51] Die!

Tetsu: …Those people were innocent; they did not deserve to die…

Abaddon: Their blood is on your hands; I gave you a choice.

Tetsu: (gulps heavily) I should have never questioned your authority…

Abaddon: Yes, you shouldn't have.

Tetsu: … (kneels down) Your orders, my king.

Oni: Tono…

Abaddon: Gather the rest of your army, we march towards Umbria immediately.

Tetsu: Ha…! Hyouji!

Hyouji: My lord?

Tetsu: Hoka no yatsura ni koko de atsumero[52]…

Hyouji: Ha!

Abaddon: Tetsu, I hereby pardon you for your past transgressions, I hope we can continue to be friends.

Tetsu: …I have no reason to hate you, my own actions brought this upon us, I know how it is, the strong ones prevail.

Abaddon: It's the world we live in sadly.

Tetsu: Not so sad for those with power.

Abaddon: Touché.

Tetsu: (cracks a small smile) And you are forgiven for killing my slave (extends his hand).

Abaddon: (takes it and shakes it) You can tell your soldiers that you are not my subjects, but rather allies, only, I have the final say.

Tetsu nods an approving nod.

Jamil: Are you okay, princess?

Morgana: Why wouldn't I be? (She looks towards the scene of the explosion and smirks).

Then she turns to look at Jamil with the same look and it brings out a chuckle out of the prince, a sinister chuckle.

Ignatos: (It is already too late for these children; their souls have already fallen too deep into the Abyss…not that I mind though).

Fulguros: What are you pondering on about?

Ignatos: It's nothing.

Fulguros: You know you can talk to me if something is bothering you.

---

[52] Gather the others here.

Ignatos: Much appreciated, if there is anything I want to say, you will be the first to know.

Fulguros: You were always a shy one.

Ignatos: On what planet?

Fulguros chuckles.

Fenris: (growls) What's taking so long? What are we waiting for?

Fulguros: What is the wolf saying?

Ignatos: I have no idea.

Fenris: Right, I forgot the lizards don't speak our language.

Wizard King, what is the hold up?

Abaddon: We are waiting for the rest to gather then we move on.

Fenris: More marching? We haven't eaten nor drank anything in three days! My people are famished!

Abaddon: Stop whining, once we reach the realm of the Shadow Demons you will feast as much as you like. Besides, who said anything about marching.

Fenris: Right … you can just move us there.

Abaddon: (sighs).

Fenris: So, these Dimnar Helertoren, are they like you?

Abaddon: Similar, we share the same God.

Fenris: Great, more delusional fanatics.

Abaddon: In a sense you are right.

Fenris: Hm?

Abaddon: They used to be Angels, but they saw that they followed the wrong God, or Goddess in their case.

Fenris: There are female Gouden now? And what is an 'Angel?'

Abaddon: Winged creatures that are basically the exact opposite of us.

Fenris: Like good Demons?

Abaddon: No, not quite like that.

Fenris: Noted…creatures that can fly in the sky, and they are not avian like?

Abaddon: No, if I had to compare them, I'd say they look like your former nemesis only much smaller.

Fenris: The outside world is all kinds of messed up.

Abaddon: Oh, my furry friend, there are so many more things that would surprise you in this world.

Surtr: Look Ymir, more tiny people, and they come in different colours as well.

Ymir: There is routte, blaer, graenne[53] (points with his finger).

Surtr: Fascinating.

Tetsu: What are these creatures? They are enormous.

Abaddon: They are called Giants, from the lands far up North.

Ymir: Demon King, Ymir wants to know what these tiny people are called.

Abaddon: Ogres, but they call themselves 'Oni'.

Ymir: Very interesting…the outside world is full of wonders; Ymir is glad he went beyond the border of his homeland.

Surtr: As am I, although it bothers me that we have met nothing but tiny people so far…

Ymir: Do not be bothered, brother Surtr, that means we are the biggest in existence, that would make us number one.

Surtr: Number One…I like the sound of that.

Tetsu: They seem simpleminded.

Abaddon: Because they are.

Surtr: Hey Brundig! Come see the tiny people!

Brundig: What?

Surtr: Come see the tiny people!

Brundig: More tiny people? No thanks! Not interested!

Surtr: They came in different colours!

Brundig: … I'll be right there.

Abaddon sighs.

Tetsu: Even their language is strange.

Abaddon: And yours is strange to them so the feeling is mutual.

Tetsu: So many different races in one place, how are we to communicate? To work together when we do not even know what we are saying?

Abaddon: That's why I'm having all of you learn Dhalsarrian.

Tetsu: We are to learn your tongue?

Abaddon: Yes, since we'll be spending quite some time at Dumah's you all might as well do something useful, my Demons will provide the tutoring.

Tetsu: But there are thousands of us, you cannot expect everyone to learn it.

Abaddon: You won't be thought individually but in groups and besides getting down the basics for at least rudimentary conversation is enough.

Tetsu: Hmmm…

---

[53] Red, blue, green.

Brundig: Where are the colourful tiny people? (The ground shakes as he runs over).

Abaddon gestures towards the sea of Oni.

Brundig: By my beard! It is true! Hohoho! Now this is a rare sight.

Ymir: Ymir thinks so too.

Soon after, the remaining of the Oni forces arrive. Once they all have gathered, Abaddon unsheathes Absharu and casts the second stance, 'Pride'. This magnifies his magical ability and therefore allows him to cast 'Mass Teleportation' on a much grander scale, and thus teleports everyone within Zhilmatu, just outside the Royal Capital, Dur-Addar.

Fenris: Why have we stopped now?

Abaddon: Because now we wait for the king of this place to make an appearance.

Fenris growls a long, displeased growl, and stretches on the ground beside Abaddon. After an hour Dumah appears with his host.

Dumah: This is as far as you go, make one more step and it shall be war.

Argyros: Not this again…

Abaddon: Dumah, I told you that your hubris will come back to haunt you.

Dumah: You do not frighten me (unsheathes his own Demon Sword, Fragarach) this is your final warning, leave now while I still feel generous.

Abaddon: I'm afraid you don't fully grasp the situation you're in, dear cousin.

Dumah: I could say the same thing for you.

Alabaster: I've heard enough of this insubordinate scum, allow me to teach him a lesson my lord.

Dumah: You? A mere grunt, means to teach **me**, a lesson? Ha-ha I'd like to see you try.

Abaddon: That won't be necessary, Alabaster, I will deal with this personally, without lifting a finger.

Dumah: Such bold words, and you say I have hubris.

Abaddon: It's not hubris if I can back it up (raises both arms) Elu Illutu Ardanatuu.

He says, 'arise army of the dead' and Dumah knowing the meaning of these words scowls, his armies too starting to look around in anticipation.

And from both sides of the Shadow Demons, out of the ground rises the armies of the fallen Dwarves and Vampires.

Demon: My lord, the dead are rising!

Dumah: I can see that! I'm not blind!

Captain: We are surrounded!

Dumah: Stop stating the obvious!

Abaddon: What will it be, Dumah? Do you still want that war?

Dumah: I do not fear the dead!

Abaddon: Do you honestly mean to risk the lives of your entire army for your ego? These are not just any dead, these are trained soldiers, face it, you're outnumbered and outmatched, there is only one outcome of all this.

Dumah: …

Amra: This is taking too long (yawns) want me to use my powers and charm him into submission?

Dumah: (stunned) And who is this?

Abaddon: This is Amra, once Queen of Vampires.

Amra: Once and future mind you.

Abaddon: Right, pardon me, 'your majesty'.

Dumah: Dumah, King of Zhilmatu it is an honour, my lady (kisses her hand).

Amra: Can't say the same.

Dumah: Defiant, I like that.

Abaddon: (By Baal what is going on here?)

Amra: Are you coming on to me?

Dumah: Does that not please my lady?

Amra: Okay, first, I am **not** your lady, second, yes it does not please me at all.

Dumah: But I'd like you to be.

Amra: Is this guy serious?

Dumah: Oh, I am always serious.

Abaddon: What are you on about?

Dumah: I will join you, under one condition.

Abaddon: Again, with your conditions, what is it now?

Dumah: This exquisite lady must become my queen.

Abaddon: (As I thought) (face palms).

Dumah: I won't have it any other way.

Amra: My dear man, you just met me and now you want to marry me? Are you insane?

Dumah: You are the most beautiful woman I have ever laid my eyes upon in my whole life, and I want to make you mine.

Abaddon: Why don't you take one for the team, huh?

Amra: Excuse me? I am not a bargaining chip!

Abaddon: You wanted to be a queen, didn't you? This is your chance.

Amra: I wanted to be your queen not to some random guy whom I just met.

Dumah: I promise, I will be just by you and lavish you with everything your heart desires.

Amra: By the Gods…could you be any cornier?

Dumah: If my way of talking displeases you, I will speak to you in any manner that you like.

Amra: Noctis have mercy, I cannot believe that this just happened to me (speaks to herself in Vampiric).

Abaddon: (Listen, accept his offer.)

Amra: (I will not!)

Abaddon: (I said listen! You only have to put up with him until all of this is over, after that you can kill him if you like.)

Amra: (Can I really?)

Abaddon: (Honestly no, Dumah is a very old and powerful Demon, despite his appearance, but you are most certainly welcome to try.)

Dumah: My lady, have you decided?

Amra: (sigh) I accept your offer.

Dumah: Splendid!

Abaddon: (Was he always like this…?)

Tetsu: Hou! Looks like we will be having a wedding, congratulations hahaha!

Amra: Congratulate me again and I will cut off your balls and feed them to the wolves (smiles).

Tetsu: Noted…are all Vampires this scary (to Abaddon).

Abaddon: Particularly this one.

Tetsu: Remind me not to piss her off again.

Abaddon: You got it.

Dumah: Tetsuzaemon, my old friend.

Tetsu: We were never friends, or has Lady Amra addled your mind?

Dumah: Do not be a sour prune, we used to get along once.

Tetsu: Until you started the siege on my borders.

Dumah: And then you decimated Dumgardu.

Abaddon: The same city you abandoned?

Dumah: Abandoned is such a harsh word, neglected is more like it.

Abaddon: Sounds all the same to me.

Dumah: The city was already overrun, sending my men there would not have changed anything, they would only be lambs to the slaughter.

Abaddon: It would have for the people you left behind! Do you have any idea how much they suffered?

Dumah: Why do you care? You are not the king of this land, I am.

Abaddon: I care, because any king that doesn't care about the safety and wellbeing of his subjects is no king at all.

Dumah: The city was already lost; nothing could have been done.

Abaddon: You didn't even try.

Dumah: You make it sound personal.

Tetsu: Is this about the slave girl you killed?

Dumah: What slave girl?

Abaddon: Her name was Asha, and she was one of yours.

Dumah: So you're giving me all this sass for some girl you barely knew?

Abaddon: You don't get it do you? It's not about that, it's about caring for your own people. I suffer day and night, knowing that my kin are treated like garbage, my Demons beaten, and my Demonesses raped, at the hands of the occupying scum that plagues my land, and I can't wait for the moment I grant them their freedom and make them masters of their home once again. Now you tell me, did you feel anything for that city and the Demons you left behind?

Dumah: (steps up just before Abaddon's face) No, I did not.

He punches him in the face, sending him down on the ground.

Abaddon: That feels better.

Dumah holding his cheek, gets up on his feet, spitting the blood from his mouth, glaring at Abaddon.

Abaddon: I promised Asha that I will put a stop to the fighting and that is exactly what I will do, from this day forth there will be no bloodshed amongst us, and all the slaves will be freed, on both sides.

Dumah: I do not keep slaves; they are filthy and unworthy to live in my presence.

Abaddon: Maybe you don't, but I'm sure some of your nobles do. There will be no more slavery amongst Demon kind as long as I live.

Tetsu: I will send a messenger back to Onigashima and let them know.

Abaddon: You do that, and you, you will kneel before Baal and ask for his forgiveness or I will have your head, I'm a Demon of my word.

Dumah: We do not do Baal worship anymore.

Dagon: Heresy!

Dumah: There is no purpose of a higher being when I am the one on top, the people need to worship me not some deity my ancestors bowed down to.

Dagon: You would hold yourself above Baal? I have never heard such blasphemy before! You ought to be drawn and quartered!

Abaddon: Calm yourself, Dagon.

Dagon: Your majesty! I cannot sit idly and listen to this heretic defile the good name of our Lord!

Amra: (Well, this escalated quickly).

Abaddon: Dumah, I am willing to overlook this misbehaviour if you agree to bring back Baal worship.

Dumah: No.

Amra: (I will deal with this) You'll either convert back or the wedding is off, my dear king.

Dumah: I'm sorry, my lady, I cannot do that even for you.

Jamil: What do you think is going to happen?

Morgana: I have no idea but whatever it is it doesn't look pretty, both Abaddon and Dagon seem extremely pissed off.

Amra: Well, I tried.

Tetsu: Non-believers will get struck by a curse!

Dumah: Yet another fanatic, what do you care; you do not even worship Baal.

Tetsu: Maybe not the same way you do, but I still know the meaning of a higher being and spirituality. Lord Ashura[54] gives us the strength and courage to win our battles and we always express our gratitude for those without faith are nothing.

---

[54] The Oni version of Baal Girruu

Dumah: Please, spare me the sermon, it is your own prowess that wins battles not because of some higher being.

Fenris: (growls) How long is this going to take? My people grow hungrier and with that more impatient by the minute!

Abaddon: Not now, Fenris.

Fenris: Yes now! Can't you settle your differences with some food?

Abaddon: I said not now!

Fenris: What is his deal anyway?

Abaddon: He refuses to bow down to Baal, he dares refuse his ancestral obligation.

Fenris: Sounds like my kind of guy.

Abaddon: Looks like you both need more convincing, Dagon, summon the Dark Lord.

Dumah: What?

Abaddon: Behold! A feat only a High Priest can achieve!

Morgana: Is he really going to summon a God?

Jamil's eyes blister with anticipation.

Dagon: Now you will believe, all of you will.

He gets down on the ground in a praying position, with his hands and forehead touching the ground and begins chanting in the old form of Dhalsarrian.

Dagon: From the Abyss I summon Thee, oh Baal, Lord of Shadow and Darkness, me Thine humble servant, me Thine loyal subject, me Thine greatest venerator, allow me to become Thy herald on this plane so that Thine voice may be heard and the nonbelievers and blasphemous heretics be rendered silent! Let those that speak against Thee Oh Baal, feel the wrath of Thine anger!

As he chants, the ground trembles, the sky darkens and the clouds thunder, and sinister winds begin to howl.

A sinister and dark energy, most foul that anyone has ever faced before envelops Dagon and makes the others – besides the Dark Demons – sick and feeble and petrified with fear, stopping the very flow of blood in their veins and causing them to grow pale.

Morgana becomes so terrified that she buries her face in Jamil's bosom as he tries to stop her shaking and shivering by embracing her.

Amra: By the Gods…What is this evil? This malice…I can't feel my blood…

Even tears surface on her eyes.

The Baal mask on Dagon's face sticks to his face and becomes akin to a real skin and he stands up from the ground accompanied with even louder tremors.

He has become a conduit for their God, an Avatar of Baal.

Dagon: Kneel!

His voice is deep and terrifying and so powerful that it compels all to bend the knee.

Dagon: You, Dumah of Shilmatu, you dare presume yourself above **me**? Your Father?

There is such a depth and malice in his voice that it hurts even the very soul, and this causes the more sensitive ones like Morgana to cry out in pain and break down in tears.

Dumah: My Lord! My Lord, I am sorry…I am sorry I did not believe! I swear I will make it up. I will atone!

Dagon: I created your kind! I brought you into existence and yet you deny me my glory and righteous exaltation! You, a lowly Demon!

Dumah: My Lord! Words cannot express how deep is my sorrow and shame from my own foolishness, I should have never doubted your splendour and existence!

Dagon: Silence!

This one is loud that now the rest begin even to physically writhe in pain.

Surtr: So, this is the master of the beldur…

Dagon: Flattery will not get you anywhere! You must prove your worth! Prove that you are a worthy son!

Dumah: I will! I will do anything you ask of me! Just say it and it shall be done!

Dagon: A thousand sacrifices for a thousand years of heresy!

Dumah: Yes! It shall be done!

Dagon: Abaddon, my son, you are the worthiest of my progeny, you have brought the most glory for my sons and daughters and to my name, I know you will succeed in your task.

Abaddon: I wouldn't dream otherwise, Great One.

Dagon: As a token of your worth, I shall grant you with a fragment of my power.

He then creates an amalgamation of dark energy around his hand.

Dagon: Produce your sword.

Abaddon unsheathes Absharu and presents it before him.

Then Dagon traces his index finger along the runes, and they change and the blade glows black and once he reaches the tip the black aura gets sucked in and it returns to normal.

Abaddon: I am eternally grateful for your benevolence my Lord and swear to use this power to bring even more glory to Your name.

Dagon: This power can only be used sparsely so use it wisely.

Abaddon: Annu, Belunum.

Dagon: And do not forget that you still owe me those one hundred souls for the protection I offered you.

Abaddon: I haven't forgotten my Lord; they will be delivered to you as soon as possible.

Dagon: Mhm…Now then nonbelievers! What sayeth thee?

A choir of voices shouts out 'we believe' all in their own tongues. For when Baal spoke, they could all hear him talk in their own language for he knew all the tongues of the world.

Dagon: My time here is over, farewell, for now!

And then Dagon comes back to his former self and the shaking stops, and the winds cease, and the skies clear up and simmer down.

Ignatos: Did that just happen…?

Argyros: Holly hell…I never really believed up until now…

Fulguros: Neither did I…

Fenris: It is true…everything you said is true…

Abaddon: Told you so.

Dagon flumps on the ground from exhaustion.

Abaddon: Are you alright?

Dagon: Yes, I only need to catch my breath…

Abaddon notices Morgana who is still shaking and approaches her.

Abaddon: It's alright, Princess, it's all over.

Morgana: No, it's not...I thought I was going to die...I've never felt like that in my entire life...I don't ever want to feel that again...ever.

Abaddon: It's because you weren't a believer, next time you'll be fine.

Morgana: Are you sure?

Abaddon: Absolutely, didn't you see me and the rest? We were completely unaffected.

Morgana: No, I was too busy fearing for my life...

Abaddon: Why can't you be more like Jamil? Look at him, he's ecstatic.

Morgana: That's because he's a freak...

Jamil: Thank you (still in a bit of delirium).

Morgana: That wasn't a compliment.

Abaddon chuckles a bit.

Tetsu: I believe we all need some strong wine after that one, I hope you have enough to fill us all, Dumah, 'old friend'.

Dumah: We'll manage somehow...

And so, they head to his castle for some well-deserved feasting and relief from all that has happened.

CAPITVLVM XIX

ADVENTVS MORTIS[xviii]

Tetsu: Where are you going to find a thousand sacrifices?

Dumah: The land of Hathasia lies beyond our borders, plenty of sacrifices to be found there.

Tetsu: Don't let the sand boy hear you, from what I can see he is close to Abaddon.

Dumah: Let him hear, are they not our allies? They can spare those one thousand lives for us.

Tetsu: They are of a different faith and by doing that we risk their allegiance.

Dumah: We don't need them; we are already strong as it is.

Tetsu: But Abaddon-dono needs their cavalry.

Dumah: I do not care, for now my needs take priority.

Abaddon: What needs?

Dumah: Abaddon, speak of the devil.

Abaddon: Do you mean the sacrifices?

Dumah: We were discussing how we are going to use the sand niggers as offerings.

Abaddon: Surely you jest.

Dumah: Do you have a better idea? Do not forget, you are in this one as well.

Tetsu: To be fair, you could offer a thousand animals, he did not specify the kind of the sacrifices.

Abaddon: No, it doesn't work that way, it has to be a mortal's blood, or we risk incurring his wrath.

Tetsu: Do you make a sacrifice to him for each favour?

Abaddon: That used to be our way, but not anymore, sacrifices are not condoned. Usually, our blood is used to entreat his favour, and if deemed worthy he will answer it. But for greater favours or even greater blasphemies (looks at Dumah) it requires much more.

Tetsu: Then your people can fill in the role.

Dumah: I will not sacrifice my own kind.

Abaddon: Since when did you start carrying about your own kind?

Dumah: Why bleed my own people when it can be done with someone else hm?

Abaddon: You brought Baal's wrath upon yourself by yourself and you, yourself will fix it.

Dumah: You would rather see your own kin die than a couple of sand niggers?

Abaddon: Kinship means nothing among us, if it did, we wouldn't be here in this manner.

Dumah: … No, I am the king of these people, and I say no.

Abaddon: You may be king, but I am the leader here and I have the final say.

Dumah: You might want to save that talk for after you win the war. I am not one of your Orcs or Goblins for you to order around as you please.

Abaddon: … (stands up) Everybody listen up!

He uses 'Herald of Doom' to enhance his voice, grabbing everyone's attention.

Abaddon: It would seem that some of you have this misguided notion that you yet hold some form of power as you did before my coming but make no mistake that this is not the case! You may govern your respective people, but it is I who am in charge! It is I who presides over all of you! It is I that has the final word in all matters! I am the King of Kings I am your Emperor!

Some cheer, some remain silent on this.

Abaddon: If anyone has a problem with that, they can take it up to my sword. I would be more than happy to take you on if any of you wishes to challenge my authority but be warned that by doing so you are facing most certain death!

Complete silence.

Abaddon: No one? Anyone? Two on one, three on one, all on one! I do not care, come at me with all you have got!

No one dares speak up against him.

Abaddon: That's what I thought, if this is the case then I expect all of you to keep your opinions to yourselves when not warranted and do as you are told! That is all.

Lindroz: (stands up) If anyone has a problem with the Dread One, they have a problem with us!

Grough: And us!

Argyros: And all of us!

The troops on his side begin to cheer his name.

He raises his hands up high and they all yell out with a mighty 'yea' at once.

Dumah: …

Abaddon sits down and smiles and all around him can see him smile as he has his hood down.

Dumah: Excuse me, I lost my appetite… (gets up and leaves).

Tetsu: Cheers! To our new Emperor!

Cheers!

Morgana: That was a mighty speech you gave there.

Abaddon: It's one of my specialties.

Morgana: I can see that; the rest almost shat their pants (smiles goofily).

Abaddon: Have you been drinking?

Morgana: So what? I'm sixteen I'm allowed to drink.

Abaddon: And you obviously can't hold your liquor.

Morgana: I've had wine before! It's just that this one is particularly strong (hic).

Abaddon: Yeah right.

Morgana: (props against him) I love you (still retaining her goofy smile)

Tetsu laughs.

Abaddon: Jamil…! Where is that blasted boy.

Morgana: I think he's flirting with Malgaras over there, whom I might add is quite dashing without his getup, it would seem all of you Demons have that going on for you…you're all secretly gorgeous (hic).

Abaddon: Alright, off to bed with you (picks her up).

Morgana: No! I will not be put to sleep like a little child!

Abaddon: I think you've had enough fun for one night, let's go (takes her towards the castle).

Morgana: Put me down, you brute! (Hic).

Abaddon: Stop squirming or I'll knock you out cold.

Morgana: Tsk…I suppose (hic) it's not so bad being carried by you in this manner (smiles).

Abaddon rolls his eyes.

Morgana caresses his cheek while smiling goofily.

Abaddon: By Baal, how much did you drink?

Morgana: Pleeentyyy!

Abaddon: This is why little children should stick to orange juice.

Morgana: I'm not a child! Stop treating me like one!

Abaddon: Compared to my age you might as well be a foetus.

Morgana: Hey! That's rude! …How old are you again?

Abaddon: Six hundred.

Morgana: Wow! You're old!

Abaddon: That's quite young for our standards, you are not considered old unless you've lived at least a thousand years.

Morgana: Like Dagon (laughs).

Abaddon: Exactly (chuckles).

And so, he takes her to her room in Dumah's castle and places her on the bed but just as he was about to leave, she latches onto him.

Abaddon: You can let go now.

Morgana: Stay, don't go…

Abaddon: You're drunk, you don't know what you're saying.

Morgana: I may be drunk, but I'm not plastered, I know what I want.

He forces her hands off him and as he turns to leave, she grabs his hand.

Morgana: Don't push me away.

Abaddon: (looks at her) Let's not do something we will later regret.

Morgana: (approaches him) I don't regret a thing (kisses him).

Abaddon: Mor –

Before he can finish the sentence, she kisses him again and as she moves away after the kiss, the left frame of her dress falls over her shoulder revealing more of her skin. Then she undoes her braid and lets her hair hang more loosely and freely, making her in her current state, under the moonlight, look like a luscious seductress and not a young girl. Seeing her in such a light, Abaddon reaches his breaking point and begins to remove his armour almost immediately and laying her eyes on his naked body, she bites her underlip in a craving manner.

And so he gets on the bed and she throws herself in his arms and they make out passionately. He lays her down on the bed and undresses her and both lay naked in each other's arms and making out.

As they do so, Abaddon caresses her body with his hands, from her breasts to her thighs and legs. Not only his hands but also his lips move around as well, greatly arousing the young girl until she reaches the desired point.

Morgana: I'm ready, make me yours.

Abaddon: Are you sure? After this there is no going back.

Morgana: I've never been surer about anything else.

Abaddon: As you want, so it shall be.

And he gently penetrates her as she gives off sweet moans of pleasure mixed with slight feelings of pain.

Abaddon: Does it hurt?

Morgana: No, I'm fine, you may move.

Now he moves his hips gently and with much passion, enjoying every thrust as does she. The feeling of his penis rubbing her insides brings her to ecstasy, to a whole new level of pleasure like she never knew existed.

At one point she begins to loosen up and even take control herself, like moving her hips on her own and switching different positions.

And thus, their joyous lovemaking goes on for hours until Abaddon is finally ready to ejaculate, and, in that moment, he did not hesitate to finish the deed whilst still inside her and she moans deeply as his warm love juice fills her womb.

Abaddon still had the stamina to go on, but Morgana was exhausted, having had multiple orgasms herself until that moment.

Morgana: My God that was…incredible (heavy breathing) …you knocked the drunkenness out of me (snickers).

Abaddon slightly chuckles.

Morgana: I can't feel my legs…

Abaddon: That's nothing, I can still go on.

Morgana: Well, sorry for only having the stamina of a normal human.

Abaddon: Oh no, not at all, you did quite well holding on for this long, most girls your age can't even last an hour.

Morgana: I'm not most girls, I'm a…prin…cess (falls asleep in his arms).

Abaddon: Sleep tight, princess, sleep tight.

Once he makes sure she is sound asleep, he sneaks out of the bed, conjures up a nightgown and goes outside on the balcony and stares at the starry sky with a glass of wine in hand.

The following morning Morgana wakes up to an empty bed, patting around with her hand and feeling only the bed sheets.

Morgana: (rubs her eyes) Abaddon? Abaddon?

Abaddon: Over here! (Shouts from the balcony).

She rushes out of the bed, puts on her dress, and goes outside.

Abaddon: Morning.

Morgana: Morning (yawns) were you here all night?

Abaddon: Mhmm, looking at the stars, or at least I was.

Morgana: Right, Demons don't sleep.

Abaddon conjures up a chair for her.

Abaddon: Sit.

Morgana: (sits down) Last night was…truly incredible.

Abaddon: It really was, for the first time in a long time for me it felt more than just sex.

Morgana: (taken aback) What are you saying?

Abaddon: I'm ready (looks at her) to give my heart to you.

Morgana: (aghast) You mean…you mean you're admitting that (gulps)…you have feelings for me?

Abaddon: I guess I always had I was just afraid of acting on it, afraid of getting my heart broken, but now I know, your feelings are genuine.

Morgana: (tears of joy come to her eyes but she stops herself from bursting into tears) So – so there is no queen?

Abaddon: There never was, or rather there should have been.

Morgana: Argyros did mention something about it, but he said that it's not in his place to tell, that you will tell me on your own when you're ready (takes his hand).

Abaddon: And he was right to say so, you should hear it from me (exhales deeply) …her name was Mayrion, she was of the Storm race, with skin so blue, bluer than the sky and hair wavier than the ocean. I found her the most beautiful Demoness in the entire kingdom. The moment I saw her my heart was hers, so I courted her. It wasn't easy but she ultimately succumbed, and we fell deeply in love. It felt like our love was eternal and would last forever so I proposed to her, and she accepted. She was to be my spouse, my queen but she…she broke my heart, she wounded me so deeply that I was never able to fall in love again.

Morgana: …

Abaddon: It happened on the day of our wedding, she was late for the ceremony so I went to look for her, and what I saw still haunts my memories…the woman I loved, naked, in the embrace of my best friend, a Demon with whom I grew up with, who I knew for my whole life…and there they were, the two people most precious to me, shagging in one of the royal bedrooms…

I could feel my heart physically break in my chest, ire, madness, disappointment, sadness…all these emotions came swelling within me at once and at the end ire won. I've never been so furious in my entire life, my whole being was bursting with anger, so I bound them and dragged them outside naked for all to see.

I took them to this pit we had where we would punish traitors, we would tie them on a pole and let the crows eat their flesh while they still live. I watched as those infernal birds picked the flesh of their bodies right down to the marrow of their bones, then I fed the bones to our Hell Hounds. And while the whole thing happened, I didn't feel a thing, no remorse, nothing, only – pure satisfaction.

Morgana: That's awful…what you had to go through, I can't even begin to imagine how that feels, being betrayed by your loved ones like that…if that ever happened to me, I…would probably do something of that nature.

Abaddon: Oddly, that doesn't surprise me (slightly smiles).

Morgana: (slightly smiles as well) But now I understand, why you acted the way you did and I neither judge nor blame you. I too would be reluctant to fall in love ever again after being betrayed like that. But I want you to know that you can count on me (squeezes his hand tighter) I promise on my life never to betray your love and trust in me, and if I ever do something to wound you so grievously, I will take my own life.

Abaddon: I know, and I trust you (kisses her hand).

Morgana: Hold me.

So, he pulls her over to his side and she is sited on his lap, and they lay like that in each other's embrace.

Morgana: You know, don't you? Who set up Merlin?

Abaddon: It was Emrys, his student.

Morgana: Emrys, that conniving snake, I knew he was up to no good, I didn't like him from the start, but Merlin saw great potential in him.

Abaddon: And look where it got him.

Morgana: I'm going to kill him myself; I'm going to kill them all, I swear.

Abaddon: But for that you'll need power, that's why from today I will be teaching you magic.

Morgana: You? I thought Dagon's going to do it.

Abaddon: If you don't want me than I'll have him do it.

Morgana: No! That's not it it's just – (squints) you're messing with me, aren't you? (Flicks him on the forehead) dummy.

Abaddon: (chuckles) You're so easy to tease.

Morgana: I thought I'd get used to your antiques by now but no! I still fall on them like a naïve child.

Abaddon: You'll get used to it, in time.

Morgana: Time…will you still love me when I grow older?

Abaddon: Of course, why wouldn't I?

Morgana: You won't replace me with someone younger?

Abaddon: There are spells that can keep you young, you know that right?

Morgana: It's not the same…eventually you'll outlive me and…we'll be torn apart…

Abaddon: There is a way, but it comes at a great price.

Morgana: What way?

Abaddon: By offering the proper sacrifice Lord Baal can grant you with eternal youth.

Morgana: What sacrifice?

Abaddon: You will have to kill someone close to you, and your father doesn't count since you hate him.

Morgana: My mother…but I hate her too.

Abaddon: Do you really? Because deep down I think you believe that she is just another victim of the old ways of Camelot.

Morgana: Perhaps you're right…

Abaddon: It's the only way, a life for a life.

Morgana: A life for a life…I guess we'll cross that bridge when we get to it, for now there are more pressing matters.

Abaddon: First things first, breakfast, you can't train on an empty stomach.

Morgana: I suppose…let's go wrap that up so we can start, shall we?

Abaddon: Alright (smiles).

Morgana: Alright (kisses him).

He kisses back and they make out for quite a while, basking in the morning sun. And so, after breakfast they go out in the courtyard and are ready for training.

Abaddon: We'll start with a basic spell; I'm going to teach you how to cast 'Aura of Dread'.

Morgana: Is that the one you used on the Oni back then?

Abaddon: Precisely, now this may be one of the most basic spells, but it can prove quite effective when the right person uses it. Depending on the mana of the user the effects can be terrifying.

Morgana: Yet it had no effect on the bigger Oni.

Abaddon: That's because some creatures, most usually those of the big brutish type are immune to it due to their fearlessness. In order to intimidate them you'll need the next level of the aura which is 'Aura of Despair'.

Morgana: Is there a level beyond that?

Abaddon: Yes, 'Abyssal Presence' with which you can intimidate mostly everyone. And finally, the highest rank is 'Presence of the Dark Lord' and it can effect anybody but the effect itself can warry depending on the individual. For instance, a higher ranked being like an Arch Mage can break free more easily.

Morgana: Amazing, I didn't know there was so much depth involved in magic.

Abaddon: You used to date a magician, and this surprises you?

Morgana: Merlin rarely talked about magic with me, because my father wouldn't have it, he wanted me to be a diplomat instead…

Abaddon: I thought as much, but no matter, now you're free to learn as you will.

Morgana: And I have you to thank for that, my prince in shining armour (smiles)

Abaddon: Stop you'll make me sick.

Morgana: (chuckles) But how will I know if it worked?

Abaddon: That's why I had this wee lad help us out today, you can come out now Nairn!

A young boy dressed in a noble outfit comes out from one of the pillars and joins them.

Nairn: Hello!

Morgana: Hello little one, I'm Morgana.

Nairn: I know, Uncle Abaddon told me.

Morgana: (smiles) Who is this kid?

Abaddon: He's the son of one of the nobles and he was quite eager to help us out in our session.

Morgana: Are you sure that's a good idea? He's just a boy.

Abaddon: He's not just a boy, he's a Demon too he can handle it, can't you, Nairn?

Nairn nods eagerly.

Abaddon: I had my father practice with me when I was even younger than him.

Morgana: You're you and he's…oh alright, if you say it's fine, then who am I to worry (smirks).

Abaddon: That's my girl. Now, you'll need to focus, channel your mana, and make it flow out of your body with your dark attribute. As a start, just making him shiver is fine.

Morgana: Easy for you to say (focuses).

After a while of focus, she expels the mana, but it has no effect.

Abaddon: You're not adding your dark element to it, again.

Morgana: I'm trying! (Focuses) how do I even do that?

Abaddon: Visualise, imagine your mana mixing with your element, like stirring a pot, blend in the ingredients.

As she does so, a small amount of dark aura begins to sip out of her.

Abaddon: You're doing fine, almost there.

Morgana: Aura of Dread! (Fails) Damn it!

Abaddon: Doesn't matter; you're starting to get the hang of it, try again.

The next time more aura begins to sip out but again it is no good.

Abaddon: Okay, watch me do it, focus, build up your mana…and release!

He casts the spell and the boy almost faints from the shock and Morgana herself freezes in place.

Morgana: You make it look so easy!

Abaddon: You okay there, boy?

Nairn: Mhmm, just a bit dizzy…

He casts 'Cure Ailment' on him, and he is good as new.

Abaddon: Now you try.

Morgana: Focus…build up…and release!

She manages well this time although it is only a weak wave.

Morgana: How's that?

Abaddon: Better, but I think it would be best if we began with 'Fear' instead.

Morgana: 'Fear'?

Abaddon: The most basic version.

Morgana: What? No! I can do this!

Abaddon: Clearly you can but it might improve your chances if you start with the most basic.

Morgana: Tsk, fine! Teach me…

Abaddon: This one is even more simple, all you have to do is focus and stun your opponent with a small amount of malintent, watch.

He does it and she only feels frightened for a small second, but that small second can mean life or death in a battle.

Morgana: Okay, that doesn't have as much impact, but it is useful, nonetheless.

She does it as well and after a couple of tries she manages to frighten the little boy.

Morgana: I did it!

Abaddon: Excellent, 'Aura of Dread' works on the same principle but on a larger scale, now try to implement how 'Fear' works and magnify its effects.

And so, she tries and tries and with each trial she gets better and better until finally she manages to successfully pull it off although still not on the required scale.

Morgana: Yes! I can feel it! I'm almost there.

Abaddon: You're picking up real fast and you learn from your mistakes, well done.

Morgana: Thank you (smiles).

Abaddon: You were great as well Nairn, good boy.

Nairn: Can we play again?

Abaddon: Of course, tomorrow at the same time, don't be late.

Nairn: Hurray! Bye-bye! (Runs off).

Morgana: Perhaps I should practice on some animal instead.

Abaddon: Isn't it more exiting this way? Practicing on a sentient being?

Morgana: Hmmm you know what? You're not wrong (snickers).

Abaddon: (snickers) Go and rest now and then we'll begin your language lessons.

Morgana: Can't wait (kisses him).

He kisses her back.

Morgana: But before I go, there is one thing I would like to know, how is it that there are only, what? Seven elements? And how is it decided to which one we belong?

Abaddon: Those are some good questions, and I can answer them as you rest.

And so, they go her chambers where she lays down on her bed.

Abaddon: Let's see now. All the seven elements come from the Gods and Titans themselves. In the beginning there were only two elements, light and dark, whose Gods were Baal, and his sister Shekinah. The other four Gods represented the forms derived from these elements: Sunlight and Moonlight, Night, and Day. Then came the Titans, from the blood of the Creator God and they carried the other elements with them, and their tribes were named after the elements. After the Titanomachia we inherited the traits from all of them, as we all came from the mixing of their blood with the Mother Earth. Next, is the matter of genes.

It is our mana that bears those elements derived from the Divine kin, for it is also born out of divine energy, and therefore those that possess more of Baal's blood were born like us and we have inherited his dark element, others his dark fire and so forth for each race. There are those who possess very little affinity for mana therefore they are called talentless, or ordinary.

Morgana: And what about the Storm Demons? How do they fit in your race? I thought Baal was the God of Darkness, not storms, or fire.

Abaddon: The Titans tell us, 'Baal was made God of darkness itself'. We have to ponder on darkness here for a moment. What does it mean, what does it entail? It does not simply mean something that is 'dark' in colour, or obscured, it also pertains to the abstract idea of it. Everything in this world has a dark side to itself. A clear sky can be darkened by thunderclouds, even a calm water can turn to a violent storm. Fire, can bring brightness and warmth, keep us comfortable and dry. But it can also burn and destroy, it is both benevolent and malignant at the same time. This is what Baal is the Lord, God of, the dark side of things. Thunder and lightning; eddies and hurricanes, are also his domain. The *Addarim* have made a cult out of this aspect of Baal, calling it *'Baalum*

Addadim', Baal of the Storm, or *'Hadadim'* in their dialect. But his office extends beyond that, to abstract things as well. Lies, secrets, are all dark things, a secret kept can bring more harm than a blazing inferno, lies too. That is why thieves and those that live in the shadows of society have taken *Baalum Etutim* that is 'of the Darkness' to be their patron. Do you understand now?

Morgana: Yes, I do, it all makes much more sense now.

Abaddon: Well, that makes me glad.

Morgana: So … this 'dark flame' your people can command, these Fire Demons, it is a manifestation of the destructive side of the regular, red flame?

Abaddon: I would say so, but it is not that simple. It is said to be a manifestation of Baal's divine spirit, his true power. We believe that is what He used to create Tiamatu, the Abyss, that is why it's called *Girru Tiamatuu,* 'Flame of the Abyss'.

For us it has a benevolent meaning, much like the good side of fire. Thus, since it holds such a meaning, many amongst the *Isarim* think that they are the 'true' *Baalim,* 'Those of Baal'. I think that's subjective.

Morgana: I agree, all those things that you have explained ultimately make up Baal as a whole, therefore, to claim that one of his progenies is the 'true' kin is like saying that trees are more of a plant than flowers.

Abaddon: I like that analogy, but unfortunately certain ideals are easy to twist to personal gains in claiming superiority and legitimacy. But that's a topic for another time.

Morgana: Do you think that Baal is his real name?

Abaddon: Alas, we cannot know all the secrets of the world, some things are not meant to be revealed. It is those mysteries that make the divine so fascinating, wouldn't you say?

Morgana: I suppose that's one way of looking at it.

Abaddon: And now I would like for you to rest (gives her a kiss on her forehead). I will call for you in past an hour.

Morgana: See you later, my love.

She stretches and turns on the side, then takes to napping.

Thusly, the daily routine of magic training and language sessions for Morgana began, but at one time Abaddon was tending to other matters so Dagon was overseeing her training and tutoring.

Morgana: A-li-shu…Abat-duru?

Dagon: Wrong, try again.

Morgana: Oh, it's – aagh! (Feels a sharp pain in her stomach).

Dagon: It is '-Turu', child, not 'agh'; again.

Morgana: Agh!

Dagon: Morgana? What is wrong?

Morgana: My stomach! It hurts! Aghhh!

Dagon: Come! Let us lay you down (he helps her on the bed).

Morgana: (winces from the pain) It hurts so much!

Dagon: Let me see.

Using his magic, he examines her body and what he discovers shocks him.

Dagon: My dear child…you are pregnant.

Morgana: What?

Dagon: You're carrying a child, Lord Abaddon's child.

Morgana: I am? (Smiles from happiness) Our baby (holds her stomach).

Dagon: You must rest now; I will tell him the good news.

Morgana: No, I want to be the one to do it.

Dagon: As you wish; now sleep.

And then he alleviates her pain, and she falls asleep. At that moment Abaddon comes in to check her progress and freaks out when he sees her all covered in sweat.

Abaddon: Morgana! (Rushes to the bed) what happened?

Dagon: Nothing to worry, my lord, she was just exhausted and in need of rest, that is all.

Abaddon: She's trying too hard, maybe I should lower her regime.

Dagon: She is quite content with how things are, doing otherwise might displease her.

Abaddon: You sound awfully worried about her, is there something you're not telling me?

Dagon: (it pains me to lie to his majesty, but I must do it for her sake) No, I would never hide anything from you, my lord.

Abaddon: You better, you know how I feel about liars.

Dagon: Oh yes, all too well.

Abaddon: You can go now; I'll stay with her until she awakens.

Dagon: That too is awfully carrying of you sire if I may say so.

Abaddon: Of course, I care about the people I love, and I wouldn't have anything happen to them, especially her.

Dagon: You are a good person, my lord, that is why your people love you, that is why she loves you.

Abaddon: You know what I say about that, don't you, Dagon?

Dagon: 'Benevolent God or a Demon of Carnage'.

Abaddon: Benevolent God or a Demon of Carnage.

Dagon: That is what makes you great.

Abaddon: Thank you…Grandfather.

Dagon: (smiles) It has been ages since I last heard you call me that.

Abaddon: Only because we don't mix personal relations when on duty.

Dagon: I know the custom, but it would not hurt to hear it more often once in a while.

Abaddon: If only Father were here to see us…

Dagon: My boy (places his hand on his shoulders) you will free him, Lilim too, you will free them all, that I am certain of.

Abaddon turns to him and embraces him as does he and when that is over with, he takes his leave.

After a few hours Morgana awakens and smiles when she sees Abaddon beside her bed.

Morgana: Were you here the whole time?

Abaddon: Indeed, I was, you had me worried. Da-my grandfather says it's only fatigue, but I don't buy it for a second.

Morgana: Wait! (Straightens up) Dagon is your grandfather?

Abaddon: Why does that surprise you so?

Morgana: You look nothing alike!

Abaddon: That's because he had to shave his head when he became a Priest and besides, he's over thousand years old.

Morgana: He said he's only thousand.

Abaddon: He lied, he's very sensitive about his age (chuckles).

Morgana: Even Demons can get age sensitive huh? (Laughs) well, since you put it that way it does make sense.

Abaddon: So, talk to me, what really happened?

Morgana: I had stomachaches, so Dagon had to sedate me.

Abaddon: Stomach aches? (Then it dawns on him) wait, don't tell me, you're–

Morgana: Yes! (Smiles) I'm pregnant! We are going to have a baby!

Abaddon: By Baal, that is great news! (Embraces her).

Morgana: (returns the embrace) I am so happy, having a child together will only bring us closer.

Abaddon: We have to think of a name.

Morgana: We don't even know the gender yet.

Abaddon: You're right, perhaps that should wait.

Morgana: Yes, let's not be hasty, like you always say, 'in time'.

Abaddon: I sound nothing like that.

Morgana: Maybe a little (chuckles).

Then he kisses her and so does she.

And the days pass, and with the child having Demon blood it speeds up its developing process and thus Morgana is ready to give birth after the first trimester. Dagon is overseeing the procedure, keeping her stable with his magic while the midwife delivers the baby and a healthy halfling boy is born.

Morgana: Let me hold him.

Now the umbric cord is cut and it is given into her arms as he cries.

Morgana: There he is, my son, my baby boy (smiles and tears of joy jut out of her eyes).

Abaddon: He is beautiful.

Morgana: Just like his father.

Abaddon: And mother.

Midwife: Have you decided on a name yet?

Both parents look at each other and unanimously say 'Mordred'.

Dagon: What a wonderful name.

Midwife: I agree (smiles) well then, I will take my leave now, don't want to spoil the family atmosphere.

Morgana: Thank you.

Midwife: No, thank **you**, it was my privilege to give birth to your son.

Abaddon: Thank you.

The midwife bows and leaves.

The boy grew at a rapid rate and within months he had already reached adolescence and then young manhood and he was ready to be trained in combat. But not all was as it seemed with young Mordred, at a young age his parents discovered that he has been gifted with a most sinister ability, death magic. Everything the boy touched would witter away and die, flowers, grass, animals even people, nothing was immune to his touch; he was like death incarnate.

This was due to the simple matter of him being something unnatural, something that was not meant to be. And so, the world rejected him, it did not want him walking its paths or smelling its flowers, only those dearest to him could hope to touch him and those were his parents for nothing is stronger than a parental love for one's child.

Therefore, his great-grandfather forged him a bracelet that suppressed his magic and he wore it at all times. When he was ready to be a warrior his father, Abaddon, made him a special suit of armour that allowed him to contain his powers and use them in a more controlled manner. Said armour was a work of art, made of obsidian steel and black gold, with a Demonic and monstrous look to it, fitting for someone like him. He also forged him a sword bearing his name and it became known as the Demon Sword 'Mordred'.

During those passing days, Abaddon's powers grew stronger until they finally reached their peak, and Morgana was able to master not two but three elements, becoming a terrible Sorceress of both Darkness and Shadow. The three of them would often spar together and during that time they learned that all magic is rendered meaningless when faced with Mordred's ability which then made him the most powerful warrior in all his army.

Now with his power fully restored, Abaddon was ready to gather the final piece of the puzzle and raise the curtain for the final act.

CAPITVLVM XX

FILIVS DIABOLI[xix]

Mordred: Father, shall we go and gather the last of the Demons?

Abaddon: No need for that, they will come to us.

Mordred: But they are quite far away and deep beneath the surface, how are you supposed to call them here?

Abaddon: You will see soon enough, my son.

Mordred: Are you going to perform some high-level summoning spell?

Abaddon: Not quite, I will be doing the summons but with no spell.

Mordred: I have to see this.

Abaddon: Then follow me my boy.

Morgana: Where are you going?

Mordred: Father was going to show me his method of calling the Subterrans here.

Morgana: Then your father will have to do it by himself because it's time for your language lessons.

Mordred: But Mother…

Morgana: No buts!

Abaddon: Come on let the boy go, it won't take too long, he'll be back swiftly I promise.

Morgana: You're being too easy on him.

Abaddon: And you're being too harsh, he's a young man now not a little child, he can make his own decisions.

Mordred: Father is right, I am more than capable to make decisions on my own.

Morgana: (squints) Fine! You have five minutes, five!

Abaddon: Better make it three, it will be over soon.

Morgana: I'm counting on that.

Mordred: Or you can come with us.
Abaddon: Of course, that's always an option.
Morgana: I guess I could.
Abaddon: Well?
Morgana: Oh alright, why not.
Abaddon: Now you will bear witness to the extent of my raw power.

And so, they climb the 'Saharu Kishpunuu', 'Tower of Sorcery' which is the highest construct in the kingdom, and they step out on the balcony. It was high noon at that time of day, so the sun was shining bright.

Now Abaddon spreads out his arms and without uttering a single spell or invocation has his mana well up inside him and releases it into the world. The mana is so potent and of similar nature like that of Baal, dark and sinister, powerful, and commanding. The surge of energy shoots up into the sky and turns it from bright blue to blood red, it darkens the light of the sun, and it spreads out into the horizon bloodying the sky as it goes. And it also spreads throughout the earth in the form of black clouds, and all can see it and feel it, and they fear what they see and dread what they feel.

The cloud of mana commands respect out of the sheer pressure and fear it spreads and they all understood that this is their king's true, original power. And they shout out in awe and admiration as they bask in his spiritual presence, some are brought on their knees for they could not stand underneath that presence. Demon, Orc and Giant alike for the first time understood what it means to be Abaddon, Kishsharrum – King of All the World.

And the mana spreads and spreads and ultimately it engulfs the entire land of Shilhumu reaching even the realm of Hathasia. It slips into the very earth, into every stone, every grain of sand, every organism inanimate or animate is covered by the clouds. And it reaches the underground kingdom of Barathruz and Albunalich the king smiles at the thought of getting a rematch with Abaddon but that smile soon turns sour when the clouds hit him like a tidal wave, and he is overcome by the same feelings everyone had.

At that moment he realised that there will not be any kind of matches for the battle was already won. Some of his people cannot withstand it and are driven mad by it even going as far as taking their own lives. And even he begins to laugh akin a madman all from this mighty presence. Even Dharmat is brought on his knees, and he goes mad from its influence, naming Abaddon a God, like the Orc Zog did before him.

And his wife and son next to him were standing there frozen from awe, unmoving, only observing the spectacle that unfolded before their eyes.

Argyros: This presence…ah it's been long, so long…

Ignatos: He is back! Rejoice people, your King has arrived!

And they roared, and the others roared with them, and the Wolves howled, and the Giants bellowed, and they all cheered the true coming of Abaddon, yelling out 'long live the king'.

Albunalich: Get ready, you scum! We are going to war!

Now the mountains part, shaking the ground as they move and where once stood the passage to the Underground Kingdom a huge rift opens and the hordes of Demons come flooding out from beneath the Earth like ants from their homes. Big ones, small ones, from all shapes and sizes all made from earth and stone, vile and grotesque looking. Thousands upon thousands swarm out until the entire land is drained from their presence. And then Albunalich stood at the helm and led them towards Shilmatu and they march unimpeded by the sunlight for the sky remains dark and bloody.

Finally, Abaddon stops the flow of mana, and the black clouds dissipate from the surface of the Earth but the sky as I said, remains the same.

Mordred: Father, that was breathtaking!

Morgana: By Baal, I haven't seen anything of this scale before, truly you're the best.

Abaddon: Ah, it feels good to be back.

Mordred: I can only hope to achieve even a fraction of your power someday.

Abaddon: You are my son, it's in your blood, don't ever doubt yourself.

Mordred: Yes father.

Abaddon: With that, the final piece of the army will soon be here, once they arrive, we will go on to gather the Hathasians and from there we go to war.

Morgana: I can't believe that it's finally here, the moment we've all been waiting for, the moment we've been preparing for almost two years.

Abaddon: Nonstop recruiting, creating, forging, training, everything we've done so far will finally be put to the test; will we break or be broken?

Mordred: I have no doubt that we will be the ones doing the breaking.

Abaddon: Agreed, there is no room for errors. Now, with that out of the way I would have you rally up everyone and prepare them for departure.

Mordred: At once father.

Morgana: Wait! What about your lesson?

Mordred: Sorry mother, this takes priority.

Morgana: Ugh, I guess you are your father's son…alright, go.

Mordred: Excuse me (walks away).

Morgana: Well, since the lesson is off the table what say you and I have a little session of our own (snickers).

Abaddon: It's like you're reading my mind.

Morgana: Lead the way then, my lord.

Abaddon: Gladly.

Then he teleports them both to their bedroom where they make love. But they are not the only ones enjoying each other's companies, others that were interested, were engaged in one final act before the sortie.

Malgaras slips out of the bed he shared with Jamil.

Jamil: Where are you going?

Malgaras: I can feel it, the time to move is upon us.

Jamil: Surely, we can spend a couple more minutes in the comfort of our bed.

Malgaras turns to him.

Jamil: I could go for another round if you like (smiles).

Malgaras: Don't tempt me, we must prepare.

He says as he pulls his hair back into a ponytail.

Jamil: Just a couple of minutes won't hurt then. Who knows, this might be the last time we spend time together like this.

Malgaras: Don't jinx it.

Jamil: It's war and wars are unpredictable; therefore, we must cherish every moment we can spare, wouldn't you agree.

Malgaras: You do have your way with words.

And then he uses Shadow Step to get back on the bed and as soon as they start kissing there is a knock on the door.

Demon: General Malgaras sir, King Abaddon requests the presence of all turtanim immediately.

Malgaras: (sigh) So much for those couple of minutes.

Jamil: Can you give us a moment?

Demon: Of course, but please, do not take your time.

Jamil: 'Do not take your time'? Who does he think he is?

Malgaras: Don't be upset with him; he is just doing his job.

Mordred: (outside the door) Where is Malgaras?

Demon: He is still inside, your highness, I informed him of the summons.

Malgaras: Shit, it's the prince! Quick! (Gets off the bed in a hurry).

Mordred: Malgaras! I am coming in!

Malgaras: Just a moment, sire! Come on! (Motions Jamil to get off the bed)

Jamil sighs.

They dress up in a jiffy right as Mordred opens the door.

Mordred: Great! You are not even in your armour yet!

Malgaras: Hello my lord…

Jamil: My lord…

Mordred: Unbelievable! There is summons order and you two are still shagging!

Jamil: To be fair, my lord, we've only received word—

Mordred: I do not care for your excuses, Jamil; when your lord calls for you, you are expected to be ready!

Jamil: How can we be ready when we've just received the orders from the soldier outside, pardon me, your majesty, but you're being unreasonable.

Mordred: How dare you speak to me in that manner? I am not your friend nor lover, Jamil.

Jamil: My lord, I –

Malgaras: That's why I told you we should prepare!

Jamil: So now I'm to blame?

Mordred: Enough! You have two minutes to appear outside or suffer the consequences (walks out).

Jamil: Cheeky brat, I can't stand him.

Malgaras: Like it or not, he is our lord's son.

Jamil: That doesn't give him the right to be a pompous arse.

Malgaras: He was right to get angry, I knew this would happen, yet I did otherwise, this is the last time I think with my cock instead of my gut (puts on his hood).

Jamil: So, **you are** making it my fault?

Malgaras: You're the one that goaded me into it.

Jamil: I'm sorry for wanting to spend more time with my lover.

Malgaras: I don't have time to argue with you.

Jamil: You're the one that's turning it into an argument.

Malgaras: See you later, make sure you come at once (takes off).

Jamil: Humph, idiot…

At the outskirts of the Royal City

Carmox: You're late.

Malgaras: I was busy.

Carmox: Stuffing that pretty boy's arse with your cock?

Malgaras: Why do you always have to be so vulgar? It's hard to imagine you're a Dhalka, or Etlu Baalim[55] for that matter.

Carmox: I'm a warrior, not a stuck up noble, the same norms don't apply to me.

Malgaras: It's good to have you back.

Carmox: It's good to be back.

Malgaras: If I'm honest, I kind of missed your vulgar remarks.

Carmox: And I missed making fun of your queer arse.

Malgaras: Heh, why are we here anyway? The others can't have made it yet.

Carmox: Normally, you would think that but look (she points towards the distance with her head).

Malgaras: What in the name of Baal is that…?

Carmox: It's them.

Lo and behold, the most unusual sight was before the eyes of all present; the Earth Dwellers of Barathruz were riding patches of dirt throughout the land as if riding ships on dry land which allowed them to move faster than usual, and they had crossed the distance in half the time it would normally take them.

Once they stood before the amassed soldiers, the king makes the patches halt and returns them to the ground with his magic.

Albunalich: Pretty impressive wouldn't you say?

Abaddon: That was quite the entrance.

---

[55] Knight of Baal in O.D

Albunalich: (kneels) We are in your service, Abaddon, king.

Abaddon: I accept.

Albunalich: I must ask that you pardon my past rude misbehaviour and inhospitality.

Abaddon: All is forgiven, frankly if I was in your position, I might have done the same.

Albunalich: That's very generous of you.

Abaddon: There can be no bad blood amongst us if we are to do battle together.

Albunalich: Agreed.

Abaddon: Come, we will have your kind properly prepared.

Albunalich: I'd rather not, we are more comfortable the way we are.

Abaddon: Surely you don't mean to fight bare as you are.

Albunalich: We need no armour (taps his chest) our bodies are already sturdy enough.

Abaddon: I'm afraid I'll have to insist, sturdy bodies are not protection enough.

Albunalich: Oh, but they are, and Mother Earth provides us with all the protection we need.

Abaddon: Oh?

Albunalich: Allow me to demonstrate.

He unsheathes his own sword and cuts off his arm much to the surprise of the others but then his arm reforms anew.

Abaddon: Remarkable.

Albunalich: As long as we are fighting on solid ground, we'll be fine.

Mordred: What manner of magic is this?

Albunalich: Earth magic my boy, primordial Earth magic, very ancient and powerful.

Mordred: Pure Earth magic…is every one of your kind endowed with this gift?

Albunalich: Indeed, I so more than the others. Nonetheless we are the children of the Earth itself, given form by the mana of Mother Earth[56].

Abaddon: We were all made from the bones of Mother Earth and the blood of the Divine Kin.

Albunalich: But you are not of the first.

---

[56] Gai'ara, rendered as Gaia in Common; one of the Earth Titans and Goddess of Earth.

Mordred: That would make you one of the first denizens of the world.

Albunalich smiles a toothy grin.

Abaddon: Why keep yourself hidden underground then?

Albunalich: Because that is where it's most peaceful, we hate conflicts.

Abaddon: Yet you are not beyond taking part in one.

Albunalich: Do we have a choice?

Abaddon: Touché.

Albunalich: And who is this curious young man?

Abaddon: My son, Mordred.

Albunalich: Son? I didn't know you had progeny.

Abaddon: I didn't, he was born recently but his Demon blood made his growth faster.

Albunalich: Demon blood you say, astonishing.

Abaddon: Which, apparently you have not even a drop of.

Albunalich: I told you before, we call ourselves 'Subterrans', or in our modest speech, *Ardan Dwelurz,* 'Earth Dwellers'.

Abaddon: I would very much like to hear more about the history of your people.

Albunalich: I'd happy to oblige however in a more suitable environment.

Abaddon: Agreed.

Morgana: I have a question.

Albunalich: Ask away, young lady.

Morgana: How do you survive that deep underground? Or do you not need any form of food?

Albunalich: We absorb all the nutrients from the earth which is abundantly rich in them for example by the decomposed flesh of animals.

Morgana: That would make you similar to trees, the way they absorb nutrients through their roots.

Albunalich: You are correct in a sense.

Morgana: Interesting.

Albunalich: And you are?

Morgana: Morgana, Mordred's mother.

Albunalich: Oh dear, aren't you a tad too young to be a mother?

Morgana: I'm old enough.

Albunalich: I don't judge, my lady.

Morgana: Tell me how is it that you speak Common? Considering the fact, you live isolated underground.

Albunalich: Oh, my lady, I know a great deal about this world beside Common, I know of Dragons, Giants, Goblins and Orcs, Faeries and Vampires and what not. Our Entomancers can communicate with insects and these curious little critters bring news from all over the place, Avalon, Baltia, you name it.

Morgana: I reckon these Entomancers are bug mages?

Albunalich: Indeed, they are.

Abaddon: You keep on surprising me.

Albunalich: What can I say? We are one of a kind.

Abaddon: I'd love to stay here and chat but I'm afraid time is of the essence.

Albunalich: Before we go, may I still receive these armours you have prepared for us?

Abaddon: I thought you weren't going to wear them.

Albunalich: Oh, they are not for wearing.

Abaddon: Hm?

Albunalich: You'll see for yourself (smirks).

And upon his behest he is brought the many armours that were supposed to be theirs and he redistributes them amongst the cleverer ones of his race and what they do next is truly surprising. Instead of donning them they absorb the minerals that compose the armours into their bodies acquiring the steel, manalith and all other components to further strengthen their own bodies and it renders the armours into useless chunks of metal.

Abaddon: By Baal…you have to be the most fascinating creatures I've ever seen.

Morgana: I second that…

Albunalich gives off a courteous bow.

Now Abaddon raises his hands and casts 'Mass Teleportation' moving all of them in the heart of Hatashia without any problems whatsoever thanks to his massive, mana reserves.

Dharmat: He is here, our God has arrived.

Azar: Husband? What are you talking about?

Dharmat: God is here…

Azar: By Mithras what is wrong with him?

Lahar: I don't know, my queen, he has been like this ever since that miasma showed up.

Azar: That foul presence, yes, I felt it too.

Lahar: I'm afraid it has messed with the majesty's senses…

Azar: Are you telling me my husband has gone insane?

Lahar: …

Azar: Well, do something! There must be something in those books of yours.

Lahar: My lady, I'm a librarian not a medic…

Azar: Then get the medic!

Lahar: He was already here…and he said there is nothing he could do…the damage has been done on a spiritual level.

Azar: In that case call a Mystic!

Lahar: …

Azar: Now what?

Lahar: …They all suffered the same fate, my queen…I'm afraid they couldn't handle the pressure and as you know our best Mystics went to join his cause…

Azar: Then this country is all but doomed…everything went to shit when that piece of filth Abaddon showed up! We never should have welcomed him to our home! Curse him! Curse him to death and all that follow him!

Jamil: Hello mother.

Azar: Jamil, ooh my sweet boy!

She rushes to embrace him but stops in her tracks when she sees Abaddon.

Azar: You…

Abaddon: Greetings, your majesty, looking lovely as always.

Dharmat: He's here! Ohhh my lord! I kiss your feet!

He kneels on the ground and kisses Abaddon's sabatons.

Abaddon: Oh dear, it would seem your father has lost his mind, get up and stop embarrassing yourself.

Dharmat: As my lord commands.

Azar: It is your fault! You did this! You poisoned his mind! You do nothing but take and take! What more do you want! You monster!

Mordred: How dare you speak to your lord in such manner, woman!

Abaddon: Hold.

Jamil: My king, please forgive my mother, she is clearly besides herself at this moment.

Azar: (slaps him) ‘My king?’ This is your king, your father! Not some fiend from a foreign land!

Jamil: Mother, I would ask –

Azar: Silence! I am your mother, and you will not shut me up!

Jamil bites his lip.

Azar: Look! Look! You even took my baby boy from me, twisted him to your own cause!

Mordred: I have heard enough of this baseless slander!

Morgana: Mordred! This is Jamil’s home, let him deal with his own problems.

Abaddon: Your mother is right.

Jamil: Thank you, Lady Morgana.

Azar: Listen to yourself, boy, ‘my king’, ‘Lady Morgana’, have you no shame? No dignity? Where is your patriotism? Have you forgotten where your true allegiance lies?

Jamil: My allegiance lies with my King Abaddon, to whom I swore my unwavering fealty upon my sword.

Azar: How…how could you?

Dharmat: Well done, my boy! Well done! I shall do the same!

Azar: Husband! Get a hold of yourself! For Mithras’ sake, man, come back to your senses!

Dharmat: Enough! You will not stop me from worshiping our true God, from this moment forth I denounce Mithras and pledge my servitude to Lord Abaddon!

Abaddon: No, I am no God, and I will not be worshipped as such, if you want to venerate someone let it be Baal instead.

Dharmat: And so it shall be!

Azar: Marduk!

Dharmat: Be silent, woman!

Ester: Brother, you’re back!

Azar: Stay back, child, that is not your brother, he is a Demon in his skin.

Ester: What are you saying, mother? That is big brother.

Jamil: Mother is feeling unwell, why don’t you take her to rest.

Azar: No! I will not be silenced!

Dharmat: Be silent! (He begins to strangle her).

Ester: Father! Father no! Stop it!

Morgana: Well, that escalated quickly.

Jamil unsheathes his scimitar and pierces Dharmat through the heart.

Dharmat: M…my son… (spews blood).

Jamil: I'm sorry, father, but you are no longer fit to rule this kingdom (pulls out the scimitar).

Azar gasps, covering her mouth.

Jamil: From now, I am the new king.

Azar: You ruined us…you ruined us all…Demon! Davian!

She curses him in Hathasian while little Ester is crying over her father's corpse.

Jamil: Take them to the dungeons.

The soldiers are somewhat hesitant to listen.

Jamil: Am I not your king? Take them away!

Azar: (spits on his face) You are a disgrace, freak!

Jamil slaps her across the face, and she falls on the floor.

Ester: Mother!

Jamil: What are you waiting for?

Abaddon: Do as your king commands.

Then the guards step up and seize Azar and Ester.

Azar: Unhand me! I can go on my own!

At that moment the middle child, Bahar, comes from the opposite corridor and sees the grizzly sight.

Bahar: Mother? Where are you taking her? Mother!

Jamil: Seize her too!

Bahar: Jamil? What are you doing? Stop this madness!

Jamil: I am king now, little sister, and I sentence you to the dungeons.

Bahar: Have you gone insane? We are your family! You can't do this to us!

Jamil: I have no need of family who do not mean me well.

Bahar: What are you talking about?

Azar: Bahar! He killed your father, he is on the Devil's side now, the man you see before you is not your brother Jamil.

Bahar: (tears show up on her eyes) … You would stand with them over your own family?

Jamil: Take them!

Bahar: Why Jamil? Why! You bastard!

Abaddon: You did the right thing, Jamil, they would've only been a liability.

Mordred: Thank Baal that's over, I was beginning to get a headache.

Morgana: You should've executed them.

They all turn to look at her.

Morgana: What? They can prove to be a bigger problem if you let them live, it's clear they hate you now and it wouldn't be a surprise if they lead an insurrection one day.

Jamil: I believe that they pose no threat from the dungeons. Perhaps some time there will straighten their mind.

Morgana: Are you sure? You saw the soldiers, they are still loyal to the queen, it only takes one to set them free and you'll have a mutiny on your head.

Mordred: My mother speaks wisely.

Jamil: Maybe so but executing my own family will only make my people resent me even more. I will take my chances for now.

Morgana: Alright, but I did warn you.

Jamil: What does my lord advise?

Abaddon: Whatever you think is best, this is your kingdom now and its subjects are your responsibility however, I do agree with you, executing them now could prove unwise.

Jamil: (nods) So it shall be. My lord, I would be honoured if you served as a witness to my coronation.

Abaddon: I see no problem with that.

Jamil: That means a lot to me.

Mordred: But we have no time for that? Can't it wait until the campaign is over?

Jamil: No need for that, we will begin immediately.

Mordred: No ceremony, no nothing?

Jamil: As you said my prince, there is no time.

Mordred: Indeed.

Jamil: (takes the crown from his father's corpse) Only His Majesty and Lord Dagon as a religious official are required to conduct the ceremony.

Abaddon: I will contact him then.

He does so telepathically, and Dagon appears.

Dagon: You called for me sire?

Abaddon: Dagon, we'll have you conduct a coronation ceremony.

Dagon: With all due respect, I am only vested in coronating under Baal's authority and since Baal worship is not official in this kingdom, I am afraid I cannot conduct the ceremony.

Jamil: It is as of today, as a prince I declare it to be so.

Dagon: Problem solved then; shall we begin?

Morgana: Wait, what do we do with that? (Points to the corpse).

Mordred: Allow me.

And then he nears the corpse and places his hand on top of it. As soon as he does that the corpse begins to rot and decompose until no trace is left of it, not even the stain of blood.

Jamil: So that is the power of death magic, amazing.

Mordred: You should stop being so easily amazed by things; it is not very mature.

Jamil: I can't help but be fascinated by all these new things I'm experiencing.

Mordred: Then you should not let it show so much.

Jamil: Perhaps you could teach me.

Mordred: No thanks, I am not interested in men.

Jamil: It was worth the shot (smiles).

Mordred: Jamil, I am not some common boy you can casually pick up, try to flirt with me again and I will melt off that pretty little face of yours.

Jamil: …Noted.

Mordred: Good.

Abaddon: Yes Jamil, you forget your place.

Jamil: Apologies my lords (bows)

Morgana: (chuckles) You're hopeless.

Jamil smiles cynically.

Dagon: May I have the crown?

Jamil: Here (hands it over).

Dagon: Kneel.

He does so.

Dagon: In the name of Baal, our great Lord I consecrate this crown and all the merits that come with it (he engraves the 'Tiamat Star' along with its sacred inscriptions in the middle of the crown) In the name of Baal, our great Lord I ask upon thee Jamil, son of Marduk, do you swear to uphold the worship of your new God and all his aspects; Etutuu, Addaduu, Girruu, in the highest regard?

Jamil: I do.

Dagon: Do you swear to do justly by your people and serve in their best interest under the guidance of our Lord?

Jamil: I do.

Dagon: Do you swear to be loyal to your one and true king under the sky?

Jamil: I do.

Dagon: Then by the power vested in me by our Grand Order and by our God and Lord Baal, with Him as a witness from the spiritual plane and our King Abaddon from the physical, I crown thee Jamil, King Dharmat the –

Jamil: No, the name Dharmat ends today, I shall be known as Padavian the First.

Dagon: Very well, I crown thee King Padavian the First (places the crown on his head).

Mordred: What does it mean? (To Abaddon).

Abaddon: It means 'Devil's son'.

Mordred: But he is – oh I see.

Abaddon: Mhmm.

Jamil smirks.

And thus, a new king was born.

CAPITVLVM XXI

ANTEBELLVM[xx]

After Jamil was crowned, he makes an address to the people, and this is what he has to say:

Jamil: My loyal subjects, my people, I am sorry to tell you that my father, your king, has perished.

The crowd immediately gasps and exclaims sadly at this tragic news.

Jamil: Unfortunately, madness had gotten a hold of his sanity and in a fit of this madness, he attacked my mother, your queen, and had I not drawn my blade he would have killed her.

More gasps come out from the crowd and shouts of disbelief, some were praying to Mithras and other Gods for comfort.

Jamil: The honourable King Abaddon that stands next to me and his family are my witnesses, and they can attest that I speak the truth.

Person: He has the 'Devil's Mark' on his crown! (Points to Jamil).

'It's true, it's true,' others began to yell out and the crowd began rabbling.

Jamil: People, calm yourself! I will explain everything!

Now booing began to rise from the crowd.

Jamil: Silence! I have not finished talking!

Abaddon: Settle down!

His voice thunders throughout and the crowd simmers down.

Jamil: Thank you, my lord (clears his throat) as of today I as the eldest child and only male heir am the new King of Hathasia and I have undertaken the name Padavian the First.

The crowd does not dare to speak in fear of angering Abaddon again.

Jamil: As my first decree, I abolish Mithras worship and our old pantheon and instate the worship of Baal.

Now the crowd cannot hold in any longer and erupts in bashful jeering and booing once more.

Jamil: Also, we will pledge our servitude to our one and true king, a devout follower of the Dark Lord who has been graced by Him personally, Lord Abaddon.

The booing intensifies and even curses begin flying in the ether.

Abaddon: People of Hathasia! I assure you that there is nothing to fear, nor there is need for despair, under my patronage and that of our God this kingdom will flourish even further, your grandeur will spread throughout the world, greater riches and prosperity will follow!

People: Our kingdom belongs to us not you! Get out! Usurper! Devil! We have only one true God and that is Mithras!

Abaddon: Worry not, you will come to revere me and my God once you witness the splendours I have to offer!

People: Where is the queen? Bring out the queen! She should rule, not you! You sold out soul!

Jamil: Sold out soul? Your former 'oh so beloved' king sold his soul as well! He struck a bargain with King Abaddon; he pledged his allegiance over a blood contract! So, he is no better!

Abaddon: Here is the contract (produces it) so you see, you already belong to me, as of course I had no intentions of allowing Dharmat free reign, this was only means to assure his allegiance.

People: Oh Mithras, deliver us from this fate! Deliver us from this evil!

Abaddon: Evil? I mean you no evil! I am assuring you that nothing will change drastically, we will be right by you, as long as you abide by the laws there will be no problem. Here, as a gesture of good will, you will not be forced into Baal worship, we have never imposed our religion to anyone however, anyone who wishes to do so is free to join our ranks. Dear people I want you to understand that I am not a tyrant, I am not a usurper, I am your friend!

Now the attitude of the crowd changes drastically and they begin to cheer instead.

Morgana: (Way to pull the carpet underneath him, my dear) (smirks).

Marekh: (Steps out from the crowd) The army stands with you, my lord, and with our new king (kneels).

Abaddon: You're the captain of the garrison armies as I recall, do you speak on behalf of the entire force?

Marekh: I do.

Jamil: Thank you Marekh, your loyalty will not go unrewarded.

Abaddon: And are the armies ready for sortie?

Marekh: Almost, my lord.

Abaddon: Excellent, notify my when the time is ripe.

Marekh: Yes, my lord.

Jamil: You may go now.

Marekh bows and leaves.

Abaddon: See that Jamil? This is how you govern people, you ought to learn a thing or two hm?

Jamil: You are a born leader sire, I may be clever, but I'm not fit to be a ruler, perhaps it would be best if you took the reins of this kingdom.

Abaddon: Nonsense, I can't keep under control all the territories I command, that's why I need someone like you.

Jamil: But…

Abaddon: No buts, you are Padavian, are you not?

Jamil smiles a bit and nods.

Dumah: Abaddon, a word?

Abaddon: Of course.

He raises his hand as he walks away and the crowd cheers even louder.

Mordred: See that, Jamil, you are nothing without my father, never forget that (says it into his ear as he walks away).

Morgana: (pats his shoulder on the way) You'll be alright, I believe in you.

Jamil: Thank you, my lady.

Morgana: Don't call me my lady, we are friends, there are no formalities between friends, right?

Jamil: Right, forgive me, Morgana (cracks a smile).

Morgana: Much better.

Abaddon: What is it?

Dumah: It is about your son.

Abaddon: What about him?

Dumah: Okay so…me and Amra were talking, and we want to betroth Morvene to him.

Abaddon: A marriage between our two families? What a splendid idea!

Dumah: So, you approve?

Abaddon: Of course I do, this will only strengthen our bond even further.

Dumah: Oh, praised be Baal, I was worried you would decline.

Abaddon: I have no reason to, you have become a more respectable Demon in the past year, and I have no qualms of marrying my son to your daughter.

Dumah: To be honest, I surprise even myself.

Abaddon: (smiles slightly) Of course, there's the question of how the two feel about it.

Dumah: We have not told her yet, but I am sure she will be delighted.

Abaddon: I hope so.

Dumah: Of course, first we must win this war and survive, preferably…

Abaddon: Why didn't you come to me sooner, why wait to the last moment?

Dumah: I don't know, I am not sure myself, perhaps if all went well, I did not want for their happiness to be ruined because of what might come next.

Abaddon: A sound argument, it would be cruel to marry them and then face them with possible misfortune.

Dumah: Indeed. What happens now? Do we launch an assault with no warning or meet them in open battle?

Abaddon: I believe it would be wiser to meet them in an open battle and wipe them out all at once, siege tactics will work against us, by the time we conquer all the lands our numbers would have dwindled.

Dumah: Agreed, head on is the best course of action, fearlessly, openly, whatever happens, happens.

Abaddon: Whatever happens, happens.

Now it should be noted that Amra and Dumah's daughter, Morvene, was named outside the usual conventions of the Vampires. To symbolise all that has transpired in her life, Amra wanted to break away from the old naming tradition and named her daughter with a name of her choosing – backed up by Dumah of course.

In the meantime, Arthur was summoned to a meeting of the rulers

Arthur: Now what? Our monthly session was last week.

Folduin: We have a good reason for reconvening again, old friend.

Arthur: Well it better be a bloody good reason because I am busy.

Priscilla: Busy with producing your Philosopher Stones?

Arthur: I have no idea what you are talking about.

Urania: Cut the façade, Arthur, I am sick of your crap, we accuse you of something, you deny it and we spin in circles until you confess so spare all of us the headache and come clean for once!

Arthur: That was a closely held state secret, may I ask how you procured such information?

Umbriela: So you admit?

Arthur: Aye, there is no point in denying it seeing as you are already well acquainted with it, so I ask again, how did you find out?

Priscilla: Your personal aide, Thomas, was kind enough to relay us the information.

Arthur: Thomas? Nonsense! He is as loyal as they come, he would never betray me!

Priscilla: Why don't we ask Thomas himself, come dearie.

Thus, Thomas appears in her hologram feed.

Arthur: Thomas Barwick! What is the meaning of this?

Thomas: I'm sorry sire…

Arthur: This is an outrage! You must have enchanted him or something!

Priscilla: I did, at first, but then he began to share information all on his own, for a handsome fee of course.

Thomas: Sire, they paid me gold, lots of gold, more than you ever did ha-ha…

Arthur: You mangy cur! I made you and your father gentry, and this is how you repay me? With a knife in my back?

Thomas: Perhaps if you weren't so stingy, I wouldn't have resorted to this.

Arthur: Blind greed! Oh Lugos, deliver me from this stupidity! Get him out of my sight!

Priscilla: You may go now.

Thomas: Yes, my lady (waddles off).

Cyril: You are in no position to speak of greed, Arthur.

Arthur: Do not preach to me, this is a clear violation of the accords!

Urania: The spy hails from your kingdom therefore there is no breach.

Arthur: You conniving snakes! You planned this all along!

Ivaldi: Yer not the only one who's good at scheming, Arthur.

Arthur: You were on this too?

Ivaldi: Aye, I knew something was going on when you lowered yer grain and look what it is, a stone more precious than anything we can dig out from the earth.

Arthur is beside himself.

Umbriela: How could you keep something like this from us, Arthur? This discovery clearly tips the balance in your favour, it is not to be selfishly guarded!

Folduin: Unless that is what he desired.

Umbriela: Arthur…

Arthur: This is not a trifling gem we are talking about; this is one of the most important artefacts in history, sought out by scholars throughout the ages and **we** succeeded in making it! **We** made it when no one else could not! It was done by the sweat and hard work of **my** magicians! Why should I so easily part with something so precious as if it were a common bauble to give away? Why should those that had not even attempted, revel in the hard work of my magicians? You expect me to just hand it over on a silver platter? I will not! If you want it make your own damn stone!

Urania: Arthur! Do you realise what this means? You are risking a serious breach in our pact! A pact that was built on mutual trust and cooperation! This is the exact opposite of everything we stand for!

Arthur: I know full well what the accords were built upon! I was the one that drafted the bloody thing! Equal trade and share that is what it stands for! And you have nothing to offer me in return for this treasure.

Urania: Age has made you dumb and senile, Arthur Pendragon!

Cyril: I know what this is, you wish to grow stronger on your own and eventually supplant us!

Arthur: Do not be a fool, Cyril Greyhide! I only wish to not be dependent on ore supply and with this I finally can!

Cyril: Your military will be one of the mightiest on the continent, we can't allow this to happen.

Arthur: What are you going to do about it?

Folduin: How about we leave you to fend on your own against Abaddon's armies?

Arthur: You wouldn't!

Folduin: I would not be so sure about that.

Arthur: I would expect something like this from Urania but not from you!

Folduin: You leave me no choice.

Arthur: What do the rest of you say?

Umbriela: I'm sorry, Arthur, but you are forcing our hand.

Arthur: This is blackmail!

Folduin: What will it be? The stone or the fate of Camelot?

Arthur: Fine! You will get the method of crafting but if we survive this, I am pulling away from the bloody treaty!

Urania: As you wish; we will not stop you.

Arthur: I will remember this!

Priscilla: It's unwise to threaten the council especially with no one to back you up.

Arthur: I will not be intimidated by cowards!

Umbriela: Enough! We are a respectable group not a den of villains!

Arthur: Respect has been long lost on this table.

Guard: Sire! You must come out, quick!

Arthur: How dare you interrupt me in my meeting!

Guard: My deepest apologies but you must see this!

Umbriela: What's the matter? Arthur?

Urania: What on earth is going on?

Now he goes outside to look at the sky and sees a message written in the clouds saying, 'I am coming. Death and destruction await you'.

Arthur: He is ready…call the men to arms!

Guard: Yes, my lord! (Runs off as quick as possible).

Arthur goes back inside to the feed to inform them.

Arthur: He's coming, he's finally coming.
Gentlemen, ladies, the day of reckoning is finally upon us, muster the armies.

Cyril: Seeing as he is openly announcing himself, he is goading us into open battle.

Arthur: And we shall ride out and meet him.

Urania: But that's exactly what he wants! We will be like lambs to the slaughter!

Cyril: This is what we've been preparing for we have nothing to fear! We have a choice: fight on the battlefield or cover in our walls and wait for him to come.

Ivaldi: I say we meet him head on like men! We have the numbers; we have the equipment! What is there to fear!

Umbriela: I will send my men to create portals for your armies.

Arthur: Most likely we will meet at the Great Desert that lies beyond Camelot.

Cyril: A fitting place, vast and spacious, plenty of room to go wild.

Arthur: Everyone, I will see you on the battlefield.

Umbriela: May the Gods be with us.

They all say 'amen' and then disconnect.

Meanwhile, back at Hathasia, after the strategic meeting:

Abaddon: Mordred, a word.

Mordred: Yes father?

Abaddon: (places his hand on his shoulder) You won't be fighting at the front lines.

Mordred: What do you mean? I am your most powerful asset!

Abaddon: You are, which is why I have a task for you, one that only you can do.

Mordred: What task?

Abaddon: I need you to go to Dhalsharri and free our people.

Mordred: Alone?

Abaddon: You can do it, all of the enemies' forces will be fighting on the front, only the garrison armies stationed there will remain, and they are a fodder to you, no one can harm you, my boy. That is why only you can fulfil this task.

Mordred: And once our people are free, I will come from the back, and we will pin them down.

Abaddon: That's the plan.

Mordred: Ingenious.

Abaddon: And they won't be the only ones accompanying you, take this (hands him over a scroll)

Mordred: This is…!

Abaddon: Have one of the Warlocks or Nigromancers perform this spell once you're done.

Mordred: (rolls up the scroll and puts it away) I will not fail you father; you have my word.

Abaddon: I know, you are your father's son after all.

Mordred smiles.

Abaddon: (creates a portal for him) May Baal be with you.

Mordred: With you as well father (smiles before putting on his helmet and then walks inside).

Morgana: Where did you send him?

Abaddon: On a very important mission.

Morgana: What mission?

Abaddon: To free our people.

Morgana: Alone?

Abaddon: He'll be fine don't worry; the garrison armies are no match for him.

Morgana: If something happens to my boy…!

Abaddon: Nothing is going to happen; don't you have faith in him?

Morgana: I do, but I hope you're not overestimating him.

Abaddon: He will be fine, I promise (kisses her forehead) come now, it's time to ride out.

Morgana: Wait!

Abaddon: What is it?

Morgana: Before we go, I want to give you this; I wrote you a poem.

Abaddon: (taking the parchment) A poem? I didn't know you write.

Morgana: Well not really, but I was feeling inspired.

Abaddon: Let's see what your inspiration has wrought; 'A New Star Shines', what a lovely title.

Then he goes on to recite the poem, and here it is in full:

In the time of peace
There yet cannot be respite,
Ruin looms
In the form of a vengeful sprite.

A malice, thought destroyed
Bids its time,
A scheme of domination
Once more employed.

Rise again from ruin

Reclaim your might,
Make them fear, and tremble
When you are in sight.

Scorned with contempt by would be allies,
Fools, thinking themselves grand
Soon they'll learn their folly,
When before a god; they stand.

Amassing a great army,
Under one banner you call
Bring the world a reckoning,
Make their cities fall.

Demons and Dragons,
Orcs and Eastern Men,
All the bile under the sky,
West Avalon; they damn.

Their shield, you will shatter;
Their arms, you will break;
Their blood, you will splatter
And make the sands quake.

For the Star of Tiamat;
For the glory of Baal;
In the name of Dhalsarria,
Build a grand Imperia.

Abaddon wraps the parchment and tucks it away.

Morgana: Well? What do you think?

Abaddon: It's amazing, encapsulates everything that has transpired up to this point. I love it (he gives her a kiss on the forehead).

Morgana: I'm glad you like it; I didn't think I would do so well on my first try.

Abaddon: You could make a career out of this.

Morgana: (laughs a hearty laugh) Do not even joke about that. Come on, we've lingered long enough.

Abaddon: I was being serious though…

And so, they go, and they stand before his armies, armed and ready to go, filling the entire area outside Akhum, a number never seen before, numbering over 190,000. 60,000 Hatshasian cavalry and 40,000 infantry; 20,000 Oni, 20,000 Shadow Demons; 20,000 Subterrans; 30,000 Orcs and Dragonborn combined; 300 of the Giants, and 300 of the Dragon kin; and 200 Giant Wolves. Everyone in their rightful positions, at the head of their respective companies. All were equipped with updated armour and weapons, enchanted by Abaddon's powerful magic and the Mountain Giants' runes.

The Undead Orcs had reinforced neck braces to prevent their heads from being looped off. Armour was forged for the Dragonkin as well and now they looked like horrifying war engines of destruction. All Dragonborn were equipped with full body armour including chainmail.

Even the Giant Wolves were armoured up as far as their build allowed it. The Frost and Fire Giants were equipped with armours laced with special alloys which allowed for heat and frost resistance. The other equipment was also enchanted with resistance to all sorts of magics. Everything was accounted for and made perfect.

Now it was time for Abaddon to make the final address.

Abaddon: My brothers! My sisters! The time has finally come! This is it! This is the moment we all have been preparing for, for the past years! This is the time when we put all of our hard work and effort into use! This is the time when we show our enemies just how powerful we are! Their day of reckoning is finally here! I gathered you all for that one purpose, to trample those that would deny me my rightful place at the top of this world! So, ride! Fly! And march with me! March to war and the world's ending! Let us bring them Armageddon! Onwards!

And with great shouting and chanting the army marches on, flowing like a river, all waving the banner of Dhalsarria – Magdabolg's face in gold on a black background, set within the centre of the Star of Tiamat.

Kur Dimatim, lowest town of the capital Dishum

At a local tavern, a couple of soldiers were enjoying their ales, amongst other unsavoury habits...

Knight: Another!

On his behest the waitress, a young Fire Demoness, with a short flaming hair, and bronze skin, brings another round of ales.

Werewolf: This young one is quite the beauty.

Dwarf: Aye she sure is! (Spanks her behind as she walks away).

Knight: Wait! Why don't you keep us company, love?

Girl: S-sorry I have to tend to the other guests (says timidly).

Knight: The other guests can wait; we want to have some fun (pulls her towards him).

Girl: I-I'd rather not sir knight…

Knight: What was that? Speak up!

Werewolf: I don't think she wants to keep us company!

Knight: That's very rude of you!

Girl: P-please let me go…I h-have to work!

Knight: You'll work when I say you'll work, ya cunt!

He slaps her and she falls on the floor.

Knight: Get up! (Grabs her violently and throws her on the table).

Faery: Savages (enjoys his beer without making any ruckus).

Dwarf: Looks like this lassie needs some attitude adjustment.

Knight: I'll make sure to properly educate her, with my cock.

The rest laugh as the knight rips off her clothes.

Girl: Please sir don't! I already have someone!

Knight: Shut up! (Slaps her again) I don't give a fuck if you have two somebodies.

Werewolf: I call next yahahah.

She starts to weep, and her tears are liquid fire.

Mordred: That is enough! Let the girl go, now!

Knight: Who the bloody hell are you?

Dwarf: He looks like a knight is he one of yours?

Knight: Don't be ridiculous, Drumni, no one of ours wears such foul looking armour.

Werewolf: Who are you? Name yourself, stranger.

Mordred: I do not have a name to give to scum like you.

Knight: Now you've done it, little shit! (Grabs his sword)

But Mordred sends out a death wave and kills everyone besides the girl.

Mordred: It is okay, you are safe now.

Girl: Thank you…thank you so much…please, may I know your name?

Mordred: My name is Mordred, I am the son of your King Abaddon, he has sent me here to set you free.

Girl: Praised be Baal…praised be Lord Abaddon!

And all nearby Demons begin chanting the same and thanking him and giving their blessings as Mordred goes around and frees them from their anti-magic shackles.

Meanwhile the allied forces of Avalon have already arranged themselves beyond the border of Camelot, them being in a combined number of 200,000 as well, all properly equipped to battle the hordes of Abaddon, just as they were, only difference was that they each waved their own banners.

Eerie silence filled the air, it was the calm before the great storm.

Arthur: This is it, people! The greatest battle of our lives! We will either stand triumphant or be buried and forgotten beneath the sands of time! For Avalon!

And they all chant 'For Avalon!' and their war cries fill in the air, breaking the eerie silence that surrounded them.

But the desert wind continues to howl and blow furiously, raising the sand in the air and obstructing visibility.

Arthur was shielding his eyes when in the distance he spots them, the waving banners of Abaddon and his advancing armies with the Dragons flying above them.

Some of the troops were gripping religious symbols and were praying to their Gods.

Cyril: Do something about the stinking weather!

Now the Sylphs, Faeries of the air, halt the wind and restore visibility. Now the board was set, and all the pieces were in place.

Abaddon was in the rear mounted on Argyros and Morgana was beside him on Ignatos and the other kings were given Dragon mounts as well and they were arrayed on both their sides.

Morgana: Arthur is mine! No one is to touch him!

'Yes, my lady' fills the air.

Abaddon: So, it begins.

CAPITVLVM XXII

DIES IRAE I[xxi]

Ivaldi: What's wrong? Why aren't they attacking?

Cyril: Maybe we should strike first?

Folduin: No, wait! I sense a foul presence in the air.

Ivaldi: Draw swords!

Arthur: Draw your swords! Arms ready!

The command reverberates throughout their ranks and the sound of steel rubbing against scabbard fills the air.

Abaddon: Are they in place?

Albunalich: Yes, my king.

Abaddon: Give the command.

At that moment a root begins to grow out of Albunalich's index finger, and it extends towards the ground and once it reaches the sand, it burrows beneath and send out slight shockwaves that are felt only by some.

Once the signal is sent, a pair of hands break the surface of the sand and pull one of the knights underground and then another and another all pulling soldiers beneath the surface, sowing disorder and confusion amongst the ranks.

Arthur: Accursed creatures, they were already waiting in ambush!

Ivaldi: Watch yer feet!

As he says that a pair of hands reaches out for him, but he stabs the ground with his sword, and they retreat accompanied with a wailing scream.

Another one reaches for Cyril, but he instinctively grabs them by the wrist and pulls out a Crawler Demon and rips it in half with his brute strength.

Now they emerge from the ground, thousands upon thousands and close combat ensues.

Abaddon: Send them a volley.

Tetsu: Archers!

The Oni archers make ready and release a volley upon the forces with flaming arrows.

Arthur: Volley incoming!

The support unit: the magicians, erect a protective barrier deflecting the arrows.

Tetsu: Second volley! Ute!

Another rain of arrows cuts the air.

Abaddon: Dagon.

Dagon: Yes, my king.

As the arrows fly, Dagon enchants them with piercing magic, and they drill through the protective barrier of the magicians and fall upon some unfortunate soldiers, but most make it through thanks to their protections.

Umbriela: I won't let you!

She uses her light magic to erect an even stronger barrier that easily deflects the oncoming arrows.

Abaddon: Umbriela huh.

Arthur: Let us send one of our own, fire!

Now arrows whiz through from this side of the desert, but Abaddon's Mystics take care of it.

Then they too enhance their arrows, but Dagon and the Mystics erect the 'Wall of Fire' spell, and they disintegrate before they can reach the soldiers.

Urania: Magicians! Prepare an attack!

Now they shoot out magic missiles, but they too do not make it through the fiery barrier.

Umbriela: Urania, that is Dagon's magic, ordinary attacks will not make it through.

Urania: I got it! Water users, fire!

Upon her command they fire watery bolts towards the barrier and both queens use their magic to coat the missiles in extra protective layers allowing them to pierce through this time.

Dumah: Brace for impact!

The units that use shields raise them up and the rest just take the impact with protective stances, and everyone remains relatively unscathed thanks to their new armours. However, there are some casualties from the cavalry whose horses end up being pierced by the bolts of water, some end up being crushed by the weight of their steed as it happened to topple on them. Some were pierced themselves. Shield-less infantry units end up with some casualties as well.

Abaddon: Time for phase two (Lindroz, it's your turn).
Lindroz: (With pleasure).

Abaddon: (Take out their magicians.)
Lindroz: (Understood!)
And amongst the fighting the Wyrms break the surface as well sowing more chaos by spreading their acidic breathes.
Ivaldi: Wyrms!

One by one they emerge in many numbers, like moles through a hole and breathe down upon them. Now their breaths where not the usual yellow, sulphuric ones but this time they were black clouds of destruction made possible through Abaddon's magic that was imbued in their armour. The troops of Avalon were prepared to face Abaddon's nigromancy, but still the black acid is potent enough to melt their armours and reach their flesh, corroding it.
Lindroz: Kill them all!
Ser Gawain of the Table Knights descends upon Lindroz with his broad sword, but the latter's armour avails him, then Lindroz polymorphs into his humanoid form and engages in combat with him.
Gawain: I've never heard of Wyrms being in possession of such magic!
Lindroz: It's all thanks to the Dread One!

As he says that he comes at him with his axe but Gawain blocks with his trusted shield and they clash with their weapons.

Meanwhile Umbriela's Hashmalim[57] *cast 'Holy Purification' to deal with the Wyrm's acidic fumes.*

One of them lunges himself towards her but that proves to be a fatal mistake as she pierces the inside of his mouth with a spear of light and ends up killing it.

Some shield wielding soldiers like the Skelthuz Bhregor and the Erelim[58] *manage to endure their breaths much better due to that extra protection and slay their foes the same way as the Angel Queen; by aiming in their mouths. Piercing spells such as 'Lightning Bolt' and 'Starlight Beam' prove very effective. Nevertheless, by emerging amongst the ranks of the magicians they did manage to deal severe damage to their numbers.*

Abaddon: (Fenris, aid Lindroz and his Wyrms.)

Now under the cover of night the Wolves under Fenris' command circle around and descend upon the mages as well.

Being unprotected by armour like the normal troops makes it easier for Fenris and his kin to sink their teeth in their flesh and rip them apart.

One of the Undine, a water Faery, casts 'Slicing Torrent' at one of the Wolves but being massive as they are he simply braves through it and swallows the Undine whole.

Ivaldi: Protect the magicians! (He yells as he embeds his axe into one of the attacking Crawlers).

Cyril: By my beard what are these creatures! They are like hundred-fold the size of our Dire Wolves!

Ivaldi: They must be from the North, bloody beasts!

Cyril: Come on, boys! Let's show them who the alpha wolves really are!

And with a loud howl the Werewolves around him including Cyril transform themselves and fall upon Fenris and his kin.

Fang and claw sink into fur and flesh as these two races tear each other apart. The Werewolves, like their lupine counterparts are protected by a special

---

[57] A rank of Angels specialising in support magics.

[58] The Angelic heavy infantry.

leather armour that expands when they transform therefore preventing it from breaking, but that is not enough to avail them as the sheer size of the Wolves make it possible to swallow them in one big gulp. Despite that however, the Werewolves are still not easy pickings as their enormous physical prowess puts the jaws of these beasts to a halt. And since it is a full moon, their strength is increased tenfold.

Fenris: So, you are those 'man wolves' we've heard about.

Cyril: And what are you?

Fenris: Can you not see? Giant Wolves obviously.

Cyril: That's what you call yourselves? 'Giant Wolves'?

Fenris: No, we call ourselves 'Ulfurtor'.

Cyril: Now, that sounds much better.

Fenris: Pity; if we were not on opposite sides, we might have become friends.

Cyril: I'd like to think that as well, fellow wolf, but unfortunately fate would not have it that way.

Fenris: Pity indeed, but I get to feel the taste of your flesh.

And with a loud roar they go at each other.

After some time fighting, a company of Faery soldiers breaks off from their ranks and goes to the help of their Werewolf companions and with their small frame and agile movement manage to almost effortlessly deal with the Ulfurtor.

Also having the Queens in the proximity as they are in charge of the Magician brigade does not help their situation as well.

Abaddon: It's time for the aerial assault, Argyros.

Argyros gives off a loud roar which is the signal for the Dragonkin, and these creatures soar to the skies and open fire.

'Brace for impact' echoes through their ranks as fire, ice and lightning come down upon them.

Some may defend from the initial attack, but the aftershock knocks them off their feet.

The magicians are too busy fending for their lives and cannot provide adequate support, but they are still great in numbers, and some manage to counter the attacks with fire, water and wind spells respectively.

Some Wizards and water mages, including Undine even erect domes of water to shield from the fire, but Dragon fire is mighty and evaporates the water. Here is where the more prominent ice casters come into place and manage to subdue the flames by freezing them.

Archers too open fire and the infantries hurl their spears at them, but they are shielded by their new armours.

Amra: I'll help out as well, this is a new attack I've been working on.

Now she pulls out her bow, creates a giant magical arrow and releases it sky high. Once it reaches above the soldiers it divides into multiple arrows and rains down upon them like countless comets.

And being infused with her magic the arrows petrify anyone they come into contact with.

Dumah: As expected from my spouse, you are magnificent.

Amra: Save the sweet talk for the bedroom.

Dumah: As you wish, pumpkin.

Amra: Guh (rolls her eyes).

To counter this threat, the Angel infantries take to the skies as well and engage the Dragonkin. Karamiel, leader of the Archons, leads the charge.

Karamiel: Advance, men! Let none of these foul creatures live!

And with a loud yell, they come down at them with their weapons of light.

As we know Dragonkin are not good at close combat and even with their armours they fell prey to the Archons.

But not all is as desperate as it seems as some Dragons do manage to defend themselves and ultimately slay their opponents thanks to their great physical prowess and enormous stature.

Now to add oil to the proverbial flame, a number of the Faeries join the fray as well and they prove to be an annoying foe to deal with due to their small frames.

One of the Faeries easily passes through the rakes of one of the Dragons and stabs it with its rapier in the throat, then using wind magic he cuts up its organs on the inside and the Dragon falls dead on the sand.

Abaddon: Dumah.

Dumah: On it.

He gives the command, and his Shadow Demons produce metal like exoskeletons from their shoulder blades, that were tucked away in their armours with magical formulae. Where once was supposed to stand wings of pearl white come out wings of black shadows.

Now they fly up to the side of their Draconic comrades and engage the Angels and Faeries in battle.

Karamiel: Look, the descendants of those that once took up the mantle of the Dark God stand against us, let us make them pay for the sins of their ancestors!

Dumah: I would like to see you try.

He unsheathes Fragarach and goes into combat.

Dumah: (Baal Belen[59], those that I kill I offer to you as sacrifice, a thousand you asked of me and a thousand I shall send your way).

The Shadow Knights hurl shadow waves at their Angelic counterparts but the latter parry with light waves of their own.

Those of the Assassin type, with their swift blink attacks deal with the Faery infantry. One attempts to stab at an Assassin with her rapier, but the latter swiftly appears behind her and stabs her through the back and as another one was approaching, he kills him with a throw of a dagger.

Now the Shadow Fiends, which serve the purpose of a heavy infantry overpower the Angels with their massive stature and brute force, smiting them down with their weapons of shadows.

These Demons were much more demonic looking in appearance as they have attained most of the physical traits of the Fiends that used to live in Shilhmatu prior to the arrival of the Fallen Ones.

The Malakhim which are the ranged infantry of the Angels open fire at them, but they protect themselves with shield of shadows, while Kesef, the leader of the Assassins deals with them one by one by exploiting the weaknesses in their armours, instantly in the midst of battle. This serves as a testament to the skills of these warriors.

Several Ishim, which are the light infantry attack Dumah all at once, but he makes a quick work of them in the blink of an eye.

[59] Lord.

He cuts the arm off one and stabs him through the mouth, he disarms another and pierces him through and deals with the rest in a similar fashion.

But that is not all, for the Demon Sword Fragarach has a terrible ability. Its name translates to 'Soul Destroyer' in the Common Tongue and as the name suggests it destroys the soul of anyone that it pierces and turns them into Shadow Warriors; slaves to Dumah's will. Another way of using this sword is destroying the soul of the opponent in the literal sense of the word, causing the death of the entity. Fragarach also has many other abilities besides these but more about them at another time.

Now these Angels have black veins show up on their bodies and their wings turn black as a sign of their corruption, and Dumah sends them forth to battle their brethren.

The Angel that had his arm cut off is oozing black bile from the severed spot which shows that his once golden blood has now been tainted.

Karamiel: Fiend! How dare you turn the children of Shekinah to your slaves! I'll make you pay!

Dumah: Stop yapping your mouth and put your words to action, Angel scum.

Karamiel: Prepare yourself!

And with a mighty war cry he charges towards Dumah and engages him into one-on-one battle.

Now since the Shadow Demons arrived to help them out, the Dragonkin have been freer to wreak havoc upon the battlefield.

Abaddon: It's time for the next wave, Jamil.

Now it is Jamil's turn to give the orders and upon doing so the Hathasian heavy shock cavalry rushes in with mighty war cries and makes their way towards enemy lines.

Arthur: Pikes at the ready! Cavalry charge!

The Spearmen take up their posts with their spears upfront ready to meet any horsemen that may break through while the heavy knight cavalry rides out to intercept the Hathasians and both cavalries meet midway.

Lance upon lance crash against armour, horsemen get knocked off their mounts and both, rider, and animal blood spill on the desert sand.

However, Abaddon's magicians cast protective force fields around the cavalry which enables them to break through the enemy knights and into their lines.

But the spears of the Skelthuz Bhregor made by Dwarven hand and imbued with Angelic enchantment will not be undone that easily thus putting a halt to the charge of the Hathasians.

For the best result they aim at their horses who even though were armoured and protected could not withstand the mighty spearhead.

They are also met with dense walls of winds erected by the Sylphs, the Wind Faeries, who cut down to shreds anyone that dares pass through.

However, their quota is fulfilled as a good number of cavalrymen manage to break through their ranks regardless.

Many were cut down in the breach but that did not matter for a way was carved open for the light and medium cavalries to rush in through the path and cut down anyone that stands in their way.

Folduin: We may use this confusion to our advantage as well! Ride forth, people of Elviun!

And upon his command the riders of the Elven cavalry set forth encircling the armies and making their way towards the main bulk of Abaddon's forces.

Seeing this, Kushsanu descends slamming his sword into the sand and creates an ice wave that freezes everything. However, the cavalry was equipped with a powerful talisman that contains the light of the Sun God Solarion and upon reciting the required chant they become enveloped with a sphere of bright sunlight which defends them from Kushsanu's attack.

Now he has no choice but fly upwards in order to dodge the charging forces.

Abaddon: Ymir!

And so, the Frost Giant steps forward and releases a devastating 'Glacial Below' but that too will not avail them as the light of the sun is powerful and it burns the brightest. Seeing as Ymir's magic is not enough his brethren join in and that seals the deal. No matter how strong the sun is it cannot hope to content with the combined might of the Giants' primordial ice magic and the entire cavalry becomes frozen solid, ice sculptures in the middle of the desert.

Abaddon: Surtr.

Now Surtr steps up and whips out Oeskbreidur, decimating the cavalry with a heat wave.

Seeing the flare from his cavalry being decimated Folduin is overcome with a sense of dread and fear.

Folduin: How frightening are these creatures…

As he is contemplating this a couple of Crawlers jump him, but he blinds them with the light from his sword and then despatches them easily.

Meanwhile in Kur Dimatim

Mordred had just finished liberating the people and was surrounded by cheerful clamouring.

But their moment of joy was broken when they hear the thumping of feet coming from the distance; the legions of the Dwarven garrison were approaching accompanied by a company of Faeries.

Demoness: Oh no, the armies are here! What will you do?

Mordred: Go back inside your homes, do not worry about me.

Demon: Young lad! Surely you don't mean to take them on by yourself!

Mordred: That is exactly what I intend to do.

As they are talking, the thumping becomes louder, and the tips of their spears become visible from the uphill.

Mordred: Go! Go now!

Demoness: Come on, everyone!

And so, the ordinary people retreat inside their homes but some of the young Demons remain.

Demon: We will fight with you, my prince.

Mordred: No, I do not need your help, I can do this on my own, do not throw your lives away needlessly, you have people that care for you, do not burden them with grief.

Demon: You speak wisely my lord, thank you, we are in your debt.

Mordred: Do not, I am only performing my duty as a future king of this land.

Demon#2: Be safe, my prince!

Mordred: Go!

As they retreat, the troops are now already in place, and they are led by none other than Haldur.

Haldur: So, you are the one that has been causing trouble for our men.

Mordred: The only ones that are causing trouble here are you lot.

Haldur: I don't think yer in a position to be a wise arse laddie. Why don't you go back from whence you came, and we'll leave quietly no harm no foul.

Mordred: I refuse.

Haldur: Don't you see the gravity of the situation yer in? You are one man, and we are many, no need to throw away yer life.

Mordred: You people, you come here, you occupy the land of my father, my homeland, enslave its people, tear down its buildings and act as if you own the place, have the audacity to get me to leave? Just who the hell do you think you are?

Haldur: Did you say your father? Is that by any chance…?

Mordred: Yes, my father is the king and rightful ruler of Dhalsarria none other than Abaddon himself, and I am her prince.

Haldur: Abaddon fathered a son? Well, that's just perfect, your father killed my father and in turn by killing you I will avenge him (draws his broadsword).

Mordred: If it is death you wish, I will gladly oblige (unsheathes 'Mordred').

Haldur: Now that I know who you are, you will die by my sword! Hiyahh!

One of the Dryads, Forest Faeries, entangles him with vines but they immediately dry out and die.

Haldur is taken aback by this, but he has no time to stop as he is already charging towards him.

Mordred dodges his attack and swings his sword, Haldur skilfully blocks however Mordred's sword rusts away the steel, cuts through it and slashes him at the side. He falls from the pain, and Mordred's magic from the wound spreads throughout his body causing him even greater pain as his flesh decomposes.

Seeing this, the troops are gripped by fear and halt their advance.

Faery: He is…eibran deag, an agent of death!

Haldur: Run, you fools! (Dies).

Frightened, they drop their weapons and flee.

Mordred: No, you do not get to flee.

Now he casts a spell unique to him 'Predatory Death' that releases a spectre of death magic in the form of a Grimm Reaper accompanied with an eerie wailing, taking the lives of everyone that it touches.

And it passes through the legions like the plague and ends them then and there and they fall lifeless on the ground, both Dwarf and Faery.

Demon: (reluctantly exists the door of his house) It is over…in an instant?
Demon#2: He took down the entire legions just like that…incredible.
Demon: Guz Baltu Malku!

Soon he is surrounded by the cheering 'long live the prince'.

And now Mordred sets his sight towards the uppermost city, Kur Mushallim Now the way Dishum was built was in five towns, in a disk shape, elevated on platforms. Each ascending city was smaller in diameter than the previous one. The platforms were built of stone and concrete, magically enhanced to hold the weight of the towns. One could get to the upper platforms via lift, or by a wide, uphill, cobbled road. In the time of its founding the city had only three circles but two more were added in the time of Abaddon's father, Demiurgos. As a whole, the city looked like a hill, and it was truly an architectural work of art. Only now, much of its splendour had been reduced due to the last war.

There is a religious significance behind the naming of the five towns and their number. The prefix 'Kur' means 'land' but not in the sense of 'earth, land' instead it refers to the land of the dead, the otherworldly realms of Tiamat. According to Dhalsarrian belief, there are five stages through which the soul of a departed Demon goes through before they reach the Halls of Tiamat and Baal. All the town names are in Old Dhalsarrian and they have been preserved as such. First is the 'Land of Tears', Kur Dimatim called as such because of the tears the soul sheds at its death, thus symbolising the grief of passing. Next is 'Kur Etutim', 'Land of Darkness' where the soul begins its descent to the Halls, by entering the entrance gates of Tiamat and moving through the darkness of that otherworld. Third is the Kur Muradim, 'Land of Descent', as the soul steadily descends downwards and downwards towards the bright light of the Girrata Tiamatuu, the Flames of Tiamat. Fourth is Kur Kasadim the 'Land of Arrival' when the soul finds itself before the Gates of the Hall and makes the last leg of the journey.

The journey ends with reaching the Grand Hall, in the 'Land of Healing', Kur Mushallim where the soul finally finds solace and peace and is healed from its pain and grief by the presence of Baal, its God. There it is reunited with its lost ones and spend out eternity in bliss and comfort. The only difference from this is that the lands are believed to move downwards, in the case of Dishum the towns move upwards so the topmost is called Kur Mushallim. That is because the residence of the king is located there, who as ruler is supposed to bring peace, and stability to his people.

Meanwhile turmoil was stirring up in the other countries as well. In Nidvelir the Drugnir, Black Dwarves, started an uprising and were laying siege to the scarcely defended cities around their kingdom.

The Drugnir are cursed Dwarves that had been living in an autonomous small kingdom at the edge of Nidvelir, near the border with the Great Dessert.

Long ago, Fafnir who used to be a great Dwarven King became so obsessed with riches that it reached a point of madness. One day overcome by greed he slew his father, his flesh and blood over a precious gem and angered Shekinah, who is also the patron deity of the household and family, and she blemished him with a terrible affliction. His appearance became that of an ugly disgusting creature and the curse was carried on to his progeny as well.

As a result, the other Dwarven Lords grew fearful of him and cast him and his family out of the Royal City by force. They were allowed to stay in Nidvelir as long as they did not cause any trouble and so he founded the small kingdom of Drugdvelir which translates to 'Dwelling of the Black Dwarves'.

However, Fafnir's rage and despise towards the rest of his kin never assuaged and his descendants carried this grudge as well. So, when Abaddon approached them in secret during the past year and offered them their kingdom back, they jumped on the offer with no hesitation.

And they were not the only ones that took up arms against their kin. The Fallen Ones, group of tainted Angels, who were also living a secluded life at the edge of Viloth rose as well against the ones that would oppress them.

The start of the war was the sign both races were awaiting because all of the armies of their homelands would be out fighting it, leaving them defenceless.

Thus, Abaddon was bringing destruction from the inside as well as the outside.

Back at Dhalsarria word reached the armies of the other towns that someone has been wiping out the soldiers and freeing the Demons and so they rallied up and soon they were upon Mordred.

Hundreds of foes stood before him, soldiers of all races most of which were Men because the royal district was in the charge of Camelot.

One of the captains steps up and addresses Mordred.

Captain: Surrender quietly and no harm will befall you, you are outnumbered and outmatched, any futile resistance will result in your death.

Mordred: My death you say? Foolish man, I am death itself.

Captain: So, you choose resistance over obedience.

Mordred: I will never obey scum like you.

Captain: Any last words before you meet your end then?

Mordred: My name is Mordred, son of Abaddon, remember it well when you leave for the Afterlife.

Captain#2: Brazen brat! Get him, men!

And the garrison forces all descend upon Mordred as he waits calmly for them to approach.

***

Just like that the battle is over, Mordred stands surrounded by the corpses of the soldiers as blood and bile flood the streets of Dishum and the air reeks of death and decay. He himself is also covered in the blood of his enemies, slightly panting for as mighty as he is his power is not without limit. Thus, he presses on towards the Royal Castle or what is left of it at least, without any further resistance as all the armies stationed there were utterly annihilated.

As he is making his way, he is again greeted by the shouts and cheers of the locals and that alone gives him strength and vigour.

Once he makes it to the castle he searches for the dungeons and finally he finds them, filled to the brim with imprisoned Demons of all races.

One of the Demonesses dressed in a very fashionable but ragged up dress, thinking that it was one of the soldiers when she hears the footsteps begins to wail and beg.

Demoness: Please, no more, I beg of you.

Mordred: It is okay, my lady, I mean you no harm.

Demoness: (looks at him through teary eyes) You are not one of the soldiers…?

Mordred: No, I am not (he says as he melts away the iron bars).

Demoness: Then…you are not here to force yourself upon me…

Mordred: On the contrary, I am here to set you free (breaks her chains).

Demoness: (falls at his feet from exhaustion) Ohhh thank you, thank you…

Then a male voice emerges from the cell next door.

Demon: Darling, who is it?

His voice sounds ragged and weary.

Demoness: A young man, he has come to save us!

Demon: Oh, praised be Baal! Finally, our prayers have been heard!

The other Demons from the cells begin clamouring in relief as well.

Mordred: Let me help you out (he helps her on her feet).

Demoness: You speak our language, are you one of us?

Mordred: Partially yes, from my father's side.

Demoness: Please, let me look upon the face of the one that would deliver us from this fate.

And then he removes his helmet, and when she lays her eyes upon him, a sense of familiarity and warmth wells up inside her, and she cannot help herself but to break down in tears. She touches his face and in her state of bliss confuses him with someone else.

Demoness: Abaddon…?

Mordred: (smiles gently) Close, I am his son, my name is Mordred.

Demoness: His son…he has a son, do you hear that, Demiurgos?

Demiurgos: I hear it, my dear, I hear it loud and clear… (tears come to his eyes as well).

Mordred: Demiurgos? Then you must be…Lilim?

Lilim: Yes child, I am your grandmother.

Mordred: Grandmother! (Embraces her).

Lilim: (embraces him as well) Ohhh, oh my sweet boy…

Mordred: What have they done to you, to all of you, it is unforgivable.

Lilim: My boy, it is all in the past now, we are safe thanks to you.

Demiurgos: Come to me, boy, let me see my grandson.

Mordred gently pushes Lilim aside and he places his hand on the wall that separates their cell, breaking it apart.

Demiurgos: Oh, dear me! You are the spitting image of your father.

He smiles gently as he releases him as well. Demiurgos was still wearing his black armour, with part of silver plating on the pauldrons, poleyns and couters, where there also were spiked like decorations. He also had a long cape of red colour. He has two, white horns with red tips, coming out the side of his head. His white hair was almost reaching his feet, and his face looks older and weathered due to the many years of rough imprisonment, but his red eyes now gleamed bright at the sight of his grandson. Mordred rarely smiled but he could not help himself in this situation; meeting his grandparents for the first time has brought him immense joy.

Demiurgos: How is your father? Is he alive and well?

Mordred: He is, grandfather, he is leading a host of armies against the usurpers as we speak.

Lilim: Praised be Baal, he has succeeded in coming back.

Demiurgos: When word reached us that he had been killed, we were devastated, all this time we thought he was dead for good, but seeing you here means that his soul survived; no one told us that.

Mordred: It was done to keep you in low spirits and obedient, but nothing of that matters now, the time of Avalon's reckoning has come and those that ruled shall rule again.

Lilim: Not only that you look like him, but you sound like him as well, I could not be prouder, he has raised you well.

Demiurgos: Every day we prayed for salvation; I never would have thought it would come in the shape of my grandson (hugs him).

Mordred hugs him back.

Lilim: Dear boy I know this might not be the adequate time but what did you mean when you said 'partly'? Does that mean your mother is of another race?

Mordred: Indeed; she is human, the once daughter of Arthur Pendragon.

Demiurgos: What?

Lilim: He would mingle with a human girl?

Mordred: I would hardly call my mother human; she threw her humanity away long ago.

Lilim: What do you mean?

Mordred: You will know once you meet her yourselves, but for now we have more important matters on our hands.

Demiurgos: Right, we still must liberate the rest here and then the other principalities.

Mordred: Tell me grandfather, how many of the fighting men remain?

Demiurgos: I am not sure, but not many I reckon, most were killed in the siege.

Mordred: That is unfortunate, but nonetheless we have to gather every able-bodied Dhalku and Dhalka alike and meet with my father on the battlefield, those are his instructions.

Demiurgos: Me and your grandmother will see to it here, you go and free the rest of our brothers and sisters. You will find Isari to the west and Addari to the east, but be warry, they too are guarded by garrison armies.

Lilim: Perhaps some of the men here should accompany you, you must be exhausted from all the fighting you did to get here.

Mordred: I will be fine; I can handle it.

Lilim: On the other hand, that won't be necessary. My magic may have grown weak from all this time in imprisonment, but I can still teleport you to *Isaria*.

Mordred: No, I do not want to put any more strain on you.

Lilim: Do not take me so lightly, boy, I am the one who fathered the one who will rule this world after all.

Mordred: (nods) One more thing, grandmother, since you can cast magic perhaps you can do something about these (hands her over the scrolls).

Lilim: These are…spells for gateways to other plains of existence…wait, I know these places, hmmm I see.

Mordred: Will you be able to do it in your present state?

Lilim: Most likely, but I'm afraid we will need something to open these gates, like Abaddon's sword.

Mordred: Will mine do then? (Shows her)

Lilim: Yes, that will do.

Mordred: Are you sure you will be alright?

Lilim: Like I said, do not take me lightly.

Demiurgos: Do not push yourself too much, dear.

Lilim: I said I will be fine; now stop pestering me! Both of you!

Demiurgos: Alright, alright! Calm down.

Lilim: For these, we will need space, let us step outside, in the meantime Demiurgos, take care of the other prisoners and I will join you once I'm done with helping Mordred.

Demiurgos: Alright.

Lilim: Come, boy.

And so, they step outside and now Lilim performs the spell from the first scroll.

Lilim: Now, boy! Use your sword to cut through dimensions!

Mordred slices through the air with his sword and a rift opens, then the rift expands, and a Faery-like creature emerges from within...

CAPITVLVM XVIII

DIES IRAE II

Now, this creature is of the utmost horrendous countenance. It does look like a Faery, but it is the ugliest one you could ever see. Its left eye is completely white and there is a scaring around it and his other one is deep purple but there is also the same manner of scar as the other one. Its lips are cut at places and its teeth are sharp and the complexion of his skin is pale. Its hair is long, and it reaches its hips, being snow white in colour. Its facial features are bony and thin as are his fingers. Its robes are fashionable but seem to be in tatters from the passage of time. And finally, it has a pair of ragged, transparent wings with eerie markings that flutter rapidly as it is suspended in the air.

Mordred: What is this creature?

Lilim: That, my boy, is a Spriggan.

Mordred: A Spriggan? I remember my father mentioning something about them, I did not think it would be this obscene.

Spriggan: Ahh! (Stretches) Out at last! (Looks at Mordred) art thou the one that set me free?

Mordred: Indeed, I am, in fact we both helped.

Spriggan: Then you have my gratitude friends, I am forever indebted to thee.

Mordred: And what may we call you?

Spriggan: I am Hyberion, King of the Spriggan.

As he says that a retinue of other Spriggan come fluttering out of the portal and fill out the outer courtyard.

Mordred: There is so many of you!

Hyberion: Aye, long ago we were sealed away in this dimension by the Faery Queen Venera who could not destroy us, so she banished us instead.

Mordred: Why would she wish to destroy you?

Hyberion: Why? Because we are malevolent sprites that's why. Not all Faeries are pure and kind. Besides, we fought on the side of Magdabulgu the Fire Demon who sought to conquer the other races.

Lilim: I know of what you speak, for as you see we are kindred of our late king. I know who you are as well, we met once briefly, though you may not recognise me as I was a young Demoness back then.

Hyberion: Tell me, what are ye called?

Mordred: My name is Mordred, son of Abaddon the current king of this land, and this is my grandmother Lilim.

Hyberion: Lilim? You are Lilim, the daughter of Prince Morlas?

Lilim: It is indeed I, wrecked by the passage of time.

Hyberion: Nonsense, thou art still as comely as I first saw thee. I remember now, it is all coming back to me afresh. I mourn for the passing of thine father, and that of thine king, Magdabulgu, but you may find solace knowing that they shall be at peace once they see you liberated. Much time did we spent in their company.

Lilim: I am much pleased to hear that …

Hyberion: And I am pleased that Lord Abaddon produced such a fine son.

Mordred: You know my father?

Hyberion: I do, albeit the time we spent together was very brief indeed. I would have liked to get to know him better, he is a fine successor to Magdabulgu. Though it seems I will have the opportunity to do so now, for he has made good on his word.

Mordred: I do not understand. Did you have some sort of an agreement? How is that possible? And how is it possible that you have met in the first place?

Hyberion: I see he has not told thee of our meeting. It so happened in Avernus, that region of Tiamat where we were banished to. Upon his death his spirit briefly entered Tiamat and we were allowed to meet. There we shared in our fates, and he told me that when the time comes, he will set us free.

Mordred: That would explain his possession of those scrolls, he is the one that created them after he resurrected himself. But wait, I did not know his soul went to Tiamat, he said he lingered here on Avalon …

Hyberion: Ah, you do not know of what happened there, but it is not my place to tell. Your father will tell thee, if he so desireth.

Mordred: Now is not the time to dwell on that, my father is fighting at the front lines as we speak, we are to join them once our task here is complete.

Hyberion: But first, thou must free mine other kindred who were unjustly banished like we were.

Mordred: I reckon that this scroll serves that purpose.

Hyberion: Let me take a look.

Mordred hands him over the scroll.

Hyberion: Very well, I will recite the incantation and thou shall use thine weapon to open the doorway.

It should be noted that Hyberion spoke to them in Old Dhalsarrian, hence his outdated speech. Now he reads the spell and once it was done another creature even more terrifying than Hyberion emerges from the other portal. The creature was riding a black horse with gleaming red eyes and steam coming out of its nostrils. The creature itself was dressed in an old-fashioned armour, having a silver cuirass with intricate designs, under which there was a chainmail shirt, and beneath that a gambeson. It had black leather gloves and tall boots; iron studded. But the strangest thing about it was that it had no head and instead black mist was exhuming from its neck and it had a bizarre weapon, a scythe in the shape of a human spine.

Now this black rider did not emerge alone for a multitude of ones like him rode out of the rift as well.

Mordred: A headless Faery, I know what you are, a Dullahan.

Dullahan: And I know what you are boy, a Demon, Dark one to be more precise.

Hyberion: Princeling to be more precise.

Dullahan: Hyberion my old friend, so good to see you again.

Hyberion: To think that we were banished to the same place. Were you also imprisoned in Avernus?

Cain: Nay, it was in another, lower region, cruel of Venera to separate us so. Come, let us embrace.

Once they do so, Hyberion introduces them.

Hyberion: Gentlemen, this is Cain Ech'Cenad[60], King of the Dullahan, and these are Mordred and Lilim, both relatives of the current king.

Cain: Lady Lilim I know, but I do not know this young man. Pleased to meet you.

---

[60] Horse master.

Mordred: Same here, your majesty.

Then Mordred proceeds to tell them both of everything that has led to this moment.

Cain: I see; so, war is upon us once again and we as once former allies must answer the call.

Hyberion: Indeed.

Cain: We rode with the Ri'Daemhaen[61] when he was alive now it would be an honour to ride with you again.

Mordred: You have my gratitude.

Cain: No gratitude is needed for such are the bonds of friendship. And we owe it to your father who no doubt has helped set us free.

Mordred: Let us go and free the rest then.

Lilim: May Baal be with you.

Cain: Beanni cui at te karain[62].

He gives him his blessing as well and Lilim opens a portal to Dur-Isatum, the capital of Isaria, and Hyberion aids her with his magic in order to sustain the portal longer and then he himself passes the last.

Now the Dullahan were the mightiest cavalry that has ever existed on the two continents, being called 'Harbingers of Doom', 'Black Riders of Death' or 'The Grimm Reapers of the Battlefield'. These headless, malevolent Faeries ride swiftly like the wind and mow down anyone that stands in their path be it a Man, Demon or Orc, everyone falls prey to their spine shaped scythes. They possess the same magic as Mordred, death magic, which is why none can withstand their assault.

It is said that one scratch is enough for the Dullahan to snatch your soul. Now set free, they ride once again to raise carnage and bloodshed. Call them what you will but one thing is clear: wherever the Dullahan rides, certain death is sure to follow.

***

Meanwhile, on the main battlefield, the war was raging in full force.

---

[61] King of Demons in Faeran.

[62] Blessings upon you as well friend.

The remnant of the Camelotian cavalry that managed to survive was pushing its way through the Hathasians.

Seeing this Abaddon orders their pike men to step up front with pikes ready and so they break upon their tips.

However, this being a heavy shock cavalry they were adequately equipped and so they managed to break through the first line of defence. But the Hathasian infantrymen were not the only ones; ranks of Onimusha were ready with their yari as a second line in defence and with a boost from their War Priests, the cavalry simply did not have enough men to break through and broke upon Oni spears.

On the other side the number of Wyrms, Wolves and Crawlers was rapidly dwindling, and the Allied Forces saw this as an opportunity to strike back.

Ivaldi: Bhregors press onwards, lights and mediums, stay behind!

Folduin: My forces shall assist you in this charge!

And so, the combined forces of Elf and Dwarf fight their way through the ranks of their enemies, soon some paladins from the Order of Lugos join them.

Now paladins are Holy Men, in this case clerics in the service of the Dragon of Light, trained in combat. They employ heavy armour and prayers as a means of defence. In other words, Paladins were people that were gifted with the talent for magic casting. Those that did not have such talents and could become neither paladin nor a magician went off to join the military in the capacity of a regular foot soldier.

Ser Lancelot and Ser Percival were amongst the charging men as well. One skilled with the spear and shield and the other with the axe, these elite soldiers lay dead the enemies that stood before them.

Another amongst the elite were the 'Twilight Twelve' the most skilled and most powerful Vampires in all Sanclunea, handpicked by the queen herself. The previous ones were killed in the battle of 'Sairn Paleon', the Silent Plain as it was known in the Goblin tongue, so these were new and hungry for blood.

But soon they found themselves under heavy fire from the Dragonkin up above, so the archers had to provide cover for them.

Elven archers of whom the Sylvan ones were the most skilled of all their kindred and all races for that matter, fulfilled the bulk of this task. Equipped with enchanted bows and arrows that were able to reach high in the sky they were true in hitting their marks.

Seeing this, Abaddon gave new orders.

Abaddon: It's time for the next wave, Albunalich, it's your turn.

Albunalich: Ni Akh'su[63]!

Abaddon: My generals, the time is right for you as well, show them hell. Remind them of the glory of our race once more!

Carmox: Finally! I was getting angsty, alright you faggots! Anukki[64]!

With that the combined forces of Undead Orcs and Subterrans descend upon the assaulting armies.

Now the Dragonkin were free to focus their fire on the archers who oh so irritated them, and the Shadow Priests of Dumah provide them with a blanket of thick darkness that obstructs the archers' viewpoint, and the Dragons rain destruction from above, using their trait to see through the veil of darkness.

However, using the purifying properties of Shekinah's light, Umbriela dispels the darkness causing Abaddon to click his teeth in irritation.

Nonetheless the damage was done, and the archers lay dead on the desert sands. Not all though, for the archers of the Vampires were lucky to survive due to their super speed so they have dodged the beams of destruction.

Now Albunalich comes down from Ignatos, and the Fire Dragon King was free to join his kin in the slaughter.

Albunalich then unsheathes his Titan sword, Balmung and raises it up towards the sky. The sword begins to resonate with an immense green light, just like it did that time when he fought Abaddon.

As soon as this was done the place between the two charging armies splits in half and opens revealing a bottomless chasm. Both armies immediately come to a halt before they fall in the abyss. But the King Beneath the Earth does not stop there and he swings his sword and then the sand begins to move, like an avalanche it pours in the chasm dragging the allied armies to their deaths.

This sword was a terrible weapon indeed for it gave Albunalich the power of everything that was of the earth; ground, rock, stone, and sand everything was at his beck and call and could be bent to his whim.

---

[63] Yes, my king.

[64] To battle!

The captain of the Hashmalim who were Angels that specialised in supplementary magic, Ramaela, casts a wall of light that separates the armies from the chasm therefore halting their descend.

Now the Blood Mages of the Vampires engulf this wall with their Blood Cocoon spell, solidifying it even further.

Dagon, now working this nigromancy, summons forth a terrible sand viper to come out from the hole and lurch over the wall, striking the armies behind it.

Albunalich is not done as well, and he increases the width of the chasm to stretch beyond the wall and many of the forces fall.

Arthur seeing that his armies are in great distraught springs forward and slams his sword, Excalibur, into the desert sand. The sword sends forth an explosion of the whitest light ever seen which nullifies the effects of Albunalich's magic, for the light of Lugos is one of purity and is not meant for harming. Now the sand return to normal which in turn causes the sand viper to be snapped in half and fall dead.

The remaining forces press onward and Abaddon's armies from the opposite end do so as well, rendering Albunalich unable to do the same trick again lest he wishes to doom their forces as well.

Arthur being of old age was quite taxed from this feat and was left exhausted. Morgana saw the flash of light and knew that this was her que.

Abaddon: Be careful.

Morgana: I will.

And then too she gets off Fulguros and he too goes to join his brethren.

Morgana turns into a black cloud and leaps forward, past the nearby battle and to the back lines where Arthur is.

No sooner than she landed, she is surrounded by her enemies.

Knight: You are a traitor to your kingdom! Die!

He falls on her with his sword, but she blasts him with a bolt of black lightning and completely destroys the right side of his upper body; he falls dead.

Other soldiers come at her at once, but she uses her nigromancy and fills their insides with black fog, smothering them.

Morgana: Out of my way, pests.

Arthur, seeing his daughter approach, calls out her name with a dry voice.

Arthur: Morgana!

Morgana: Arthur! Come and face me!

One of the paladins comes to his side and by touching his shoulder, he casts 'Healing Light' on him, and he is invigorated.

Then he shouts, 'To the king! Rally to the king!'

Gawain, who was fighting Lindroz nearby, hears the cry although faintly and wishing to rush to his liege's side he seeks to finish the combat quickly.

Lindroz trained well this past year in his knight form and was able to give Gawain a run for his money which is why the duel was at a stalemate till now.

Now Lindroz strikes with his tail at Gawain meaning to trip him, but the latter sees through this and cuts off his tail. But Lindroz being of the Dragon folk regrows his tail and manages to seize his ankle and hoist him up in the air.

He was meaning to embed his axe in his skull but Gawain blocks with his shield in time, and Lindroz is forced to toss him before he has the chance to retaliate.

Now Gawain throws his shield at Lindroz, but he deflects it with his buckler and sneers at Gawain. But little did he know that this was no ordinary shield for it comes back like a boomerang and strikes Lindroz at the back of his head, making him dizzy from the impact.

This gives Gawain enough time to act and with a mighty leap he is before the Wyrm with sword through his chest; The Great Worm of the North was no more.

Lindroz: Well…done…

He says as Gawain pulls out his sword and he falls on the ground.

Gawain: You fought well too, Ser Wyrm, please, tell me your name.

Lindroz: Lin…droz.

Gawain: I shall remember it for as long as I live.

Lindroz: Yours?

Gawain: Ser Gawain Irvine of the round table.

Lindroz: Ga – wain…I will carry it with me in the afterlife (Frigga…I will be joining you soon).

That is his final thought as he lets out one final sigh and perishes, upon his death returning into his Wyrm form.

Now Gawain was free to hurry towards his king.

On another side of the battlefield the duel with Fenris Wolf and Cyril, King of Werewolves was over; Fenris laid dead on the sand, with his jaw split in half. He was a ferocious Wolf and fought hard and strong, but the might of Cyril was not to be undone.

Cyril: Neka Myeseczka odvyedit dushoy tvoyu u mira, priaetlyu[65].

With that, he blesses his soul and returns to the battlefield.

Up in the skies, the Angels and Demons were still clutched in a ferocious battle. Neither side was ready to let go and neither side showed signs of weakness.

Dumah was still locked in combat with Karamiel, but it was by no means because he could not deal with him but because he was shamelessly toying with the captain of the Archons.

Karamiel: Enough! Fight me seriously like a true warrior!

Dumah: But I still haven't had my fun yet.

Karamiel: You scum! How dare you mock me?

Dumah: I dare because I can.

Karamiel: That is it! I've had enough of you; it is time to bring the hammer of Divine Punishment upon you.

Dumah: Uuu how scary, by all means show me this 'divine punishment' of yours.

Karamiel: You have mocked me for the last time! Now behold what a champion of Shekinah is capable of!

Now he raises his sword, and it begins to glow with an immense light. As soon as that happens countless swords of light arrayed in a spiralling fashion appear around Dumah.

Dumah: I see.

Karamiel: There is no escape for you! You will be judged by the Swords of the Heavens!

---

[65] Let Lunaria carry your soul to peace my friend.

He descends his sword and all the other swords come onto Dumah, but he has braced himself by enveloping his dark wings around him.

The swords beat down on him furiously and when the few final swords descend, an explosion of light occurs that illuminates the entire sky.

Karamiel: That will teach you to mock the powers of Light.

Dumah: Then you must suck at teaching because I did not learn a thing from that, but perhaps I did, I learned that you are astoundingly weak.

Karamiel: Impossible! How are you unscathed by that?

Dumah: That is a good question, I guess I am too powerful for you to handle.

Karamiel winces in frustration.

Dumah: Just how many years do you think I have been alive boy; you still need to suckle some more on your mother's titty to come on my level.

Karamiel: Impertinent!

Dumah: Enough! Now let me show you what real power looks like.

Now the darkness from his wings expands and in it forms obscene creatures with many eyes and sharp teeth.

Karamiel: What is this devilry?

Dumah: I know some magic too you see.

Karamiel: I've never seen such disgusting magic before!

Dumah: And you never will, ever again – Zhu Akalu[66].

Upon his command, the creatures spring forward. Karamiel tries to defend himself but finds his right arm missing which makes him distraught. Then his other arm goes missing too, then his leg and so forth until the creatures in the darkness swallow him whole and he is eaten alive.

Dumah: Time to deal with the other pests as well.

Angel: The captain has fallen!

Dumah: Do not fret; you will follow with him soon enough.

Now he extends his hand with the sword forward and casts 'Aralu Napshatii', 'Requiem of Souls' which is another one of Fragarach's abilities. What this spell does is releasing the souls that have been devoured by the blade and unleashes them upon his enemies. These souls fly about with chilling, eerie moans until

---

[66] Devour him.

ultimately, they force themselves into the Angels and possess them, making them Dumah's puppets.

Dumah: I will have to restock now, and as fortune would have it there is a bountiful abundance of souls here for the taking (snickers sinisterly).

Now a good bulk of the Angelic hosts end up being possessed and soon brother falls upon brother and sister falls upon sister once more, now even in greater numbers.

The tide turns upon them with the addition of their corrupted brethren and they end up being pushed back.

Upon seeing this Umbriela is deeply grieved but her hands are tied at the moment for the battle upon the sands is just as fierce.

Meanwhile the hour of Arthur's reckoning draws ever closer, but lo! Ser Gawain has made it to his king's side.

Arthur: Gawain!

Gawain: Fear not my lord, I will deal with Morgana, I will not let you bear the burden of slaying your own child.

Arthur: No! She is my responsibility! I have a duty as a father to deal with her personally.

Gawain: I understand your feelings my lord but having to kill your child will weigh heavily on your soul, please! Allow me to take on that burden!

Arthur: Who said anything about killing?

Gawain: Surely you do not mean to reason with her? My king, she is beyond saving at this point!

Arthur: Even so – I must try.

Mordred: Well, well look who it is, none other than Ser Gawain, the Sword Champion of the Table.

Gawain frowns.

Arthur: Morgana! Cease this madness!

Morgana: I don't listen to you anymore, Arthur, I am a free woman now, free from the shackles you and that wretch of a place I used to call home imposed on me. No longer do I need to worry to whom I will get married, for I am with the one I love now.

Arthur: What are you saying? Abaddon is using you!

Morgana: You're wrong, he loves me, and I am his queen now, and not only that, but we also have a beautiful son as well.

Gawain: What?

Arthur: You sired a child to that Devil? How could you! That is sacrilege!

Morgana: Not for me it isn't. And he is not a Devil, he is kind to me, sweet, caring, loving, showers me with kisses and affection, something you never did, something you never showed me, so how can you understand?

Arthur: I may have not showed it as I should have but I do love you; I still do, you are my daughter –

Morgana: Don't call me that! I'm not your daughter! I never was! You only saw me as a political piece to marry off for more men! As a means to your own desires! I was daughter to the King Arthur but not the man himself…

These words strike a chord in his heart, and he is brought to tears. In that one moment he has come to realise how wrong he was all this time with her, how he never was the father he should have been.

Arthur: (weeping) I am so sorry child, so sorry…you speak the truth, I never treated you as a father should, I see that now…but I am willing to change if you would let me, please come back with me, after all this is over I will convince the others to pardon you and we can start over as a true family, me, your mother, you, the three of us together.

Morgana: It's too late for regrets now, besides I have no intentions of going back nor did I ever have, my place is here with my betrothed. You lost me the moment you executed Merlin, knowing he was innocent.

Arthur: …There was no proof, I could not act on emotion alone.

Morgana: You didn't even let him defend himself! You and all those other old farts just outright convicted him! Had he been given the chance he could've proved that it was Emrys who framed him! Merlin was a great sorcerer, and he could've proved it easily!

Arthur: You know all too well that magic and state matters are separate! Only physical proof is accepted and there was none!

Morgana: And there it is! Clinging to an ancient, old-fashioned system and believes! It's because of that we are here on opposite ends, Arthur! You lost your daughter to stupid rules set ages ago by men who didn't know any better! As long as that system stands nothing will change!

Arthur: It is not in my place to change tradition and bring insult to my forefathers like you do now!

Morgana: (shakes her head) You will never change, how can you when you're not even prepared to change the system that has ailed you.

Arthur: Tradition is greater than us, it is not something that can be changed so easily!

Morgana: You didn't even try!

Arthur: …

Morgana: (sigh) Why don't we just end this farce, I didn't come here to make amends, I came here to take your life and take it I shall!

Then she fires a bolt of lightning at him but Gawain blocks with his shield.

Morgana: Stand down, Gawain!

Gawain: No, my lady, I will not!

Morgana: Then you shall die with him!

Now she extends her hand and begins to drain the enchantments from his armour with her black magic. Being powerful as she is now this is done in an instant and Gawain finds himself broken by a torrent of black lightning before he can deal a blow.

Arthur: Gawain!

Morgana: Humph!

However, this being a battlefield means that one cannot simply stand by and have a 'nice' conversation without being assaulted and Morgana finds herself in that predicament, surrounded by the weapons of other soldiers but she creates a plasma shield around herself that blocks all oncoming attacks and then explodes in a flash of lighting blasting them away.

Arthur: Stand down! Do not interfere! … I will deal with her.

Now with a heavy heart, the old king of Camelot steels himself for the fated duel.

Morgana: (conjures up a sword of black lightning) Doy[67], Arthur!

---

67 Come.

Arthur: Madu me fy mlentyn[68] (mutters) Hagh!

And so, they clash for the first and last time...

Meanwhile, on the opposite side of the battlefield, the previous assaulting armies were going at it each other pretty strongly.

Now it was hard for the Vampires and the others for that matter to cleave off the heads of the Undead for their necks were protected with sturdy braces unlike last time and so many fall by the hands of these nigh immortal creatures.

But the mighty champions like Lancelot did not fall, instead they were the ones doing the falling.

With his trusted spear Ascalon he brought down many-a-foes.

Now Abaddon had a spear champion of his own, the one we all know, Malgaras. He himself was despatching enemies left and right, spilling guts and blood on the desert sands. None could withstand the might of doom.

Soon these two warriors were face to face.

Lancelot: You seem skilled with the spear.

Malgaras: As do you.

Lancelot: Name yourself, warrior.

Malgaras: Shouldn't the one asking the question name himself first?

Lancelot: Per our customs the one who is addressed first, should answer.

Malgaras: Well, this isn't Camelot, is it?

Lancelot: No, it is not.

Malgaras: You don't strike me as an ordinary soldier, are you perchance Ser Lancelot Germaine of the Round Table?

Lancelot: Indeed I am.

Malgaras: I've heard of you from the Lady Morgana.

He shudders at the mention of her name.

Lancelot: How is our lady?

Malgaras: Great, she is a mother now.

Lancelot: Not only does she flee with the sworn enemy of our land, but she also bears him a child, I hope swift justice finds her.

Malgaras: You can stop hoping for it for she is the most powerful woman in the world, technically speaking.

Lancelot: Justice always finds those deserving.

---

68 Forgive me my child.

Malgaras: Someone who accuses another on false accusations has no right to preach about justice to me.

Lancelot: I see my name is not the only thing you've heard from my lady. It is an unfortunate thing what happened to the sorcerer, but the law is the law, and we must abide by it.

Malgaras: Even when the law itself is unjust.

Lancelot: (snickers) I am no lawyer, sir knight…

Malgaras: Malgaras, my name is Malgaras.

Lancelot: Malgaras, neither am I a preacher, I am a warrior and my purpose in life is to fight for my king and country, that is all there is to it.

Malgaras: Then you won't mind me laying you dead like the good soldier that you are.

Lancelot: You are welcome to try if you can.

As he says that, both he and Malgaras get jumped from the back by enemy soldiers and both impale them with their spears at the same time without even turning back.

And once their assailants lay dead, they go at each other in silence. Alabaster himself was busy with bashing the skulls of his opponents.

Many soldiers felt pray to Halnadu the Pain Bringer; their enchantments were mighty but those of Halnadu were mightier.

Now the captain of the 'Twelve', the mightiest champion of the Vampires took it upon themselves to stand up to this behemoth.

Surprisingly enough they were no man but a woman, a tall woman and one of great skill and strength, nonetheless. Her feet were quick, quicker than any Vampire and her strikes were precise and deadly. Selene was her name, and she was also a woman of few words, but no words were needed between these two for both knew what must be done and immediately fell on each other upon meeting.

Both Kushsanu and Amra as well were doing their fair share of damage as well.

Now Kushsanu would have met with difficulty for his foes were warded with anti-ice enchantments, but Abaddon foresaw this and strengthened his abilities so now his ice was no ordinary one, but black and terrible and was able to freeze whomever it touched with a mere strike.

Elves, Men, Vampires and Dwarves were turned into statutes of glittering black ice and then shattered to pieces.

His shield had the same affinity and it turned to solid ice anyone that dared strike it. Thanks to this fearsome ability he was met with little resistance with the only ones actually able to fight back being the Paladins of Pyrhas and Lugos, of the Men and of Solarion of Elves. Nonetheless the powerful ice gave Kushsanu enough edge to even lay down these warriors as well, for not only his shield and sword but his breath as well was that of dark ice.

His onslaught went on until he met with his biggest hurdle yet; a champion of the Elves, a paladin not of Solarion but of Lunaria, the Goddess of the Moon, for she was a Drow or a Dark Elf and all Dark Elves followed the cult of the Moon.

Equipped with a short sword wrought in moonlight and a silver starlit shield this maiden of Lunaria makes her stand against the Winter General of the Wyverns. Her name: Lumien, which stood for 'daughter of the moon', and she was no ordinary paladin, not because she was a captain but because she was a princess, daughter to the King of the Drow, Illuvinnan. Her armaments were a gift from King Arathur to her grandfather, as a token of gratitude for the introduction to Lunar magic.

Kushsanu: If you fight me you will die, little Elfling.

Lumien: Your words frighten me not, spawn of darkness.

Kushsanu: You've seen what happens to your comrades, I don't wish to slay someone as comely as you.

Lumien: What is this? An enemy offering compliments to their opponents? How surreal, surely, I am not the only female that has crossed your path.

Kushsanu: But not one as beautiful as you.

Lumien: Save your sweet words fiend for I have no need of them, now are you going to do battle or sweet-talk me to my grave?

Kushsanu: Pity, seeing you has stirred my heart but alas I serve my Lord Abaddon and as my enemy I must slay you, if you wish not to retreat.

Lumien: I will neither flee nor retreat, now prepare yourself.

Kushsanu: Then I must bid you farewell, maiden of the moon.

Lumien: 'Tis you that will be parting this world!

And with a mighty war cry and a raised sword, she falls upon him.

Now Amra was met with no resistance at all from anyone for her opponents were dealing with a magic never seen before and were not adequately prepared to face her.

She fought with her bare hands for she was in no need of a weapon besides her bow; her hands and otherworldly strength were all the weapons she needed for close combat.

With her mighty punches she incapacitated the soldiers who were foolishly rushing her and pried their armours open with sheer force and dealt the final blow with her venomous claws.

Now these soldiers were also equipped with chainmail beneath the plate armour and as it was a doozy to go through all that layer of protection she mostly went straight for the face.

Of course, all of the armours were properly enchanted against physical strikes, but what made Amra's punches unique was not her strength alone but her psychic abilities as well for as you know she is able to emit psychic waves that are able to shatter almost anything.

And who would be brave enough to stand against the Lamia, for many-a-soldiers even fled from her, but her very own dear cousin Priscilla, who I might add was beyond herself when she saw her and Amra was equally surprised.

Priscilla: Amra…? (Wide-eyed).

Amra: Priscilla…?

CAPITVLVM XXIV

DIES IRAE III

Priscilla: You're…alive?

Amra: Alive and well, as you see.

Priscilla: So, my eyes are not deceiving me, or are you a corpse raised from the dead by him?

Amra: No dear cousin, it is I in the flesh. But more importantly, why are you here? Where is Luzira? Where is my little sister?

Priscilla: Luzira is…she is… (chokes up).

Amra: No…no… (shakes her head in disbelief).

Priscilla: I am so sorry… (tears well up on her eyes).

Amra: It was you! You killed her to get to the throne!

Priscilla: I would never hurt her, you know this! We were like sisters, the three of us!

Amra: Then who did?

Priscilla: …It was an assassin of Camelot, 'The Phantom'…

Amra: Arthur…

Priscilla: Know this, he acted on his own, none from the council wished it!

Amra: Why? Why do such a thing?

Priscilla: …She meant to come to Abaddon's side, she did not think we could win.

Amra: So he killed her, and you let him go for it, because you all knew he did the right thing even though it was wrong.

Priscilla: No! We all voted 'nay' except Haldur, but still!

Amra: Abaddon was right…they all pretend to be our friends but secretly they wish us dead.

Priscilla: I don't justify it, but Morvene brought it upon herself…

Amra: How dare you!

Priscilla: Well maybe if you didn't side with the enemy none of that would have happened? If you were alive, why didn't you return!

Amra: I had no choice! It was either that or die and besides, I am indebted to Lord Abaddon for he bestowed me with great power.

Priscilla: Listen to yourself, he slaughtered our people, and you take his hand?

Amra: **I** slaughtered our people! With my own pride and vanity!

Priscilla: Amra, please, come to your senses, it is still not too late, join us, join me!

Amra: No, I cannot.

Priscilla: Please, let us be sisters once more.

Amra: Sorry, this is my life now.

Priscilla: You would rather die a traitor in a foreign land?

Amra: I don't intend on dying, I have a daughter to live for now.

Priscilla: I have a niece… (smiles).

Amra: Too bad you won't get to see her.

Priscilla: Is there no other way…? Must we fight?

Amra: Unless **you** join me.

Priscilla: You know I can't, as much as you can't; I am queen now…

Amra: Then we fight, and you will die here, after which I will kill the rest.

Priscilla: It won't come to that.

Amra: I was always the better one in combat.

Priscilla: People change, I'm not the same I used to be.

Amra: I'll be the judge of that.

Now family falls on family once more.

Meanwhile, Mordred and his newfound allies were making their way to the royal palace of Prince Jamaz, ruler of the Fire Demons.

Any resistance they met on their way was crushed beneath the hooves of the Dullahan's horses and the mighty magic of the Spriggan.

Once they storm the palace a gruesome sight awaits them; the people of the court were being raped and molested and beaten when they resisted. Prince Jamaz was chained to the throne and made to watch as these acts of debauchery unfolded before his very eyes, even his own wife was amongst those being molested.

When Mordred saw this, horror and rage overcame him.

Hyberion: Ag na Deuthe[69]…

Cain: Muchadh!

Savages, they called them, but they were too busy to notice them barging in. It was only when Mordred's voice thundered throughout.

Mordred: Seize this madness at once! Defilers!

Everyone stopped what they were doing and looked upon the young prince.

Jamaz: Allies… (mutters).

Knight: And who are you?

Mordred: I am your death!

And in his rage, he unleashes a powerful death surge, controlled one, and soon their enemies laid dead on the floor. The magical chains turn to rust, and all are set free.

That attack takes quite the toll on him, so he begins to feel slightly more fatigued.

Cain: Death magic is a powerful one, you should not use it so recklessly, friend.

Mordred: I am fine, do not worry about me.

Jamaz: Dalilu adanishkim annum[70], you saved our lives.

Mordred: No thanks needed, as the Mar Sharruu[71] of this land, it is my duty to take care of my subjects.

Jamaz: Mar Sharruu? You are the son of King Abaddon?

Mordred: Indeed I am, my name is Mordred.

Jamaz: And I am Jamaz, come, embrace me Ahu[72].

And they fall into a brotherly embrace.

Jamaz: Who are your companions?

Cain: I am Cain Ech'Cenad, and this is Hyberion.

Jamaz: Faery Kings, the ones that fought with my grandfather?

Hyberion: The very same ones, lad.

---

[69] By the Gods …

[70] Thank you very much my friend.

[71] Son of the king.

[72] Brother.

Jamaz: Then as our friends and allies you have my gratitude as well as my welcome.

Hyberion: You have our thanks for your kind words as well.

Jamaz: I would offer you food and wine but as you see we are not exactly in a welcoming state…

Mordred: There is neither need nor time for a feast, war is upon us, and my father needs us on the battlefield.

Jamaz: Say no more, we will muster every remaining man and set forth at once.

Mordred: Thank you.

Jamaz: I'm glad that the time has finally come for us to reclaim our homeland.

Mordred: Now all that is left is to liberate the Addarim and then we will be ready to launch our assault from the rear.

Angel: Demon scum! We should have killed you the moment we stepped into this place! Hiyah!

One of the garrison soldiers attacks them in a fit of rage but Jamaz in the blink of an eye vanishes in an ember of flames and reapers before the Angel, lifting him up by the head. His hand flares up with the Blue Flame of Baal and the soldier is instantly turned to cinders.

Mordred: Impressive.

Jamaz: I'm no prince in name only.

Mordred: So I see.

Jamaz: I would be unworthy of my title if I couldn't do at least this much.

Mordred: Well said.

Jamaz: Come Malku, let's gather the rest.

And so, they go and rally up every available male and female of the Fire race that are able to fight and are ready to set forth for Addaria.

Their forces include the Shakatim, Incinerators, Fire Demons of smaller stature, quick and nimble in their movements, their name is derived from their special trait, 'Incineration' which releases a surge of highly combustible flame upon contact and is able to turn even the sturdiest objects to ash in a matter of seconds.

There are also the Niprumutim, 'Blaze Knights'. They are equipped with armours gilded with red gold, and with great designs of black gold, though their splendour had much waned in captivity. They fight with flame-forged weapons that can sear through any steel.

And lastly, the Hanizbatim, The Misbegotten Ones, or simply Fire Fiends, named as such for their appearance is quite monstrous. They are big, strong, fierce and fear no foe. Their blood contains much trace of the various beasts and fiends that Baal created for the purpose of the Titanomachia, hence their more fiendish appearance. Their weapons are made of pure Tiamatian fire, and they are also possessing of an arsenal of flaming attacks, such as their breath.

These three units comprise the elite forces of the Isarim.

Their magic casters are called Isaptim 'Pyromancers' and their handling in fire magic is without equal.

Now the combined forces of Demons and Faeries march on to the land of the Storm Demons.

They were transported there thanks to Hyberion's magic whose Spriggan had to empower him so that it would not be too taxing on his person.

The situation in Dur-Addadum, the capital, was no different than in the ones in Dishum and Dur-Isatum.

The garrison armies put up a valiant fight but were crushed nonetheless by the overwhelming might of the combined forces.

Prince Harthan greatly welcomed the recue army and soon his forces joined them as well.

There are elite units within it that excel in one of their three, major elements. The Shibmutim, 'Gale Knights', who excelled in fighting with pole arms and wind magic. Their armour is fully plated and silver with gold. The Shagantim, 'Thunderbreakres' a light infantry unit that fights by transmuting their bodies into lightning allowing for quick and deadly attacks. And lastly there are the Ezgubilim, 'Tidebringers', a heavy infantry unit serving as a vanguard. They have the ability to envelop their tridents with water and deliver heavy blows. Due to their water infused attacks and unbreakable defence with their great shields they indeed liken to a mighty tidal wave, hence their name.

Their armour is decorated with iridescent metallic pieces in the shape of fish scales, and Sea Serpent fins on their pauldrons.

The most powerful magic caster of this race is called an Addaptu, 'Storm Cleric' and they are masters of wind, water, and lightning, able to conjure up powerful tempests be they hurricanes or hails.

At last, they were met up with the army of the Dark Demons led by Demiurgos and it was time for them to march on to the battlefield.

Hyberion: What will it be gentlemen? Shall we march onwards or shall I teleport ourselves to the place.

Demiurgos: I say we go by a proper march; it would not feel right otherwise.

Harthan: I agree with Lord Demiurgos, let us do it the traditional way.

Cain: As much as I would love to agree to that idea, it is not plausible at the moment, the distance is far too great.

Mordred: Then how about this, we shall march for some part of the way, symbolically, then we shall be teleported there, sound good?

Cain: Aye, I can agree with that, not only do we save stamina but time as well.

Mordred: Then it is settled, what say the rest of you?

The rest shout out with a unanimous 'aye'.

Hyberion: Setting forth doesn't seem right without a chant. Cain, do you still remember that old one we used to sing?

Cain: How can I forget?

Hyberion: Take it away, old friend.

With Cain taking the lead, they begin chanting what they used to sing when they first rode off to help Magdabolg, and this is what they sang:

Over the mountains we ride, we fly
To the help of our brother in arms
Great Demon of fire,
Forged in the North
We ride, we fly to stack on your pyre
Make it higher and higher
By the Gods above to be seen
None to stop you will ween.
By the Gods above to be seen
None to stop you will ween.

Great is your might, great is your rule
Everyone who stands in your way is a fool
Beacon of light, beacon of might
Plunge your foes into fright.
For the iron sceptre and rod,
We ride, we fly for Baal, your God
Of fire and blood,
There will be a flood.
Of fire and blood,
There will be a flood.

Come thither, their corpses wither
Stomp on the ground, shrivel the mound,
We bring darkness and death
Together at last, we'll rule the rest.
Masters we'll become of the West
You Kishsharrum with fire and doom,
'Room-doom-doom'
Rule King, rule!
'Room-doom-doom'
Rule king, rule!

Now with the combined numbers of all races this already became a sizeable army and with great chanting they set forth to do battle.

At the other side on the battlefield the set battles were well underway.

First let us have a glimpse in the combat between the two spear-wielding champions. Lancelot had a slight advantage over Malgaras for he had also a shield which aided him greatly in blocking his attacks but Malgaras despite not having one was dual wielding his partisan which allowed him to dish out mightier and swifter blows.

Now you would think that Malgaras' 'Shadow Step', which allowed him to move faster than any human being, would provide him with a significant advantage but, Lancelot was not just any soldier for he and the rest like him were trained to counter the threats of such abilities. And by using his keen instincts as a highly skilled soldier, he was able to accurately defend against his advances.

But that was a problem in itself, for Malgaras' swift assaults kept him in the defence and unlike Demons, Humans have limited stamina.

Malgaras: What's the matter? Getting a bit tired?

Lancelot: You wish, this suit of armour has been properly equipped with an invigoration enchantment which will keep me going for a few more hours.

Malgaras: Too bad, I could keep on going the whole night.

Now Lancelot lunges at him but Malgaras counters with his own spear and they cancel each other out.

He moves in to strike him with his shield, but he swiftly dodges out of the way.

Another one difficulty that Malgaras is facing is that Lancelot being fully encased in armour has no openings left from where he can cast his 'Doom' ability which is slightly irritating for him.

Now Demons are not the only ones equipped with special weapons, soldiers like Lancelot to compensate for their lack of usage of magic are granted with magical weapons and Ascalon was one of them.

Said to be once wielded by a powerful warrior saint, once activated it grants the user the ability to move at unimaginable speeds.

And now Lancelot does just that with uttering the proper incantation, sacred inscriptions appear along the spear and Lancelot becomes surrounded by a bright aura.

Lancelot: This is where I begin my counterattack.

Now Lancelot moving swiftly like the wind itself comes upon Malgaras and a battle of great speed ensues. In fact, Lancelot is moving so fast that he creates afterimages.

Moving at speeds almost impossible to follow with the naked eye, their clashes cause sonic booms to be created throughout the air.

For the longest time it seems that they are at a stalemate until Malgaras enacts what is to be the decisive blow.

Now he uses his black cloak that is not just any cloak but a magical one and it being made of dark magic he turns it into a waving mass of blackness, throwing it right at Lancelot's visor.

So, what he does is he raises his shield and with his other hand tries to remove the veil of darkness that is obscuring his vision.

Malgaras uses this to his advantage; he attacks Lancelot from the side and the soldier moves instinctively trying to defend himself by waving the shield in that direction which leaves him wide open.

Realising his mistake, he reaches for Ascalon so he can lunge it forward and ward off Malgaras, but it is a moment too late for the cunning Demon had moved faster and his partisan, the 'Salmu Deberu' was making its way through the opening in his visor, and the next thing Ser Lancelot saw was permanent darkness.

Malgaras: Rest in peace, Ser Lancelot Germaine of the Round Table.

And he was off to find another pray as Lancelot slumped over dead on the sand. Meanwhile, Alabaster was exchanging fierce blows with Selene. Both of these robust warriors were giving their best and neither seemed to be budging.

Alabaster: You're quite strong, I like tough women.

Selene says nothing to that.

Alabaster: Got nothing to say back? Not even 'thanks, you too'?

Selene: A battlefield is a place for combat not for idle chatting.

She says with a poised voice and attacks him after she is done saying it but Alabaster blocks it.

Alabaster: How about if we both survive this, I make you, my woman?

Selene: No thank you.

Alabaster: They all say that until I introduce them to my giant meat stick.

Selene: Gross.

He pushes her off with his brute strength, but she jumps right back at him with a swift attack but due to his larger stature he tanks it and grabs her by the arm. Then he sets his mace aside and grabs her with his other hand, rending her arm asunder and tosses it.

Selene does not even make a sound but simply reattaches her arm using blood strings and whacks him on the head resulting in him letting her go.

Much to Alabaster's surprise he feels a bit dizzy from that last attack and to further his surprise he feels that there is a little dent at the spot, and not only there but also at the last place she hit him as well.

Now Alabaster begins to worry for no one has able to put a dent in his armour as of yet and he thought that its magical properties were beginning to wear off. Or maybe it was Selene's weapon itself, he could not say for sure.

In his moment of confusion, he finds himself toppled on the desert sand with Selene on top of him, bashing at his helmet with her mace with a calm expression like some coldblooded psychopath.

Alabaster was right, his helmet was beginning to cave in, and he could feel the blows clearly against his head.

Now this was due to the fact that the weight of the mace coupled with the Vampire's unhuman strength were overwhelming his armour.

Alabaster knew that Vampires had great strength, but he never knew that someone could reach to this level which was almost as his.

He tries to whack her off with Halnadu, but she stops his attack with her bare hand. Now this scrawny Vampire was holding his weapon at bay and was slowly but surely bashing his brains in relentlessly. It was a matter of time before the helm completely gives in and his brain matter lay spread on the cold desert sand.

With his other hand he starts to punch Selene in the face in the hopes of knocking her off, but the Vampire does not budge and seems completely unfazed by the blows.

He tries to kick back up on his feet, but he felt too dizzy for that venture. He could now feel his consciousness slowly leaving him, but he was not about to give in; he was a Destroyer god dammit! And he would be damned if he let some scrawny Vampire get the better of him.

So, he steels himself and with his new resolve the Demonic runes on Halnadu begin to shine and now Selene could feel her arm being crushed inwardly towards her torso, but the mad lass just keeps on pounding his head and does not even flinch when Halnadu reaches her torso and completely obliterates her top right half.

Blood and innards spill all over Alabaster and finally the pounding stops, so he flings what is left of her aside.

However, with her left side and consequently her heart being intact, she begins to regenerate.

Seeing this Alabaster immediately flings himself on his feet and smashes Selene's remains into a bloody pulp, hitting her a couple of times for good measure until nothing is left but a bloody mush.

Alabaster: Crazy bitch…almost killed me… (breathing heavily).

And so, he waddles onwards bashing the skulls and spilling brain matter and goop from any unfortunate soul that crosses his path. As he moves through his victims, for a moment he feels dizzy and tries to shake it off, but that leaves him open to the assault of yet another Vampire who whacks him across the head with his war hammer. Blood begins to spill over his eyes, and they become clouded. The Vampire standing before him makes a sucking motion with his mouth and begins to drain the blood spilling from his head, that is being drawn through the eye sockets of the helmet. This was an elite type of Vampire, an Exanguinator, who possessed the rarest of vampiric abilities of sucking blood remotely, even drawing it from the pores of the skin. As the Vampire was focusing on draining Alabaster from his blood, he fails to sense and react to Malgaras' partisan that finds its way through his mouth, from the back of his head.

Alabaster: Who's there …?

Malgaras: It's only me, you're welcome.

Alabaster: Cover me, I need to wipe the blood from my face.

Malgaras: You need a treatment, fall back and have someone patch you up.

Alabaster: No time! Cover me!

Frustrated, he stands before him. Alabaster removes his helmet and grabs Malgaras' cape, using it as a towel.

Malgaras: What are you – ugh! You're irredeemable!

Alabaster: Just shut your mouth (flings the cape aside and puts his helmet back on).

Malgaras: You've lost a lot of blood; you **must** fall back!

Alabaster: No (he pushes past him and trudges on).

Malgaras: Aghh! Idiot!

Seeing as there is a treat by the Allied Forces to move forward, Abaddon orders the next wave to be send in and so the Oni army and what remains of the Hathasian infantry enter the fray.

With flaming swords and war cries they descend upon their foes and slice them up. Tetsuzaemon is finally ready to let loose for he was getting impatient and so he unsheathes his trusty Muramasa.

Now this Demon Sword is of great power just like the ones we have seen so far, and its ability is to inflict curses. Along the blade of the sword there are several characters engraved on it and each one represents a specific curse and there are twelve in total. There is the curse of 'Baku' which can bind the persons movement and even rob him of his senses, then there is 'Shi' which grants instant death to the one being pierced, 'Dokuji' which turns toxic the blood of the stricken and so forth. 'Shi' is the most powerful but it also consumes the most mana so it must be used in a case when all hope seems lost.

Thus, many warriors fall beneath the might of this great weapon.

With the addition to the Ogres and Hathasians the Allies begin to be pushed back further and their rear guard sees no other option but to join in as well and so the Werewolves and Dwarves that were fighting in the back go in to support their brethren.

Support comes in the form of their magicians as well for now they had much more room to breathe because the Giant Wolves and Wyrms' attacks were dwindling as well as the Crawlers'. But also, the elite units of the Volkodakians find their way there. They include the Shaman-Warriors and the Spiritualists. The former are shamans who combine their lunar magics with melee weapons, even their claws when they transform, and can unleash devastating attacks.

The latter are also fighters who summon the aid of lunar spirits in the shape of spectral wolves with whom they can deal deadly combination attacks.

The most formidable off all however, were the armies of the Subterrans who refused to go down due to their unfair ability of constant regeneration.

Not only that, the Basher and Champion classes boasted great physical prowess as well, which added to their threat levels and enabled these siege engines to brave through the lines of soldiers unscathed and make their way to the rear where the support units were.

Now Olwen, whom is to say the Queen of the Sylphs and the Court of Autumn steps forth and conjures up a massive tornado in an attempt to halt these beings and thwart their advance.

She uses her magic to keep the mass of wind into one place so that it does not affect her allies.

Her kin and fellow Queen of the Summer Court, Brigitha, adds her flame magic and sets the tornado ablaze creating a pillar of spiralling inferno.

The intensity of the flames proves greater than their regenerative ability and the Demons end up being burned to a crisp.

Albunalich, seeing that his troops are in distress, steps forward and uses his magic to raise the sands along the tornado, covering it and dowsing the flame entirely.

Urania: That Demon spoils us yet again.

Umbriela: He is quite powerful, the magic he uses is no ordinary earth magic I can feel it, we need to stop him.

Brigitha: I would go but his magic counters mine.

Olwen: I will go.

Iliana: I will accompany you as well, sister, together we shall beat him with ice and wind.

Eireann: I will go as well.

Olwen: No, you stay behind in case they need you here, we are more than enough.

Urania: Go my sisters, but exercise great caution for he is a formidable foe.

'Yes, your majesty,' they both say in unison and fly off.

Now, Iliana was the Queen of the Undine, that is to say Water Faeries and of the Winter Court. Eireann was the Queen of the Dryads and the Court of Spring.

Now a couple of things need to be said about the Faeries. Their land, Faeran, is divided into two, major courts: the Seelie and Unseelie one. The Seelie are the 'benevolent' sprites, whereas as the Unseelie are the 'malevolent.'

As a tradition, the Faeries of the Seelie Court always pick a High-Queen as a Ruler Supreme. This tradition stems from an old teaching of theirs. Namely, the Seelie Faeries have a tutelary Goddess whom they call Nadar Mather, 'Mother Nature'. According to this teaching, Mother Nature is the feminine, physical aspect of the Creator, whereby the earth, the waters, the forests, and mountains were created.

Therefore, within her are contained the Four Elements of Nature: Fire, Water, Wind, and Earth. Hence the Gods of these Elements are said to be her children, and by them the Seelie Faeries. The Elements of Light, Dark, and Lightning are considered part of the masculine, spiritual aspect, and are not venerated, as the Seelie Faeries are more concerned with the visible, physical nature. This division of feminine and masculine stems from the duality of the Primordial Gods.

In light of this, a High-Queen is seen as someone who embodies the ideal of the Nadar Mather, so it has to be a female. Now the way a Ra'ard, is elected is by age and so, the eldest of the four queens takes the place. Then, she must undergo a specific ceremony to prove her worthiness. Once passed, she ascends to the throne of the Seelie Court, and is blessed by the power of the Four Elements. This office is not hereditary. If the High-Queen births a daughter, or if she already had one, she assumes her previous place as a ruler of her home court. If it is a son, then they act as a King Regent until such time comes when a daughter is born. The Faery Kings have no real power, they are simply king consort. With the Unseelie Court things are much different.

Now seeing as their plan to halt the Subterrans has been stopped, the fire users cast a massive 'Raindrops of the Phoenix' which rains down drops of fire that invigorate their allies and allow them to keep on fighting.

But Dagon and his Mystics will not be undone and with a combined effort they nullify the fire rain.

Then the Entomancers from Albunalich's side conjure up a cloud of locusts and launches it at their foes and it obstructs their view.

They also mix up infernal mosquitos within the plague of locusts that suck the blood dry out of the soldiers that are not completely covered by armour.

However, the Angelic Hashmalim combine their efforts and send out a blast of cleansing light that destroys the clouds of pests.

While this exchange of magic was going on other things were underway as well like the family feud between Morgana and Arthur.

Arthur might have been an excellent swordsman, but Morgana was no slouch either having been trained by his best sword instructors and Abaddon himself. But it is no ordinary sword he wields but the Sword of the Dragon itself. It is called by that name because when the king of Camelot, Bethor III presented it to the White Dragon Lugos it was imbued with his life essence, in order to help him end The War of the Five Kingdoms. Since then, Bethor took up the name Pendragon and it was handed down to the line of kings ever since.

Indeed, Camelot was only one of the five kingdoms that comprised the land, which was once known as Thyrodyn, and when Bethor III ended Y Cadfel Kyryadol, The War of the Five Kingdoms and united them, they all became assimilated into it and now the name encompasses the entirety of the land.

Now Arthur with it dispels Morgana's dark sword and moves in to strike her down but his heart grows heavy, and he is unable to deal the final blow. Using his moment of weakness, she intends to strike him down with lightning, but his regal armour will not be undone so easily, and his life is spared. Finally, he steels himself, alas with a heavy heart still he plunges Excalibur into Morgana's chest.

But instead of falling on the ground dead, she smirks and dissolves into a mist of shadows that surrounds Arthur and using her nigromancy she takes the shape of a black serpent and coils around him.

Morgana: I will squeeze the life out of you!

Arthur: By the grace of Lugos the Wise, you shan't be availed!

He means to activate Excalibur's light once more and dissolve her magic, but before it can take effect Morgana casts an evil illusion on him through her eyes which shows him a vision of a burning Camelot, buildings falling and people dying, Guinevere, his queen and her mother as well.

This breaks his already weighted heart for he knows that despite being an illusion this is the fate that awaits them, and so Excalibur escapes his grip and falls on the ground.

Now Morgana opens her mouth, and her tongue takes the shape of a sword, and it goes straight through Arthur's forehead, ending his life.

Upon seeing this, the knights begin to shout out 'the king is dead!', 'the king is dead!' Some even break formation and with a grievous cry rush at Morgana in an attempt to avenge him, but the evil sorceress who has now taken human shape again casts the penultimate version of 'Fear', which is 'Abyssal Presence', and all around her freeze in their tracks like statutes. Then she casts 'Corporeal Shadow', which causes the soldiers to be killed by their own shadows.

She tries to pick up Excalibur, but the sword burns her hand, and she drops it on the sand.

Morgana: Accursed blade! (Kicks it beneath the sand) may you rust there with no one else to wield you.

Then she turns towards the corpse of her father and looks down on it.

Morgana: Goodbye Arthur, and good riddance.

Now she assumes the shape of a dark cloud and travels back to Abaddon's side.

Morgana: It's done, my love, Arthur is dead.

Abaddon: Well done, my dear, I never doubted you for a second.

Morgana smiles.

Abaddon: And what of the sword?

Morgana: Buried beneath the sand.

Abaddon: I should seek it out later, it's unwise to let such a powerful weapon unattended.

Morgana: By that time, it would've sunk to the depths of the desert, my love.

Abaddon: I'll have Albunalich dig it up for me, should he survive that long.

Morgana: But why? It's not like we can use it.

Abaddon: Not to use it, my dear, but to destroy it.

Morgana: I see, that is wise, I suppose.

Abaddon: Of course it is.

Morgana: And what of you, my love? How long do you plan to stand on the sidelines?

Abaddon: Not for long, after I launch the final wave, I shall make my move.

Morgana: I wonder how Mordred is doing.

Abaddon: I'm sure he is just fine and making his way here as we speak.

Morgana: You're right it's such a foolish thing to worry about him, he is our son after all, no one may touch him.

Abaddon: That may be so but it is a parent's instinct to worry about their child so I wouldn't say is foolish.

Morgana: Of course, how could I ever think it to be foolish.

He kisses her hand in a comforting manner as she is sitting behind him on Argyros.

In the meantime, Kushsanu was having his hands full with Lumien, the Drow princess.

The light from her star-spangled shield was negating his dark ice, so he had a hard time disposing of her.

And from her moonlit sword she was expelling beams of concentrated moon light that he had to avoid so most of the time he was on the defence.

Now she casts a spell and from her sword come out magical projectiles in the shape of crescent moons in succession, but Kushsanu shields himself with his own shield.

While being under attack, Kushsanu deduces that the best course of action would be to separate Lumien from her sword and deal the final blow.

But this was easier said than done for she was a formidable warrior despite being a princess.

Now she continued her onslaught by creating illusions of herself with the help of the moonlight and the three of her, including herself attacked him head on, switching places in the process as to confuse him.

This tactic may have worked on any other soldier, but Kushsanu was originally a Wyvern therefore he had a keen sense of smell, so he was able to sniff out the original and successfully guard against her attack.

This worked in his advantage as well for now being so close to her he was able to unleash his icy breath upon her, but she manages to put up her shield just in time and shield from the breath. Then by banging the sword on her shield she creates a bright flash of light that blinds Kushsanu and temporarily renders him immobile.

Now this was not just any blinding light, so he found not only that his sight was incapacitated but also his hearing and smell as well.

Kushsanu: What have you done to me, Elfling!
Lumien: Nothing much, I merely robbed you of your senses.

Then he feels a sharp pain surge through his chest, and he knows that his life is at an end.

Lumien: And your life.

Now Lumien feels the same pain he did for in her moment of cockiness she had let her guard down and allowed the dying Winter Knight to plunge his blade through her as well.

Kushsanu: I guess that goes for the both of us.
Lumien: Curse you…fiend.

And so, they both lay dead, with each other's swords in their hearts. On another front there was also the battle between cousins.

Priscilla was attacking Amra with her rapier in a quick succession, but Amra was evading and parrying every single move with her bare hands.

Now she means to hit her with a psychic wave but Priscilla being of royal blood as well cancels it out with a wave of her own.

This moment necessitates Amra with the right condition for a direct eye contact so that she may cast 'Gorgon's gaze' upon her cousin and turn her to stone.

Then she gives her a flick and shatters her to pieces making this match short lived.

Amra: You may have gotten better, cousin, but I'm still the best.

She looks at what is left of her and ponders.

Amra: Perhaps I should have kept her as a statue for the main hall…oh well.

Then she begins to walk away but then something dawns on her, so she goes back at the statue and uses her psychic powers to reform the statue and uses one of her poisons to serve as an adhesive.

Amra: Perfect, good as new.

Now she picks it up and flies it off to Abaddon.

Abaddon: What is this?

Amra: This is what used to be my cousin Priscilla, now she will serve as a decoration for my palace.

Abaddon: Surely you jest.

Amra: I'm dead serious, it would be such a shame to let this fine piece of art go to waste.

Abaddon: Good grief…

Amra: Therefore, could you do me a favour? Be a dear and pop this back at the palace, will you?

Abaddon: (snaps his fingers and it gets teleported back in the royal castle) done.

Amra: Thank you very much.

Abaddon: Anything to get you back in the fight.

Amra: You're always a sweetheart.
Abaddon: Get out of my sight already.
Amra: Ta-ta! (Flies off).
Morgana: She can really be obnoxious at times.
Abaddon: More like all the time (sighs and shakes his head).

Yet on another side, Abaddon's own female champion, the general of the Abyssal Knights, had found her match in the form of Ser Percival Godwyn of the Round Table but that is a match for the next chapter...

CAPITVLVM XXV

DIES IRAE IV

Now Carmox and Percival were locked in a tight combat falling upon each other with their weapons; one with his axe and the other with the broad claymore.

Now her sword, named Mashbanu which means 'Oblivion Maker', was made out of Obsidian Steel a material which can only be found in Dhalsarria and is many times sturdier than normal steel thus making it a capable weapon for blocking attacks as well. However, as it was not made for defensive purposes the blade is susceptible to damage. Ser Percival was a tall buff guy, his armour made him look even bigger, kind of like a human version of Alabaster so his attacks were quite hefty and at most times it threatened to throw Carmox off her feet.

However, she patiently was looking for an opening she might exploit, and that moment presents itself. As Percival was swinging his axe towards her, she meets him with the exact same force and both attacks cancel each other, and this creates an opportunity for Carmox to push back Percival with 'Dark Pulse', a spell which unleashes a mighty surge of dark energy. However due to his sturdy armour he is only moved back a few steps, but that is enough for Carmox now to launch a counterattack. In the middle of her assault, she casts an incantation, and her hands, including the sword become wreathed in deep, purplish darkness and she slams against his weapon.

Percival, who had heard of the feats of these Knights, nevertheless was not expecting such enormous display of power and was visibly taken aback. The blow had almost knocked him off his feet, but he had managed to stay his ground. Now he too casts an incantation, 'Blessing of the Black Flame' and the blade of his axe is now wreathed in powerful, black fire, summoned from Avernus, the Fire Plane. Him being of the Godwyn clan, from the line of Godrick, was also a Paladin of Pyrhas, the Fire God, and his axe was a family heirloom that once belong to that same Godrick, his grandfather twice over, once hailed as the 'Red

Lion'. Like his position in the Round Table, the weapon and calling were hereditary as well.

Now the Black Flames give an enormous boost to his axe, and he repels Carmox, then follows with a swift swing that hurls a fireball in her direction. It hits her in the torso, and she is blinded by the blast that spreads around her helmet. Percival capitalises on this opportunity and comes in with a two-handed attack at Carmox's torso, but she deters him by shooting an eldritch beam in his direction which he is forced to deflect. Then, she follows up with a massive, slashing wave of darkness sent from her claymore which Percival disperses by meeting it with a burst of black flame from his axe, swung in an arc.

From behind the blast emerges Carmox, wielding her sword with both hands and they clash again with their weapons. In the midst of the clash, the blade of Carmox's claymore turns into a cloud of darkness that spreads around Percival's axe and snuff out its flames. The darkness rapidly envelops his body as well, and he ends up being lifted in the air, by Carmox who directs the cloud with her hilt.

Carmox: You are fucked now, knightly boy.

Percival: I would not celebrate so early.

The darkness begins to constrict him, and he can feel his flesh being torn apart inside his armour, but he fights against it, and casting 'Pyrhas' Divine Immolation' sends forth a surge of purifying flames that burn away the slicing darkness of the blade. Then, he gathers the tongues of flames on his axe and comes slamming down with a fiery attack. Carmox leaps to the back in an attempt to evade but she is caught in the aftershock, nevertheless. This causes her to lose her footing, but she uses the sword that has now reformed, to prop herself.

Percival was gripping the handle of his axe, which was now pointed towards the ground, and he seemed as if though he was in prayer. Then, a flaming tongue erupts from beneath the sand around Carmox's feet and seeks to entangle her, but she swipes away with Mashbanu. Then, another appears, and another, chasing after her as she is trying to evade being caught. Percival's prayer continues – he was channelling the Divine Fires of Avernus. The flaming tongues that were emerging around Carmox like flaming vines now rise high in the air and then conjoin together, forming a pillar of fire around her. The pillar begins to swirl and enclose rapidly around her, but she already was contemplating her salvation.

She casts 'Shadow Walk' and her body becomes a mass of shadows, which she had hoped would allow her to phase through the flaming pillar, but the divine flames were serving as a prison and were burning away the whisps of shade – the sensation was excruciating. Her attempt failed she decides to try something new before the flames completely consume her. In that form, she also channels the power of Tiamat through prayer and her shadowy body becomes merged with that of the darkness of Baal, which was summoned through her body as a medium, and now there were iridescent shimmers of darkness of different purples beneath the thick, black shadows.

Now she spreads out her arms and the darkness spreads, taking over the pillar and turning it black – she was fighting the divine will of the flames with that of her own. Percival perceiving this understood what was happening and sought to counter it by changing his prayer. Now his flames that were being consumed turned to the Black Flames of Phyras, which were of pure, black colour, and were eating away at the invading darkness – it was a battle of two wills. But ultimately Carmox's prevails, and the purple darkness swallows the black flames, and it is extinguished. There is a blast of energy in the form of wind, and there stands Carmox, corporeal.

There is a moment of stillness – Percival picks up his axe in one hand and straightens up, meeting Carmox's eyes and then – lo! Suddenly a violent surge of dark energy in the form of a massive wave is released from the tip of Mashbanu towards Percival, who has no hopes of availing himself. The energy surges through, and past him extending in the battlefield and even engulfing others. Being under that darkness, Percival suffers the effects. His armour begins to corrode and rust, as the Abyssal darkness was eating away its magical essence. Not only that, but also his body begins to darken as his life essence, his soul, was being corroded as well, for such was the nature of Baal's power.

He tries to preserve himself with a final incantation – 'Phyras' Divine Flaming Mantle' which protected the body with benevolent, divine flames, but they too could not avail him as the darkness was snuffing every attempt of the flames to cover his body. They would ignite and sputter, ignite and sputter, until finally the surge is expended, and he falls on his knees, holding on to the rusted handle of his axe. His breathing was laboured, and his life cut in half; his armour was blackened by rust. He tries to get up, but his ankles break from brittleness, and he falls back on his knees. Carmox, strides forward and stands before him. Her black armour with demonic designs made her look that more terrifying.

Percival: Mighty … and cursed is the power of your dark God …

Carmox: Do you know why? Because unlike yours, he is a fucking, true God.

Percival: Are you trying to say that … we are at fault for having deified the Titans …

Carmox: The results speak for themselves, look at where that has gotten you, down on your knees like a whore giving head.

Percival: … A woman should know better … than to use such language.

Carmox: I'm no fucking woman, I'm a *Dhalka.*

She swings her claymore and easily decapitates him.

Carmox: Say hi to bloody Hedwig when you see him in The Scarlet Lands.[73]

With her task at hand now finished, this 'Battle Queen' sets her sight on new prey. Meanwhile Albunalich was being assaulted by the two Faery Queens who had previously attacked him, and despite having the numerical disadvantage, he was holding out pretty well.

With his magic he was able to create powerful plants that negated the effects of Iliana's ice magic and the sand seemed to free itself when frozen. But his attacks did not have effect on Olwen as well, for her wind magic was blowing all of his attacks away and the powerful winds cut through the different plants he threw at them.

Then Iliana switched to pure water magic which dampened the sand, so it grew heavy and crumbled, rendering it useless for attacks, the same happening with his normal earth spells.

This was beginning to frustrate him so now he summons up a bunch of bizarre looking plants with big flower petals and large gaping holes in their centre.

Now these flowers release fumes of poisonous clouds, but this does nothing for Olwen casts 'Vacuum Winds' and the clouds begin to congeal into one place and then she sends them flying away from the rest to a safe distance.

Then Iliana casts 'Rainfall' and creates a cluster of cumulus clouds above their area which begins to drench the sand making it completely unusable in case Albunalich dared to use it again.

---

[73] The name given to the Fire Plane – home of Phyras.

Seeing their master in a pickle, his Entomancers send a cloud of infernal cockroaches which are nasty, resilient, carnivorous critters, their way in an attempt to impede them but this blows back in their faces as Olwen with her guiding currents sends them back at the casters themselves.

Now the powerful Warlock casts 'Vermin Bane' on them and the roaches drop dead on the ground. Then he decides to lend a hand to the Earth King and personally joins his side.

At this point Abaddon feels like it is time for the final wave, and he sends forth his Dragonborn, led by Andrakos.

They join up with the Oni and the remaining Undead at the front and unleash hell upon the gathered armies.

With their elemental weapons and breath attacks they overwhelm the combined forces of Men, Elf, Dwarf and Vampire who were already worn out by their previous fights. Even more blood and gore now stain the sands.

The other members of the elite groups desperately try to hold off the new wave but one by one they meet their end.

Magicians cast support spells like crazy and archers release numerous volleys in an attempt to help their comrades.

Those that can use earth magic summon Earth Elementals as additional battle numbers. Fire, Water, Wind and Lightning Elementals are being summoned as well to help in the fight. The Sanclunean Phantomancers call in the aid of all sorts of Wraiths.

However summoning Earth Elementals proves to be a bad move as Albunalich's Geomancers use their magic to wrestle control over them and turn them against their allies.

The Dwarven Stonemasons now step up, creating defensive walls and towers for the archers and magicians as they did not have much room to breathe before.

Also, the Wyrms and the Wolves were forced to retreat for their numbers had gone dangerously low, with only a handful Wyrms and but a pack of Giant Wolves remaining.

Werewolf: Tzare! Potrebyemo za nim![74]
Cyril: Ne! Pustyi gi![75] I don't want to bring them to extinction, come, we join the front ranks now!

---

[74] My king! We should go after them!

[75] No! Let them go!

Werewolf: Da Tzare!

The Sylvan Elf Rangers use their 'Sharpshooter' ability to take out foes from high up the towers that were provided by the stonemasons.

Now the Dragonkin recognising this strategy from before, turn their attention towards the towers and immediately dive down to topple them down.

But this time the masons are not alone and their stonewalls are reinforced by powerful, five layered barriers, and the Dragonkin find themselves unable to break them down and many fall toppling on the ground themselves.

They are rushed immediately by the Werewolves who pile atop of their giant heads and rend them asunder with their combined might. A pair of Werewolves pry open the maw of a downed Dragon, allowing one of their Shaman-Warriors to finish it off with a lunar beam.

Fulguros: Do not attack the towers! Idiots! Fall back!

As he is shouting his orders a volley of 'Guided Arrows' find their way into his maw and pierce him dead. The Great Tempest Dragon King in his final moments realises what has happened and his eyes go wide with shock as he begins to plummet to the ground. In his final moments he closes his eyes and images of his family, of Fragora and their little drakes, flash before him and he slumps dead on the sands of the Desert Sea

Argyros, seeing this from the distance lets out a loud woeful sound filled with grief and pain.

Tonitros: Fahrisss![76]

Ignatos: Neyyy!

His eldest son flies down by the body of his dead parent and with tears in his eyes releases the same gut-wrenching roar as Argyros.

With ire in his eyes, he turns towards the archer towers and releases a torrent of lightning to no avail for they are protected. But in his rage, he disregards this and continues firing his breath attack.

---

[76] Father!

Ignatos: Tonitros! As Ni Rataros![77]

However, being blinded by rage, he does not heed his warning and a single arrow finds itself in his left eye causing him to writhe in pain. The sensation of burning pain snaps him out of his madness and he knows to retreat but not before he throws one last sorrowful glance at his father.

But luck would not have it, and before he can retreat, a dozen Werewolves leap at his maw and pin him down on the ground with their unnatural strength. He begins to struggle but the Blood Mages conjure up Bloodforge Dragons to hold down his arms and legs.

Ignatos fires a stream in order to liberate him but some of the Blood Mages shield them with a wall of blood. It does not hold much longer; however, it gives Ivaldi enough time to come rushing in with his axe and embed it into Tonitros' head from the inside as the Werewolves are holding his mouth wide open.

Thus, both son and father laid dead beside each other, in a foreign land, far, far from home...

Ymir: Lord Abaddon, when does Ymir and his brood get to fight? Ymir wants to break some bones as well.

Abaddon: Your question comes in the right time my friend for now is the time, go forth, all of you and break what's left of their forces.

Then all the Giants let out a mighty bellow in a unison and this roaring cacophony thunders throughout the entire area, signalising the march of the Giant folk, shaking even the stone constructs on the other side.

With equally loud rumbling they move out to do battle. First go the Mountain Giants, then behind them follow the Frost Giants freezing the very sand beneath their feet and behind them are the Fire Giants with their scorching steps, making the sand sizzle and churn.

As these titans of destruction march forth, they grab the attention of all their foes.

Soldier: What in the name of all the Gods are those?

Folduin: So those enormous creatures are finally on the move, this does not bode well...

---

[77] Get out of there!

Once they reach within fighting distance they unleash their fury, squashing everything in their paths with their feet or bash them with their weapons.

Now with the arrival of the second part of the final wave, what was left of the advancing force now is completely pushed back against the defensive walls.

The magicians open up entry gates so that they may pass through to the other side and being safe with the barriers also in place they are granted safe passage for no evil creature may pass by it.

Now the Stonemasons conjure up stone ballistae atop the walls that fire gigantic stone arrows at the giants, but they do no damage for they freeze or melt away upon impact and are unable to pass through the enchantments of the Fjaldortoren.

Frost Giant: Why do we stop?

Fire Giant: I do not know.

Brundig: There is a magical barrier protecting this place but no matter, we'll bring it down.

Then the Mountain Giants, now being equipped with black, plate armour, begin to hammer down upon the barrier with their enchanted weapons, but it does not give in for it is a five-layered barrier which is the highest level.

Ymir: Stand aside, Ymir will take care of this.

And lo and behold! With one strike of Ymir's club, 'Isulfur', the barrier turns to solid ice and then with another mighty blow it shatters down leaving the stone walls vulnerable.

Ivaldi: Prepare yerselves!

Now Brundig and his lot once again come crashing down this time on the walls and even though they are self-repairing, the Mountain Giants are with no equal when it comes with the magic of enchanting for it is their speciality, and plus it being given boost by Abaddon it proves too much for the magic of the Dwarves, and the walls come crashing down allowing the onslaught to continue.

The normal army like the Dragonborn come storming in and start attacking anything in sight.

Surtr with his Oeskbreidur turns to cinder anyone he deems a foe.

None are able to withstand him as his fire burns straight through their fire enchantments and their armours and they lay dead in a pile of ashes.

Argyros: I should be there as well!

Abaddon: Not yet.

Argyros: What are we waiting for! The battle is almost over!

Abaddon: I said not yet.

Argyros: Gah!

Morgana: Patience, friend, patience, our Lord is wise he knows what he's doing.

Argyros: I find myself at my wits end by every passing second.

Abaddon: I understand how you feel but you will wait for my command.

Argyros: Ugh…very well.

Olwen: (glances towards the rear) They've broken through the defences! They are killing everyone!

Iliana: Whatever shall we do?

Dagon: You will do nothing.

Then he casts 'Abyssal Chains', wrapping them in place.

Iliana: You know that these chains won't hold me, Demon!

Then she proceeds to freeze them, but it does not work.

Dagon: Not this time.

Now before she had a chance to freeze them, Dagon had turned them into fiery ones and mere ice could not hope to freeze the flames of the Abyss, and so they both begin to scream in agony from the burn, cursing their own folly for letting their guards down. They might have been powerful spirits, but Dagon had much more battlefield experience, unfortunately for them.

Dagon: If Queen Venera could see you now, the pathetic disgrace that you have become she would turn in her grave. Master Albunalich, if you will.

Now Albunalich conjures up several sand spikes from now the normal dry sand that imbed themselves in the two queens and kill them.

Dagon: And that is the end of that.

Albunalich: You have my gratitude.

Dagon: Nonsense, it was a pleasure to assist someone as yourself.

Albunalich gives him a polite nod.

Dagon: Now then, shall we head to that direction as well?

Albunalich: After you.

And they both head to where the rest of the armies are clashing.

Now the magicians, pooling their powers together create Water and Fire Wardens respectively on their own in order to combat this giant threat.

The Water Wardens engage the Fire Giants but once their fists make contact they evaporate, and the Giants turn them to steam with their fiery weapons. The same happens with the Frost Giants who freeze the Fire Wardens with no difficulty at all and shatter them apart.

Seeing as this has no effect, they make new ones and enhance them with armour, in the fashion of the Giants again.

One of the Water Wardens that is now protected with a thick layer of ice armour slams his fist against Surt's face, but it has only slight sizzling effect.

Surtr: How dare you touch the Great Surtr's face! Raagh!

With a mighty scream and fist, he punches it and blows away the entirety of its upper half and the rest falls on the ground.

You see Abaddon was expecting this, that is why he had armours with ice and fire resistance respectively be built for the Giants.

Seeing as the Elemental Wardens have no effect on the Giants the magicians begin to despair, even more so when Brundig's lot descended upon them, deeming it wise to take them out first seeing as they were the most troublesome.

They hack away at them, tearing through both protections and limbs.

It is then when the last remaining paladins of Solarion step forth with their radiant weapons and begin to hack in turn at the Frost Giants. The ones in the service of Lugos would help as well had their light been one meant for harming.

Now the Elven Sun-Bearers which is the Elven magical unit of the Light Elves starts shooting concentrated beams of sunlight at the Frost Giant as well in an attempt to aid their kin and with their combined efforts they succeed in taking down couple of them.

The Archmages of the Sun-Bearers even manage to slay two Frost Giants on their own, with powerful sun spells. Some maim them by aiming at their exposed spots.

One of the paladins, slashes at his kneecap and then another joins, and another repeats the same, with one of the Light-Bearers finally searing off what is left of it and the creature finds itself on the ground.

The nimble Elves climb its massive posterior and jam several blades at once through his skull, killing it.

However, this does not come without repercussions for the cold emanated from the Giant leaves them with severe frostbite, despite their 'Sun Orb' protection.

A couple of the Dragonborn take notice of their state and they fall upon them. Being frostbitten makes it difficult for the Elves to defend themselves and they become easy prey to the devastating lightning breath attack of the Blue Dragonborn as their frozen parts shatter from their bodies.

Urania sees how desperate the situation is and decides to break from the back and step up more to the front where the Giants are.

Now she is in her winter state which allows for the manipulation of water. This is an ability only the High Sovereign may possess; access to all types of magic available to the Four Faerie Courts. Each time she switches she takes on the properties of the respective court.

She flies up and releases a magical torrent of water towards Surtr who she deems to be the leader of the Fire Giants, however he seems to be unaffected by this and simply shrugs off the attack, laughing at her face.

Surtr: Tiny woman thinks she can extinguish the Flames of Surtr, but none may do that! I am fire itself! Now perish beneath my scorching heat!

Now he leans forward and like Laufey, Ymir's son, did before when he faced Abaddon, he releases a magical beam of scorching magma straight at her, but she seems unharmed as well, as the magma slides off her body creating only vapours from her watery countenance.

Surtr is visibly taken aback by this and enraged as well; how could this tiny creature be unaffected by his fire?

Urania: Your flames may be strong, An Taine, but I have the grace of Muun on my side. *At that moment she begins to invoke an incantation offered to the same Muun*[78] *she mentioned, who is the Goddess of all the waters, for Faeries*

---

[78] Originally Min'u'un, Queen of the Water Titans who fought in and survived the Titanomachia.

worship all the deities connected to nature. However, this leaves her vulnerable, so she erects a sphere of water around herself to protect her and additional Faeries swarm in to protect their queen.

Surtr now comes in swinging with his flaming sword and the Undine create barriers of water in order to halt his attack, but he cuts right through them, and they perish in a cloud of steam and vapour.

A second line of Undine now invoke spells to cast more powerful barriers, yet these do not completely stop his next attack as well for he manages to destroy several of them before it comes to a halt.

One of his kin foolishly attempts to attack Urania from the rear, but a torrent of water juts out from the sphere in the shape of a sea serpent and bites down on his forearm, extinguishing his flame and causing the hand to crumble and fall off. This causes the Giant to scream out in both pain and fear.

As Urania was nearing the end of her incantation her waters were becoming more potent and the flames of the Giants would not avail them. Ymir and his Giants smash against the sphere, but it does not waver neither does the water freeze over.

Surtr angrily comes down upon it with an overhead attack, but his blade becomes wedged in the waters and only manages to create vapour and steam.

Some of the Angels offer the blessings of Shekinah as well and once the spell is finished, she casts 'Racht na'Faraig', 'Rage of the Sea'– and a row of magical circles with Muun's sigil rotating in the middle, appear on the left and right side of Urania.

Surtr looks wildly around him as do the other Giants when out of the circles come massive torrents of holy water, bright and shimmering, in the form of mighty sea serpents, they crash down on the Giants, and Surtr who was in the middle of it takes most of the brunt of the attack as these mighty waters sweep around them.

The force is so intense that even the ground units become affected and are swept by the current.

Umbriela who was at the moment locked in a double combat versus Amra and Dumah, gets her attention taken by what has happened and even the married couple glances downwards. It truly is a fierce sight.

The Frost and Mountain Giants come out mostly unscathed by the attack but the Fire Giants although standing have their fire extinguished, once bright and burning with hot magma now they had the countenance of a dried-up lava.

Surtr looks around at his brethren in bewilderment as they are desperately trying to reignite themselves and their weapons only to fail miserably.

Now this spell was a very ancient and powerful one hence the time it took to cast it; its sole purpose was just that, cleansing any impure flames that may plague the good people in Muun's service. Try as they may the Giants' flame was lost at least for now, and their infernal home of Surtrheim was many a miles away...

Brundig: Well, this this doesn't look good.

Ymir: Ymir agrees.

Surtr: No! Nooo! This is not how it was supposed to be! I was supposed to burn the world! I was supposed to make ashen snow fall from the sky! I will not end here!

Then the next thing he sees is a flash of bright light and then complete darkness as his head is pierced and shattered by the lance of Jomael, one of Umbriela's generals. The bloodied and exhausted Angel with his last strength had hurled his spear at the vulnerable Giant and slew him.

Surtr's lifeless body slumps on the sands with a mighty sound, creating almost an earthquake, falling upon ally and foe alike.

The few thousand remaining soldiers cheered in ecstasy, but Jomael's victory is short lived as Ymir in his rage, at the loss of a brethren, unleashes his ear splitting 'Glacial Bellow' and freezes him in place and then shatters him into pieces.

Ymir: Vig da alla[79]!

Angrily shouts Ymir as the Frost Giants stomp their feet and create patches of freezing fields.

The Fire Giants keep on fighting fearlessly as well despite having their flames extinguished but come to a swift end for now the soldiers can fight back and slay them. Ivaldi rushes at one of the Giants with his axe but his blade meets the sword of Tetsuzaemon.

Tetsu: Show me how a King of the West fights.

---

[79] Slay them all!

Ivaldi: Get out of me way, ye wretch!

And they begin to clash.

Urania still in her Winter Form now conjures up tempests of snow that pile upon the Giants and freeze them in place.

But Ymir will have none of it and he uses his own primordial ice magic to dispel the hail causing Urania to cringe from frustration and now she assumes her Summer Form.

Urania: Now to deal with you!

No sooner when she had finished saying that when a powerful dark, purplish beam comes crashing down from the sky, breaking the ground between them.

Urania lifts her arm in order to shield herself from the blowing sand as do the others as the sand is blown away all around them from the impact.

They all look upwards towards the source of the blast and see him; Argyros, the Black Dragon King flying above them and what appears to be a tiny shiny dot coming off him and descending towards the ground.

Tetsu: So, you have finally decided to show up yourself (grins).

Folduin: Abaddon!

The Elven King, all covered in blood and gore, his once beautiful golden hair now smeared crimson red, hisses through his teeth as he makes the nastiest look an Elf can make.

It was none other than the Etu Dhalsharru, the Dark Demon King himself, descending from the sky in a godly manner, black cloak waving about him and his armour shimmering dimly against the shine of the early dawn.

His troops begin to cheer the arrival of their king and master with loud shouting while his enemies were frozen in fear.

Argyros immediately sets his sights on the archery towers and proceeds to destroy them with great fury and anger.

Volleys are fired upon him, but he brushes them off like mosquito bites and rains death upon them instead.

Now Abaddon sets his feet upon the cold sand as all eyes are on him, watching his every move, waiting to see what he will do next.

He approaches Surtr's smashed head and looks around at the remains of what used to constitute his silly noggin; it was good, most of the pieces were still there.

He stretches out his hand and the pieces begin to reform and take shape and travel to his headless corpse.

Urania immediately recognises the workings of his necromancy and means to interrupt him, but Ymir and Brundig block her way with weapons at the ready.

Now Abaddon places his palm atop Surtr's head and recites an invocation.

Umbriela manages to fend off the couple for the time being and begins to fly towards Abaddon, desperate to stop him from doing what he was about to do. However, her flight comes to a halt when a group of Shadow Demons block her path. She struggles to fight them off and proceed but their numbers prevent her from doing so and she is held in place.

In her rage she releases a burst of holy energy, so potent and powerful that the whole sky lights up and the Demons surrounding her dissipate into nothingness, armour and all.

However, it is a moment too late as Abaddon had already finished his spell and says these final words.

Abaddon: Surtr, son of the primordial flames, by the power granted to me by Baalum Belum Shilatim Etimma Baalum Ilum Dhalatim Tiamatimma[80], I command you to rise and be reborn with the Girratam Tiamatim!

Now Surtr's eyes that once burned bright red flare up with an intense blue colour and once his veins that ran with scorching magma fill up with blue, infernal flames. The reborn Giant slams with his left hand and straightens up, then he gets on his feet and as he does, he picks up Oeskbreidur and enflames the blade with the same fire.

Abaddon: From now on you will be known as Surtr Beldurson, Surtr of the Blue Flame.

With a loud shriek, he announces his presence and as he does his whole body now becomes enflamed with the Isatu Tiamatuu and emanates a wave of scorching heat.

---

[80] Baal Lord of Shadow and Darkness, Baal God of Demons, and the Abyss – in O.D

Abaddon: No water may dowse you; no ice may freeze you and no ground may extinguish you, go and burn, burn them all.

Umbriela: Abaddon!

He looks up at her and smirks a sinister smirk beneath his hood.

CAPITVLVM XXVI

IGNIS ET SANGVIS[xxii]

The newly reborn Giant swings down his sword now burning bright with the blue flames of the Abyss and unleashes a torrent of flaming tongues throughout the area turning those around him in instant charcoal.

Seeing the searing might of the fire, Urania shoots a torrent of water in an attempt to douse it, but it does not work just like Abaddon had said.

The flames stretch and soon they reach the magical units in the back, setting Mages, Wizards and Light-Bearers alike ablaze.

Now the air is filled with the horrible sensation of burning flesh and charred robes, mixed with the awful reek of melted metal.

Abaddon chuckles beneath his hood as Umbriela, teeming with rage, rushes at him, her trusty sword, Nahad'hodesh, the 'Wrath of the Heaven', in hand.

With no one in her path to stop her she immediately finds herself face to face with the Demon King, the archenemy of the free folk, who has blocked her attack with his own Absharu, 'The One Who Destroys'.

Abaddon: You're looking lovely as ever, Angel Queen.
Umbriela: Save your snarky remarks, Demon!

She backs away and comes at him with another swing which he also parries.

Abaddon: I guess there is no need for words then.
Umbriela: None at all.

Seeing this, Dumah intends to intervene and land a hand, but Amra grabs him by the shoulder and holds him back.

Amra: Do not interfere, husband, he has got this.

Dumah: If you say so.

Amra: We have more pressing matters, like cleaning up the rest of this filth.

Dumah: Better get it done then, we do not wish for our noses to be clogged any longer than they should.

Amra: Those remarks make me glad I married you.

Dumah: Aw, that warms my heart.

As they exchange words, a couple of Angels rush at them but are quickly despatched. Below, the raging Giant continues to wreak havoc and at this point the remainder of Abaddon's armies simply sit back and let him do his thing.

A couple of the Wizards that remain use their psychokinetic powers in order to contain the raging fire and they manage to do so in spheres of telekinesis. The Avatars that draw their powers from the Goddess of Water, call upon her divine waters to cleanse it but the fire is so strong, as if it came from the Abyss itself and they only manage to subdue it to a small degree.

While all this is happening Ymir and his Frost Giants, coupled with their brethren from the mountains deal the final blow to the rear guard of Werewolves, with ice and enchantments.

Mighty as they are, the warriors of Volkodakia cannot hope to contend with these Titans of mass destruction.

What is left of the allied forces, seeing these unstoppable forces of nature at hand begin to lose hope and their hearts waver within their chests. Some of the Knights even lay down their arms and beat a hasty retreat.

One by one, soldiers from the other races follow their example as well and turn to flee for dear life.

Both Angel and Demon take their scuffle to a halt as they observe what is happening amongst the ranks.

Umbriela: No! Come back! Fight! Fight for your lives!

Ivaldi: Fight, ye cowards! Form ranks!

Folduin looks around him as well as even his own troops run away from the battlefield.

He yells at them in Elven to stand their ground and fight, but his words are muffled beneath the shouts of his generals who keep yelling 'Vetalite! Vetalite! Peradite!'– 'Retreat! Retreat! Fall back!'

Abaddon: Well, would you look at that, it would seem that your armies are finally falling apart, look at them, desperately fleeing for life, frightened, lost, defeated.

Umbriela: Curse you, Abaddon! And curse your infernal machinations!

Abaddon: You can curse me all you want but it won't change the fact that you've lost this war.

Umbriela: At least I will find solace knowing that you are dead!

Abaddon: Stop it, jokes don't suit you.

She angrily fires a magical blast at him, but he casts 'Shield of Reflection' and so the blast simply bends and swivels around him, hitting the ground instead and exploding.

Now her sword flares up with immense energy and she unleashes a wide surge of searing holy light in his direction, but a thick patch of darkness forms behind Abaddon and begins to engulf the light, eating away at it, and in a brief moment it is completely snuffed out.

Or so it seems, but then small cracks begin to appear from inside the cluster of darkness as rays of light protrude from within and finally the light bursts forth forcing Abaddon to move to a safer distance.

Umbriela continues her assault by creating swords of holy energy as she casts 'Storm of Swords' and hurls them at Abaddon in great succession.

He immediately reacts by casting 'Shadow Form' turning his body into a mass of shadows and so the swords whiz through him.

Now it is his turn, as he raises his hand and Umbriela is surrounded by magic circles on all sides. This spell is called 'Abyssal Destructive Formation' and it sets off the circles, creating a chain of dark powered explosions that flash with a dark, purplish colour.

Once the explosions die out Umbriela emerges with small bloody cuts as she has casted 'Quick Heal' to rapidly heal the wounds on her body.

Meanwhile as Ymir sees the remainder of the armies fleeing, he raises his hand and massive walls of ice emerge from the sand blocking their path.

In an act of desperation, Mahazael, the Archangel of the Ophanim, asks of the troops around him to buy him some time as he attempts a ritual, a spell of the highest level and only available to him and the Queen herself.

Now this spell requires a ridiculous amount of mana to perform and time, there is a small chance of success as well, which is why he had not cast it before. But this time the outcome outweighed the risk.

And so, a few Elves and Humans form a protective circle around him as hordes of Abaddon's armies move into action once more and come down upon them.

Out of the swarming Undead Orcs, Dragonborn, Oni and Subterrans, emerges Alabaster with his battered and caved in armour.

With his mighty mace he makes his way through the ranks of the soldiers of Camelot and towards Mahazael in an attempt to thwart his ceremony.

But it is too late as the Angel finishes his ceremony and the spell is cast.

Now this spell is called 'Trumpet of the Seventh Heaven' and is a summoning spell that beckons a Heavenly Guardian, a Celestial from the Heavenly Halls of Shekinah.

A moment of anticipation happens and it would seem that the Goddess of the Light has heeded the call of her followers, as the clouds part and the sky is torn asunder by a massive, illuminating ray of light, accompanied by the sound of mighty trumpets and great tremor.

All present turn their eyes towards this phenomenon as from the Celestial plane, descends an Angel of the Yazata[81] *order, a Celestial of massive proportions, twice the size of Surtr, dressed in a gleaming, golden, heavenly armour, flaming sword of golden, luminescent fire, and shield in hand, and a wingspan of a thousand eagles'.*

'It worked,' mutters Mahazael before he collapses on the ground from exhaustion.

Abaddon: Oh dear…that does not look good.

And he was right, as the Yazata swipes with his mighty sword and the ice walls come crumbling down like a house of cards.

He swings his sword in arc once more and this time it is Abaddon's troops that are burned by the holy flames.

---

[81] Guardian Celestial.

The Dragonkin and Shadow Demons that are up in the sky are forced to retreat as they cannot bear the light that is emanated from the Angel.

The soldiers that were stopped by the walls from escaping now turn and face their foes once more with a newfound courage.

Alabaster, who was in the near vicinity of the call can feel his armour being damaged just by being in the presence of this entity and turns to retreat.

But the Yazata, sensing his greater mana signature comes down with its flaming sword and pierces him whole, pinning him on the sand.

Halnadu falls from his hands as for the first time in his life fear comes over him as he is overtaken by a sense of imminent death. He wildly looks around, desperate to meet the look of his master but is unable to do so in the midst of all the fighting that is going on around him, as the holy flames begin to consume him and drag him to his demise. But instead of screaming in agony and pain he accepts his fate calmly and perishes with these final words.

Alabaster: Forgive me, Lord Abaddon, I was not able to serve you to the end.

At that point the flames completely consume his body leaving not even a trace behind, cleansing his soul as well; resurrection for this loyal, behemoth of a Demon was possible no longer.

Abaddon senses the passing of his dear general and feels a slight prickle in his heart.

In this moment of absentmindedness, he leaves himself open for an attack from Umbriela, but he quickly recovers and deflects it.

Albunalich: That giant winged creature, how do we stop it? It is twice the Giants' size.

Dagon: Leave that one to me, I shall handle it.

As the Celestial Angel walks upon the sands, the forces of darkness are compelled to walk away from him as the holy light is something they cannot handle, which creates a moment of counterattack for the allies.

Abaddon notices this and 'blinks' away to a safe distance then flies up in the air. Before Dagon has a chance to act out his plan, Abaddon raises both of his hands and on the ground appears a big magic circle with the Tiamat Star in the middle; he performs a dark summoning spell and the circle glows, and as it does the ground beneath it crumbles and out emerges a pillar of blue fire, reaching almost to the sky, but the pillar is merely an interlude as what really comes out is a Demon from the Abyss itself, an Ifrit, a malevolent Abyssal of the highest level, of the same proportions as the Yazata, wroth in the Flames of Tiamat, with wings of fire, large curly horns, flaming hair that waves around, equipped in an onyx, infernal armour, wielding a sword of pure flame.

As soon as these two entities lay eyes upon each other a clash of titans, in the literal sense of the word, begins.

With the Celestial's attention now distracted by the Ifrit, Abaddon's troops are free to move again unimpeded.

Amongst them are his other Generals; Malgaras, Andrakos and Carmox, who although weary and bruised as well are still alive and kicking.

Leading the final charge, with the Giants at their backs they completely overwhelm what is left of the armies and wipe them out.

By this time, it is already late in the morning as the sun is beginning to shine brighter, now clearly revealing the heaps of bodies from both sides, the bloodshed, piles of guts and entrails, broken weapons and armour, laying there, dotting the landscape of the Desert Sea.

The rest of the army that managed to flee before, now nearing the border of Camelot was forced to a stop by a loud rumbling sound.

Dwarf: Wait! Do you hear that?

Elf: Hear what?

Dwarf: Horses…

Vampire: I can hear the rumbling sound quite clearly but horses? That's impossible, all of our cavalry was present at the battle!

Dwarf: I know the sound of hooves when I hear it, laddie, and those are definitively horses!

Man: Look! Something black approaches from the horizon!

Dwarf: What do your eyes see, master Elf?

Elf: My eyes see only – kuolor …

Vampire: Death…

Now they can hear the sound of neighing horses, huffing angrily and releasing clouds of steam from their nostrils, they can see their burning red eyes and the stomping of their hooves as they stride on the sand.

They clench their weapons in preparation, with trembling hands and trepidation as they look upon the headless figures that are atop these horses, wielding aloft spine shaped scythes.

Cold sweat drips from their foreheads as they face these creatures of whom they only heard stories, only few amongst them, the eldest ones have actually seen them with their own eyes.

Dwarf: For death and glory!

Yells out the dwarf in attempt to lift their spirits as he charges off, right before Cain Ech'Cenad, the King of the Dullahan, who was at the helm of the charge, swoops in and separates his head from his shoulders.

The rest of the Dullahan soon follow behind him and break upon the band of deserters, moving them down like a farmer mows his crops, for no enchantment or armour could withstand the magic of the Headless Horsemen.

Behind them still, followed the rest of Dhalsarria's armies along with the Spriggan. King Hyberion had teleported them there midway like they had agreed upon. Now the few hundred unlucky souls that had broken off from the main army were laid to waste by the charging Dullahan and the Dhalatum[82] *led by Mordred.*

Not so far away from them it was time for the final battle of this bloody war.

Abaddon was facing off Umbriela who was now joined by the remainder of the rulers that were Folduin, Cyril and Urania.

Ivaldi had fallen in his battle against Tetsuzaemon. The Oni Shogun had managed to graze his cheek with Muramasa and strike him with the jibaku curse which rendered him completely immobile and then deal the final blow with the blade through his eye socket.

What was left of Abaddon's forces now were watching this intense clash of crowns, so to say, as the other clash was going on in the background.

Jamil: Don't you think you should lend him a hand?

Morgana: No, he's got this, I'd only get in the way.

Jamil: Maybe you put too much faith in his abilities?

Morgana: Look at them, his foes are bruised and weary, at the very limit of their mana supplies, trust me, this will be a short battle.

Jamil: I will trust you then.

---

[82] Plural of Dhalku – Demons.

Jamil says with a weary heart because as it seemed like his entire army was wiped out; he could only spot a few Hathasians here and there mixed in the mishmash of creatures.

Abaddon: This brings back memories, doesn't it, not very fond ones I must say but memories, nonetheless.

The rest do not say anything only stare intently at him.

Abaddon: How very cold of you, not even saying hello.

Still nothing from the rest.
Cyril cracks his neck left and right.

Abaddon: The last standing of your warring kin, how tragic, but don't despair, you can find solace in the fact that soon even your civilians will follow you in the halls of your ancestors.

This is the final straw for Cyril and with a loud howl, he leaps at Abaddon, who vanishes from the spot and reappears next to him, slashing with his sword but Cyril grabs the blade and stops the attack.

He comes swiping down with his massive claws, but Abaddon repels him by blowing him away with a surge of dark energy.

Umbriela immediately casts 'Mass Cure Wounds' and heals up Cyril and the rest.

With new vigour, Folduin joins the fray as well with his own longsword, lit up with the fire of Solarion.

They begin to fence and now Urania who casts 'Nature's Blessing' on herself to restore some of her mana by drawing in from the nature, while still in her Summer Stance, hurls a fire ball at Abaddon.

However, he dispels the fireball and manages to kick away Folduin.

Cyril jumps in and they both attack him at the same time, but he succeeds in managing them both.

Now Urania shifts to her Autumn Stance, gaining a windy like complexion. This time she casts 'Autumn's Lament', which causes yellow leaves to fall upon the target. Whatever the leaves touch, that place begins to rot and decay for Autumn is the season of passing.

Upon seeing the leaves, the two Kings step back from Abaddon who takes the brunt of the spell.

Some of his armour begins to form rust but at a very slow rate and he casts 'Cloak of Darkness' on himself which coats him with a very thick layer of dark mana that reduces the effects of a spell.

Nonetheless he sees himself at a disadvantage and is ready to activate one of Absharu's stances.

Abaddon: Absharu: Etum Sebu: Haddanu![83]

He incants in a quick succession and the inscriptions on the blade begin to shift and change and now the sword glows with a sickly green aura.

The rulers know what this means as they have seen it before. This ability of Absharu allows Abaddon to turn the tides on his opponents when he is facing with a disadvantage, as it boosts his magical and physical prowess significantly.

Cyril pounces at him and while he is in mid-air Umbriela casts 'Holy Strength' on him which doubles his physical power.

Nevertheless, Abaddon is able to beat him away with his hand and he falls on the ground.

Folduin comes with an overhead swing only to find his blade stopped with a bare hand and Abaddon unhurt by the Solar flames. He pries the sword from his hand and jams it in his throat with such ferocity that it cleaves his head straight from his body.

The seemingly lifeless body falls on the ground, but something feels off; Folduin's body begins to shift and waver, and Abaddon immediately recognises the spell, it is 'Fata Morgana'.

Folduin, who was not a stranger of the arcane ways, being able to cast spells in the sphere of his affinity, was clearly behind this mirage.

This immediately puts Abaddon on guard allowing him to react accordingly as the real Folduin was coming at him with a stabbing motion from his rear, so he ends up being side stepped.

As he whiffs the attack, Abaddon quickly casts 'Soul Sap' which makes his hand ethereal, and he reaches inside Folduin's body and begins to extract his

---

[83] Seventh stance: Envy.

very soul but manages to only grasp his attacking hand before Umbriela casts 'Friendly Blink' on Folduin which teleports him by her side.

He ends up being saved, however his right arm is now rendered completely unusable and there existed no healing spell in this world that was able to restore a piece of a lost soul. His arm now goes limp and loses its colour.

Folduin: Agh! He got me…he got me good; I am no longer fit to assist you. If only I was ambidextrous…

Umbriela: It's alright, you did well, leave the rest to us.

Folduin: No, I was careless and now it has cost me my arm.

Cyril: Isn't there something you can do? A spell? Anything?

Abaddon: Unfortunately, once a piece of a soul, or entire soul for that matter, is lost, there is no getting it back, even by means of necromancy.

Cyril: You will pay for this!

Abaddon: I highly doubt that.

He blinks next to Cyril and slashes with his sword, however Cyril, using his heightened Werewolf senses dodges out of the way, finds his footing and immediately leaps off in a counterattack.

Now it is up to Umbriela to join in the close quarter fight, and so they both flank him on each side, but Abaddon once again uses 'Shadow Form' to become intangible, alas Umbriela manages to stop herself in the last minute and avoids colliding with Cyril.

Cyril however whizzes through Abaddon but finds purchase on the ground and with swift agility turns to face him, slashing with his claws.

Urania now in her Spring State, again quickly casts 'Bestial Frenzy' on Cyril to empower him further. He also strengthens his claws with lunar magic and now they glow with a cold, pale light.

Cyril's claws find their mark, but he only manages to scrape his armour. However, as he is in frenzied state he keeps clawing at Abaddon.

Umbriela uses this opportunity to throw at Abaddon a spiritual spear, enhancing it with her magic to make it bigger,

The spear travels to Abaddon but he, still under the effect of Envy, extends Absharu at the direction of the spear, mutters under his breath and activates the Avarice stance of the blade and now with its cyan blue aura it absorbs the spear much to the Queens' surprise.

Umbriela: Cyril, get out of the way!

By her warning, Cyril manages to react and retreat as Abaddon extends his other hand towards him and shoots the spear at him now with a dark attribute, however the weapon is faster and finds its mark through Cyril's chest. His leather armour and thick hide might have availed him had it not been fired at him through the effects of Avarice. The Werewolf King falls on the ground in a pool of his own blood.

Folduin: Cyril!

Urania: Heal him!

But before Umbriela has a chance to react, Abaddon casts 'Iron Maiden' on the fallen Cyril.

Now from the ground beneath him appears a coffin made of dark matter with spikes on the inside and a grotesque looking female head on the top, and it coils around him. Umbriela tries to dispel it, but Abaddon negates her spell. After a few moments the coffin snaps shut, and it drips with thick, blackish blood.

Abaddon: Two down, two to go.

Urania: Bastard! You bastard!

Abaddon: Too bad this will not be a repeat from one hundred years ago, my darlings.

Folduin: It is up to you two now, be careful.

Urania: You don't have to tell me that.

Umbriela winces.

Urania: Briela, can you buy me some time?

Umbriela: I told you not to call me that in public!

Urania: Now is not the time for that, can you or can you not buy me some time!

Umbriela: How much do you need?

Urania: As much as I need!

Umbriela: Tsk, fine, but see that it does not take long, I am not doing so well myself.

Urania: I know but I'm counting on you!

Abaddon: (This might prove troublesome).

Right as he finishes, he finds Umbriela right at his face with her Nahad'hodesh.

Urania: (begins chanting) God of Fire, God of Wind, Goddess of Water and Goddess of Earth, Gods of Nature by your name I call upon you; Pyras, Boreas, Muun, Eire, lend me your aid…

Meanwhile, as the clash between the Angel and the Ifrit is still ongoing in the background, sending tremors and shockwaves throughout the area, Surtr sees that the Ifrit is having trouble dealing the final blow and decides to land a hand.

Ifrit: Stay out of my way! (He yells at him in Abyssal).

Surtr: I have no idea what you just said but I wish to help.

The Ifrit spits on the side and continues to do its battle.

Now Surtr is up to the waist of this entity but stands his ground regardless and without fear swings his Oeskbreidur at the Celestial.

The Yazata blocks with its sword and with its shield blocks the Ifrit's attack.

Seeing itself surrounded, it lets out a deafening shriek with the sound of celestial trumpets and temporarily incapacitates both fire creatures. This allows it to bash the Ifrit away with its shield and push Surtr away.

Now Ymir, not wanting to be outdone by his flaming counterpart joins as well and freezes the sand bellow the Yazata by slamming his club down, in an attempt to sweep him off its feet. However, the flame of the sword is so intense that it melts the ice away.

This slight moment allows Surtr to swing his sword and land a hit on the Yazata's arm, but he only manages to indent it and anger the creature.

It swings towards Surtr but the latter blocks with his sword, although slightly giving in under the pressure. The Yazata strains and Surtr can feel his sword cracking and breaking.

With one final strain the Yazata cleaves his blade in half along with Surtr's arm clean from the shoulder.

Before it can deal the final blow Argyros shoots a breath attack from his position grabbing its attention.

As it is distracted, now Surtr grabs Oeskbreidur from his severed hand and slashes at the tendril right behind the Angel's kneecap. An inferior creature he may be, but the blade is still wrought in the flame of the infernal plane and a gush of bright liquid spurts forth from the tendril. However, that is not enough to bring it down and, in its anger, he smacks Surtr with the pommel of its sword and sends him flying, yes flying across the air a few metres away and he falls flat on his back with a big thud.

Now as it faces towards the Ifrit in its rage it fails to see the Abyssal's flaming blade as it comes towards it and pierces it through his face.

The Yazata falls screaming on his knees and perishes in a flash of light.

A loud cheer fills the air as the troops celebrate the Ifrit's victory and Umbriela is left with sorrow at the loss of her Celestial kindred.

The Ifrit walks up towards Surtr and gives him a hand, the Giant takes it and finds himself on his feet.

Ifrit: Thank you.

Says the Ifrit in Abyssal and vanishes in the same flaming pillar as he appeared.

Now as Abaddon was engaged in a sword combat with Umbriela, Dagon in his stead attempts to disrupt Urania's ritual but the elemental forces that surround her at this moment prove troublesome.

Morgana tries to pitch in as well with her magic but that does no good either.

Dagon: It is no use; she is well protected.

Morgana: Whatever she is doing, it does not look well! We must stop her!

As they clash, in a spare moment, Abaddon activates the sixth stance of Absharu – Lust. This ability gives Abaddon advantage when he is facing female opponents. And so, he blocks one of her swings and without making any other movement repels Umbriela with a surge of violent energy, sending her flying through the air.

Now his attention is turned towards Urania who seems to be at the end of her invocation. But Abaddon does not seem nervous nor in a rush, in fact he smirks beneath his hood at this moment, as he is about to face whatever the Faery Queen has to throw at him.

Umbriela fires a magical blast of holy energy at him, but he cleaves it in half with Absharu, that is now glowing with a pink aura. The blast separates and explodes into two separate sides.

Urania: (This will completely drain me of my mana, but I don't care! Even if it costs me my life, Abaddon must be stopped!).

Umbriela, nearing her last drops of mana as well, casts a high-level spell of entrapment 'The Cage of Hadagh', which as the name suggests, entraps the opponent in a cage of dense, unbreakable energy. But much to their surprise, Abaddon yet again does not seem affected, in fact he allows himself to get caught.

Umbriela: (Something doesn't feel right about him…what is this feeling?).

Right before she is about to cast the spell, in the distance emerge Mordred and his armies.

He sees his father in a predicament and raises his voice towards him.

Mordred: Father!

Abaddon: Stay where you are!

Both their voices echo throughout.

Urania: Demon! Be gone from this world! Fearg na Deithe!

And thus, she casts the most high-level offensive spell at her disposal: 'Ire of the Gods'. Now four magic circles appear around Abaddon: red, blue, green, and silver, each bearing the sigils of the four gods in the centre. They spin around, bleeding into each other and congealing, in the end unleashing a tempest of sheer elemental energy which beats down upon the entrapped Abaddon with great fury. There is not a clear shape of these forces as it is pure unadulterated elemental magic, raging in that one spot.

Demiurgos: Abaddon!

His father yells out in desperation towards his only son, fearing deeply for his life. However, Mordred, Morgana, Jamil and the rest remain calm knowing and anticipating what is to come.

Mordred: Do not worry, grandfather, he will be just fine.
Morgana: Any time now…

The violent storm begins to simmer down and the two Queens, especially Urania intent to see Abaddon's mangled corpse, and truly so any other person would be surely dead from such a spell but not this one.
From the eye of the storm comes out a muffled:

Abaddon: Absharu Gamru Rebu: Lamassu Tiamatuu[84].

A flash of light, black, with flashes of purple lightning rips through the polychromous elemental tempest and disperses it.
Out of the chaos emerges Abaddon looking completely different: two pairs of jet-black wings protrude from his back, his upper torso was now clad in shining onyx armour similar to that of the Ifrit, his lower half covered in a black, battle skirt that goes down to his feet, his crown now forming a half halo around his head from the back and Absharu itself oozing with black, infernal energy.
Everyone looks wide eyed at this phenomenon; some from excitement, some from awe and some – from fear…

---

[84] Angel of the Abyss.

EPILOGVS

QVID VLTRAM IACIT[xxiii]

Urania: What magic is this? So foul…so sinister!

Umbriela: It's not like any magic from this world.

Folduin: Because it is not, it comes straight from the Abyss itself.

Abaddon: You're right, this power was granted to me by Lord Baal himself, and you should feel honoured to have a taste of it first-hand.

Umbriela: Baal himself you say? Curses, how are we to face such a thing?

Urania: Perhaps if we too called for our deities?

Umbriela: There is no time for that!

Abaddon: The time for conversation is over, this ends now.

He extends his hand towards Folduin and he immediately begins to contort in pain, as he feels his insides burning and churning. Wounds open from all over his body and blue flames flicker from within.

Umbriela: Stop this now!

She rushes at him with her sword, but he waves with his wings creating a powerful gust and blows her away with sheer magical pressure.

Urania casts 'Healing Shell' on Folduin which encases him in a water shell with healing properties, but the flames are just too strong.

Now Abaddon twists his hand and clenches his fingers into a fist after which Folduin begins to burn even brighter and finally implodes in a burst of fire, burned pieces from his entrails falling on to the ground.

Urania: No! Malacht or[85]!

In her fit of rage, she summons four elemental guardians and Umbriela with her magic encases them in celestial armour and they attack Abaddon at once.

However, before they can even connect, he releases a surge of dark energy, and they dissipate into nothingness.

With her last drop of mana, Urania summons an Oread from the Wind Plane to battle Abaddon, but the Wind Spirit does not stand a chance as it is killed with a single swipe of Abaddon's sword. The blade unleashes a surge of a dark wave and cleaves it in half diagonally.

He now turns to Umbriela, who for a moment seems fine but then she begins to choke up, grasping her throat as she struggles for air.

What Abaddon was doing to her was not robbing her of her breathing apparatus but something viler and more sinister; with his new dark and more potent powers he was corrupting Umbriela's celestial essence, the very core of her being, turning it into a dark and evil matter. Soon, black bile begins to ooze first from her mouth, then her nose and ears and finally from her eyes. The black gooey matter cascades down her face, seeping into her celestial armour and garments, dirtying, and defiling her. Now, not just from there but all pores on her body begin to excrete it, turning the once fair Angelic Queen into a disgusting mess.

Urania: Fiend! If you are going to kill her, do it quick! Don't make her suffer!
Abaddon: No.

Grief-stricken, she entangles Umbriela's sword by the hilt with her vines and swings it towards Abaddon, who grabs the blade with his hand and shatters it with no effort whatsoever.

As Umbriela's contamination spreads even further, her wings begin to turn into the same substance and melt away into a pile of a dark, necrotic matter. With her last grace corrupted, she falls lifelessly on the sand.

---

85 Curse you!

Urania: (tears in her eyes) O Doythe! Craelach Doythe! Er throyg seyne in? Muan, Gayoth…ayinne! Saheil in! Ney in fleyngt! Saheil m[86] – (speaking in an ancient form of Faerian).

Before she can finish that word, Abaddon swings Absharu towards her and severs her body in half at the waist with the air pressure itself. She falls on the ground, sundered, entrails and blood spilling on the sand. With sad watery eyes, she looks up at the morning sky and before death takes her, she utters these final words.

Urania: Er…throyg…seyne…

And light fades from her silver eyes, turning dull grey.

Now, Abaddon sends forth a surge of pure dark energy at her and obliterates her completely, leaving not even a trace behind.

With that, his power dissipates, and he returns to his normal visage. He does look normal, but he finds himself strangely over exhausted; perhaps his newfound powers did not come so cheap?

Much rejoicing ensues with the official end of the war, cheers of all sounds, loud and quiet; deep and low fill out the entirety of the area.

'Abaddon! Abaddon!' booms in the air.

Jamil: My lord…that was…I have no words…

Morgana: We did it, my love, we won.

Grabs her by the waist, pulls her in and kisses her.

Mordred and his host approach closer now that the bout is over.

Mordred: Father, congratulations, you did it.

Abaddon: I see you succeeded as well; I knew I could count on you.

Mordred: Of course, I would never fail you.

Morgana: Well done, my son.

He cracks a gentle smile at her.

'My king,' both Harthan and Jamaz say in unison and kneel before him and as they do, the rest of the Demonic host follows suit.

---

[86] Oh Gods! Cruel Gods! Have you forsaken us! Muun! Boreas! … Anyone! Save us! Do not let us suffer! Help m-

Jamaz: You and your progeny delivered us from century of suffering and humiliation, we will work ten times as harder to repay you.

Abaddon: Arise, my fellow Dhalatu, your fealty up to now is more than enough, I wouldn't dream of demanding more than you have already given me. What I did was what any just and noble ruler would do for his people, and I couldn't possibly ask for any sort of repayment, only that you serve me as you have before.

Harthan: Your grace is truly boundless, oh King!

He embraces them both in a brotherly embrace and they return the hug.

Out of the crowd, his father, Demiurgos, emerges with wavering eyes full of tears of joy.

Demiurgos: My son…

Abaddon: Father…

And they fall upon each other in the tightest embrace, tears streaming from both their faces.

Demiurgos: My sweet boy… I missed you so much…

Abaddon: You too…

Mordred does his best not to shed tears but try as he may, a few manage to escape his eye sockets.

Even Morgana's usually cold demeanour, softens in the presence of this touching scene. Seeing how both, father and son, are so close, brings her to tears as well for this is the image of familial love, she never used to have, nor will she ever have.

Dagon: Demiurgos…

He approaches with spread arms and his mask down. Demiurgos immediately embraces his own father as well.

Abaddon: Father, how is mother?

Demiurgos: Alive and well…as far as she can be considering…

Abaddon: …

Demiurgos: She is waiting for us at the castle.

Abaddon: I can't wait to see her.

Demiurgos: She as well (pats his shoulder and notices Morgana as he does). Is this the bride to be?

Abaddon: Indeed, come say hello Morgana.

Morgana steps up closer and introduces herself.

Demiurgos: (nods) We will talk more at a more suitable location, my dear.

Morgana: I would like that (courteously bows and smiles).

Demiurgos returns the bow.

Hyberion: Well, it looks like we were hardly needed, I'm afraid.

The Spriggan King steps up deeming it to be the right situation for he did not want to squander the touching family reunion.

Cain straddles along on his horse beside him.

Abaddon: Hyberion and Cain Ech'Cenad themselves, I am honoured to be in your presence.

Cain: The honour is all ours, young king, for thou hast succeeded where we all have failed.

Abaddon: None of this would have been made possible without the aid of my trusted allies (waves his hand towards the remaining leaders) and the guidance of our Lord Baal. So, it would be unfair of me to take all the credit for myself.

Cain: Of that I have no doubt, but ultimately it was thee who brought all these people together under one banner, and that credit is thine alone.

Abaddon: Of that you are correct (slightly chuckles). I am interested though, how did you two come to be banished?

Hyberion: Well, you see, after Magdabulgu was defeated, we fled far up north, into Orc territory. We found a cave in this mountain range where we stayed hidden for a while, but unfortunately it was guarded by an Oread. It was a tough opponent to beat alas we managed to subjugate him, and I imprisoned him into a prison of manalith. I spend some time researching how to control it, however eventually we were found out before I could finish. We fought but couldn't resist Venera's forces much longer and the result was as you know it.

Abaddon: So, you are the one who imprisoned it? It all makes sense now.

Cain: You know of this spirit?

Abaddon: Yes, one of my turtati[87] faced it into battle, it was being controlled by the Goblins who came to occupy the mountains, and now he is restored to his former position.

Hyberion: Goblins? Now that is hilarious (slightly chuckles), in any case thine turtanu is lucky to have survived.

Abaddon: Not so lucky now…

Hyberion: Sorry to hear that…it's difficult when you lose good men…

Abaddon: Even more so for the second time…

Suddenly, a violent wind begins to blow and raise the desert sand in the air.

Hyberion: What is this? An attack?

Mordred: Look! Over there!

And at the place he points, a spark of blue flame appears and spirals upwards, at last taking the shape of a person.

Before them now stood the flaming, incorporeal form of the one Demon whom only few knew personally, the Demon whose face adorned the Dhalsarrian national banner, the First Demon King Magdabolg. He was wearing a cuirass of obsidian steel, vambraces and greaves, strapped with leather belts, a purple waist cloth was hanging up to his knees, and a long cape, reaching up to his heels.

Demiurgos: Your highness (mutters silently and gives a courtly bow).

Magdabolg: Greetings, fellow Dhalatum and others alike, I assume by now ye all know who I am.

The Demon speaks in a courtly but jovial manner.

Hyberion: Ahum Rabi[88], how long has it been.

Magdabolg: Ah you two, so glad to see ye still alive and well, which is far from what I can say for myself (laughs).

Cain: I don't know what you are talking about thou seemest very much alive to me (laughs).

General laughter ensues.

Magdabolg: Ahatunum, Ilutnum[89] (turns to Jamaz, who gives him a nod) I would love to stay and chat and reminiscence of the old days but I'm afraid that

[87] Masculine plural of 'general'.

[88] Old Friend.

[89] My friends, my family.

I run on borrowed time. Baalu Belum was gracious enough to allow me brief audience with ye so I cannot linger at mine leisure.

Abaddon: Let's not keep you then, speak your mind, great king.

Magdabulgu: Indeed, mine deeds may be great but thine go even beyond, Abaddonu Seher[90]. I have watched thine performance from the world beyond and you never ceased to amaze me. Like my dear friend said, thou hast succeeded where all of us have failed. Thou hast united all these races together and defeated the joined forces of Avalon once and for all, and now this continent is thine to rule.

As thine predecessor, I could not be prouder. Thine father may have not wished it during his ruling days, but I am so pleased to see that my dream of subjugating the inferior peoples of this land hath lived on and finally hath been fulfilled through thee. I am also pleased to see the homage thou hast paid me by leaving mine visage on the banner but mine rule, mine time, hath long ended. Now it is thine time, thine rule, it is the Adanu Abaddonuu La Magdabulguu[91].

With that, he burns of the image of his face off one of the banners and it becomes replaced with the face of Abaddon, much to the amazement of the others.

Magdabolg: Yours is much worthier to grace our banner.

Abaddon: Truly, you honour me.

Magdabolg: Nay, you honour me, you honour all of us and our Lord.

He salutes him.

Magdabolg: Guz Baltu Baalum! Guz Baltu Dhalsharri! Guz Baltu Sharrum! Guz Baltu Abaddonu!

The rest also chant the same words in unison.

Magdabolg: May thine rule last forever more, mine descendant. Before I go, I will leave thee with a piece of warning, beware those long thought dead, they still haunt this world. Farewell.

And with that he disappears with a flash.

Mordred: Even those beyond the grave come to congratulate your success, you truly are the greatest.

Abaddon: I guess I truly am (cracks a smile).

---

[90] Young Abaddon.

[91] The age of Abaddon not Magdabolg.

Mordred: Though, what do you suppose he meant with those words? It seemed rather ominous.

Abaddon: I'm not quite sure … (I wonder …).

As he thinks that he shares a meaningful look with his father and grandfather.

Morgana: Might telling us what got you so silent?

Abaddon: Nothing important, no use pondering on that for now. Come, everyone! Let us count our dead.

As this is going on, Abaddon spots the empty, charred, armour of Alabaster, with a big gaping hole in his back.

Abaddon: Sittu Salamu, old friend…

Mordred: Can you not revive him again?

Abaddon: No, I'm afraid not, his soul had been completely destroyed.

Mordred: Sittu Salamu, you were a brave warrior.

Abaddon: Kakama.

Mordred: Kakama.

They say the equivalent of 'rest in peace' and 'amen' as they pay their respects.

Abaddon: So many have fallen, but we honoured their deaths with victory.

Mordred: Father are you feeling alright?

Abaddon: I'm fine why do you ask?

Mordred: You seem a bit off.

Abaddon: It's just your imagination, there's nothing wrong with me.

Mordred: If you say so.

Abaddon: I say so, now move along.

Among the dead they spot the corpses of both Dragons, father, and son, lying next to each other.

Abaddon: (sighs heavily) (I'm sorry little ones, but at least you have your mother…) (closes Fulguros' eyes).

After all that they reconvene and state their findings.

Dumah: That's more than half of our entire troops…replenishing the armies will take time.

Abaddon: No matter, we can spare that.

Brundig: What happens now Tonungur? There is too many to burry.

Abaddon: I will take care of that; the bodies will be transported to their respective kingdoms and be buried as heroes.

Mordred: You needn't overexert yourself father.

Abaddon: Nonsense, it is my duty as their king to see to it.

Morgana: I will lend a hand as well my dear.

Hyberion: As will I, I have done my fair share of dabbling with necromancy.

Abaddon: I appreciate it.

Hyberion: It's the least I can do for arriving so late.

Brundig: And what of us? You said we can be free after this.

Abaddon: And you are, I liberate you from your service, you may return to your homestead, but there is still work to be done should you decide to stay.

Brundig: More work?

Abaddon: Their armies may have fallen but their kingdoms still stand, as long as that remains, true and complete victory cannot be obtained.

Brundig: I understand, but these people here were soldiers, we will not partake in the slaughter of innocents.

Abaddon: Then go, be free.

Brundig: Farewell Tonungur, may we meet again.

Abaddon: Farewell jarl.

He gives him a final nod and walks away and to his side gather the remaining of his kindred.

Myrtis (Fenris' daughter): We will head back as well, we are grateful for the carnage you allowed us to taste and the different flesh, but as the new leader of my kin I must salvage what few remain of us if we are to survive.

Abaddon: I completely agree, and I thank you for your service, should you need any help from me you know where to find me.

Myrtis: Thank you, Tonungur.

And with a bow, the Giant Wolves make their way back as well.

Abaddon: What about you two?

Ymir: Ymir and his kind will stay and help the Great King crush the rest.

Surtr: We will stay as well, I have a debt to repay the Great King for bringing me back from the dead, and with that burn the world like I said I would.

Abaddon: Good.

With their goodbyes now said, Abaddon and the rest of the Necromancers using their magic make the bodies of their fallen soldiers sink into the magical circles which appear all around the desert plain.

Dumah: Abaddon.

Abaddon: Yes?

Dumah: Did you remember to offer those sacrifices to Baal Belen as you were supposed to?

Abaddon: Do you take me for a fool?

Dumah: It was not my intent to insult but seeing as how you were reminded by him the last time; I took it upon myself to do the same.

Abaddon: How very kind of you to check on me, you're finely fulfilling your duty as a loyal believer. I commend you but it was not needed, for I have already fulfilled mine accordingly.

Dumah: It's just that I did not see you kill a hundred foes, that's all.

Abaddon: The rulers that I slayed are worth a hundred sacrifices, and more. Are you satisfied with that answer?

Dumah: Humph, whatever you say. I'll say no more of it.

Abaddon: Now with that we are done here, it is time to move on to the final step. Onto death and ruin.

Mordred: We met with the leaders of the Fallen Ones and the Drugnir on our way here, they had succeeded in taking control over their respective homelands.

Abaddon: Which would make our next task far easier to accomplish, excellent.

But before we set off there is one more thing I need to accomplish. Albunalich, find Arthur's sword for me.

Albunalich: It should not be too hard to do.

Like last time, a root extends out of his index finger and burrows beneath the sand. The root then branches out and the other roots expand throughout, searching for the sword. After a while he is able to sense the essence of Excalibur, and the root that is closest wraps around the handle and drags the sword all the way back to Albunalich.

Abaddon: You never cease to amaze me.

Albunalich: What are you going to do with this?

Abaddon: Destroy it.

He taps the blade as it lays on the sand with Absharu's tip and activates the 'Avarice' stance. His sword begins to suck out all of Lugos' essence remaining and when it is done Excalibur becomes just another, ordinary sword. Abaddon bends down and picks it up.

Abaddon: Jamaz, if you will.
Jamaz: Gladly.

He takes the sword from him and using his ability he begins to melt the sword. Excalibur begins to glow as it turns into molten metal, the liquid steel dripping over Jamaz' hand but it does not hurt him at all. In the next few moments Arthur's glorious sword, heirloom of Camelot kingship is no more, turned into a pool-melted metal upon the sand.

Now Abaddon looks about the gathered there and points Absharu towards the direction of Camelot and his armies march forth with great shouts.

Once they reach the capital of Londwyn, having burned down, and destroyed everything in their path to that point, Surtr Beldurson brings down the main gate with a mighty swing of his sword.

Stone and wood crumble down on the ground and a cloud of dust rises in the vicinity. Abaddon's troops move in and quell any resistance offered by what is left of the armies inside, ensuing in a scene of unprecedented carnage and destruction. The Dragonkin breathe their fire and lightning from above toppling down buildings and houses, the Giants with massive swings lay to waste everything that lays in their path, from stone to body none are spared.

Abaddon: Damatum, Awilatam, Abratim, Shehrukku Daku! Nishunukku Balatu![92]

With a mighty war cry his armies set to task; anyone that stands in their way is cut down mercilessly. Within minutes, death and destruction fills the capital of Camelot. The streets flow with the crimson red of its citizens and piles of debris. Bodies dot the cobalt streets left and right; from young to old, from children to adults.

Seeing all of this unfold, Abaddon reminiscences of the time he first resurrected.

---

[92] Children, women, men, kill them all! Let none live!

Abaddon: I told you, didn't I, Arthur, that Camelot will be the first to fall.

As he says this, a burned down spire from a building, falls on the ground. Blazing inferno engulfs the city giving the scenery an even more ominous look.

Morgana stands next to her beloved, looking around alongside him and revelling in the undoing of her once home city.

Morgana: Beautiful, is it not, my love?

Abaddon: Indeed it is, (looks at her) this is my first time seeing someone take pleasure in the destruction of their home.

Morgana: What a silly thing to say, this place stopped being my home a long time ago.

He smirks.

Mordred: So, this is Camelot huh. I have to say it does look pleasant, but it must be reduced to rubble. I would say too bad but really, it is not.

Abaddon: (places both arms around them) We did it, we won.

Morgana: There is one more thing I have to take care of.

Abaddon: Go on.

Morgana: It should be over soon.

Gives off a smirk and then, using her magic, she takes on the shape of a flying, black Dragon and takes off towards the royal castle, joining in the destruction the Dragonkin sowed along the way.

She makes it to Merlin's tower where Emrys was looking outside the window at what was happening below with a bewildered look on his face.

As he does this, the draconic visage of Morgana slowly shows up from beneath the window, causing him to retrace his steps towards the inside of the room in fear.

When their eyes lock in, he immediately recognises the look behind the serpentine eyes.

Emrys: La-lady Morgana…

Morgana: Hello Emrys.

Emrys: …

Without uttering another word, Morgana spews forth her fiery breath at him but he shields himself with magic, then he strikes back at her with a lightning bolt, but she is unscathed.

Morgana: That won't do.

Now, Emrys out of fear bolts toward the door before Morgana spews forth another blazing stream but he escapes through it.

She then reverts into herself, enters the room and goes after Emrys, who has locked the door with a spell and now was running down the hallway.

But Morgana will not be thwarted by a mere locked door, so she bursts forth from the room, breaking the door in thousand pieces, sending splinters flying all over.

Morgana: Oh Emrys! Fitting from a rat to scurry on away from the face of danger! But you won't escape me!

With her nigromancy she summons two Ghouls to chase after Emrys, and being speedy creatures moving with the shadows themselves, quickly close in on him, who was just making a U-turn along another hallway. But before they can get their claws on him, he transforms into a sparrow and flies away from their grasp.

He manages to sneak away from the castle and just as he thinks he has achieved freedom; a black gauntlet snatches him in its grasp.

Abaddon: Naughty, naughty birdie, where do you think you're flying off to?

He begins to chirp nervously, and wriggle and Abaddon tosses him on the ground and the magic is dispelled.

Emrys: Please…spare me!

Abaddon: Sleep now.

He casts a sleeping spell on him, and he falls fast asleep. Then he binds him with ethereal shackles.

Abaddon: I'll let Morgana deal with you, filth.

Morgana: Did you find him? (Addresses the Ghouls).

They both shake their heads in negative and she dismisses them with a click of her teeth.

Morgana: Where has that rat gone? Tsk, no matter; I'll find him later, now while I'm here, I might as well tend to my other task.

With that, she climbs the stairs towards where the royal chamber is and finds the door unlocked.

Inside, she finds her mother, Queen Guinevere, calmly sipping on tea as she watches the destruction unfold outside the window.

Guinevere: Do what you must.

Morgana: What? No 'Oh my poor child! So good to see you! I've been so worried!' nothing?

Guinevere: (takes a sip) But you are not my child, are you? (Turns at her).

Morgana: I suppose you're right.

Guinevere: All I see is a stranger, wearing the face of my once beloved daughter.

Morgana: I suppose you are right again; after all, I'm not the Morgana you used to know.

Guinevere: … I wept for you; you know. Day and night…I begged the Gods, any God, to bring you back to me but…they never did, they either did not want to hear my plea or…there was nothing left to return.

Morgana: My, you are on a roll, mother, everything you say hits the mark. True, your daughter died the day she left this place. Your precious Morgana was gone so no wonder no one heard your call (smirks).

Guinevere: Are you pleased? With what you have done? With the Hell you have wrought upon us.

Morgana: I couldn't be happier (still smirking).

Guinevere: … I do not blame you; I blame myself and my inability to stand up to Arthur, my own weakness as a mother and a queen…

Morgana: You can blame yourself all you want it won't change a single thing, it won't turn back time and sure as hell won't change your own idleness and behaviour like a muppet. But that's okay, I wouldn't want it to change, in fact I'm grateful, because if it weren't for all those things I wouldn't be where I am right now; living a happy life as the most powerful woman alive, with the man whom I love and my son, all three of us standing at the summit of this world.

Guinevere: Good…I'm glad that you could make my daughter happy when we could not, she deserves it.

Morgana: Yes, she does.

Guinevere: …What happens now?

Morgana: Now you will be bound and taken captive until you fulfil a higher purpose.

The queen then offers up her wrists without any resistance whatsoever.

Guinevere: Whatever fate you have in store for me, I am ready.

Morgana: Evermore the obedient one, aren't you?

She binds her, walks up to her, and pushes her out of the window.

Guinevere falls, and as she does, she closes her eyes as she expects to hit the cobalt floor beneath but instead, she finds herself in a dungeon.

With that, Morgana finds her way back to her beloved.

Abaddon: Look who I found for you, my dear, he's yours to dispose of as you see fit.

Morgana: (spits on Emrys' face) I already know what to do with him, but that comes later (teleports him to the dungeons of Dumah's castle as well); first, we have to finish this.

Before they set out, they are interrupted by the sound of approaching footsteps. Turning, they see the figure of a hooded man.

Abaddon: Who are you? Reveal yourself.

The man takes off the hood and it is revealed to be Sir Orwell.

Morgana: I know you! You're one of them, 'The Black Crow', Damian if I recall.

Damian: It is indeed I, your majesty, though the last time we saw each other you were but a wee lass.

Abaddon: 'Black Crow' an assassin huh, don't you think you're taking the wrong approach here, showing yourself in the open like this.

Damian: I do so because my intention is not to sneak around. I want to make you an offer.

Abaddon: An offer? Let's hear it then.

Damian: It is clear that the war has been lost, the King is dead no doubt, if I had to guess killed by your own hand, Lady Morgana. Therefore, it is naturally for me to put myself in the service of the next rightful ruler of Camelot, which is you.

Morgana: Are you being serious? Despite me being the rightful ruler, I brought this kingdom to ruin, killed its people, yet you'd still serve me?

Damian: My service is to the king, not the kingdom nor the people. What you do with it is no concern of mine.

Morgana: Well put but, I will have to decline, sorry, I just don't trust you.

Damian: Pity, me and the 'Crow' could've been of much service.

Abaddon: Our intelligence network is more than enough; your service is not needed.

A hidden blade subtly slips into his hand, but before he can make a move he is frozen in place. Abaddon freezes him in place by his presence alone, which to him it seems like something most vile and grotesque, twisted and menacing, as if it had crawled from the Abyss itself. This image, this feeling is enough to make his muscles stiff, and using this opportunity Abaddon 'blinks' at his side, piercing through his chest with his hand, holding his heart from the other side, and he squeezes it.

Abaddon: Foolish.

Morgana: We should find the rest of the 'Crows' and dispose of them as well.

Abaddon: Let them be, there is no place they can hide behind anymore.

And thus, both join in on the destruction of Londwyn as well, with their powerful magic.

Within a matter of hours, the capital city was reduced to ruin and its citizens exterminated. After that, a systematic destruction of the rest of the land ensued; not even the tiniest village was spared.

When Camelot was no more, half of them went north towards Elviun while the rest moved on south towards Faeran, from there to Volkodakia until they reached Sanclunea and finally they stop at Dhalsarria.

The same fate befalls these lands as it did Camelot, utter ruin, and complete extermination of their populace. The luscious green forests of Faeran, its wintery scape, the tranquil scenery of the deciduous woods, was now turned into a scenery of burning trees, black snow, charred grass, and death, so much death as the remaining Faeries fell dead upon its land as they futilely tried to resist.

In Volkodakia they were met with resistance in the form of the Druids: a peace-loving kind of Werewolves that lived secluded in the forests and along nature, with the unique ability to change their shape in all sorts of woodland creatures not just wolves, but their resistance proved as futile as the Faeries', and they too were laid dead upon the forest soil they loved so much.

These days marked the end of the other races of Avalon; just like Abaddon had said he had delivered, none were left alive, none were left to stand against him, none could oppose him.

***

Mordred: We did it, father, we finally did it, this world is ours, now we can rebuild it in our image.

Abaddon: It's going to take a long time, my boy, but we will indeed make Avalon a better place, better than it ever was, without the scourge of its former races.

Mordred: Are we going to divide the lands amongst the other rulers?

Abaddon: That would be most wise, for now Camelot will fall to Jamil as his father was supposed to get it anyway, Nidvelir will now be run by the Drugnir, Viloth by the Fallen, Amra will take her rightful place back at Sanclunea and for the rest we will figure it out (smiles at him).

As they are talking, Surtr approaches them.

Surtr: Great Abaddon.

Abaddon: Yes Surtr?

Surtr: I have burned the world like I said I would and now I am not sure of what to do next, should I stay with you or go back to Surtrheim, I find myself conflicted.

Abaddon: Surtr my friend, thinking was never your strong suit, just do whatever your gut tells you to do.

Surtr: But…my gut does not speak…

Abaddon and Mordred sigh simultaneously.

Abaddon: Do…whatever it is you feel like doing, whatever compels you the most.

Surtr: I feel like…staying here, with you, you did give me my second chance and it does not feel like I have repaid my debt yet. Besides, I might get the opportunity to bring other worlds to ash one day.

Abaddon: If you decide to stay then I'm more than happy to welcome you into my ranks, permanently.

Surtr: Yes, I would very much like that (gives off some sort of a smile).

Abaddon: Then allow me to officially welcome you in my service.

He creates a huge ethereal hand with his magic which Surtr shakes.

Abaddon: And how does the rest of your kin feel about all this.

Surtr: They wish to go back to our homeland; they say they are not strong enough to yet follow you.

Abaddon: After that crushing defeat, who can blame them for feeling like that.

Surtr gives off a low mournful groan.

Mordred: I suppose that is where your dilemma stemmed from, you were conflicted whether to follow your kind back or stay here with us.

Surtr: Little prince speaks truthfully.

Abaddon: I won't hold it against them, they are free to do as they wish but let them know that they are always welcome in Helheim.

Surtr: I will do that, thank you.

He bows his head and goes to say goodbye to his kinsmen.

Now Ymir steps up as he was waiting for Abaddon to finish up with Surtr.

Abaddon: And what might I help you with?

Ymir: Ymir only wishes to say vertr sardur, Great King.

Abaddon: So, you are leaving as well?

Ymir: Ymir agreed to help you in your war and that is what Ymir has done, with Ymir's role over he has no longer a purpose to serve here; therefore Ymir will go back to his icy Niflheim. Besides, the weather here does not really suit Ymir.

Abaddon: If that is your wish then I won't keep you, I thank you greatly for your service, your loyalty won't be forgotten.

Ymir: (nods) Vertr sardur, magnar konningur[93], stay strong.

Abaddon: Vertr sardur venir min[94].

And Ymir walks away and as he does, Abaddon calls out to him once more.

Abaddon: Ymir!

Ymir: Yes?

Abaddon: Should the need arise; can I count on your strength yet again?

---

[93] Farewell great king.

[94] Farewell my friend.

Ymir: Always.

He gives him a deep, respectful bow and continues walking.

Mordred: Looks like everyone has left for their homelands.

Abaddon: Not everyone, Jamil is still here, somewhere.

Mordred: Well Jamil is…a special case.

Abaddon: I second that (chuckles).

Mordred chuckles as well.

Morgana: What are you two giggling about?

Abaddon: Nothing important.

At that moment Lilim's voice tears through.

Lilim: Where is he? Where is my son?

She comes rushing down to the outer courtyard and Abaddon turns to her.

Abaddon: Mother!

Lilim: Oh, my boy!

They fall in a deep embrace.

Lilim: I missed you so much, I thought I lost you forever…

Abaddon: I'm here now mother, I'm not going anywhere, ever.

Lilim: My sweet boy (caresses his cheeks).

Abaddon: I feared for your fate, and father's too, I didn't know whether you were alive or worse…every night I prayed for your wellbeing and now here you are.

Lilim: And we are here to stay for as long as Baal wills it.

She kisses his forehead and gives him another hug, after which she notices Morgana.

Lilim: (breaks away from the hug) So, you are the one they call Morgana, the human that stole my son's heart.

Morgana: Indeed, I am, your highness, pleasure to finally make your acquaintance.

Lilim walks over to her, lifts her chin, and inspects her closely with her bright lilac eyes. Morgana does not do or say anything, but she simply lets this play out.

Lilim: My grandson was right, you do hardly feel like a human, I would say there is more malevolence coming out of you than any Demon I know.

Morgana: Thank you, I'll take it as a compliment.

Lilim: I like this one, darling, you may keep her.

Morgana: Pardon me, your highness, but I'm not sure I like how that sounds. The way you say it makes it sound like he needs your permission to be with me.

Lilim: I am his mother, am I not?

Morgana: And he is a grown Dhalku and doesn't need his mommy to make decisions for him.

Lilim: Mind your tongue, girl.

Morgana: No, your high – nay, Lilim, I will not. Like it or not, I am the one who's going to marry your son, so you better show me some respect.

Mordred: Mother, grandmother, let us not get hasty, shall we?

Abaddon: Yes mother, I don't need anyone's permission to be with the person I choose, I am the king of this land and not the prince.

Lilim: (purses her lips) If your soon to be bride wants to get respect, she has to bloody well work for it (walks away).

Mordred: That went well…

Abaddon: We haven't even gotten to the wedding and things are off to a 'great' bloody start (sigh).

Morgana: Don't worry, dear, she just needs time, I'm sure she'll warm up to me eventually.

Demiurgos: There you are!

Abaddon: Oh, for Baal's sake! One after another…

Demiurgos: We can finally get to know each other better.

Morgana: I would like that (smiles).

Demiurgos: (kisses her hand) Pleasure to meet you, my dear, allow me to formally introduce myself, I am Demiurgos, the father.

She smiles.

Demiurgos: My, what a radiant smile you have, fitting for a young and gorgeous girl such as yourself.

Morgana: Thank you.

Demiurgos: She is a fine one, this one, Abaddon always had the taste for the young and fresh (smiles).

Abaddon: (Oh for the love of…) Yes father, we all know that; you don't need to point it out.

Demiurgos: Right, of course (cracks a small smile) so! When's the wedding?

Abaddon: We haven't decided yet.

Mordred: Wait, you do not mind that she is a human? I remember you acting quite revolted before.

Demiurgos: Yes, I did but seeing her now, up close, it's just as you said, she hardly feels like a human.

Morgana: I'm so glad you all pick up on that!

Demiurgos: Who knows? You might have more of a Demon blood flowing through you than you know.

Morgana: You can't be serious, right?

Demiurgos: Of course not! I'm only kidding my dear ha-ha.

Morgana: (sigh) I can see now from whom has Abaddon gotten his sense of humour from (mumbles).

Demiurgos: What was that?

Morgana: Nothing (smiles).

Abaddon: How about tomorrow?

Morgana: What's that dear?

Abaddon: The wedding, how about we hold it tomorrow?

Morgana: Tomorrow! That soon? But where will we do it? This place is a mess!

Abaddon: I'm sure we can manage something.

Demiurgos: We do have magic on our side.

Morgana: Magic can't fix everything.

Abaddon: No, but it can help us make it functional at least.

Morgana: I suppose you're right, fine tomorrow it is then!

Abaddon: Splendid!

Demiurgos: Ahem, as much as I understand and admire your enthusiasm, especially yours my son, I cannot help but think that tomorrow is, well … too hasty. We have just been freed from a century of virtual slavery and imprisonment, the people have not had the time to properly recuperate and gather their senses. If we push the wedding on top of them the next day, they will be absolutely staggered.

Besides, there is also the issue of burying our dead and the days of mourning. So, in light of all that I would suggest that instead of the next day we hold it the next month, in two months even, maybe three. That should also give us enough time to properly rebuilt and prepare, at least to be decent enough for an occasion such as the royal wedding.

Abaddon: You speak justly father, I got carried away with my emotions and did not stop to think about all the other circumstances that surround us. Very well, I believe a reasonable date would be in three months.

Morgana: I agree, it should be more than enough time to properly prepare, and like father Demiurgos said – may I call you father? Or is it too soon?

Demiurgos: Nonsense, you most certainly may do so (smiles).

Morgana: (smiles back as acknowledgement) like you said, to look decent.

Mordred: Sensible conclusion, a royal wedding should look the part, and it is not like you are in a hurry to get married.

Demiurgos: I'm glad you all agree. Now, allow me to be the first to congratulate you!

Abaddon: Thank you father.

Morgana: Thank you!

Demiurgos: It is my pleasure (smiles brightly) I could not be any happier, my son is finally getting married.

Abaddon: Yes…finally…

Demiurgos: Let that be, it's all in the past (places his hand on his shoulder).

Abaddon: You're right (squeezes his hand).

Demiurgos: I will go and let your mother know.

Abaddon: I'm sure she'll be thrilled (smiles a half-smile).

With that he pats his shoulder and walks off.

Abaddon: Which reminds me, Mordred, we need to talk.

Mordred: About what?

Abaddon: How do you feel about Morvene's hand in marriage?

Mordred: Dumah's daughter?

Abaddon: Do you know any other girl by that name?

Mordred: No, I mean –

Morgana: Hold on! Who brought that up?

Abaddon: Dumah did, and personally I think it's a splendid idea.

Morgana: Well, it doesn't matter what you think does it!

Abaddon: Calm down, nothing's been decided yet, it's all up to Mordred and her in the end, it's not like I'll force him into marrying her.

Morgana: Well? What do you have to say boy?

Mordred: Truth be told I… I always had an eye for her (slightly blushes).

Abaddon: Did you now?

Morgana: First time hearing about this!

Mordred: That is because I did not know how exactly I should go on about it.

Abaddon: My son, a fierce warrior, but too shy to talk about his feelings.

Morgana: You're not the one to talk.

Abaddon: I had my reasons.

Morgana: Mhmm.

Abaddon: Anyway, this isn't about me it's about him. That's reassuring to hear my boy.

Mordred: But what if she does not feel the same way about me?

Abaddon: You won't know until you ask her yourself, right?

Mordred: **Me**?

Abaddon: Certainly not I, you're the one who's supposed to marry her, son.

Mordred: B-but I have never talked to a girl in that way before.

Abaddon: It's easy, nothing to worry about, you just have to tell her how you feel and see how she responds, if it's favourable, then you'll pop the question.

Mordred: So, I just tell her how I feel? Just like that?

Abaddon: No use beating around the bush, is there?

Mordred: I –

Morgana: Tsk, don't listen to your father, he doesn't know what he's saying. First, you'll ask her out on a walk and talk her up a bit, just general conversation, see how it goes. Mind the way she acts and talks, if she seems fidgety and bashful at times it means she also has some feelings towards you, then you will express how you feel. If she seems dismissive and blatant in her replies, walk away.

Abaddon: That is such a roundabout way.

Morgana: Oh please, surely you didn't straight up ask that girl to marry you back then.

Abaddon: Well, of course not –

Morgana: There you go!

Abaddon: Humph.

Mordred: Thank you, I will try and do my best.

Morgana: Go for it, dear, surely, you'll do fine (gives him a smile).

Mordred: I shall go and look for her at once.

Abaddon: Good luck, my boy.

Mordred: Thank you, father.

Morgana: Do you think he'll succeed?

Abaddon: Honestly, I have no idea.

And so, Mordred went to look for the princess Morvene, whom he found in the presence of her parents, who had asked from Dagon to bring her here to Dishum with his magic. He did like Morgana told him and they went for a stroll through the city, but with it in ruin it was hardly romantic alas, that was not really the purpose of this endeavour. They talked and got to know each other better than before, for they had dealings earlier in their lives but not ones so personal.

All went well and Mordred finally steeled himself and told her how he felt. Much to his surprise, she reciprocated these feelings; it turns out she had her eye on him for quite some time as well, and therefore, his marriage proposal was accepted, and it was decided that a dual wedding shall be held in the three months' time.

For now, the burials needed to be taken care of. The first that was laid to rest was the mighty Alabaster, for whom his mace, Halnadu, and his empty suit of armour were sent beneath the earth instead of his body for there was nothing left of him. His father, General Alygoros, who headed the defences in the siege on Dishum, followed after him soon. Already being a Demon of old age, his heart gave away from grief; he could not bear to lose his son a second time. After Alabaster followed the other valiant fighters in Abaddon's service. Kushsanu was buried in the tomb alongside Frigga and the rest of the Wyverns; Fulguros and Tonitros in their respective homeland.

Now Fragora and her brood were devastated at the loss of both their family members, and they grieved a lot. It will take them a long while to get over this heavy loss. The Hathasian soldiers were buried at the Akhum cemetery with all honours. After that followed three days of mourn per the national customs.

After all was set and done, there was the issue with Emrys which was resolved quickly.

He was taken to the Burtu Timmatimii, which is to say the 'Pit of Stakes' where traitors were tied and left to the mercy of the Demonic crows and ravens of Dhalsarria, who were creatures twice the size of the normal corvus genus and sprouted two heads with serrated beaks able to cut through the flesh and sinew like butter.

A murder of them was circling above as they were waiting to descend on their new prey. Some were perched on the stakes and were waiting with anticipation, their fully red eyes filled with carnivorous lust.

Emrys: Please! Let me atone! I am more useful to you alive than dead! I know things! Things no one else knows! I can show them to you!

Morgana: Oh, you mean this little thing (produces the Philosopher's Stone).

Emrys: Yes! That! I can show you how to produce it!

Abaddon: So, this is the most advanced alchemical achievement sought out by alchemists and magicians alike.

Emrys: That's correct, your highness!

Abaddon: Most certainly this can prove quite the useful artefact, but you know, we don't really need you alive to unlock its secrets.

Emrys: But…but…

Abaddon: Feast on his flesh.

He addresses the infernal birds, and they descend upon him and tear into his flesh with their serrated beaks, ripping out chunks with great ferocity, plucking out his eyeballs, ears, nose as he screams in excruciating pain and anguish.

Abaddon: Make sure you leave him at least half-alive.

Now he sits on the edge of the pit and observes this feast of crows with Morgana sitting next to him, her head propped against his shoulder.

Morgana: You were right, there is something oddly satisfying about this (smiles slightly).

Abaddon: Isn't it though?

Morgana: (chuckles) Oh how I longed for this day…

Abaddon: I wonder what sort of potential Merlin saw in this wretch.

Morgana: I can't help but wonder the same…

Abaddon: Well, whatever the case may be, now he has been avenged, all that wronged him are dead, well, mostly dead (slightly smiles).

Morgana: Why do you need him almost alive though?

Abaddon: I'm going to feast on his soul and find out the secrets of the stone.

Morgana: (perks up to look at him) You can do that?

Abaddon: Mhmm.

Morgana: You know what? I'm not even surprised (chuckles).

Abaddon: It's a nigromantic spell, I can teach it to you, if you want.

Morgana: Really? Although eating souls sounds rather repulsive.

Abaddon: It is, however, very useful.

Morgana: Something to think about, in the meantime I will leave the soul eating to you.

They both laugh a bit at this.

With that, after a while when Emrys has been left a mangled mess on death's door, Abaddon goes down to him and consumes his soul and with it all its memories, gaining the knowledge of producing the stone.

Abaddon: So that's how it's done, interesting (looks up at the corvi) you may proceed.

And as he walks back up, the birds fly back to finish their meal.

After that eventful afternoon, that night a council was held amongst all the rulers where it was decided who gets what. As Abaddon and Mordred have discussed before so it was done. Camelot was given to Jamil, Amra was reinstated as a ruler to her kingdom, whose citizens were the only ones spared from the genocide on her behalf, but she instead gave it to her daughter to rule who was thrilled by this mighty gift. Faeran was divided between Cain and Hyberion, Viloth to Dorochiel, leader of the Fallen, Nidvelir to Nurri the Drugnir King and Volkodakia fell to Andrakos the Dragonborn, turning it into the first ever Dragonborn kingdom.

Elviun was decided to be a colony for the Demons of Dhalsarria.

Next followed the three months of rebuilding and recuperation. It was the season of summer which allowed for a pleasant working climate. Builders worked diligently to repair the damaged building. Help was sent from all over the allied kingdoms to help in the restoration of Dhalsarria. Most help came from Sanclunea and Viloth who were the two, closest kingdoms to Dhalsarria. The Vampires in fact were most eager to help since the wedding of their princess was in question.

Now the Vampires did not take too kindly to the change in climate on Avalon, in the sense of rule. Most were against Abaddon's dominion and that of the changed Amra, as of course, it is not easy to simply forgive and forget centuries of animosity. Though a part of them saw no other way but to conform and gave way to the new change, those that did not showed visible sign of disdain and so had to be put to death as a precaution. Those that conformed, in time melted into the society that was forming at large and became fully supportive of their future rulers, especially Morvene. Being a kind, young woman, she won their hearts rather quickly and they grew quite fond of her.

As a result, when the day of the dual wedding finally came, many Sancluneaans found their way to Dishum for the celebration. Not only Vampires but other races as well were there to celebrate. The city was now brimming with joy and laughter and thus had become completely opposite of how it was three months ago. Much work was still left to be done however, but at least the city looked pleasant and presentable as they had hoped. Homes were decorated with flower arrangements, beautiful decorative tapestries, and other handicrafts.

The ziggurat, the holy temple of Baal, was fully rebuilt with the help of magic where the wedding takes place in the traditional fashion of the Dhalsarrians. The ceremony was to take place inside the main sanctum which was located at the very top. It was filled with surviving Dhalsarrian nobles who were dressed in traditional clothing per their customs. Sancluneaan and other nobility and royalty was present as well. Tetsuzaemon was there as well as Jamil, Dorochiel with his twin sister Gabriela, Cain and Hyberion, and lastly Nurri, the Drugnir King.

There were five maidens, Demonesses, standing at the sides of the sanctum, also wearing black vestments embroidered in gold, but their faces were veiled, with a thin, crimson veil, and on their heads, they had a circlet made of silver etched with sacred inscriptions. The maidens were arrayed in such a way that they formed the Star of Tiamat: two were standing in each of the far corners of the north side, two on each right and left side in the centre, their backs facing the walls, and one at the entrance. All five were holding candlesticks that were lit.

Soon, the four make their appearance, dressed in traditional, Dhalsarrian wedding clothes. The male one consists of a black, satin tunic that went up to the knees, embroidered with gold at the edges of the sleeves, neck area, and the knees, interwoven with intricate designs and patterns. The edges were also decorated with tassets. Two golden bracelets, bedecked with sapphires adorn their biceps, and they have vambraces made of gold. Each vambrace held a big, sapphire in the centre, and they too were decorated with intricate designs.

Around their waist there is a big belt that covered their stomach as well. It is of royal blue colour, rimmed with gold, and embroidered with sacred inscriptions in gold. It also has tassets. On their shins they also have golden braces with sapphires, and on their feet, they wear sandals. Over their chest there is a woollen, crimson cape, with tassets and highly ornamented with embroidery at the back.

Atop their heads there is a sacred, wedding tiara. It consists of a circlet made of gold whose front piece was raised above the brow and came to a pointed end some five centimetres above the head. The top is consisting of a crimson, velvet cloth, which was welded to the circlet. The women also wear a similar circlet but theirs has a veil that goes down to their waist, and it is royal blue of colour. It was rimmed with gold, and it also had tassets. The rimming was embroidered with intricate patterns. Religious symbolics were carved onto the circlets.

Now the female garment consists of a black, sleeveless tunic also satin and rimmed with gold, in the fashion of the male garment, only theirs goes down to the ankles. There is a crimson, woollen shawl with tassets, highly decorated and rimmed with gold, going across the torso. Over the hips there is also a highly ornamented shawl, decorated with tassets. As accessories they have a golden belt, carved with religious symbols and writings in Old Dhalsarrian. In the middle of the belt there is the Mul Tiamatuu with a large sapphire in the centre of it. Around their neck was clasped a golden circlet, and golden, flowing earrings adorn their ears. On their legs they wear sandals which are held in place by bands of gold, conjoining at a leg bracelet. One band was running down the middle and was connected to a ringlet on the middle toe, and two ran down on the sides of the ankles. On their face they have make up consisting of black eyeliner and red lipstick.

Upon making their entrance the five maidens start chanting in unison and vociferously a hymn, accompanying the betrothed as they make their way towards Dagon who was standing before a bronze statue of Baal.

This is the hymn that was sung, in Old Dhalsarrian.

Kaddu Keshdu Alkashunu
Abaddonu Sharrum Kallatnumma
Mordred Malku Kallatnumma
Edukki Sagu Alkaba
Shalplanish Ilunim Inatam

Baragu Baragu, Baragu Karbar Udu
A Abunum Belum Baalum, Karbar Lakullum.

Meshukku Na A Belum
Nismu Muhrunum Nismu Muhrunum
Pannum Na Emu Ashu Qulerunu
A Amarukku Baalum Rabum Ilum,
Gasatamka Qadatti
Emekunum Lequki.

And here is the translation in Common.

Here they come to tie the knot,
King Abaddon and his bride
Prince Mordred and his bride
In union to become one, under the eyes of our God
Blessed is this holy day, holy day, holy day,
Oh Lord Baal Father of us blessed let it remain.

Scorn us not Oh Lord, hear our prayer, hear our prayer
Turn not Thine face for we shall despair,
Look upon us Oh Baal, Great God, hallow Thee these marriages
Take them in Thine care.

Once they reach him, they kneel, and the chanting stops. Now Dagon begins the ceremony in Old Dhalsarrian.

Dagon: Dearly beloved Dhalsharrim, Lamashtim, and people of other races, friends, and family, we have gathered here in this holy place to bear witness to the sacred union of our Abaddonu Sharrum Morgana Malkama Mordrded Malku Morvene Malkama.

Taking note that Lady Morvene is of a dual faith, so that we may not transgress in the eyes of her other God and patron, Lord Noctis, I have been vested by High Priest De Wrais to conduct the ceremony in His name as well.

Before we begin, let us give thanks to our Gods, especially to our Lord Baal, who after a century of torture and imprisonment hath sent us our king, Abaddon, as His deliverer, and who under His guidance hath rid us of our enemies for good.

Let us also give thanks to them for reconciling our two people, who until recently were mortal enemies but now are as one.

Thus, they spend a minute in prayer giving thanks.

Now, without any further ado I shall commence the wedding rite. The betrothed shall repeat after me the sacred vows. First, we shall begin with our Sharrum.

And these are the vows that Abaddon was bid to repeat.

Dagon: Dost thou Abaddon, solemnly swear, under Baal, thine God, that thou shalt honour and cherish thine wife to be, Princess Morgana?

Dagon: Dost thou solemnly swear to ever uphold her honour and defend it against those who would tarnish it?

Dagon: Dost thou solemnly swear to be faithful and loyal to thine wife, to never cheat and lie to her, to never slander and debase her good name?

Dagon: Dost thou solemnly swear to never raise thine hand against her and never defile her against her will?

The same procedure is repeated with Mordred, and then with the women. Though with Mordred and Morvene, Noctis too was inserted.

Dagon: With the vows complete, I pronounce ye husband and wife.

Ovation erupts from the gathered.

Dagon: And now we shall offer our prayers to our Lords.

He bids the maidens to come and they, step by step begin making their way to the married couples, chanting as they approach, a hymn to entreat Baal.

Once they arrive, they stop with the chant and sit around them with bend knees, forming the Tiamat Star, and they place the candelabra before themselves.

Dagon: Oh Lord Baal, Greatest of Gods, Abyssal Father, the Beginning and End of us all, in Thine name and in that of Tiamat hear my prayer. Let these four be blessed with perpetual bliss and uninterrupted happiness for the rest of their lives. Let them not be led astray and let not their hearts waver, but to remain true to each other. Vows they have taken and vows they shall uphold. Keep them and protect them, Kakama.

Kakamu resounds throughout.

Dagon: Lord Noctis we pray to you for your child Morvene, for the same benevolence as that of our God Baal, who is Thine brother by blood, and by domain. Please, let no harm find her in her love, grant her the wisdom and strength to uphold her solemn duties as a wife and as a lover. Protect her and her husband from those that would seek to see them in ruin: false friends, and homewreckers. Kakama.

Another 'Kakama' resounds. Now the newlyweds are presented with a sacrificial bowl and an agla – a ceremonial dagger, both inscribed with sacred inscriptions. They then slit their wrists and jointly fill out the bowl, letting their bloods to mix. Once it has been filled it is set before them.

Dagon: Lord Baal, Lord Noctis, accept this gift of blood as a seal to this holy ceremony and as a sign of our devotion and sincerity.

There is a moment of pause where they all wait with much expectation. Then a cold breeze passes through the sanctum and snuffs out the flame of the candles, after which another grave silence follows. After a few minutes the blood in the bowl begins to ripple and spill, then it begins to flow in the direction of the five maidens, outlining the Star of Tiamat, and at the end an enclosing circle around it. Once the Star has been drawn the candelabra lit up anew, this time with the blue, Abyssal fire. But the fire did not burn alone, it was instead accompanied by wreathes of shadows that emanated from the bottom of the candleholder and swirled around the flames – both Gods had heard their prayers and answered favourably.

Immediately the sanctum was filled with sighs of relief by Vampires and Demons alike, followed by cheerful ovations. The parents of Abaddon and Morvene were the loudest and most enthusiastic, clapping with tears in their eyes, especially Lilim and Demiurgos who finally got to see their son married after the first, unspeakable, failed attempt. The newlyweds look at each other and share smiles – the ceremony was a success.

There was much merriment and joy making that day; people were drinking, feasting, and laughing. There has not been this much joy in this land for a very long time. All people from all walks of life, from nobles to peasants were welcome at the grand ball that took place afterwards. It was not just Dhalsarria but great celebrations were underway in Sanclunea as well.

On that day, Jamil gave back the rule to Camelot to Morgana as a wedding gift, saying that he was content to rule only his own kingdom and that the lordship over Camelot was his father's dream not his.

With that Camelot also was decided to be repopulated with the people of Dhalsarria, making it the second colony alongside Elviun.

Now with his marriage and his mother being the Queen of Camelot, Mordred's titleship expanded and now he was Mordred, Prince of Dhalsarria and of Camelot and King of Sanclunea.

The celebration lasted for three days and three nights. After those few days, Abaddon was standing on a cliff at the edge of Faeran, which overlooked the vast stretch of ocean. The waters bellow crashed against the cliff, foaming with the impact, and gleamed beneath the bright sun, as he was looking away in the distance, thinking, wondering...

Mordred: (approaches) What are you thinking of father?

Abaddon: Have you ever wondered what's beyond this vast body of water?

Mordred: I do not know, more water?

Abaddon: That's what I used to think as well, but what if there is something else, like an unexplored land, waiting to be conquered.

Mordred: You are thinking of conquests again?

Abaddon: I can't help it, it's in my blood, I'm not satisfied with being confined only to this place, I need the thrill of blood.

Mordred: You have a wife now, a peaceful life, Avalon is yours, like you wanted, maybe it is time to put a stop to these ventures of yours?

Abaddon: Perhaps you're right, but something compels me to stretch out my grasp beyond.

Mordred: What if there is nothing there and really it is all just water?

Abaddon: That's what I want to find out.

Mordred: Even if and that is a big if, there is some unknown land beyond, what if it is some place that is better off left unknown?

Abaddon: Wouldn't that be something?

Mordred: (sigh) I see that you have already made up your mind, how do you even plan on getting across this ocean? We do not know how long it goes, surely you do not plan on crossing it with your magic.

Abaddon: Which is why I started working on something.

He hands him over a scroll of blueprints of some weird never before seen contraptions.

Mordred: What in Baal's name is this? It looks like a riverboat, but only bigger.

Abaddon: I did use the same principle as with boat-making and expanded on it.

Mordred: Incredible, and do you have a name for this curious contraption?

Abaddon: I call it – 'ship'.

Mordred: 'Ship'? A curious name for a curious contraption. When will we start working on these?

Abaddon: Next week; I have to spend some more time with your mother; otherwise, my life is forfeit.

Mordred: (chuckles) A wise decision, you do not want to anger her.

Abaddon: No, I do not (chuckles slightly).

Meanwhile, in an unknown place in an unknown land, an unknown servant was relaying his findings to an unknown lord.

Lord: What tidings do you bring me?

Servant: He has won the war, sire, just like you said he would.

Lord: But of course, I would not expect anything less from the great Abaddon.

Servant: And now just as you have foreseen, sire, he sets his sights even further beyond the confines of Avalon.

Lord: Yes, yes, he will be here soon, I can feel it, and I shall be waiting patiently for his arrival.

He lets out a loud laughter which sounds more like a cackle that echoes throughout the halls of his abode.

A mysterious lord in a mysterious land...

END NOTE

---

[i] The Wheel of Fortune Turns

[ii] Beginning of the End

[iii] Cruel Fate

[iv] Lord of Monsters

[v] New Order of the Ages

[vi] What All Want

[vii] Seed of Evil

[viii] Bringer of Pain

[ix] The Enemy of My Enemy is My Friend

[x] Precautionary War

[xi] Breath of Dragons and Power of Demons

[xii] Apple of Discord

[xiii] A Song of Flame and Frost

[xiv] Land of the Big

[xv] Diverse Feelings

[xvi] A Night to be Remembered

[xvii] The Miraculous Blast of the Trumpet Calls All Before the Throne

[xviii] Advent of Death

[xix] Son of the Devil

[xx] Pre-war

[xxi] Day of Wrath

[xxii] Fire and Blood

[xxiii] What Lies Beyond

Ingram Content Group UK Ltd.
Milton Keynes UK
UKHW022310290523
422450UK00006B/57

9 781398 425767